Mythic Winter

A Science Fiction and Fantasy Anthology

Edited by
E. R. Donaldson & Nate Battalion

MYTHIC WINTER
A Science Fiction and Fantasy Anthology

All stories within are copyright © 2022 by their respective authors. All rights reserved.

Publication copyright © 2022 by Eric D. Roath and Mythic North Press LLC

This is a work of fiction. All characters and events portrayed in this novel are either fictitious or used fictitiously.

Cover art by E. R. Donaldson

Illustrations by E. R. Donaldson, Rionna Morgan, H. R. Parker, Aishatu Ado, and Austin Abbamonte

Some illustrations made with the assistance of Wonder.AI

https://www.mythicnorthpress.com

ISBN: 978-1-954177-35-2

TABLE OF CONTENTS

Foreword

In case you might not have guessed, here is my confession: I love winter. Though you can find something magical in every season, there's something about winter that sets my imagination alight. Maybe it's all those years of conditioning around the Christmas holiday, or maybe it harkens back to my roots growing up in the woods of northern Michigan. Regardless, there's nothing quite like the first snowstorm of the season to get me inspired.

Maybe you can see it now: a cold winter's night, snowflakes cascading outside while you're snuggled safely indoors. Maybe there's a fire crackling in the background, or perhaps some heavy blankets on your favorite recliner. A cup of coffee, tea, or hot chocolate sits steaming on your end table. It's time to cozy up with… come on, you know this one:

A good book.

That's how this project came to be. I wanted to craft a project that was perfect for each and every science fiction and fantasy lover out there. I knew, however, I couldn't do it alone. That's why I've pulled together eleven of my favorite authors in the speculative fiction space to help me with the tasks. I assure you: they did not disappoint.

Mythic Winter is, by design, an eclectic mix of speculative fiction stories. In these pages, you'll be transported to magical realms, walk the path of larger-than-life heroes, and travel across the stars to yet-undiscovered worlds. Whatever your favorite subgenre of science fiction or fantasy, I guarantee you'll find something here perfectly suited for you.

You may see some familiar faces on the author list, though I bet there's plenty more you've never heard of. That was another part of this project that was very much by design. This anthology features some of the newest voices in speculative fiction.

My hope is that you'll find your new favorite author somewhere on these pages. If you like what you've read, make sure you check out the biographies included at the back of the book. There you'll find out how to connect with the authors featured in this anthology, along with any other published work they've put out there for your enjoyment.

So, without further ado, I will let you get on with your journey. Please enjoy the stories we've crafted for your reading pleasure. I hope you get as much pleasure from reading them as we did from crafting them.

Sincerely,

E. R. Donaldson

First Blood of Winter
— *A Tale of the Silent North* —
By Hank Ryder

The old world is dead. Consumed by the forces of darkness. All that remains of her people are the broken survivors from the four sentient races: Elves, Dwarves, Orcs, and Humans. Once mortal enemies, these four peoples banded together to flee to the only refuge left to them.

Even the sharpest rays of the harsh winter sun failed to pierce the frozen canopy overhead. Last night's snowfall still blanketed the forest floor, muffling every sound save for the distant thump of a woodcutting axe striking a log and the mirthful laughter of three small children. All else was silent beneath that frosted veil.

Thunderous hoofbeats broke the peaceful mid-afternoon silence. The distant silence echoed off trees and bounced off rocks as it wove its way through the forest to a small cottage occupied by a pair of adults and a trio of children. All three young girls had the same brown freckles adorning their green-tinged faces. Their ears were elven-sharp, and fledgling Orc tusks had begun protruding from their bottom lips. Busy playing in the dirt–giggling as they rooted around hunting for worms–they did not pick up on the sudden alarm that sparked on their parents' faces.

The girls' parents locked eyes.

The father was a tall, muscular Orcish man with long dark hair braided into locks. A hint of gray had crept into the roots of his beard, but most of his hair was still black as a shadow. He bore the marks of his age with pride, for an Orc past his prime was, indeed, a rare sight to behold.

The mother was a willowy elven woman with short blonde curls and piercing blue eyes. Her age was inscrutable, for that was the nature of her kind. Naturally, her beauty was matched only by her grace. Her only deviation from the typical elven features lay in the battle scars adorning her body, which she bore with the same regal elegance most Elves might wear silver laurels and ornate gowns.

In the old world, the very notion of an Orc and an Elf marrying and having children would have been cause enough to have their families slaughtered. 'Race traitors' they would have been called, their bodies hung from trees or burned for their heresy. It was for precisely this reason that the family of five had fled the old world.

Yet some of the old prejudices, and thus many of the old dangers, persisted even in these frigid lands.

A thousand words passed between the Orc and Elf in that single glance. Possibilities were weighed and measured. Fear, protective instincts, acceptance, and readiness echoed across the lovers' faces in a flash. The questions of who might be headed their way, the dangers posed by any newcomers, and what should be done about it were all left unanswered.

A wordless decision was reached between mother and father.

As one, they sprang into motion.

"Girls, go inside and help your mother with supper," commanded the father. The white tusks protruding from his lower lips gave his voice a gruff tone no matter how he tried to soften it, so he gently added, "Whichever of you peels the most potatoes can pick out tonight's fairy tale."

The girls squealed with delight and darted inside to begin their work.

Despite the potential danger galloping their way, the father felt his cheeks curl back into the hint of a smile. Their joy was his greatest treasure, and he took no small amount of pride in knowing that their lives thus far had been filled with warmth and ease; utterly lacking any of the savagery he and his wife escaped from.

As their beautiful mother corralled his daughters inside the cottage with a fond smile plastered across her timeless face, her gaze shot first out into the woods where the rhythmic thunk of an axe striking a tree still echoed, then back to her husband.

A silent question played across her face. *Should we?*

He shook his head ever so subtly. *Leave it,* he seemed to say; and turned away from both his cottage and the spot in the woods his wife was motioning towards, his sight drifting toward the road.

The urgent drumming of hoofbeats drew nearer with every passing heartbeat; an urgency that spoke to fear on the part of the hunted, and fierce determination on the part of the hunter. With this rapidly dwindling distance came a new sound. The unmistakable snap of spells being fired through the trees. Flashes of bright lights: orange slashes, red bursts, and teal beams; confirmed the father's suspicions. Spell-fire like that could mean only one thing.

"Shepherds," The father snarled under his breath. *Of course.* Be they hunters or prey, the presence of even one Shepherd would bring nothing but trouble.

Inside the cottage, the mother fussed over the girls just enough to keep them focused on peeling the potatoes. "Mama will be right back," she promised as she disappeared into the bedroom. When she emerged a moment later—a bow and quiver slung over her shoulder, an elegant sword sheathed on her hip, and a battle axe in her hands--the girls were too busy with their potatoes to notice. "Keep peeling those potatoes, girls!"

The mother returned to the doorway and whistled sharply—perfectly mimicking the call of a bird that was not known to nest anywhere within three thousand leagues of their cottage—tossing her husband his axe.

Hearing the call for what it was, he reached behind him and caught the deadly weapon without even turning to see it, such was his trust in his wife's accuracy. He flourished the mighty weapon into a sturdy two-handed grasp. Despite all the many years that had passed since he had needed it, the father admitted to himself that it felt *right* in his hands again. Like something had been missing until now.

His wife unslung her bow and readied an arrow, moving with fluidity and grace as she came to stand at his side. "Now this brings back memories," she said with a flirtatious smile.

The Orcish man—a husband, a father, and once, long ago, a warrior—turned to his beloved wife and returned her smile. For the briefest moment, the past decade and a half faded like smoke before a strong breeze. He was once again in his prime, staring at his beloved elven bride-to-be as they stood side by side–clad in metal and leather instead of cloth–ready to face down an army of shadow spawn along the shores of the old world.

But that was so long ago now, and he bore the marks of his advancing age with far less immutability than she. Along with the threads of gray dotting his coarse beard, his arms and shoulders were not quite as broad as they had once been. By contrast, his wife appeared largely unchanged, aside from a thin scar across her cheek which did nothing to mar her otherworldly beauty but instead–to his eyes at least–only brought it into sharper relief.

"*Such* memories," he agreed. "Let us hope the years have not dulled our skills."

She smirked. "Sweet Nakkagar, please tell me that you do not fear that age has robbed you of your savagery. Though I sincerely doubt it, my handsome and *strong* husband, you are more than welcome to hide behind me if you truly believe that to be the case. As for me, however? A few years of quiet comfort could not hope to weaken your wife. My aim is as sharp as ever!" Though she spoke her words with confidence, he knew her far too well to believe her.

Her eyes were moving quicker than they had that day on the beach in the old world, and her scent had changed, her pheromones betraying her anxiety. Fear and stress in small doses along with the heady scent of a person who had resolved to kill: *that* he remembered well. But something new had joined the bouquet.

A hint of protectiveness accompanied that pungent aroma he associated with her motherly side. It had filled their cottage many times since their children's births, often during frightening storms or on rare occasions–such as this–where strangers rode up to their doorstep and threatened their small oasis of peace.

He glanced back at their cottage, fear and worry etched across his face. Yes, it had been many years since they had last fought, and yes, their bodies were still strong enough to handle many threats regardless of that time. It was also true that they had more to lose than they ever did back then.

"I do not doubt it, my beloved. While it is true that the years may not have been as kind to me as they have you, my tusks remain sharp, and I have strength enough yet to lift my axe. With you at my side, dear Yeena, I could fight through the sieges of Kadumas and Icharog once again to keep our family safe. How shall we greet death, my love?"

The hoofbeats drew nearer still.

Yeena smiled, remembering the old words. "Together, no matter what comes our way?"

"Together," Nakk agreed, "come what may."

Mother and father locked eyes once more and nodded, reassuring themselves as much as one another that they were ready to meet whatever dangers were headed their way.

And they did not have to wait long.

Five horses came galloping around the bend in the road, barreling down upon the small cottage at top speed. Four of their riders–a mix of Humans and Orcs–wore comfortable travel clothing and light armor. Two of them carried swords. A third had a bow and arrow already strung and pointed back the way they had come. The fourth was toting a staff topped with an arcana crystal. Brown knee-length coats billowed about their armored torsos as they sped down the road, fleeing from what?

Their leader, a dwarven man, was clad in finer fabrics, adorned with silver and gold ornamentation, and wearing a bronze crown indicating his high status. Regardless of their attire, each rider's attention was on the road at their backs and not on where they were going.

Behind them came a trio of new riders: an Elf, a Human, and a Dwarf. All three wore white coats and bronze pauldrons emblazoned with the feather-and-eye symbol that marked them as Shepherds, keepers of the peace. Though, gazing upon these encroaching figures and seeing the violence that they brought with them, it was no overwhelming sense of *peace* that Nakkagar and Yeena felt rising into their throats like bile. On the contrary. Judging by the speed of their harried pursuit and the white puffs of hot air wafting from their horses' mouths as they rode, these Shepherds did not appear to have kept any peace for themselves, it seemed.

One of these Shepherds, the Elf, raised his wand and fired off a spell. An orange arc of light leaped from his wand tip and raced up along the road, catching the rear-most rider squarely in the back. The rider howled in pain as he tumbled from his horse and crashed into the underbrush, his sword glinting in the sunlight as it spun away. The coppery scent of blood wafted to the Nakkagar's nostrils a half-second later.

With a cry of frustration, the Dwarf leading the pack barked some command over his shoulder and the rider holding a staff suddenly swiveled in his saddle. The rider lifted his staff with both arms and aimed at the incoming Shepherds. A deafening crack of spellfire split the forest's calm as the rider fired off a blast of his own. The teal light of the spell was many times the size of the one that had claimed his companion and sped back down the road like a broad river speeding through a narrow passage.

The dwarven Shepherd raised a wand of his own and the tip glowed white. An ivory wall of hardened light formed between the incoming Shepherds and the destructive blast they were riding towards. The teal blast broke against the blinding white light and sent a shockwave rippling through the forest on either side of the roadway, cracking tree trunks and sending rocks flying. With a whoosh, the barrier dissolved into a puff of vapor, broken apart an instant later by the Sheperds' merciless steeds, which bore them right through the space where the barrier had existed without any sign of slowing down.

With a roar, the mage with the staff began conjuring a new swirl of teal energy, pouring more of his mana into it, preparing to unleash an overpowering wave that might just break through the Shepherd's defenses.

Nakkagar and Yeena had a choice to make here. Would they enter the fray or let things play out? If they chose to involve themselves, who would they side with? Hunter or prey? They decided—in that silent way they had—upon siding with the hunters. The peacekeepers.

Their first target was the mage. His doom was heralded with a whispered oath.

"Oh no you don't," Yeena vowed.

As she said this, the elven mother stepped past her husband, drawing taut the string of her bow and releasing an arrow so rapidly that even he—who knew better—saw no way she had even taken aim. Yet, her arrow slipped through the air with all the grace of a trout speeding through a river and found its mark all the same.

Arrow pierced flesh and bone, leaving only death in its wake.

The mage toppled from his saddle with a hole through his skull.

Voice tinged with panic, the regal Dwarf shouted a command, and his remaining two lackeys shifted their focus forward. The archer aimed at the mother and fired a retaliatory arrow. With a mighty swing, the father stepped between his wife and the incoming arrow; cleaving it apart and sending two halves to the ground on either side of them.

"Thank you, dear," said his partner.

"Anytime, my sweet."

All the gathered energy from the fallen mage's spell still clung to the air around his staff, resonating powerfully as it continued to gather vaporous streams of multicolored light from all around the forest and began building to a disastrous crescendo. In a few more seconds that severed spell would unleash a blast of unpredictable magic.

Odds were good, due to the nature of the spell the now-dead mage had been conjuring, that it would be destructive. With no one left to direct the magic, however, the precise nature of the outcome was anyone's guess. It might turn all the trees to glass, transform all the snow into a flock of birds, or some other strangeness. Weirder things had resulted from out-of-control magic.

The third Shepherd, a Human woman, stopped her horse and leveled her wand at this surging concentration of magical mist. She gripped the wand with both hands to steady herself before unleashing her spell. A stream of rainbow light leaped from the gathered energy and connected to the tip of her wand.

"*Yah!*" She jerked her wand like she was cracking a bullwhip and all of the pulsating mist suddenly vanished as it was drawn into the woman's wand.

Her eyes glowed and a blinding radiance emanated from her body as she refocused her aim and let loose a flurry of new spells. A dozen strong green bolts streaked through the air, speeding past the fleeing Dwarf and his pair of lackeys to impact the terrain on either side of the roadway. Vines sprouted from every point of impact and grew rapidly; forming a green-hued cobweb that the trio of fleeing riders rode their horses directly into. The vines tangled the horses' legs and brought them all to a sudden halt, pitching all three of their riders further along their intended trajectory.

Foul fates awaited each of the men as their flight came to its inevitable end.

Death found the archer with a broken neck right near the edge of the property line.

It came for the fighter next, who rolled to his feet miraculously unharmed and immediately brandished his sword. He came for the Orcish stranger who appeared as if from nowhere to his eyes. Defending his home and his family, the Orc brought his battle axe down through the man's collar and into his chest with as much mercy as he might show a wooden log that could keep his family warm in the bitter winters that plagued this Silent North.

All at once, the air was thick with the coppery scent of blood. Acting on thousands of years of ingrained instinct, the Orc took a deep breath to savor the aroma of battle.

The Dwarf benefited from his people's hearty nature and thick skeletons. His fine clothing was scuffed from the fall, and he was covered in a light dusting of frost, but he seemed otherwise unharmed from his unceremonious tumble. He rose to his meager height and looked up to the axe-toting Orc who just cut down his last man and the elven woman who had slain his mage.

Behind him, the elven Shepherd sent a slash of orange magic through the vines, clearing the path for him and his partners to come galloping through.

With a yelp, the Dwarf turned to the couple and fumbled with something in his pocket. Silver coins spilled out of his meaty fists as he took several steps toward them.

"Please, this ain't what it looks like! These bastards killed the real Shepherds, took their gear, and have been hunting me to the ends of the North just for trying to make an honest living! But they'd be no match for you! Cut them down and you'll have more money than y've ever seen in all your lives. *Please!*"

Upon one of his pudgy fingers was a golden ring with a fat black crystal—the symbol of the local crystal baron. A tyrant who ruled over this patch of the Silent North with an iron grip and a goldlust like none other. Just under a year before this, Nakk awoke one morning to a column of smoke rising from the west. A few hilltops over lay the smoldering remains of a ranch that had been their closest neighbors. Good folks, with kids. The baron drove them off 'his' land like they were scavenger-hawks eyeing up his next meal.

Nakkagar and Yeena did not even need to glance at one another this time.

They were of one mind.

"Hold your lies. Your greed will not save you from the consequences of your own actions, Grimhorn." The mother hissed out with no shortage of venom in her voice.

Baron Grimhorn paled. "You know my name?"

Both the elven and dwarven Shepherds rode up and dismounted with practiced ease, keeping their wands level with the crystal baron's chest as the Human Shepherd hurried along to catch up.

"Your name *and* your crimes are no secret around these parts, Grimhorn," Spat the dwarven Shepherd disdainfully. "You'll find no sympathy from these hard-working folk."

Grimhorn scoffed even as he backpedaled away from the pair, trying not-so-subtly to place the couple between him and the encroaching Shepherds.

Nakkagar strafed to the side, dropping the head of his battle axe into the dirt and placing his hands peacefully on its handle to indicate that his part in the coming fight was that of a bystander only. One glance at the bisected man laying at his feet was enough to elicit a tip of the hat from the elven Shepherd as he and his partner continued stalking towards Grimhorn, the leaf-shaped spurs on their boots clinking with every step.

"Mighty kind of you to stay out of it, friend," the Elf noted. "May I ask why?"

The father nodded his assent. "Grimhorn here raised our monthly tithes seven times in the past two years. He's bleeding us dry faster than even the Old Kings of Kadumas. If half the shit they say about what he's been doing to the local goblin population is true," he grimaced, even after his experiences in the Old World it seemed the people's capacity for cruelty was an endless font of wretchedness, "then the sooner he's off my property and behind bars, the better!"

His words earned him an approving glance from the Dwarven Shepherd and another respectful nod from the Elf. Nothing but reproach filled the eyes of the portly baron, however. Silver coins continued to spill from his fists as he scampered back, littering the dirt with currency stamped with his own likeness.

"N-now listen here, you miserable sods! You've got me all wrong. I'm no villain, see. I'm an honest businessman! There's good money in mining arcana crystals is all it is. Honest! People see my success and they decide that I must have acquired my wealth illicitly. But that's not the case at all! I-I just—"

"Oh, be silent!" The Elf hissed. The tip of his wand gleamed with an orange hue as he casually, almost dismissively, flicked his hand toward the Dwarf and sent a slash of razor-sharp air particles arcing out. It was the same spell that he had used to shred through the vines a mere moment ago, and to end the life of that first fighter before that.

The spell struck Grimhorn squarely in his chest and cut through his coat with ease, shearing through the fabric and sending his polished wooden buttons down to join the silver pieces littering the ground. The spell rebounded off the fancy silver-hemmed black vest he wore beneath his coat; deflected by some magical protection likely woven into the vest's very fabric. The spell shot off into the woods and harmlessly severed a few branches overhead, scattering snow and causing very little harm.

Growling in frustration, the Elf fired off a second spell, a mirror copy of the first. Grimhorn flinched as if in turning away he might spare himself the pain of the spell's impact. But the Shepherd's aim was true. The second slash deflected off the enchanted vest and careened straight over the father's left shoulder, sailing past him harmlessly.

Behind him, he heard his wife grunt in pain. A sickly sweet scent filled his nostrils. Elf blood. He turned to his wife and the small joy of participating in a battle once more—even one so short—faded to ash in his mouth as he saw where the Elf's second spell had landed.

Behind Nakkagar, unbalanced by the impact of the spell or perhaps his clumsy effort to avoid it, Baron Grimhorn tripped over an errant stone and fell backward; spilling coins all over himself and the cold soil he fell upon. His pained grunt from the fall was followed up by a sudden gasp of air as the Dwarven Shepherd caught up to him.

A fat boot to the chest kept Grimhorn flat on his back, and the Dwarf's wand pointed at the crystal baron's reddened face kept him spluttering but unable to form any words. The irony that the arcana crystal resting in that wand's handle had likely been mined by enslaved goblins in one of Grimhorn's many mineshafts, was not lost upon either the Baron or the Shepherd.

Behind them, their Human partner trotted up and dismounted, gathering the leads of their horses and waving her wand in a simple pattern. Green light emitted from where she pointed, and a gnarled wooden post sprouted from the half-frozen dirt. Using this, she quietly secured the horses and moved to support her fellow Shepherds.

She sneered at Grimhorn. "You really thought a dozen hirelings could keep *us* back?"

If the Baron was capable of forming a reply, he did not share it.

The Elf sauntered up beside the Dwarf and spat a glob of bloodied saliva on the ground, clearing his mouth so he could speak and voicing his opinion of Grimhorn in the same fluid motion. Efficient. "Well, well, Baron. Captured at last. How long have you been evading justice?"

Grimhorn scoffed, abandoning all pretense of politeness in favor of open scorn. "What 'justice' is that, good *Shepherd*? I recognize no one's authority to take from me what I have *earned!* I've carved myself a comfortable home out here, with my own two hands! To the Bleakwinds with you if you've got anything to say about it!"

"*Your* own hands? Ha! You enslaved those poor goblins in droves and had them build that hideous town upon the graves of their ancestors. You've no respect," shouted the Dwarven Shepherd.

"Who needs respect when you've got money?" Grimhorn asked, eyes darting every which way in a vain search for some path to his escape.

Even as the conversation between the Shepherds and their cornered quarry began heating up, the mother reached out for her husband as he rushed to her side. She gripped his shoulder tight. Too tight.

"Nakk?" Her voice came out a touch sharper and an octave higher than usual.

The father's breath caught in his throat as he reached up to her arm and steadied her, intent on guiding her back into the cottage and tending to whatever minor wound she had acquired. The scent of his wife's blood was never an easy thing for him to deal with, but after their years of fighting, he knew it all too well.

"Collecting new scars already, my love?" He teased. "At least you'll have something to remember me by when our children are grown."

She attempted to smile back, but her eyes wavered, losing their focus. A slight whimper escaped her as her bow slipped from her fingers and fell to the snowy ground at her side.

Nakkagar's world slowed to a standstill as he glanced at his wife's fallen weapon.

Never had he seen her disarmed. Not in the halls of Icharog. Not on the shores of Tar Voral. There was no man, beast, or shadow in all the Old World that had managed to leave the infamous Yenaria of Quain without her signature weapon. Yet now it lay upon the snow in the Silent North. A symbol of her eternal precision that was suddenly reduced to just a thing the moment it left her grasp, losing all of its former meaning in an instant.

Her face had lost its golden flush, darkening to charcoal.

A single glance down at her stomach told him all he needed to know.

Elven anatomy spared little room for redundancies, having decided many ages ago what 'perfection' meant and sticking to that elegant design more stubbornly than any dwarven king under any mountain ever named. As such, Elves had very little in the way of spare blood flowing through their veins. Though she possessed a timeless beauty she, like all Elves, was extremely fragile. Blue ichor spilled from a gash across her stomach, already soaking through the front of her dress and reaching her knees.

She wavered slightly and gave him a weak smile.

"I think you're going to have to take care of dinner tonight, Nakk."

The haft of his battle axe thunked to the cold dirt and the lovers fell to the ground together, he to his knees and her into his waiting arms.

"Yeena?" His deep voice escaped his lips in a tremulous whisper.

"Easy, darling. It was an accident."

Nakkagar knew his brutish figure had given many people the impression that he was a thoughtless oaf, but he was no simpleton. An accident *might* have been forgivable. Maybe. But what that Elf did was thoughtless. He knew Grimhorn's vest would reflect his second spell and cast it anyway. That was no accident.

"That *Elf* did this," He stated, a rage building in his chest. "It was his spell! I'll—"

Her once-golden finger pressed into his sage lips, wordlessly quieting his wrath. "Hush, dear. I need you to listen to me very closely." Her fingertips brushed the coarse hair of his beard with a tenderness he did not feel worthy of. "Temper that rage inside of you and look after our children. They're going to need you now more than ever."

"No, *no*! Yeena, don't say that. The Shepherds! They can heal you!"

She shook her head sadly, her voice losing strength by the second. "Look again, Nakkagar. Do you see any healers in their midst?" She motioned feebly, almost disdainfully, towards the three Shepherds. Indeed as Nakk observed them he noticed not one of their pauldrons bore the marks of healers. These were all hunters.

Yeena continued. "Gone are those brief days when the Shepherds rode out to solve all the North's problems and heal the wounds of tyranny. They are no peacekeepers anymore, my sweet. They are only out here to chase bounties and keep things quiet."

Indeed, even as she lay dying in her husband's arms in clear view of all three Shepherds, not one of them made any move to assist them. Their focus was solely on their quarry.

Yeena coughed and gripped Nakk with both hands. "Don't go mistaking *quiet* for *peace*, for they are not the same thing, dear. Steer clear of them, you understand me? They're nothing but trouble. Now," she grunted softly, in pain or perhaps in fear, "take me inside so our children say goodbye to their mother, then bury me out back and plant a tree over me. And you *look after our family*. Turn away from those Shepherds. Let them leave. Don't look back at them, now, you hear me?"

He nodded, but that was not good enough for her.

"Swear it!" She gripped him as well as she could for as long as she could, waiting for his answer, but if one came she never heard it. After all the long years of battle–most of his life, but only a faint flicker of Yeena's lifespan–that those brilliant blue eyes had seen, they fell dark just outside her cottage whilst their daughters, fruits of a long-forbidden love, were peeling potatoes in the kitchen. The arms of her lover tightened around her as if he could squeeze her soul back into the empty shell she had already left behind, to no avail.

Death found her in her husband's arms, and he lifted her from the frigid ground outside the small cottage that they had built together. Left behind, with his knees sunken into the cold dirt, Nakkagar tilted his head back, hot tears streaking down his chilled green cheeks, and let loose a wordless cry.

Denial, rage, grief, and raw anguish ripped free from his throat with such power that it shook the vultures from their roosts, scattering them into the Bleakwinds far above and what feeble sunlight failed to keep back the winter's chill.

Nakkagar's cry drew the attention of his daughters, all three Shepherds, and Baron Grimhorn in the same instant. Somewhere in the distance, the thunk of that axe finally halted.

Grimhorn paused in the midst of some grandiose speech Nakk had entirely missed, one of his grubby little fists raised with a hefty nugget of crystal in its palm. Whilst the dwarven Shepherd's expression was very nearly a snarl, the Elf's eyes lingered on the crystal for three fractions of a second too long before he looked up to see the source of Nakk's sudden outburst.

As they all looked up, Nakk was already on his feet: battle axe in hand with his eyes locked on the elven Shepherd. It was *his* spell that rebounded off of Grimhorn's vest and hit his wife. The mother of his children lay dead at his feet, and the one responsible was but a few meters away.

He would have justice.

"You!" he said, his target clear from his unwavering focus upon the Elf.

Grimhorn and the Dwarven Shepard exchanged a glance as they realized they were between the Orc and the focus of his sudden ire. As Nakk stepped over the split halves of the neatly bisected Human man, both Dwarves set aside their ideological differences to clear themselves from the Orc's path.

For his part, the Elf drew himself up taller, his own gaze drifting back to the chunk of crystal in Grimhorn's fist rather than the towering Orc stomping towards him. Both of the other Shepherds had their wands at the ready and were waiting for a cue.

Nakk drew up, nose-to-nose with the Elf, and huffed hot air in his face. "Your spell killed my wife," he growled out.

The Elf finally lifted his gaze free from the crystal nugget to address Nakkagar. His dispassionate tone dripped with insincerity. "Did I now? Ah, how unfortunate. Tragedy strikes often up here in the North, my friend. It's just the way of things."

Nakk's slit-pupiled eyes narrowed dangerously. "'Just the way of things,'" He repeated in a calm voice.

"Indeed," the Elf replied curtly. "Now if you'll allow me: we have a fugitive from justice to apprehend here. I would hate to see such a fine upstanding citizen such as yourself get locked in a way-station cell over a simple accident like this. Please excuse me."

The Elf tried to sidestep the Orc, only to be caught in Nakk's mighty grasp.

"You. Killed. My. *Wife*. I will have justice."

The Elf issued a condescending smirk. "Round these parts, friend, I *am* justice."

Nakk spat in the Elf's face. "Then I will have *vengeance*."

Shepherd and father locked eyes and, for the first time, truly assessed one another. Neither liked their odds of survival but both were willing to commit to the forthcoming conflict for their own reasons.

"Oh, enough." The Dwarven Shepherd suddenly surged into action, closing the distance to Baron Grimhorn in three furious strides. With the tip of his wand pointed in the other Dwarf's face, he snatched the chunk of crystal out of the Baron's hand and stepped back. Carefully interposing himself between Nakkagar and his Elven ally, he held up the crystal, offering it to Nakkagar.

"Here." He said, pressing the fist-sized nugget of arcana crystal into Nakkagar's hand and silently willing the big orc to accept the peace offering before things got any further out of hand. "Take it, friend. For your troubles. I know it won't bring her back, but it'll keep you and your daughters fed and warm on these long winter nights. One less thing to worry about as you grieve. Please, take it. There's been far too much fuss over this bastard Grimhorn today as it is already, I'd hate to see even more blood spilled over a mess he caused."

Nakk glanced back at his cottage to see his three daughters standing on the porch: their eyes locked on their mother's ashy corpse. Emotion welled up in his chest and spilled onto his cheeks at seeing the happy little worlds they had held behind their eyes buckling beneath the stark weight of reality. After all the work he and Yeena had put into keeping them safe and sheltered, the cold world had finally revealed its ugly face.

He swiveled his head around to look at the Elf.

The Shepherd only had eyes for the crystal resting in the Dwarf's palm.

No thought was given to the pain he had caused. No lines of remorse were etched into the Elf's face. Just blatant goldlust as he stared down at the fat payday his Dwarven partner was so urgently pressing into the father's grasp.

Sniffing disdainfully, Nakkagar took the crystal, and what small comfort it provided knowing that he had taken something the Elf wanted. "This doesn't even begin to cover what you stole from me today. You owe me a debt of blood and joy you will never be able to repay. But that look on your face? That'll keep me warm in my grave." He stepped back.

"All of you: get off my property. *Now.*"

Nakkagar pocketed the crystal nugget and took several paces back, keeping his grip on his axe and his eyes on the Shepherds.

It was here that Grimhorn made his play. He looked up at the Elf and asked, "You're not just going to let him talk to you like that while he's holding that payday, are you? C'mon. You could just reach out and *take* it. No one here could stop you. Besides, what's a little blood on your hands? Are you not the great Ionar Ferovan?"

"Quiet!" Hissed the Human Shepherd, her voice an uncoiling viper leaping out to strike. "Ferovan is a legend. He's been a Shepherd longer than I've been alive and has more arrests under his belt than half our order combined. He would never betray our code for a chunk of shiny rock."

Grimhorn winced. "Arcana crystals are not mere shiny rocks, oaf! They are the most valuable resource in the known world! Look at this," He kicked a few of the silver coins he had scattered earlier, "all these are mere copper pieces compared to the price that a single fist of crystal can fetch. There's not a damn thing in all the North more valuable than what that Orc has in his hand." He then glanced up at Ferovan proudly and laid out the final piece of his plan. "How well do they pay legends nowadays?"

Ferovan's expression darkened. "Now that you mention it, Dwarf. Not very well at all."

"Ionar?" The dwarven Shepherd said in a questioning tone. "We have a code."

"Ah yes, the code. I…" Ionar Ferovan, the living legend, paused for a moment, his eyes darting between his partner, the Baron, and Nakkagar with his fistful of crystal. After a second he started chuckling to himself as if he could scarcely believe what he was about to do. "You know, I'm old enough to remember how the old world was back before it started cracking at the seams. There were folks back then, like us, with *codes*, morals, what have you, and I tell you: decency is always the first casualty when the skies darken and frost approaches, friend."

Both his Dwarven companion and the Human Shepherd exchanged worried glances. Neither had ever heard Ferovan speak like this before.

"I have rode clear across the North, end to end, trying to uphold peace. Embody justice. Punish wickedness. And for what?" He scoffed. "The North is beyond saving, friends. Maybe we all are!" His focus shifted first to Nakkagar, then the Dwarven Shepherd, and finally to Grimhorn as he asked three simple questions to which he clearly expected no answer. "What is good? "What is right? What is wrong? These things do not matter anymore. Not here, in this frozen wasteland we've all fled to. No, all that matters now is what we're capable of. What we want, and what we're willing to do to get it.

Ferovan's face split into a mirthless smile that did not reach his cold, dead eyes as he shook his head like a dog clearing water from its ears. Years of struggling against the weight of the North, clinging to the role of a peacekeeper as the death toll mounted—as the frost closed its icy fingers around his heart—shook free as the last gasp of the good man Ionar Ferovan finally succumbed to the Silent North.

Too long had he fought for a goal beyond himself, he realized.

Peace was a myth. But gold? Gold he could have in spades.

The power to take whatever he wanted rested in his hand. A length of wood tapered to a deadly point with a few small pieces of arcana crystals embedded in the handle. With his wand, at his age, with his experience? He could have whatever he damn well pleased.

"Well, friend, I'm sorry to say that what I want most in this sorry world is that chunk of magic rock our toothy widower friend has in his mangy paw. What I'm willing to do for it is the same thing I've been doing for decades; the only thing I'm good at, really. And you most definitely cannot stop me."

The Elf pivoted in place, planting his right foot into the frigid soil.

His wand tip lit with an icy glow and teal energy ensnared the Dwarf, whose eyes widened in betrayal for the split-second he had left before Ferovan's spell took hold. An ivory gleam faded from the tip of the Dwarf's wand as his half-formed spell died with him. No barrier sprang to life. No teal blast uprooted Ferovan. So swift and complete was the Elf's betrayal that all the Dwarf had time to do was flinch.

With a ripping motion, Ferovan stole the heat from every particle surrounding the Dwarf, leaving him petrified and encased in ice by the sudden cold snap. Red embers swirled about Ferovan's wand as he completed his turn, kicking his left foot back and sending his coat swirling up from the sudden motion as he leveled his wand at his Human partner.

She had enough time to shout and point her wand his way, conjuring tendrils of barbed vines from the cold earth in an attempt to ensnare the Elf where he stood, but she was too late.

A gout of flame erupted from the tip of the Elf's wand, a release of all the pent-up friction he had absorbed from around the Dwarf's rapidly-freezing body, and reduced the Human Shepherd and her vines to nothing but ash.

Grimhorn had taken the opportunity to book it into the woods. Ferovan let him run. He could chase the portly baron down in no time. Now alone and free to do as he liked, Ferovan turned back to the Orc.

Nakkagar spared one last glance for his daughters, who looked so much like their mother, before gripping his axe in both hands and swiveling to face his wife's murderer.

The Elf holstered his wand and drew a sword from his hip in its place."Here, Orc. Come take your vengeance, if you can!"

Nakkagar and Ferovan rushed toward each other.

Three small voices cried out in terror as clashing steel begot sparks and flesh surrendered to the cold bite of the blade. Warm blood splashed on frozen snow, and death descended for yet another visit to the same frozen patch of dirt.

Footsteps began tracing their way toward the cottage.

For all its frigid brutality, the Silent North also hosted a bounty of new resources for the refugees of the old world. Chief among these was Arcana Crystal; a material so magically conductive it allowed even those without a

*hint of the Gift to wield the powers of mages and sorcerers in the palm of
their hands. A force equalizer that made certain people rich, and made the
North a lot deadlier.*

The boards of the cottage's front porch creaked as two footsteps retreated down its steps.

With a sagging sigh, the man sat down on the steps and wiped the blood from his face with a rag he had found inside. He took the same rag to his blood-smeared weapon and let his eyes rest upon the ashen body of the elven maiden lying in the center of the frosted-over yard.

Footsteps broke the quiet, crunching through the snow, and the man tilted his chin to the east to watch the newcomer approach. From out of the woods strode a young man with a woodcutting axe in his hands. His hair was as dark as shadow, braided into Orcish locks that fell down his back.

Just like his father. Eyes as piercing blue as his late mother's scanned the woods as he approached. Elven ears and Orcish tusks, green skin and brown freckles the same as his three sisters; all of whom now lay dead at Ferovan's feet.

The boy took in the scene of his ruined home as he came to stand in his own yard, surveying the carnage in numb assessment. A Dwarf stood frozen near the property line, wand outstretched and pointing off into thin air. Behind him, bare soil and charred brush surrounded a blackened skeleton. Nothing but open flame could melt the frost up here, not this early in winter anyway. Four bodies littered the road: strangers, all.

His mother and father lay side by side facing in opposite directions. Her bow lay well out of her reach, her sword still unsheathed. His father's axe rested beside him, having fallen from his dying grasp. Red blood mixed with blue as they both gazed sightlessly into the heavens.

The boy's younger two sisters, Yerena and Nolla, were strewn across the front porch, their throats slashed. Presumably the eldest, Nakia, had made a run inside to arm herself and been cut down as she fled, for he could see her boot through the doorway.

Only one person remained breathing: the Elf wearing the Shepherd's mark on his bronze pauldron, with a sword resting across his lap. He wore a white hat and a white cloak, attire befitting a Shepherd, both stained gray with ash and splattered with the blood of the boy's family.

Shepherds were supposed to be peacekeepers, not murderers.

The boy met the rogue Shepherd's gaze evenly and gripped his axe a little tighter.

The rogue Shepherd sighed. "Damned if I've ever seen a colder set of eyes on one so young. Five hundred years I've walked this world, and I swear: the faces of the damned look younger and younger with each passing decade." He shook his head side-to-side. "You look like you've got an ingot of vengeance burning in your chest, boy, and not a lick of sense to temper it with."

He rose from the porch and took three strides away from the cottage, sheathing his sword across his hip and unholstering his wand instead. Enough blood had stained his hands this day, and that older Orc had been a real nuisance with his axe. The Elf saw no reason to step any closer than was necessary to end the day's bloodshed.

The boy lifted his axe, his blue eyes narrowing to dangerous slits as his jaw set. Whatever came next, he was resolved to see it through.

Ionar Ferovan stared down at the child—no older than twelve and yet *so* ready to take up arms against him—and halted. With one flick of the Shepherd's wrist, an orange flash of arcane light, a spray of blood against the snowy forest floor, and that boy would be as dead as the rest of his family. Problem solved. No witnesses left to tell the story of how a Shepherd betrayed his oaths for a fistful of crystal.

Just him and his payday. He grew very still for a long while. The boy's grip on the axe never faltered. Ferovan's eyes drifted to the father's corpse.

That man had given Ferovan a real run for his money. For a second, he thought he might not survive. It had been an… *exhilarating* sensation. Life-affirming. To feel his blue blood course with desperation again after too long being asleep in the saddle? He'd searched too long for anything that could give his ponderously slow life new purpose. He had almost found it during his duel with this boy's father.

Almost.

But the man was past his prime. This child, however…

The beginnings of a plan flowed together in Ferovan's mind. "I'll tell you what, boy. You want your vengeance?"

The boy's green lips curled up in a snarl over his one good tusk—the other having yet to grow in properly and giving him a lopsided innocence Ferovan could not help but find endearing—and he nodded.

"Alright then: I'll make you a deal. I'll train you how to be what I am. A Shepherd. Once a year, I'll give you a shot to kill me. You fail, I scar you but keep you alive and train you harder. You succeed and you'll have your vengeance. Sound fair?"

Again, the boy nodded.

"Good. Just one quick thing first. I can't have you speaking a word of all this," he gestured to the corpses surrounding them, "to anyone. I have a reputation to uphold, you see? So. Any last words?"

Ionar leveled his wand at the boy's throat and waited.

The boy's gaze drifted to each of the corpses littering his homestead in turn before settling back upon the Elf and hardening into cold steel.

"Before we get started, I need you to know that I will be burying my family before I go anywhere with you. While I'm busy doing that I want you to remember just six names for me. That's all that I ask. Let me bury them and remember what I'm about to tell you." He did not phrase this as a question, nor did he pause to give Ferovan a chance to refuse. "My sisters' names were Nakia, Yerena, and Nolla. You slaughtered them like *animals*. One day, sooner than you think, you will beg me to be so kind."

Ferovan's eye twitched, and something deep inside the Shepherd's mind whispered to him; urging him to end this here and now before it went any further. But he abstained. Simple curiosity stayed his hand.

The boy continued. "My mother's name was Yenaria Skullpiercer. It was said that her arrows never missed. My father was Nakkagar the Brave, who stood alone at the bridge of Tor Voral and held back the shadows for three whole days. My name is Nakkan. You killed my entire family. And I only have one question for you, *you oath-breaking sack of shit!*" He then asked a question Ionar was not soon likely to forget. "How far down do you want to be buried?"

Ionar Ferovan lowered his wand and breathed out, stifling a slight chuckle as he pondered what his life had come to. He licked his lips and his head tilted once in a slight shake like he was still shaking loose some old pieces of himself. But it was too late. The boy, Nakkan, was right. He *was* nothing more than an 'oath-breaking piece of shit' now.

Well, he put himself in these shoes, might as well strut.

After a second of contemplation and a sharp inhale, Ferovan raised his wand once more.

"Well said, boy. You've raised my expectations of you. Let's see how well you live up to them when you see what I have in store for you." He flicked his wrist and fueled a spell with his own mana; giving form and function to the magical energies swirling around them in abundance, unseen to all but those with the gift… or those wielding a wand.

A slash of orange light whipped forth from the tip of his wand and connected with the boy's throat. The second flick of Ferovan's wrist coiled the spell back inside his wand, leaving a shallow-yet-vicious red line across Nakkan's throat.

Ferovan grunted slightly as he channeled the coiling energy within himself and reforged the deadly spell into a new shape. Already the boy's lifeblood spilled forth and soaked his tunic, a strange purple ichor that was neither fully Orcish nor fully Elvish. How curious. Ferovan's next spell slammed into Nakkan's neck with a bright emerald flash; searing the wound shut.

"Speak," The rogue Shepherd commanded.

The boy known as Nakkan, now kneeling upon the cold soil and clutching at his throat, opened his mouth and attempted to form words. All he managed to produce was a strangled rasp devoid of all meaning or coherence.

"Good. Now you are as silent as the North itself." Ferovan strode to the boy and kicked him; sending him sprawling. "Get up, boy! I have one last loose end to take care of. Your education, and our bargain, begins upon my return. You have until then to bury your family and prepare those horses for a hard day's ride. Whatever you don't manage before I'm finished will remain undone forever. Do with this time what you will, for it is the last measure of kindness I shall *ever* bestow upon you. Your life is mine. Is that clear?"

Nakkan tilted his head down in mute acceptance, though as his chin rose Fervoan saw nothing but fiery defiance burning in the boy's eyes.

Ferovan snorted. "Hold on to that ember of rage as long as you can there, boy. The North *will* snuff it out one day. I can't help but wonder what you'll cling to when the memory of your dear departed family no longer keeps you warm inside… what were their names again? I'm afraid I wasn't listening as attentively as I ought to. Would you mind repeating them for me?"

A flash of anger crossed the boy's face and Ferovan sneered.

"Thought not. I'll be back around shortly."

The rogue Shepherd departed on horseback with his eyes set on the trail left by Baron Grimhorn, leaving his silent companion to his solemn duty. When their paths crossed again he vowed to make that boy's life a living hell. The wrathful flame burning in that boy's eyes was a force of nature matched only by the icy grip of indifference in the Elf's heart.

"Live long enough, see enough merciless winter, and sooner or later even the brightest sparks of hope and fury get snuffed out by this… the Silent North."

Winter Holiday
By Nate Battalion

"He really wants us to go out in *that?*" Rini asks as she stands beside me at the door to our little log cabin, watching the snow pour down from the gray sky.

"I have to, at least," I say. A phantom gray line extends out from my feet, disappearing into the blizzard a few feet away. I know where it goes. "Unless you want to eat plain rice for breakfast today."

"Did that for dinner yesterday," she says. She's staring off into the distance, the same look we all get when we're reading something from our implants.

"You know He doesn't like it when we run out of cooked rations." I hold up a finger and bob my head back and forth as I quote the memo He sent us last week. "'The morale of the colony is an important factor considered by the company and is one of the pillars of healthy coexistence on the planet.'"

Rini knows the company's tag line and recites it with me at the end of the memo, rolling her eyes as she does: "Safety, necessity, positivity."

"The caravan should get back today," she says, going to the basin and pouring water to wash her face. I have the same information she does in my implant, but there's something real about speaking the words aloud; something that calls back to everything we lost when they jammed these chips into our brains and shot us down onto this rock.

"Hopefully they got everything we needed," I reply, taking my parka off the peg by the door and throwing it over my head. It's getting ragged around the edges, and the drawstring around the hood broke weeks ago, but the Administrator hasn't approved a replacement to be made yet, so I'll have to deal with it.

"Hopefully they're all still alive," Rini says, leaning over the basin and staring at the water, a chill wracking her body as the water on her skin cools. My sister Mabel—Rini's best friend—went with the caravan. She is just as anxious as I am to see her return.

The Administrator is watching the caravan through their implants, keeping tabs on their progress, doing His best to make sure they're safe, that they don't get lost, and that they don't lose anything along the way. But this planet is harsh, and there's no telling what or who could have waylaid them. The tinge of bitterness in Rini's voice is there because, try as we might, the Administrator never tells us beforehand when something bad has happened to a caravan. He tells us only what we need to know, when we need to know it.

The waiting, not knowing, is always hard on Rini. Mabel is the colony's socialite—a fast-talker, a negotiator—so the Administrator almost always assigns her to go on a caravan.

"Hopefully," is all I can manage to say.

I zip the parka all the way up, pinching the edges of the hood between my fingers, and turn to Rini who is still staring at herself in the water.

"What's your first job of the day?" I ask, shoving my feet into my old boots.

"Logging," she says. When we landed here, she knew nothing about living life on a company-owned colony, but she's adapted well to it. The muscles on her arms and shoulders are hard, growing stronger each day with the brutal labor and intense sparring sessions we're required to do.

"Still? Don't we have like, ten cords stored?"

My implant sends out a tiny vibrating pulse, a gentle reminder that I should be on my way to the task I've been assigned, but I ignore it for the moment.

"Yeah, but I don't have any other assigned jobs right now, so chopping wood it is. Besides, the generators use a ton of it, especially in this cold."

"All right," I say, shrugging my shoulders even though the puffy poncho hides most of the motion. My implant vibrates again, stronger this time. "Well, good luck. Stay dry," I say, and turn away to step out into the snow.

The cold hits me, a bitter blast to the face and hands, the latter of which I hastily shove into my pockets as soon as I get the door shut behind me.

The ghostly gray line of my priority job extends out in front of my feet, turning the corner of the nearby hut. I follow it around the corner, stepping from one snow-covered flagstone to the next in a vain attempt to keep my boots from getting bogged down in the soft packed snow. Two shadowy figures pass across the slender main street of our colony, hunched over in their own winter gear. The snow is coming down so hard in the pre-dawn gloom I can't really see who they are.

I cross the street to the main cabin, making my steps as long as I can. The door to the cabin creaks as I push it open, the cheery interior of the meeting hall shining out to meet me on the doorstep. I kick the snow and mud off my boots at the door, then pull my parka off and hang it on a hook. The gray direction line crosses the room in front of me and goes through the door at the far end of the grand hall, into the kitchen.

"Hey Burk." One of the two people seated at the table in the middle of the room waves to me. Kilo and Max are having breakfast early today, I wonder why the Administrator got them out of bed so early.

I return Kilo's greeting, crossing the room to lay a hand on each of their shoulders. My implant buzzes again, more insistently this time.

"What're you having for breakfast today," I say cheerily, even though I can clearly see the bowls of plain rice and quinoa sitting in front of them.

They smirk back at me and chuckle. "An artisanal preparation of grains," Kilo replies, lifting a spoonful of the bland food.

"Hey, at least it's hot," I say, clapping him on the back and causing him to spill the spoonful of rice he was holding.

He grumbles good-natured insults at my back, which I ignore as I turn to head into the kitchen. "I'm supposed to cook you pawns some food," I say. "My only assignment today, so I guess we're stocking up!"

"Great," Max says. "So we can look forward to fresh food tonight and frozen meals for the next month." He pauses to look at something on his implant, sighs, then bends to shovel the last few bites of rice into his mouth.

"Prioritized?" Kilo looks up at Max as he stands and stomps over to the door.

"Yeah." Max stuffs his arms into his coat, his mouth compressed to a tight line. "Prioritized, like I'm doing something *super* important that absolutely has to get done right now in that blizzard."

"Haven't you been digging out that old machinery for the past two days?"

Max jams his feet into his boots, which were standing up by the door. "Yep," he grumbles. "Apparently that's critically important right now, definitely needs to happen before the sun even comes out."

"Of course," I say. "Gotta make sure we have components for the air-conditioner units."

"Hey man, the company charter says on a colony with this climate He's required to put AC in bedrooms, barracks, and meeting room by the end of the fourth quadrum. It's cold now, but Winter Holiday is next week, and it only gets hotter from then on."

"Ah yes, 'Winter Holiday,'" Kilo rolls his eyes. "The company-approved a December 25th celebration that's definitely not Christmas." He raises his glass of water and downs it like a mug of beer after giving a toast.

"Definitely not," I reply. "Can't afford the royalties on that."

"Do we even have the components for that many units?" Kilo turns back to Max at the door.

Max holds up his calloused hands. "Hey, I just do the digging. Ask the Administrator or check the inventory yourself." With that, he turns and disappears out the door, the sound of the snowfall waxing and waning as he opens and closes the door.

I go into the kitchen, the gray line at my feet puffing away as I finally reach my destination. My implant buzzes a pleasing little chime, my "reward" for following orders like a good little colonist.

Kilo's voice drifts in from the main room. "Are you coming back here for S.P.'s Holiday party tonight?"

I turn to the stove and flip it on, then pick up a sack of cornmeal off the pallet in the corner, walking through the ghostly holographic image projected by my implant of the bigger, nicer stove that the Administrator has planned for us to build. I seriously doubt whether any of our builders will get around to that since we already have a functioning stove. The plan will probably sit there until the Administrator gets fed up with the plans cluttering his screen and either deletes or prioritizes it.

"Come on, man," I call back to Kilo, heaving the bag of meal up onto the counter, "you know S.P. and I don't get along."

"You don't have to talk to him; just show up! We'll all be here, it'll be fun. Where's your holiday spirit?"

"If it's S.P.'s party, I'll have to talk to him sometime. Besides, the caravan's coming home today, and I'm sure Rini will want to hang out with Mabel. She probably bought goodies or gifts for Christm… *Holiday*." I turn to my work, measuring out the cornmeal and putting it in a pot to boil.

"Oh yeah, right." Kilo shovels the last of his food into his mouth and stands. He picks up both his and Max's bowls and brings them into the kitchen, tossing them into the sink and giving them a quick scrub.

"Well, if you change your mind, be here at the 18th hour, I…"

My implant chimes, a message appearing in ghostly text in my vision: *A caravan has arrived safely.*

"Eyyyy, there it is." Kilo grins at me after reading his own version of the notification. "Safe and sound, ain't that nice?"

"Yeah, a relief for sure," I say, staring down at the pot.

The door opens and three more people enter, shaking the snow from their coats and stomping their boots off before coming in.

It's Roper, Jingo, and S.P.: our colony's three hunters. Each carries a rifle under their arm, which they lean against the wall before heading to the cooler to pick up food.

"Come on," Roper grumbles, "Plaingrain-TM again?" She holds the frozen bowl of food up, waving it at me through the kitchen's serving window. "Burk, please! We're suffering here!"

I can't help but grin. "I'm working on it," I reply. "I'll be here all day. If you want something better, go out there and bring it back."

Jingo punches her shoulder as he walks by, tossing his bowl of grain into the heater. "Maybe if we complain hard enough, Admin will send us a pod with real food in it. Maybe some painkillers too; something from a Sparkleworld, maybe." A dreamy look passes over his face, thinking of the shiny planets in the inner core with their advanced tech, vacation spots, and draconian politics.

"Yeah, right," Roper scoffs. "Even if they have sparkle food and meds at headquarters, He would never send it down here to us. We're just pawns to him."

My implant sounds an alarm in my mind. Everyone in the room stands transfixed, staring at the alert superimposed into all of our visions.

Incoming raid.

Roper, Jingo, and S.P. hustle back to the door, food forgotten, and pick up their rifles, piling out the door and into the night.

Kilo and I look at each other.

"You?" Kilo asks me.

I shake my head, my eyes wide as we stare at each other. The Administrator didn't draft either of us to defend the colony.

"Maybe… Maybe it's just a bear or something," Kilo finishes putting the dishes into the drying rack beside the sink, his motions mechanical.

My implant buzzes the three drum beats I know and dread. I've been drafted. My vision sharpens as my implant's combat mode kicks in. I spring into action, and Kilo's on my heels as we sprint to the door and throw on our gear. He must have been drafted too.

Kilo pauses a moment to read a notification. "I'm going for Go-Juice," he says, his voice quavering as he shoves his feet into his boots.

That makes me pause for a moment. "It's not just a bear." If the Administrator is approving Go-Juice, whatever's here to raid us must be bad.

A rattling sound rolls over the sound of the wind: automatic machine gun fire punctuated with high-pitched pops of small arms and occasionally the lower boom of something exploding.

"That sounds like mech fire," I say, my eyes as wide as Kilo's in the gloom. Did someone in camp—or maybe the caravan—stumble across and awaken some of the old machines?

"Grab me a gun and meet me at the line!" Kilo runs off into the storm.

My implant buzzes a three-beat rhythm, and a jolt runs up and down my body, causing me to tense up. My stomach knots, because I know what that sensation means and how bad it is for me.

The Administrator has issued me a Direct Combat Command—DCC—allowing my implant to take control of my body. That either means something extremely dangerous is nearby that the Administrator is keeping me away from, or there's something extremely dangerous He needs me to do.

The implant begins to control my movement. I dive back through the door, kicking up snow behind me. As I hit the ground inside, I hear the distinct popping sound of bullets slamming into the metal-sheeted walls. From the floor, I kick the door, slamming it shut. Without my input, I hop up and scramble across the room. I take hold of the table in both hands and flip it on its side, sliding it over to bang up against the door.

Not good.

Next, I go into the kitchen and into the back room where the cleaning supplies and tools are kept.

I grab the aerosol can of high-acid cleaner off the top shelf, then dig around on the opposite side of the closet until my hand closes on the cutting torch.

I can tell where this is going, and I really don't like it, but I've been DCC'ed, and I don't have a choice in the matter. Somewhere above me, out in orbit on the company's headquarters space station, the Administrator is controlling my body directly through his own implants.

I can hear a scraping sound outside, something sliding across the wall toward the door. Sounds like something sharp. I have only seconds to…

Apparently, wait around for it to break down the door. I just stand there, in the middle of the room. Has He forgotten about me?

I can't move. I'm still DCC'ed, but the implant isn't directing my body to do anything. I stand in the middle of the meeting room, amid scattered remnants of whatever had been on the table, holding my can of flammable spray and my cutting torch.

The scraping reaches the door, and the latch clicks. The door moves a fraction of an inch and bumps against the table.

I really would rather have something bigger to fight with, like that snow shovel against the wall over there, or a metal broom handle, or that broken pickaxe hung in the tool closet. What's an improvised flamethrower going to do against a mech anyway?

If the Administrator has gotten distracted with something else going on elsewhere in the colony, will my implant even let me defend myself when that thing gets in?

The door crashes open, flinging the table across the floor to crash into the chairs nearby.

Automatically, my hands come up. Before I can even see the enemy silhouetted against the backdrop of snow, I squeeze the sprayer, and a thick stream of the cleaning gel shoots out. With my other hand, I click the cutting torch on and bring it up to the stream. My finger lets off the sprayer. The last bit of the gel catches fire, and it follows all the rest to splatter against the chest and head of the figure in the doorway as it barrels through the door at me.

I realize why the Administrator had me prepare a flamethrower.

I see now that my assailant is human—or, at least, was at one time. He's naked to the waist with wires and tubes poking out all over his body. One of his hands has been replaced with a power claw, the triple-bladed weapon already wet with someone's blood.

My implant buzzes again, the same three-beats of a DCC, and my body unlocks, back under my own control again. I guess the Administrator deems the situation under control now.

I would argue that point if I could.

Because he's not wearing a shirt or a helmet, the cyborg can't strip them off to get the burning gel off himself. Somehow, he doesn't seem to care. He charges forward, even as he burns—his face a twisted mask of wrath as he glares at me through the flaming gel on his face. He must be hopped up on some combat stim, juiced out of his mind by whoever sent him on this raid.

He slashes the air with his power claw, trying to catch me as I backpedal and vault the counter-top into the kitchen. The claw slashes through my parka, spilling pale white Plasticotton like entrails as it tears the back of my coat to shreds.

I just need to keep away from him. *It*. As I slide over the counter, knocking the sack of cornmeal off to scatter on the floor, I reach up and flick the latch on the hatch above me. The heavy partition swings down and slams right into my attacker's face as he tries to follow me over the counter, knocking him back into the room beyond. Hastily, I fasten the hatch and run to the open kitchen door and look through. The cyborg is picking himself up off the floor, patches of flame still burning over his body and head as I slam the kitchen door and look around for something to bar it.

There's a broom standing behind the door, so I pick it up and wedge it through the door handle and against the counter-top. It'll probably only take him a moment to break that down, but it's a moment longer than I had before.

Now's my chance to re-arm myself, so I hurry through the kitchen to the back room. I reach for the pickax on the wall, but my eyes fall on something better. Someone left a sledgehammer back here.

I heft it and go back out, just in time to see a clawed hand punch through the thin composite of the door, tearing a jagged hole in it and waving around. The hand disappears, and a face appears, peering through at my improvised trap.

The claws come back through and swat at the broom handle, but I've reached the door again and I'm ready to fight. I cock the hammer back and wait until the cyborg's elbow comes through the hole, then I bring the steel head smashing down.

A loud pop and crack sounds as the joint dislocates and then shatters under the hammer blow. An eerie silence follows, the cyborg not crying out in pain, or even grunting. It makes no sound. The destroyed arm just hangs there, halfway through the hole in the door, swinging gently from side to side.

That definitely did some damage, but it couldn't have killed him. Did the fire finally finish the job?

"Burk! Burk, are you in there?" Kilo's voice comes through to me from the main room. "I think it's dead. I brained it with a crossbow bolt and it isn't moving."

Adrenaline has my heart in my throat. I swallow and take a deep breath. "I'm okay," I call out. "I'm coming out."

My hand is shaking. I take hold of the broom that's still wedged against the door, then think of a better idea. Even dead, I'd rather not have to slip past that thing through the narrow doorway. I unlatch the counter hatch and lift it, hopping up and throwing my legs over.

A few feet away, the cyborg hangs, arm stuck through the hole in the door and head pinned to it with a brightly colored bolt.

Kilo's crouched by the door, a compound hunting crossbow in one hand and two long guns over his shoulder. "You okay?" He looks me over, then motions for me to crouch beside him.

I nod shakily. "I got DCC'ed right after you left. He had me barricade the door. Otherwise, it would've caught me outside in the open."

Kilo returns my nod. "I got DCC'ed too, right after picking up the rifles. He made me pick up this crossbow, and now I know why. Had to be quiet." He motions to the door leading out into the rain. "I saw bullet holes in the door."

"Yeah, something shot at me as I came back inside. Maybe they're gone now if they didn't shoot at you."

"Maybe. Here, turn off the lights. We might be able to see out better."

Kilo passes me one of the rifles, one of the colony's high-powered hunting guns that we mostly only use to keep the megafauna away. We go around the room flipping off all the lights, then meet back up at the door.

"They'll be watching the door," Kilo whispers, "Try the window."

Inching up to the Plastiglass, I peek out into the swirling storm. "I see it," I say.

Even through the storm, I can see the telltale red glow of a mech's optics facing us. It's far out, up the side of the mountain, peering over a large rock.

A muzzle flash makes me drop back behind the solid wall, but nothing strikes the building.

"I think it's shooting at the main battle," I call across to Kilo.

"Can you hit it from here?"

"Yeah," I reply, scuttling in a crouch back to the metal table and dragging it to the window. "I need something to set the bi-pod on though."

Kilo moves to help. We get the table standing upright again and the rifle's bi-pod set up on it.

"I don't know if the window is gonna mess up the shot though," I say, getting behind the gun and sighting through the optic at the faded red light off in the haze of snow.

"I can break it before you shoot," Kilo replies. "I'll just smash it out with my stock."

"Good. I'm almost ready." The three-toned chime sounds in my brain again, and my hand goes to the dials on the optics, readjusting them in a way I can't understand.

Apparently the Administrator has taken a real interest in me today. Kilo stands up and smashes out the Plastiglass pane, then ducks out of the way.

As soon as he gets clear, my finger pulls the trigger. The gun kicks against my shoulder and the deafening report echoes around the interior of the meeting hall. Instead of sighting the result of my shot, I yank the gun around, pivoting down to one side of the table so my rifle is aimed out at an oblique angle, directly into the center of the colony. I put my eye to the sight, and wait, staring through the haze outside at the empty side of one of our shacks.

"Burk," Kilo interjects. "What's up?"

I can't move. My eye glares through the optic, finger poised just above the trigger. The Administrator must know something I don't, because I can't see anything out there.

"Burk, what…oh!" Kilo must realize why I can't respond, because he cuts off and gets up, moving behind me and sighting out the window back to where my original shot went.

"I think you got him," he whispers, coming around into my peripheral view again. "Something out there is smoking, and I don't see—"

A shadowed figure passes into view in my scope, shrouded in the dark of blowing snow. I pull the trigger and once again the report echoes though the building. Kilo jumps in surprise, startled by the sudden boom.

The three-tone chime sounds in my head as my body unlocks again.

"I'm back," I say, shaking out my trigger hand and returning it to steady the rifle and survey the result of my shot. "Whatever it was, it's super dead now."

I scan the debris of the mech I shot, which is scattered up the street and against the wall of the building behind it. It has to be a mech. There's no blood anywhere. As powerful as this rifle is, if that had been an organic, there would be blood splattered everywhere.

A notification pops up in my vision: *Raid repulsed, report for emergency triage.* A ghostly gray line appears at my feet, leading out the door into the blizzard.

"Let's go," Kilo says, throwing his rifle around his shoulder and heading out the door.

I follow suit, gathering up the forgotten crossbow and bolts off the floor where he left it, and hustle out the door after him. The bitter cold smacks me in the face and the wind blows up the tattered back of my parka, chilling me instantly. But I can't dwell on that.

Is Rini safe? Mabel? Max, or Roper, or Jingo?

Kilo and I hurry up the road, intent on getting to the scene of the main battle as fast as possible. In silence, we pass the remains of the mech I took out with my second shot. The lower body lays with legs sprawled in two directions, while the torso is scattered in a hundred pieces and fetched up against the wall behind it.

"Nice shot," Kilo mutters, surveying the wreck.

Figures materialize out of the gloomy haze, the rest of the colonists standing at the rough wall of sandbags we use as a barricade on this side of the town. My stomach turns to ice as the ruins of our defensive line resolve out of the dark in front of me.

The bodies of our attackers are strewn about, two human cyborgs and two mechs. These must have charged the battlements, getting over the walls before they died.

"Burk!" a voice cries in the distance. "Over here!"

I hurry over to the figure crouched in the snow, hunched over a body lying in a pool of blood. It's Max, and he's wrapping a large bandage over the severed stump of an arm on—Rini. He's working on Rini.

I sink to my knees in the snow beside her. Her blue eyes are glassy, staring at a patch of blood in the churned snow a meter away.

"She's in shock," Max says. "Help me here!" I must be in shock too. I stare dumbly at the roll of medical tape he pushes at me. "Burk, she's bleeding out!"

I reach out, taking the tape from him and helping him wrap her arm tightly with the bandage. I can see he's already put a tourniquet over her elbow. We work in silence for a moment. I can do nothing but stare at the stump of her arm.

Max wraps the tape tight against her arm, just below the tourniquet. "I think she'll be okay, he says.

Rini mumbles something. I lean closer to hear her, but she's staring blankly into the distance again.

"The caravan is all dead," Max whispers. I finally look at him and see that he's got a bloody bandage strapped over his right eye. Angry red slashes extend down past the bandage onto his cheek and chin. "They didn't make it to the barricade."

He motions with his head over the wall. I stand and look out. About a hundred meters down the rough-cut road, silhouetted in the spotlights the defenders turned on, there are more bodies. Humans and pack animals, it looks like.

"I need to see if anyone survived," I say

Max stares at me for a long moment. "Go ahead, I'll stay with her 'till you get back."

I climb out and start walking down the road, past a few broken bodies of mechs and bloody corpses of cyborgs. My implant buzzes, reminding me I'm not doing my proper duty—not following orders—but I need to see. My mind is in a haze, just like the snowy fog around me.

I walk down the line of bodies until I find her: sixth and last in the caravan.

Mabel is face up in the snow, staring up into the sky, her arms and legs outstretched as if about to make a snow angel. I can't see a wound, but the front of her clothes is dark with blood already hardening with frost.

There are no words.

I sink to my knees beside her, my hand unconsciously going out to caress her cold, pale face. I reach to close her eyes but stop at the last moment. She loved the stars, I think she would want to look up at the sky one last time.

My breath hitches. I'm finally coming down from the adrenaline of the fight. My whole body begins to shake, and finally, the tears start to fall.

A roar sounds ahead of me, causing me to lift my eyes from my sister's face. A drop pod is landing in the road up ahead. Perhaps it's another cluster of mechs, coming down to finish the job. I can't seem to bring myself to care.

I look back at Mabel's face, but there are letters obscuring my vision.

A single word: *Prioritized.*

The gray line extends from my feet down the road toward the drop pod.

We always knew the Administrator didn't care about our feelings, but this is a new low. My sister lies dead on the ground, and He expects us to just carry on?

My implant buzzes.

"Go to hell," I mutter. I know He can hear me.

My body seizes up, the three-tone chime sounding in my mind. If I could scream, I would, but I can't. He makes me stand up, every fiber of my being resisting this. All in vain.

I step around Mabel's body and weave my way through the rest of the caravan's corpses, down the road to the oblong gray alloy of the drop pod.

The indignity of this, the inhumanity.

I key in a code I don't know to the panel on the side of the pod. The access hatch pops open.

Before this, I could not have believed anyone to be so callous that they—

I lift out a long Plastisteel case and open it. Inside, nestled in foam is a shining alloy prosthetic arm ending just above the elbow—exactly where Rini's arm now ends.

I set the open case down on the ground and reach into the drop pod again, pulling out a small square box. Cradled in the foam of this case is a glittering eyeball, with monofilament wire spilling from the back and a glinting metallic blue iris staring back at me. The same color as Max's remaining eye.

There's one more box in the drop pod, at the very bottom, stuffed behind vacuum-sealed packages of what looks like food.

It's wedged in tight, and I struggle to lift it out, banging it back and forth as I lift it free. The scattered gravel on the road crunches as I set it down and open the lid. Six silver cylinders lay inside, each about the size of a water-ration bottle.

It can't be.

I barely notice as my implant chimes an all-clear and my body unlocks. I reach down and lift one of the cylinders out of its cradle. There's silver lettering on the side, and I have to squint to make it out in the gloom.

Tri-phasic Chlorodoxiquin/Postmortal Organic Nanite Injection Serum—Administer within 1 hr.

I've never seen one of these before, but I know what it is. It's Sparkleworld medicine. It raises the dead.

Six cylinders, six bodies lying in the snow behind me.

A message appears in my vision, direct from the Administrator.

Happy Winter Holiday.

Frost Fiend
By E. R. Donaldson

Niklaus stood before the icy gates, sword on his back and axe in his hand. A foul wind swept up, whipping his scarlet coat all around him. It was a gift from the townsfolk a fortnight past, issued when he'd declared his intended destination.

"Take this," the crone had directed, proffering her wool-lined gift.

With his current cloak in tatters, Niklaus had accepted the offering graciously; sparing only a moment to balk at its unusual color. "Why the red?"

The woman seemed confused and taken aback by his question. Recovering herself, she said, "It was made for one of the men from the south—some chief of those who bring the new religion. 'Saints,' I think they call 'em."

Niklaus had scowled at the reference, even though it seemed somehow incorrect. He didn't like being compared to the cowards of the new religion. Though their Christ had conducted plenty of miracles in the south, none of them seemed inclined to bring His benevolent grace northward. None except *one*, anyway.

He'd accepted the gift nonetheless and was now glad for its protection against the icy winds. Niklaus drew his scarlet cloak tighter about his muscular frame, even as the storm buffeted his long white hair and tangled beard.

What wouldn't he give for a scarlet cap to match his coat right about now?

Setting the pain aside, he stomped his way through the snowdrift to reach the icy gate. Pounding one black-gloved fist against the frozen barrier, he bellowed out, "*Illinthius*. I know ye be here. Open these gates and face me, coward!"

A moment of chilling silence passed.

Niklaus opened his mouth to issue his challenge anew but came up short when a distant and terrible laugh rumbled out of the darkness, carried along on the blowing snowdrifts. The gates chimed a discordant ring like that of clinking glass before shifting of their own accord. The snowpack in front of the gate groaned plaintively as frosted iron swung outward, leaving the path open before Niklaus.

Fear clawed at his heart, and not for the first time, he buried it beneath a fresh layer of inner fortitude. Niklaus knew what he was getting into. He was not the first to challenge the Frost Fiend. Hopefully, though, he would be the last.

"*Hope is not a plan,*" whispered a voice in his mind—a voice that wasn't there; *couldn't* be there. It was the missionary's voice, of that Niklaus was certain, but that made no sense. Gabriel had been dead for many seasons.

This didn't stop the apparition of the dead missionary from laughing. "*You're about to walk into the crystal fortress of a greater demon,*" Gabriel noted, "*and you find it surprising that the voice of a dead man speaks to you? I believe we've established there are supernatural forces in play here, my old friend.*"

Niklaus grunted, trudging forward in the ankle-deep snow. Not directing his comment anywhere in particular, he stated, "Aren't ye supposed to be in the arms of yer precious savior? It was all ye spoke of in life. Here I was thinking ye'd be at peace. Why ye be bothering me, spirit?"

Another spectral laugh. "*Let's just say I've been given special dispensation. My Lord truly hopes that you will succeed.*"

Niklaus scowled. "Does that make ye some kind of Holy Ghost? Like the one ye kept blabbering on about?"

"*I see my 'blabbering' did not resonate with you, for if it had, you would know that's not the case.*"

"Then what're ye here for?"

There was a pause where all Niklaus heard was the sound of his own boots crunching in the snow and the howling winds. When Gabriel spoke again, he seemed to proceed cautiously. *"I know what you're planning. What I told you was true: you cannot beat this creature through strength-of-arms. You will need to adopt a different tack, Niklaus."*

Niklaus spat. "I brought that damned trinket ye gave me." He hefted his shoulder bag for emphasis—just in case the spirit was somehow watching him. "After I cut off the bastard's head, I promise to put that demon's skull right in next to it. Nice and snug."

Despite Gabriel not being present, even as an apparition, Niklaus could feel his disappointment. *"At least you have it,"* Niklaus said with finality, falling silent.

The ensuing silence made Niklaus question his mission even more. It had seemed so simple at first: a sell-sword and raider seeking retirement from his life of violence. He'd found work, married a younger woman, and built a life.

All that was taken from him in an instant. The seemingly endless winter had culled over half his village two moons prior to the arrival of Illinthius' wretched minions. Even though Niklaus—along with all the other warriors of his village—had successfully destroyed the invading force, the damage was already done.

In their naiveté, they had thought themselves triumphant heroes returning to their families to announce their overwhelming victory. Niklaus had thought it too. How foolish they had been.

The village was all but destroyed by the time they returned. They expected to return to food and drink, to warm hearths and a heroic feast. Instead, they were welcomed by sounds of violence—not of pitched battle, but of an unopposed slaughter. Debris from buildings and townsfolk alike: strewn across the grounds like snow scattered by the harsh winds of winter. Gabriel— one of Niklaus' closest friends, despite their differing philosophies—had perished in the attack, as had Niklaus' wife. Left with nothing else, Niklaus went north in pursuit of the only thing he had left on this Earth: *vengeance.*

That vengeance was his only source of warmth as he trudged past the frosted iron gates. The path, at first, didn't seem all that different from the one leading to the gates: just a snow-covered road of hard-packed soil and stone overhung by ice-laden trees. It took a few more minutes of walking before something took shape.

Two somethings, in fact. Twin figures stood defiantly, half-shrouded in shadow, unmoved by the buffeting winds. They had the shape of men and were clad in mottled leather armor. Each held a spear in their right hand and a buckler strapped to their left forearm. They stood as solid as the frozen rock under their feet.

As Niklaus neared, he saw their frost-covered faces were slack and without expression. Their eyes were glazed over, staring sightlessly in front of them.

Dead. Yet still standing… waiting.

Niklaus did not have to wait for the beings to move and recognize them for what they were. He'd seen scores of these creatures in the towns and villages ravaged by Illinthius' destructive hand. Some of his own men had even met this foul fate in his long journey here. Under most circumstances, they were the only things left standing at the end of an attack. But they were not survivors. Not really.

Wights—the undead servants of Illinthius. This pair stood guard before a crystalline archway set within a wall that stretched as far as Niklaus could see in either direction. Undoubtedly this was the entrance to Illinthius' fortress.

Niklaus scowled and spat upon the snow. "Too afraid to come out and face me yerself, demon? Ye send yer minions in yer stead?"

Booming laughter cascaded out from the crystal archway. "How amusing. Deal with these frigid corpses first, pest. Maybe then we'll see if you are worthy of my attention." At the demon's taunt, the two undead warriors shifted position as if they were but puppets whose strings had just been pulled taut. Built-up ice crackled off their limbs as they shook free the stiffness of death and sprang to this dark approximation of life. Both undead servants brought their spears over the top of their bucklers and prepared to charge.

Tightening the sack over his shoulder, Niklaus cracked his neck. He slid into a crouch, one hand held out in front of him, the other readying his axe to strike. "Fine," he growled. "Needed something to get me blood flowing anyhow."

The pair of wights began to shamble forth, in no hurry to begin a dance with death, a dance they had already lost. Niklaus did not wait for them to come to him. He charged, heavy footfalls forcing their way through the snowdrifts with ease. He veered left, and the closest opponent stabbed out at him. Batting the thrust aside with the back of his axe, Niklaus spun. His weapon came back around, finding the undead creature's neck and cleaving through it. The wight's head spun bloodlessly away as its body collapsed in the snow.

The second creature slashed out with the tip of its spear, exhibiting a speed that belied its rigid appearance. Niklaus darted backward, leaving the weapon piercing through nothing but air. He rushed forward to counter, even as the wight thrust at him again.

Niklaus ducked to the side just in time to avoid this second, heavier thrust. With his free hand, he grabbed the haft of the spear and jerked the monster sideways. Despite seeming so surefooted before, the wight stumbled off balance. Roaring in triumph, drawing upon the anger that had guided him so far, Niklaus brought his axe squarely down on the creature's skull.

Another moment of chilling silence, broken only by the sound of Niklaus removing his axe from the second wight's fragile skull.

With both monsters now lying motionless in the snow, as corpses should absent the influence of Illinthius' dark sorcery, Niklaus howled out into the night. "That's the best ye've got, demon?" He didn't stop to take a breath. He marched onward through the crystal archway, up the stairs beneath, and into the fortress beyond.

The error of his boasting became obvious when he entered the main hall. Score upon score of dead, frozen figures stood in the corridor—some clad in nothing more than civilian furs, but plenty of others armed and armored like the pair of guards at the entrance. Niklaus didn't need to hear Illinthius' echoing laughter to know that he'd allowed himself to angrily, even arrogantly, trudge right into a trap.

Cursing, partially at the industriousness of his quarry but also largely at his own foolishness, Niklaus returned his axe to his belt and drew the massive greatsword from his back. His eyes went not to the legion of undead rounding their unseeing eyes toward him, but to the stairs at the end of the hall. Atop that grand staircase stood a set of banded double doors, embossed with a demonic symbol at their center: Illinthius' throne room.

Niklaus readied himself for his mad dash. Though he might be able to contend with this army of wights, the effort would sap precious strength from his body. Living in the North had taught Niklaus from a young age not to expend more energy than he could safely spare, and there was no telling how many multitudes Illinthius yet held in reserve throughout the numerous side passages of his fortress. If Niklaus tarried too long, he might soon find himself buried in a horde of undead. If he attempted to fight them all instead of pushing on to his true target, all he would accomplish would be adding his own body to their ranks. He needed to move quickly, efficiently, striking only where it served him best. No unnecessary motion taken. No effort wasted. Such was the way of the North.

With a furious battle cry, a reminder to all these shambling corpses of what it meant to be alive, he charged: his focus upon the far side of the chamber and the staircase leading to the door, on the other side of which lay his prey. He was so close.

Gabriel, if you're listening, my vengeance is at hand. Hope you and your savior are watching.

The wights moved to intercept him, their frozen joints crackling like so much frozen meat as their master maneuvered their frosted cadavers into action like puppets. Niklaus spun, cutting down the first pair of wights that stepped into his path. Still whirling, he carved through another and separated the head of a fourth before his momentum slowed. He shoulder-checked a fifth, scattering its bones across the cobbled floor, and grabbed a sixth by its tunic. With a grunt of effort, he sent it hurtling into a trio of its compatriots.

Taking a quick breath, Niklaus assessed his progress. The distant stairway seemed to taunt him as surely as the demon's laughter had. This would not be as easy as his ordeal at the gates. As he had suspected, wights were pouring steadily from every door and side passage. If he lingered too long, he would be overwhelmed.

So, he hefted his sword and pressed on. The wights moved mercifully slowly but in an unending tide. Every step of progress was hard fought. Though the creatures never came within arm's reach of him, the sheer weight of his blade and fatigue from his exertion weighed heavily upon him; turning his mad dash into a spite-filled slog. He filled the air with frost-ridden bones and obscenities levied against every one of his enemies, the mothers that bore them, the fathers that failed to teach them how to fight so they might've lived a little longer and spared him the effort of dismantling their accursed corpses. Above all, he cursed Illinthius for using his twisted magics to raise these wights from their rightful graves.

By the time he reached the stairs, his breath was coming in heavy, ragged gasps.

With the advantage of the high ground, one of the guards upon the stairs stabbed down, just barely catching Niklaus on his off hand. Searing pain mingled with frigid chill. Niklaus' sword clattered to the steps, the ring of steel upon stone resonating like a bell through the hall, signaling the remaining undead that this living embodiment of wrath was, at last, losing some of his terrible momentum.

The breath that escaped him rose as a puff of frost before his face as his eyes hardened. His lips pulled back in a snarl.

Immediately his axe was in his remaining hand. He severed the arm of his attacker, driving his shoulder forward to knock the wight to its back. Another guard lunged forward, stabbing with its frozen spear.

Niklaus, grunting in pain, lashed out with his damaged arm. He grasped the spear, halting it inches before it would have pierced his chest. With a defiant roar, he pivoted sharply; using the spear shaft to fling the wight into its cohorts at the base of the stairs. The undead warrior stumbled, lost its grip on the spear, and rolled helplessly into the milling throng below.

The path to the doors was now clear. Still holding the captured spear with his injured hand, his axe with the other, Niklaus bounded up the steps and slammed his shoulder into the portal. The iron doors squealed plaintively as they swung open under the impact. Niklaus crashed to the crystal floor.

Yet, he didn't stop. The army of wights was shambling up the stairs behind him. He rallied to his feet, drawing the doors closed. Once they were in place, he slammed his stolen spear through the handles, locking the doors in place.

Pounding resonated from the other side of the iron barrier, but it was half-hearted. The makeshift lock would hold.

Niklaus slumped to his knees. He examined his injured forearm. The gash, tinged with frozen specks of red, had already turned black. He flexed his hand, finding he could still move it, but not without pain.

Gabriel's voice came to him like a half-remembered dream. *"How bad is it?"*

Niklaus grunted. "Still here, are ye?"

"Why would I leave when you're so close to your goal?"

The question galvanized Niklaus' flagging will. "He's close then?"

"See for yourself."

Looking up, Niklaus found himself in another darkened corridor. This gave way to a great chamber beyond, separated from the entry hall by a curtain made of frozen chains.

There he is, Niklaus thought. That fire of vengeance burned all the brighter in his gut, melting the ice in his heart and granting new life to his aching limbs. He rose to his feet, still holding his axe in his right hand.

"And you still have the artifact?" Gabriel pressed.

Biting back his annoyance, Niklaus checked his shoulder straps. His black leather sack was still affixed to his back. "Yes, spirit, I have your trinket." He waited for some reply, but Gabriel remained quiet. It seemed that hefting that stupid orb into battle like some kind of good luck charm was enough to placate the missionary's ghost.

Niklaus stalked forward, determination radiating from every step. Using his axe, he swept aside the frosty curtain and passed into the heart of Illinthius' domain.

This final chamber was broad and circular, crafted from the same strange mix of crystal and stone that comprised the rest of the fortress. Icy statues were spaced around the chamber at regular intervals. Some of them, Niklaus realized, were crafted to resemble the warriors of the surrounding regions—complete with their respective arms and armor and posed as if they were ready to strike. The others were warriors too, but unlike any Niklaus had ever fought against.

"Frozen memories of those who have come before you," boomed a voice from the center of the chamber. "Would-be champions, now reduced to nothing more than trophies for my chamber."

Niklaus turned his attention to the speaker. Sitting upon a throne of ice and crystal in the middle of the chamber, waited Illinthius.

The Frost Fiend was massive, dwarfing Niklaus' massive frame half-again. His shoulders, back, and arms rippled with jagged spikes. Similar protrusions thrust out from his knees and elbows, and his hands terminated in jagged claws like daggers protruding from his thick fingers. Though vaguely human in shape, there was something distinctly draconic about his visage.

Illinthius' reptilian maw stretched too wide for any human jaw. "Well done, Niklaus Clauson. As you can see, my triumphs are numerous, but those arrayed about this chamber are only those who've proven valiant enough to reach my inner sanctum. Countless more have failed to reach even where you stand now. I look forward to adding your likeness to my collection." He indicated, with taloned fingertips, to an empty alcove awaiting a new statue. One of many such spaces still lining the circular chamber, awaiting new champions to inspire fresh effigies.

Niklaus couldn't decide if the demon's boasts were just that, or if they held some grain of truth. These statues could have been anyone. Illinthius could be lying. Ultimately, it did not matter. "I'm here to rid this world of ye, demon. Talk as much as ye want. Ye'll only delay the inevitable."

Illinthius laughed again, though this time it was tinged with something else. Weariness? Annoyance? "Very well." He rose from his throne. "I'm nothing, if not sporting. You've traveled so far, I imagine you deserve *some* kind of reward." He spread his arms wide. "The first strike is yours, warrior. Aim true, for you will not land a second."

This had to be some kind of trick. Even if it was, Niklaus couldn't resist the temptation. He unhooked his sack from his shoulder, letting it fall to the icy ground. His empty sword sheath was next to follow. Freed of his burdens, he rolled his shoulders, stretching his muscles and stiffening his resolve. He drew in a deep breath.

All his pain, all his rage, and all his strength were channeled into a single, howling war cry. He raced forward, black boots echoing against the crystalline floor. With all his might, he swung his axe overhead and brought it down directly into Illinthius' chest, burying the blade to the haft.

Niklaus yanked back on the handle, hoping to ready a second strike. The axe held fast in the demon's torso. Illinthius didn't even flinch.

The demon lowered his draconic head. "Pathetic." Moving faster than Niklaus' eye could track, Illinthius lashed out with one clawed hand. The blow caught Niklaus on the side, sending him sprawling, tumbling, sliding across the crystalline floor.

Dismissively, Illinthius tore the axe from his chest, tossing it in the opposite direction. "I hope you got that out of your system," he growled. "Now, if I have your attention, I'd like to introduce you to our audience this evening."

Still reeling from the blow, Niklaus managed to lift his head to see Illinthius snap his fingers. Another figure—a wight, based on its appearance— stepped out from behind the icy thrown. The undead creature stepped forward, marching diligently to stand in front of Illinthius.

The demon caressed the figure's shoulders gently. "Do you recognize her, Niklaus? Unless I'm not mistaken, she's someone incredibly important to you."

At first, Niklaus did not recognize her. Then, on further study, he finally managed to find something familiar about that too-pale complexion.

The eyes were too pale, a dead shadow of their former brilliance. Her long, lush curls hung lank and matted with frost. Her once-full, strong figure, was now emaciated and flaccid. Still, there was no mistaking her.

Niklaus barely managed a whisper. "Margrete?"

Illinthius' laugh regained a hint of its former mirth. "Go say hello to your husband, dear Margrete. He's come a long way to see you."

The wight stepped forward obediently. Step by torturous step, she closed the distance between her and Niklaus. Niklaus struggled to his feet, still not believing the horror he was witnessing could possibly be true.

But it was. In her final paces, he saw what faint echoes remained of Margrete's beauty. She was still clad in the thin shift she had been wearing the night the wights had plucked her from their cabin. Her lips, now tinged blue, were the same lips he'd kissed before swearing he'd return to her.

He'd failed her that night, and now that failure stood before him in all its horrific beauty.

"This can't be real," he sobbed quietly. "She *died*."

"No, Niklaus. She did not die. She has merely been transformed. Now her beauty shall live eternally under my power." Illinthius paused, feigning consideration. "You could join her, you know. As you've witnessed, my army is desperately short of valiant warriors. I have no need of another trophy for my throne room. What I could use is a *real* warrior."

The offer wasn't tempting in the slightest. All temptation lay two steps in front of Niklaus. He closed the distance. Reaching up, he caressed Margrete's frosted cheek. Her flesh was cold but held the same familiar softness. Her dead eyes moved, meeting Niklaus'. A hint of something lay behind that cloudy sheen. Remembrance perhaps?

Her lips moved. "Niii… klaus," she groaned. "I… love… you… Ni… klaus…"

It was more than Niklaus' heart could take. With a wail, a sob of fury, Niklaus reached for the last weapon he had on him: his hunting knife. Caressing the back of Margrete's neck, he drove the blade up under her jaw.

Margrete's corpse twitched twice before sagging in his grasp. Niklaus held her close, lowering her gently to the ground, weeping openly. His warm tears frosted over as they met her undead flesh. The sheer frigidity of her form burned him, even through his black gloves and thick red coat. He held her only tighter.

Illinthius huffed in annoyance. "I'll take that as a 'no.'"

Hearing the demon's voice again roused Niklaus from his grief. He stood, all sorrow forgotten. Now, all he had was rage. He rushed toward Illinthius with nothing but his hunting knife.

Annoyed, Illinthius held up a single hand. A blast of ice and wind stopped Niklaus in his tracks before flinging him backward. He collided with one of the statues which, despite its icy appearance, felt as hard as steel. Even as they both toppled over, the statue failed to so much as chip.

The world was still spinning as Gabriel's voice broke through. *"Niklaus, you can't do this on your own."*

The dead missionary was right. He needed a weapon. He turned to the side to find the nearest frozen statue holding a vicious, double-bladed battle axe. Niklaus slid the weapon free of its icy hold and hefted the weight. This would work.

Illinthius unleashed another frosty blast. Niklaus braced himself against the pedestal which had housed the fallen statue. He gritted his teeth against the icy wind, taking one step forward. Then another.

"You're a determined one," Illinthius chuckled. A frozen sword appeared in each of his hands. "Come then: let us test your mettle."

As the magical winds dissipated, Niklaus charged. His borrowed axe came around in a vicious swipe. Illinthius dodged, but Niklaus did not relent. He spun toward the Frost Fiend like a whirlwind unleashed, the broad blade of the axe flashing again and again.

Illinthius slapped the blade down as one might a biting fly. He thrust a sword towards Niklaus' face. Niklaus dodged, bringing his axe back around for another swipe. Illinthius readied his second sword to block.

Axe met sword. Steel met ice. A shrill cry echoed across the chamber. Niklaus felt the impact down to his very bones. He could only groan in pain as the blow—a blow *he* had issued— threatened to crumple him.

With a dismissive grunt, Illinthius released his blade and backhanded Niklaus across the face. Niklaus bounced across the crystal floor, body cracking and flesh bleeding, as he was brought up near the icy curtain at the entrance.

Though his bones had not broken, Niklaus felt shattered. It was his will that had been cast to pieces upon that crystalline floor. Cold realization set in: any blow he struck upon Illinthius would hurt him more than it would hurt the demon.

Gabriel had been right. No mortal could stand against this creature.

"There's still time."

Niklaus suddenly became aware of the pressure against his back. He'd been pushed up against the nearest wall, but he'd somehow managed to bring along his leather sack. It was wedged between the crystalline wall and his broken figure.

Illinthius took a step forward. Then another. "Poor, poor Niklaus. Did you really think you stood a chance?" Another step. "You are not half the warrior I expected. You are strong, yes, but strength alone poses no threat to me."

As the demon's taloned footsteps drew closer, Niklaus tried to rouse himself. He pushed himself up. Collapsed. Tried again.

"At least some warriors brought an element of skill to our confrontation. You're nothing but an undisciplined barbarian—lashing out with not but rage to guide your blade. No form or artistry, just brute strength and stubborn will. Did you really think your anger could rival that of one who was cast out of Heaven? You think you know hatred, Niklaus? You think you know rage? I assure you: you know *nothing*."

Niklaus fumbled for the bag. He managed to secure a strap. He tried to rise again and failed. He fell upon his back.

"Still, you've made it this far, Niklaus. That has earned you something. Know that, instead of leading my immortal armies, you will forever decorate my throne room—yet another challenger who failed to prove himself worthy."

Illinthius reared back to strike. A jagged blade of ice jutted forward from his wrist. He swung downward, aiming for Niklaus' heart.

Niklaus yanked the bag over his chest, holding its leather-wrapped contents out like a talisman.

The sound of shattered glass and cracking ice pierced the air. Niklaus felt the blow pierce his bag and the object within. He locked his arms in place, holding the artifact aloft.

"What...?" Illinthius whispered. "What is *this*?"

Niklaus looked at the bag. Though Illinthius' arm was buried to the elbow, more than sufficient to break through to the other side, the back side of the sack remained intact. With the last vestiges of his strength, Niklaus held the artifact before him, still enshrined in its leather carrying-case.

It worked. The artifact Gabriel had given him had stopped Illinthius' killing blow. By the looks of it, it was absorbing him.

"*No*," the Frost Fiend growled, yanking his arm back. It was no use. He appeared trapped. Even his gargantuan strength failed to yank the artifact from Niklaus' rigid grasp.

"*It's almost done,*" Gabriel whispered in Niklaus' mind. "*But he is not captured yet. You must channel the power of the artifact. You must draw him in.*"

And how do I do that? Niklaus wondered.

"*Pray, Niklaus. You must pray.*"

Resurgent dread seized Niklaus' heart. *Pray?* He'd never prayed to the old gods, much less this new one. How was he supposed to…

"*Like I taught you, Niklaus.*"

Now it was conviction that chilled Niklaus' soul. He'd never paid much attention to Gabriel's ravings. He'd only listened enough to get the old missionary to stifle his incessant prattling. Was now the time that he'd pay the price for not listening closer to his dearest friend?

Then, almost as if by magic, something came to him. It wasn't a prayer, but a piece of poetry that the missionary had read to him. Of Gabriel's so-called "scripture," it was the piece that resonated closest with Niklaus. Whenever he'd think of it, he'd have Gabriel repeat it to him.

It was this poetry that he recited now. "The Lord… is… my shepherd," he grunted. "I… shall not… want."

Warmth radiated from the sack. Illinthius' reptilian eyes widened further. "No…"

Feeling newfound strength, Niklaus continued. "He maketh me lie down in green pastures. He… leadeth me beside… still waters."

"*Heathen!*" Illinthius spat. "You know not what you speak. Do not play at powers you yourself do not believe."

That same conviction clawed at Niklaus' heart. Yet still, he continued. "He restoreth my soul. He leadeth me in the paths of righteousness, for his name's sake."

The heat beneath his hands grew. Illinthius stumbled. Looking in the demon's direction, Niklaus saw that Illinthius had been drawn into the sack up to his shoulder. "No, no, no!" Illinthius roared. "Empty words from a nonbeliever! This cannot be happening!"

The next lines were Niklaus' favorite part. They, more than anything Gabriel had ever preached, stuck out in his mind as clear as sunlight breaching the clouds. "Though I walk through the valley of the shadow of death, I will fear no evil: for thou art with me."

Illinthius roared. Light poured from the space where his body and the sack intersected.

Niklaus finished the poem. "Thy rod and thy staff, they comfort me. Though preparest a table before me in the presence of mine enemies. Thou anointest my head with oil. My cup runneth over. Surely goodness and mercy shall follow me all the days of my life, and I will dwell in the house of the Lord forever." Upon finishing, Niklaus added a final, "*Amen.*"

The demon screamed. Light radiated from the artifact, shining through the dark leather sack. There was a rush of wind, and Niklaus was flattened. He lost his grip on the bag.

The sack with its encased artifact hovered above him, shining like the sun. Screaming all the while, the demon was drawn up and into that radiating ball. The earth quaked. Niklaus thought he might pass out.

Then, as suddenly as it had begun, it was over. The sack shuddered once and fell upon the crystalline floor. Niklaus stared at it in disbelief. It had worked. He'd done it.

No… not him. He'd failed. Failed miserably. Something else had saved him.

"You did well, my friend," Gabriel whispered. *"Farewell."*

Farewell? "Gabriel?" Niklaus asked. When there was no answer, he shouted, *"Gabriel!"*

It was no use. The missionary's spirit had fled. Niklaus was left alone in the chamber with nothing but his bag and the artifact contained within.

Slowly, painfully, he rolled over, reaching for the leather bag. He reached into the sack, fishing for what he knew had to be there.

When he withdrew the glowing orb, there was no sign that it had been breached—not even a dent upon its smooth surface. The kay'leh was completely unmarred. Now, though, instead of appearing as an inert glass sphere, a hazy smoke wafted from inside.

It had happened just as Gabriel had foretold: the Frost Fiend was trapped inside this prison, never to escape until someone released it.

Now, only one question remained: what to do with it?

Niklaus sat on that crystal floor for a long time, contemplating the question. He thought of burying it but could not imagine himself digging a hole deep enough to satisfy his conscience. No, he would bring this artifact far away. Maybe then, and only then, he'd think of burying it.

But where?

Only unto the ends of the earth, he thought, a soft smile gracing his bloodied lips.

There was tale of a place up north, across the frozen sea, that represented the true edge of the world. Most thought it was the point where the Earth ended, the point where one might walk right off into the void itself. Others, though—a *scarce* few—whispered that it was the point where, if you kept walking north, you would suddenly find yourself returning to the south.

Whichever of these was true, it was the most distant place Niklaus could think of. *That's where I'll hide it*, he decided. *What better place for an ice demon's prison than the farthest reaches of the North?*

S⊦RANDED
By Ameera Rashid

White used to be my favorite color, but now, as I peeked through the small glass window of my escape pod, the color seemed like a death warrant. The endless snow stretching through the horizon painted an ominous picture, the hissing wind promising my approaching demise.

Winters were rare where I came from, and snow was even rarer. The only time I ever felt the sensation of cold was when I held ice, and those little experiences had hardly prepared me for what I was now going through. Even the confines of this metal egg couldn't shield me from the glacial climate of the Earth. The warmth seeped continually out of my body, the snow outside drinking it in.

Why was it so cold? I was told to expect a mild climate upon landing. It didn't make any sense. During my weeks-long training, I was prepared to face any hindrances that might interrupt my mission. And yet, no one warned me about the cold.

Scratching the tip of my chin, I tried to figure out what could've gone wrong. I was given specific co-ordinates to land on Earth and investigate the area for any Primitive survivors. Even though it had seemed unlikely to find anyone here a millennia after the apocalypse.

One glance at the unending mounds of snow was enough to confirm my suspicions on the matter. There was not a thing alive out there.

Was it all a test? Or, by any chance, some cruel joke to send me on a fool's errand? The thought was more terrifying than death, but I wouldn't put it past my people; not when I had to face such discrimination for being a Primitive.

No! I shook my head. There had to be a mistake. I must have accidentally landed on the wrong planet or something. I wouldn't know for sure until I analyzed the equipment back on my ship which, of course, I currently didn't have access to. *All the more reason to go out and find it.*

But the cold had left my body lethargic. I shrank in my seat and waited, which was a stupid thing to do considering what precious little time I had. The only way I'd survive was to go out in the blizzard, find my spaceship, and fix it before my resources ran out. I didn't have a second to waste, especially because help would never reach me here; not when I was so far away from my home planet, Aleron.

Why did I ever think I could pull this off? I wondered as I worked up the nerve to unlock the hatch door, its metal grip ice-cold against my small fingers. It had seemed so much easier back then, almost heroic, to think I would get to sail across the universe and visit Earth: the planet where my ancestors once resided before the apocalypse.

On top of that, if I successfully reported my findings, I would not only get my freedom back, but I would prove to everyone that I was no less than any Hybrid. Even if I was an unevolved Primitive, we were not all that different after all. In the end, we were all just human beings.

I was thrilled when I was chosen as a candidate for this mission, despite my status. I poured my heart and soul into my training. I was willing to give it my all, just for the sake of a better life.

Yet, as I shivered and shrank in my seat, my mission seemed to be the least of my concerns. The worst part was having no idea where my spaceship ended up when it crashed. Fortunately, I was able to eject myself with the escape pod before I got hurt, but there was no telling in what shape my spaceship might be in. If it was broken beyond repair, I could be stranded here.

My colleagues, being Hybrids, would never waste precious manpower and resources on a rescue mission for a lowly Primitive like me. I prayed I would find my spaceship somewhere soon, and that it would be in good shape. If I couldn't...

I shuddered, not being able to decide which was worse: being stranded alone on a frozen wasteland, or taking too much time to get to my spaceship and having to go back without any findings.

A chill went down my back. Resisting the urge to shrink even more, I pinched my cheeks until they hurt, not willing to waste any more time thinking. I'd find my spaceship, complete my mission and go back. With a firm, determined nod, I loosened the safety harness and gently pushed open the hatch door.

It was cold enough to freeze cells, perhaps even atoms. The moment I emerged from the escape pod and stood upright the icy wind hit me like a slap, piercing through my spacesuit like a thousand burning needles poking into every inch of my skin.

I trudged through the thick mounds of snow without any sense of direction. My spaceship was nowhere to be seen. With the fog blocking most of my view, I was forced to walk aimlessly for a while, each step harder than the last one. If only I had Hybrid eyes like everyone else on my planet, I would have been able to see through the fog. Another reminder of me being an unevolved Primitive.

As I continued to flounder, I could feel my body fighting for control against the chill that had found its way within me. Only a few minutes had passed, and drowsiness was starting to take over me. At this rate, I knew I wouldn't last long, but I was still hoping for my spaceship to appear by some miracle. Besides, if I went back now, even the metal egg wouldn't be able to shield me against the cold.

So, I kept moving. I didn't know how long I walked, but it was getting harder to stay upright. I could feel the last remaining dregs of my warmth surrendering. If only I could close my eyes for just a moment...

I did not remember falling, but the next moment I found myself lying face-down in the snow. I could no longer fight it. The cold finally robbed me of the last whispers of heat within my bones.

They say your life flashes before your eyes when you're about to die. Maybe that was what was happening to me. As I lay in the middle of the blizzard, I remember seeing my mother. Her glowing silver eyes, akin to any other Hybrid, gazed upon me with disdain. I knew it was disdain because it was the same look she always wore whenever she regarded me: her greatest disappointment.

Hybrids rarely conveyed emotions. The most you could get from them would be the ghost of a smile or an infinitesimal crease of the brows. Not that they were incapable of using their facial muscles, they just didn't see it as a necessity. It was hard to believe that their ancestors once used to be ordinary Primitives like me. Their passage through the wormhole after the apocalypse might have evolved them for the better, granting them preternatural abilities—but it came at a cost. They stopped being human.

I still excused the lack of empathy in my family due to this very reason, but my mother was different. She always went out of her way to give me that particular look of contempt, just to show me how much she despised having me. She made sure it was the last thing I'd see before she sold me to the lab, and I was locked up.

I had sobbed all night long, much to everyone's wonder, because that was the first time most of those Hybrids got to see such a blatant display of emotion. I was nothing more than a test subject. My fear, anxiety, and sadness were all intriguing mysteries for them. Looking back on it, it was pretty foolish of me to believe that the glowing eyes were the only difference between Hybrids and Primitives. The worst of it all was their inability to feel anything but disgust.

I squeezed my eyes shut in an attempt to forget, but more memories intruded my thoughts. Every loss, every regret, every crushed dream... I saw it all while the chill continued to seep in. My last thought was of embracing it, as I let the cold finally take over.

I woke to the sounds of a crackling fire and multiple, soft voices engrossed in a deep conversation. I was too dizzy to make out the words. My eyes seemed to be glued shut, so I decided to stay as I was, snuggling in the warmth beneath my heavy quilt, savoring every moment, until the oddity of my situation finally struck me: this wasn't home.

It was never cold in Aleron, so I never enjoyed the warmth there either. Now, though, as I found myself cherishing the heat emitted by the crackling fire, memories tumbled back into my mind one by one: my mission, Earth, the crash, the escape pod, the snow…

My eyes tore open. It took a while for me to adjust to the glow of the fire before taking in my surroundings. Despite the illumination, the rocky ceiling and walls of the cave were so far away that they were nothing more than blotches of darkness. There was no sign of an exit.

I noticed the fur blanket wrapped around me and the rug I had been sleeping on. When I tried to run my fingers along it, I found my limbs were tied. That prompted me to finally turn my attention to the two figures sitting across the fire.

They seemed to have noticed I had awakened, and hence immediately halted their conversation to observe me. I did the same. One of them was a middle-aged man with a buff build, a strong stubbled jaw, and a fierce aura. The other one was younger: a dark-skinned woman, appearing to be in her twenties, petite and graceful in a unique way. Both of them wore white fur cloaks.

The woman offered me a warm smile, and the action was enough to make me raise my brows in shock. Never in my life had I ever seen anyone smile so broadly. Even I had stopped doing so after years of schooling my face to remain indifferent just so I could fit in.

As odd as it seemed, it was also a bit refreshing to finally meet someone like me.

"You're Primitives..." I mumbled.

"We prefer the term 'Humans,'" the man replied.

"Oh, don't be so uptight, Enzo! She just woke up." The girl shoved the man playfully, before turning her attention to me. "Hi, I'm Astrid, and this is Enzo. We found you outside the cave. You were almost frozen to death, so we bought you here. You're safe now."

I didn't answer. Instead, my mind was busy piecing everything together. They had found me outside the cave? I looked up. "What planet is this?"

Astrid and Enzo exchanged a glance.

"Shouldn't you know that already?" The woman chuckled.

I did know, but I wanted to make sure.

"It's Earth," Enzo answered.

So, I was in the right place after all, and there truly were Primitive survivors here. I couldn't resist a sigh of relief. A little while ago, I thought I was going to die. Now, here I was: alive and in possession of the information I'd come here to get. If I could only find my spaceship, I'd be able to return. There was hope again.

"What's your name?" Astrid inquired, interrupting the silence.

Instead of answering, I held out my hands. "Untie me first."

"Oh, sorry about that, but I can't." She gave me a genuinely apologetic smile. "We have to make sure first you're not hostile."

"Or a Parasite," Enzo added.

"Yeah," Astrid nodded. "A Hybrid."

Shock hit me like a tight slap. "You know about the Hybrids?"

"Well, duh." Astrid smiled. "It's been decades since someone from Aleron has come here, but that doesn't mean we're less informed."

I shook my head, unable to clear my disbelief. "You know about Aleron too?"

Both Astrid and Enzo shared a knowing glance. I clenched my hands. Just because we were in an actual cave, I had naively believed these people to be illiterate cavemen. Yet, they seemed to be well-learned about the greater details of the galaxy.

None of it made any sense. How? It didn't even make sense for them to be alive. The planet was a total wasteland.

"Never mind that," Astrid chimed. "Tell us about yourself."

I had no desire to share anything about myself, but I thought it best not to offend these people when they clearly had the upper hand. Besides, small talk was the only way I might get more information about the Earth people. This woman seemed chatty enough to spill everything.

I feigned a defeated sigh. "What would you like to know?"

"What's your name?" Astrid asked once more.

"Mabel," I answered, truthfully, having no need to lie about it. "How long are you going to keep me here?"

"We'll untie you after you meet our Commander. We'll take you to her."

"Where?" I pressed. "When?"

"You'll see where, and as for when," she turned her head to a dark mass sitting at the far back of the cave, and shouted, "As soon as Luc is done being a gearhead."

"I didn't ask you guys to wait for me," A voice shouted back from the dark.

"And leave you alone on the surface?" asked Astrid. "The Commander would kill us!"

I squinted my eyes at the structure which I had assumed was just a rock a moment ago, and gasped aloud. "That's my spaceship!" I jumped up or at least tried to. Since my feet were tied, I ended up collapsing back on the rug. "Don't touch that!"

"Luc's only trying to fix it," said Enzo. "We found it in pretty bad shape, so we bought it here. Although, it was hell to drag that thing all the way to the cave."

I should have been happy, even relieved that finding my ship was one less task on my plate. Now I wouldn't have to bother searching for it, but the thought of some random guy twiddling with my spaceship enraged me, though I didn't let my anger show.

A figure jumped down from the darkness and stepped forward into the light. The guy, Luc, was a blond kid in his late teens. He appeared to be the same age as me, but unlike me, his form was emaciated. He was wearing a similar white fur cloak as his colleagues.

Maybe it was because he was in my spaceship, but I disliked him instantly, though something did pique my interest: the book he was holding. I could only catch a glance, but the title was intriguing enough to convince me to eventually read it: *The Origin of Hybrids*. I made a mental note to steal that book before leaving. It would reveal so much more about the Earth Humans and what they knew about the Hybrids.

"Let's just go. I'm sure my sister is waiting for us," Luc said. "I'll come look into the ship more tomorrow. Remind me to bring my tools next time."

"Finally!" Astrid rose, stretching her back.

Enzo fished out a knife from within his cloak and approached me. "Relax, I'm just cutting the ropes." He sliced the bonds around my feet but left my hands still tied. "No funny business," he grumbled, pointing the knife at my neck.

My captors led me in the opposite direction of my spaceship. I reluctantly followed.

We stopped when we reached a wall. Luc stepped forward and started fidgeting with something, but it was dark so I couldn't properly make it out.

In the next moment, the wall split in the middle, and blinding light leaked from the crack. When my eyes finally adjusted, I realized it was an elevator door.

Astrid shoved me inside, not unkindly, but I still felt a wave of panic when the door slid shut and we started to descend.

Underground. Of course, now it made sense how they'd survived. I still didn't have a clue as to how technologically advanced these people were, so I had no idea what to expect.

Yet, as soon as the elevator halted and the doors clicked open, I was left gawking at the well-lit view like some idiot. Astrid and Luc laughed at my reaction. Even Enzo cracked a smile.

"Surprised?" Astrid asked.

Surprised was an understatement. I was downright flabbergasted. "It's... a city?" I didn't want to admit it, but there was no other way to describe it. Countless house-like structures stood all around, and the elevator had landed us on the roof of one such place. I tried to measure up the size of the settlement, but aside from giant pillars, there were no walls as far as my eyes could see. Hundreds of people busily wandered the streets. If it weren't for the absence of the sky, I might've believed I was on a different planet. This was not what I expected Earth to be at all.

"Let's go," Enzo said, interrupting my thoughts. "The commander is waiting."

They left me inside an interrogation room with my hands chained to the table while I waited for their Commander—who took a hell of a long time to show up—but I didn't mind waiting.

Each second I spent there, I carefully went through all the new information I'd gathered and planned my next move. When I first found the Primitives in the cave, I thought I had hit the bullseye and I was content to go back home where a new, improved life awaited me.

But the underground city changed it all. At first, all I wanted was to buy back my freedom in exchange for my findings. but, with this, the Hybrids on Aleron would give me a freaking promotion.

I couldn't resist a smile. My mother would be mortified. I *loved* it. I was going to get this information back home no matter what.

The only question that remained was, "how?" It had been stressing me since I stepped into the elevator. Breaking out and getting to the surface was hard enough on its own. Even if I somehow managed to pull it off, my spaceship would be another problem. I knew it was in bad shape, and it could take me weeks to fix it. *Too* long. I'd be caught by then.

After some careful and thorough contemplation, I came up with a plan. I had to play nice with the Commander and convince her to let me fix the spaceship. It was a long shot, but it was the only way.

Before I could decide how to do so, the doors of the interrogation chamber flew open, and the Commander walked in.

Not sure why, but I was expecting someone old and rugged with an aura of wisdom. I was certainly not expecting a middle-aged gorgeous woman with blonde hair and clear eyes. For some reason, her features seemed familiar.

She was also clad in white from head to toe and had a woolen shawl wrapped around her shoulders. My eyes didn't leave hers for even a second as she entered the interrogation room and sat on the chair across from me. She didn't look away either.

For a long while, neither of us spoke. We scrutinized each other. The competitive side in me was tempted to win the staring contest, but I reminded myself to play nice. I twisted my features into the most devastated look I could muster and blinked at her innocently. "Can you please tell me what's happening? Why did you lock me up?"

The Commander's eyes narrowed. She pressed a palm on the table and spoke in a low, threatening voice. "Here's how it's gonna go: I'll be the one asking questions and you'll tell me everything I want to know. Maybe then, I'll *consider* taking the chains off. Is that clear?"

A chill crawled down my back. Winning this woman over would be harder than I anticipated. I managed a nod.

"Good." She leaned back in her seat. "It's Mabel, isn't it?"

Another nod from me.

"So, Mabel, how did a Primitive like you manage to get your hands on that spaceship? And why did you choose Earth of all places?"

I couldn't help but notice how her eyes glazed at the mention of my spaceship. With a gulp, I answered carefully. "I come from a wealthy family. I was treated like a black sheep most of the time since no one wanted a Primitive around, so I decided to leave. It was always my dream to sail across the universe. When I asked for a spaceship, my father was more than happy to oblige so he'd get rid of me. As for why I chose Earth, maybe because I wanted to see my roots."

I thought I did a great job lying, but the Commander's demeanor shifted. It was colder now.

"Bullshit!" She slammed her hands on the table. "I'm sure you can already guess, but I'm not a very trusting person. Despite that, I decided to trust you. You'll soon realize it was a wrong move to lie to me." She shook her head disappointedly. "I thought we could bargain. We could have exchanged some information, but now that I know you're a liar. Your word is worth nothing. Now, you'll have to first gain my trust before we make some kind of deal."

I bit back my frustration, trying to figure out how she managed to see through my lie. The Commander was quick to answer my unspoken question. "Your father couldn't have bought you that spaceship, it has the military seal on it."

I whipped my head up in shock.

"Yes, I know what an Aleron military spacecraft looks like." She smirked. "In fact, I know a lot more." She placed a book on the table. It was the same one Luc was carrying earlier: *The Origin of Hybrids*. "I can even bet I know more about your people than you do yourself."

I shot down the urge to lunge across the table and snatch the book.

"I could've willingly shared that information with you had you cooperated." She shook her head as if the whole thing was a waste of time. "Maybe a few days in a cold cell would make you more honest." She rose to her feet. "I'll be back soon."

I watched helplessly as she turned to the exit. This meeting couldn't have gone worse. Not only did I fail to bring up the spaceship, but I also made her suspicious of me.

"Wait!" It was a pathetic attempt to salvage the situation. I didn't expect her to listen to me, but surprisingly, she did stop. "The spaceship, what are you going to do with it?"

"That's none of your concern anymore."

She started to turn again, so I spoke immediately, "Let's face it: we *both* need that spaceship. Whether you trust me or not has nothing to do with it."

"What makes you think I need it?" The Commander raised her brow.

"The fact that your underlings risked their lives by going into that blizzard and dragging it to the cave explains itself."

"Fair point." She gave a slight tilt of her head as if she was going to listen to what I had to say.

I planned my next words carefully. "I'm the only one who can fix it."

"You're underestimating us again. You may be a human, but those Parasites sure rubbed off on you."

"I saw one of your lackeys messing with it. If you won't let me fix it, at least don't let anyone else tamper with it."

The Commander turned fully towards me. "Luc is a capable mechanic. He's the best we have."

I was a little taken aback by the sudden shift in her tone. It sounded like pride. It suddenly reminded me of what I had heard on the surface. Astrid had mentioned something about not leaving Luc on his own or the Commander would kill them. Luc had then mentioned his sister.

Suddenly, it hit me. The familiar features and the blonde hair started making sense. Luc was her brother.

"You think he can fix the spaceship on his own?" I asked. "Isn't he just a kid?"

"Aren't you as well?" Without waiting for an answer, the Commander whirled and stalked out of the room.

I slumped my shoulders at the disastrous meeting. but, without meaning to, I had come up with a plan. A smile curved my lips. I knew how I was going to get out.

The Commander wasn't lying when she said my cell would be cold. It took a while for me to get used to it. Compared to the blizzard though, this cold was nothing. Besides, I convinced Astrid—who occasionally came to check up on me— to give me a blanket.

Since there were no windows or lights in the cell, the only way for me to know how much time had passed was by counting the meals. Having nothing else to do, I did just that. Although the food they provided seemed strange at first, it took little time for the taste to grow on me. Unlike the nourishment consumed on my planet, these provisions were prepared with some sort of seasonings to refine the taste to its finest. I looked forward to eating it each time.

I made sure to eat every last bite. Aside from the addictive taste, I needed to regain my strength.

There wasn't much else to do. Every third day, they'd let me out to take a bath before sending me to the interrogation room, where the Commander drilled me with questions. I didn't dare lie again, and I ended up spilling all about my mission. A small price to pay for freedom, because—if I were to escape—I needed her to trust me completely. I also needed to appear weak so, when it really mattered, they'd let their guard down. I made sure to cough and sneeze and act sick every time I was around someone.

The routine continued for a little more than three weeks before my opportunity finally arrived. I was in the middle of yet another interrogation when Luc interrupted us, bursting into the room. His eyes sparkled with excitement. "It's done!" he announced. I didn't have to guess what he was referring to.

The Commander rose from her chair. Judging from the look on her face, it was a monumental occasion. Probably because for the first time in a millennium, the Earth people had a way off the planet.

"There's a slight problem though," Luc admitted, just as I was expecting. "I can't access the controls." He turned towards me. "It needs her retinal scan."

There it was: the moment I had been waiting for. Although I hated that the entire plan depended on Luc fixing the spaceship, it turned out okay since he actually managed to do it.

The Commander regarded me. I was pretty sure she was pondering whether she should bother making me cooperate or just carve out my eyes.

I coughed multiple times and rubbed my chest. "I'll help you, just get me out of that cell. *Please.*"

"That's all you want?" Her eyes narrowed, her voice suspicious. I was making this too easy.

I pretended to consider. "I also want you to tell me everything you know about the Hybrids." I coughed.

The Commander smiled. Her suspicion dissipated. "All right." She turned to Luc. "If she unlocks the controls, would you be able to access them again without her help?"

He nodded. "I'm guessing yeah."

"Fine," the Commander spat. "Get Enzo."

They made me wait in the interrogation room for another fifteen minutes. When a guard finally came to get me, instead of taking me back to my usual cell, he took me to the roof. All was going according to plan.

If the Commander was indeed wise, she'd make me give up control of the spaceship now—when I was weak and desperate. Little did she know, I was one step ahead.

I quietly followed the guard to the roof of the building where the elevator awaited me. When I ascended to the surface, for a second, I mistook that I was in a different cave from the one I came in. There were people everywhere. Lights shimmered and multiple armed guards surrounded the spaceship.

Apparently, the Commander wasn't taking any chances. As soon as they noticed my arrival, all eyes settled on me. I made sure to slightly limp the rest of the way. The Commander gestured forward. "Go right ahead."

The guard beside me stayed behind. In his place, Enzo shadowed me all the way to the spaceship, pressing the barrel of his gun to the back of my head. I knew he was only trying to intimidate me, but it worked.

What if I failed? This was my only shot. My heart fluttered in my chest.

When I made it to the hatch door, I peeked inside and saw the controls fired up. A sigh of relief escaped me. It was, indeed, fixed. My freedom was so close. I could almost taste it.

"Keep moving," said Enzo, nudging me forward, the metal barrel still stuck to my head. I made a show of extreme effort as I climbed the stairs with my escort right behind me.

The inside of my ship was a cluttered mess. Tools were scattered all over the floor. Some of my rations were sitting outside, half-eaten, which enraged me. I'd need those on my way back. Luc was standing by the giant screen, fruitlessly trying to hack into the system.

When he noticed me glaring at the half-eaten food, he apologized. "Sorry about that. I just wanted to see what it tasted like." He stepped back from the screen to make room for me.

I carefully stepped forward, highly conscious of the gun behind me.

"What are you waiting for?" Luc asked.

"I need..." I slowly turned to speak, and suddenly, I sucker-punched Enzo. Before my escort could recover, I snatched the gun from his hand and pointed it at him, simultaneously using my other hand to twist Luc's arm. It was a blessing that he was so frail, or else I wouldn't have stood a chance against the two of them.

"Back off," I shouted, slamming the gun into Luc's jaw before putting the muzzle on his face, "or I shoot him!"

If Luc was any ordinary mechanic, Enzo wouldn't have hesitated, but him being the Commander's brother, the muscled man froze.

"Raise your hands, and slowly back down from the ship!" I ordered.

Enzo reluctantly started backing away.

Some of the soldiers, having heard the commotion, climbed up the steps. When the Commander was informed of Luc's life being in my hands, she barked the order at her men to stand down and not endanger her brother's life in any way.

Once everyone exited my ship, I pressed the gun into Luc's back and followed him to the stairs, where I made him lock the hatch door. All the while, I muttered into his ear that I'd pull the trigger in a heartbeat if he even attempted to escape.

The rest was easy. I switched the gun's settings and used it to taser Luc until he passed out and then got to work. Fortunately, the cave exit was right in front of the spaceship, covered by a large curtain of animal hide. I didn't have to bother maneuvering the ship before launching it in the sky.

In less than five minutes, the spaceship rose from the ground, burst through the exit, and shot up into the sky. I peeked through the window and saw the Commander and her men glaring at me from below. I grinned for the first time in a long time, still not believing that I actually managed to pull it off.

It took a while to clean up the cluttered mess, but I didn't mind. When I was finally done, I decided to tie up Luc, since I expected him to put up a fight when he woke up. It turned out I was too late. The moment I whirled from the screen, I gasped, finding him awake. He glared at me. The look in his eyes made me shrink.

His usually friendly demeanor was replaced by cool fury. "You must be feeling so smart, thinking you fooled us all. Don't you?"

Under normal circumstances, I might've retorted, but three weeks of being stranded on an unknown planet made me sympathize with him— especially because I was the one responsible for potentially putting him in a similar situation. I bit my lip and didn't respond.

Luc took my silence as an invitation to continue. "My sister wanted to carve out your eyes, but I convinced her to trust you; all because I thought you were human. But you're no different than those Parasites you came from: a stone-cold bitch!" He spat the words. "You'd think I would hate you, but I actually pity your ignorance. You're taking us to the home base of an enemy you know absolutely nothing about."

My hands clenched. It was all I could do to ignore him.

"All for what?" he went on. "So you could run back to your pretend family that doesn't even want you around"

"Shut up!" I suddenly screamed. I had told the Commander about my family to gain her sympathy, but I had never expected it to be thrown in my face, which was precisely why I ended up snapping at Luc. "How can you assume that I don't know anything about the Hybrids? I may not be evolved, but they're still my people! I spent my entire life with them! And you leave my family out of it. You know nothing about them. Just because they can't express their emotions doesn't mean they don't care about me...!" I might have kept shouting, but something dawned on me. Despite everything they did, here I was defending my family. Like the sentimental fool, they accused me of being. My eyes flooded.

Luc smirked, satisfied that his words hit their mark, and I felt the urge to burn the look off his face. "It'll be funny when you'll realize that the joke is on you. When you know the truth about those things which you refer to as 'your people.' The fact that you think they are *evolved* shows you know nothing." He put the word "evolved" in finger quotes. "You wanted to know the origin of the Hybrids, didn't you? It was part of our deal. The only reason no one told it to you yet is because Astrid and I convinced my sister to break it to you gently over time. But now, I'll enjoy the look on your face when you'll learn the truth. So, let me tell you."

As much as I wanted to know what he was about to tell me, the look of grim satisfaction on his face gave me an uneasy feeling.

"Do you know what kind of creatures used to live on Aleron before the humans went there?" he asked. "Alien bugs. Not the ordinary kind of bugs, but leeches and parasites who can't survive more than a few months without a host."

I frowned. This was the first time I heard of something like this. So far, it sounded more like a theory than a fact.

"Why do you think humans chose to go to Aleron during the apocalypse?" Luc went on. "And how did they even manage to leave without the proper tech? Because those aliens reached out to us *first*."

He let that idea linger for a moment before continuing. "It was all a setup! They took advantage of the apocalypse. In offering their planet as a safe haven, they had successfully captured thousands of human hosts to stretch out their own lifespans. Most of the humans were brain-dead almost immediately after those things crawled into them, but some people still had a little control over their bodies. So, to prevent those people from figuring out what was going on, they made up this story about human evolution. They called this new race 'Hybrids.'"

I was frozen. My brain went haywire trying to process everything I'd just heard. A thousand questions reverberated in my mind, but Luc had more to say.

"And now you'll ask me, 'How could people from Earth possibly know all this when we've never even left the planet?'" Luc rubbed his hands and grinned. "Oh, you're going to love this part. Do you think you're the first Primitive to be offered the job to investigate Earth? Well, you're actually the thousandth. Every time a human baby is born on your planet, there are bugs already waiting to take it. In a few rare cases, every decade or so, some humans are born who can't be taken over by the bugs. We call them 'Immunes,' but the Hybrids refer to them as—you guessed it—*Primitives*."

"You're lying." It was only a mumble. Tears seeped out of my eyes. I was shaking. As much as I didn't want to believe everything—deep down, I already knew it was the truth.

Luc had that sadist look on his face. "If you don't believe me," he reached for his backpack which was lying with the rest of his tools, and pulled out the same book the Commander had shown me: *The Origin of Hybrids*. "Read it for yourself." He threw the book over to me. "It contains information directly from all the previous Immunes that were sent on Earth for missions similar to yours over the millennia. They also had unexpected malfunctions with their gear: just like you. Over the centuries, all the spaceships that arrived blew up on impact with the surface. Yours was the first one that crashed and survived because the snow cushioned its fall. Besides, your entire mission was pointless, because the Hybrids already know we're alive. The only reason they haven't killed us yet, and even bother to send back the Immunes, is because they still need us alive for some reason."

"*No*..." I slumped down and wrapped my arms around my head.

Luc did not relent. "Every person you've ever known in your life is just a walking corpse. A *puppet*! Why else do you think they didn't warn you about the cold?"

WINTER MARKET
By Wren Murphy

I

Nathalie felt magic in the air. It had rippled around her like a puddle in a rainstorm for almost half a day now, each burst stronger as she moved further along the road. The sensation had begun as soft feathery strokes along her wrists and neck, but it had continued to strengthen until it felt like a heavy weight on her chest. It was not unusual to feel magic throughout the land, at least in the parts she had already traveled. Unlike others, Nathalie knew its pull. She could ignore it most of the time.

With a deep breath, she focused, keeping her attention trained on the cobblestones as she followed the twinkling lanterns beside them. After a few more moments, the heavy sensation disappeared from her chest, buried under the winter chill as it bit at her cheeks with a searing cold wind. She kept warm by burrowing deeper into her wool cloak, only pausing for a short moment to brush the snowflakes from her nose. Frostbite would not slow her, nor would the darkness of the night around her. Her intuition had directed her along this road—pushing her away from the main routes of travel to those ways off the beaten path—and Nathalie trusted herself. Her instincts had never failed her, and she had learned a long time ago that her gut was her most useful tool. After all, she had been right about many important things—the devastating drought and ensuing famine two years past, the trio of assassins that had infiltrated the harvest ball that next year, and most recently, the man who called himself her father, King Leandre of Vaihane.

It had not been a surprise to learn of his deception, or rather, her mother's infidelity. Nathalie was no heir of the king, had never been, but hearing it spoken aloud had stung more than she had expected it to. Nathalie was just a bastard the king had taken pity on. She still had yet to decide if the king had loved her mother enough to see through her lies, or if he loved Nathalie more than he hated the pain her mother had caused him.

It was easy to see she did not belong in Leandre's bloodline. His hair was the color of straw, his eyes dark like warm chestnuts. His nose was strong and crooked from being broken a few too many times in combat, but prominent nonetheless. Nathalie's older brother, Nicael, looked just like the king—damn near a splitting image. And then there was her, Nathalie, the odd one.

She was a good ten inches shorter than her brother. Her body curved like a pear, while the king and his son both stood tall like an oak tree. Her hair resembled brewed coffee with a slight auburn tint in the sunlight, and it was as thick as a horse's mane too. Her eyes were a strange color: a pale green with golden flecks in the center near the iris. Nathalie looked nothing like Leandre, not even a smidge, and so it came as no surprise when she finally discovered the truth. She wasn't of royal blood. Not even close.

"The palace might've felt suffocating, girl, but it was warmer than the inside of a boar's ass at least," Merle said as he trudged beside her, his armor clanking from their packs attached to the back of his horse. It sounded like an orchestra in the dead of night, the clash and clang of metal-on-metal echoing until her skin crawled.

"How you know the temperature inside of a boar's ass is beyond me, but I'll take this arctic hell over the palace any day." Nathalie glanced over her shoulder, nodding at the horse. "Care to fix that racket, or shall I do it for you?"

Merle scowled, his expression more cold than normal. The knight was not the most friendly partner, nor was he the most verbose, but he had volunteered to escort her through the mountains to Stadora. Nathalie would have preferred to travel alone. However, despite her new found knowledge of the king and her parentage, Leandre still demanded an armed guard to ensure her safety over the pass. After all, it was standard procedure for all of his royal emissaries.

"You're still such a brat," Merle muttered while he adjusted his coat. It fell over his broad shoulders and nearly matched the grayed edges of his dark hair. He was easily her brother's age, if not slightly older, but with a particularly wry smile, he sometimes seemed rather youthful. He directed his horse to stop, moving behind it to adjust their supplies and better secure his armor. "You've refused to follow the main roads, and now we're going to freeze to death over your stubbornness. Where are we, *Princess*?"

Nathalie wrinkled her nose. She loathed her title even more than she used to, knowing it was nothing but a lie, and Merle knew it. She saw the joy in his eyes at her discomfort even now as they sparkled from several steps away in the pale lamp light.

"I saw a town just over that ridge. We'll stay there for the night and decide where we'll enter the mountains in the morning," she replied.

"Could've been in Stadora two days ago if you hadn't hijacked us off the main roads. Now we're in the middle of nowhere—and for what reason, Nathalie? Just because?" Merle tugged on his horse's reins, encouraging the animal forward again. "Or was this another case of your feminine delusions talking? Need I remind you, the last time we listened to your 'gut', I nearly had my head cut off by a goblin!"

"'Twas an accident, and you should've been watching where you were going anyway."

"Ah ha!" Merle said, a gloved hand raised as he pointed at her accusingly. "So, it *is* because of a hunch. Your father will hear about this the minute we return to—"

"My father?" Nathalie laughed, a dark, empty sound. "For all I know, he is dead—a deadbeat, a dead end. I have no father."

Merle hissed, his distaste obvious to Nathalie as she watched him. "The king would have your head if he heard you speaking like this. Consider yourself lucky you'll have to wait longer to witness his ire because of your detour from the main roads. You would be wise to remember who raised you, who loved and cared for you since you were a babe. Most in your predicament would be grateful. You *should* be grateful."

Nathalie frowned. She should be grateful, but she was not.

Another warm sensation ran along her spine, and she froze, pausing her bubbling retort with her words just on the tip of her tongue. The hair on the back of her neck stood up, and she waited, still, feeling the pull of the warmth until it settled on her chest like a heavy weight all over again. It encouraged her forward, lured her further along the path, deeper into the thicket of trees ahead. She hadn't been wrong. Magic covered every inch of this place.

"Shut up, Merle," Nathalie muttered. "There's something ahead."

Her booted feet crunched the foliage underfoot, but instead of focusing on Merle and his delightful company, her eyes studied the trees ahead. She searched them, looking for something, only to find them empty. The darkness made her uneasy, but the electric tingle over her skin had her yearning to run with abandon down the path. Nathalie was smart enough to know better.

The last time that had happened, Merle had almost lost his head to a goblin's blade.

II

Sir Merle Llywelyn carried a rabbit's foot in his left hand. His fingers caressed the silky fur over and over, again and again, until there was a worn spot in the hide. His stomach bubbled uneasily, anxiety beginning to run rampant like an army of butterflies in his chest. There was only one explanation for his feelings: he did not trust *her*.

Princess Nathalie had always caused him grief. From fighting off suitors to running headfirst into a goblin grotto two summers past, she caused more trouble than she was worth. In Merle's experienced opinion, the princess was bad news—the *baddest* of bad news—and she was worse than any other companion he had ever had.

However, Merle could not, in good conscience, send the woman out into the world alone just to get killed because of her own carelessness. He had too much loyalty to allow that to happen, especially since Nathalie was the only reason their kingdom would prosper once King Leandre finally handed his crown to his moronic son—not that Merle would ever openly admit that to anyone, including Nathalie herself.

It was well-known throughout the kingdom just how stupid the king's heir was. Merle hypothesized the king had kept Nathalie's bloodlines secret for as long as he had because his son was incapable, but it was not Merle's place to do anything more than speculate. He was just a knight, a simple, honorable man of the Order, loyal to his people and his homeland. He did not entertain the dramatics of others and their extramarital affairs.

Instead, Merle entertained the wiles of this insane woman.

He was not convinced his current situation was any better than the last outing he had taken with Nathalie. She barely spoke, and when she did, it was often crude and short. She refused to explain herself or allow him to use a map. When he questioned the direction she led them, the daggers in her eyes scared him more than her own mother's worst glare. In Merle's opinion, the princess had no tact, no sense of responsibility, and she was selfish, only caring about herself and what served her. She was absolutely, positively the most incorrigible human being in the kingdom. It was unfortunate that he was also in love with her.

"Oh Divine, bless me," he muttered to himself, looking up at the smoky clouds floating in the sky. He could barely see them. The trees had grown denser as they had traveled further into the woods, but he hoped his strained prayers were heard. He did not wish to die on this day, nor the next day or the day after that. In fact, Merle wanted to grow old and retire peacefully into his golden years.

With Nathalie around, he knew that peace was a stone's toss across the sea away: *impossible*.

"What are you whispering about back there? More stories about boars' asses?" Nathalie asked.

Merle dropped his gaze from the sky, watching as the wind brushed her hair into her face. Nathalie recovered, swiping the pretty strands out of her eyes and away from her mouth with her gloved hands. Merle sighed, shoved the rabbit's foot in his pocket, and pinched the bridge of his nose while he squeezed his eyes momentarily shut.

"Your witty quips are most becoming, Princess," Merle replied and opened his eyes. He took great pleasure at the moment when Nathalie flinched at her title. She despised it, and in his own form of repayment for the distress she caused him regularly, the knight milked it for everything it was worth. "Perhaps they will ensnare your next victim in your web of false securities. However, if you must know what I was whispering about, I was reciting a prayer."

"A prayer for what?"

"My sanity, so that it remains intact while I follow you to Stadora. This route is asinine." Merle was not wrong. The route *was* asinine. They had crossed no other travelers for nearly two days now, and the last settlement they passed had been occupied by hermits taking residence in a small collection of abandoned houses older than the king himself.

They were lost, but Nathalie refused to admit it.

"You're asinine, Merle," Nathalie snorted, her laughter bubbling up and around him like a high-pitched song. It was stunning to hear in person, in a most complementary way. She was truly beautiful when she let her guard down, but Merle knew better than to sink into that false sense of ease. The last time it had happened, he had nearly lost his head to a goblin's blade.

"How am I asinine? Do you even know the meaning of the word?" He lifted his chin in a brave display, but Nathalie waved him off.

"I am smarter than you think. Please stop fretting. You are stressing the horse. I told you there was something ahead. See that light over there?" Nathalie pointed off into the distance, and sure enough, she was correct. Pale light flickered in the distance. Merle took a deep breath and caught the savory scent of food cooking.

It still made him uneasy. The air felt thicker here. His skin crawled as he looked around at the dark trees, and the shadows from the lanterns played tricks on his eyes. "And you're certain goblins aren't involved this time?" He meant it as a joke, but his voice cracked, and Merle swallowed the lump in his throat.

Nathalie seemed to soften, her shoulders falling before she nodded. "Trust me, Merle. I do not intend on encountering a goblin tonight."

They fell silent, the night wearing on them and forcing a yawn from Merle occasionally as they continued along the cobblestone path. Gradually they broke through the thicket of trees, entering an open meadow. The light grew larger, splitting into several small fires surrounded by wagons and tents. Merle heard an uplifting melody echoing in the dark. Nathalie hastened her footsteps.

"Look! A bazaar!" Nathalie pointed at the camp, and Merle squinted. Sure enough, people moved around, hopping from tent to tent, cart to cart.

"A bazaar? In the middle of nowhere?" Merle had never seen a thing like it before. In the middle of a lonely forest during the darkest part of the night, people laughed, conversed, bartered, and exchanged goods with one another. It was a sight he would have expected in the middle of a city during broad daylight. Not here, wherever they were.

The closer they approached, the stranger it seemed. Lanterns similar to those which had decorated their path through the forest now hung from ropes, dangling between the shanty-like structures hastily squeezed together.

Blankets and canvas draped over fragile wood frames, torn in places and patched in others.

The people were a myriad of shapes, sizes, and colors. As Merle listened, he heard their voices. Their accents seemed strange and foreign, yet they spoke the same dialect of Common as he did. He remained suspicious, even after a pair of them tied his horse to a hitching post and even more so as they wove between the first stalls. It was easy to merge into the chaos without being noticed, and regardless of his own wishes, Nathalie seemed determined to explore.

The Princess grabbed his hand and tugged him behind her, dragging him into a large burgundy tent. Incense clouded his vision and burned his eyes, the scent of sandalwood so thick he felt his nose tingle with a sneeze. He freed his hand from Nathalie's grasp and rubbed his sleeve over his face, while Nathalie unburied herself from her cloak.

After a short moment, they both turned in circles, looking at the offerings around them. Ornate furniture decorated the small space. Golden embellishments stood out against a dark hardwood, and the chairs bore cushions of turquoise silk stuffed with down. Jars of poultices and bundles of herbs resided on tables and end stands. Crystal trinkets sparkled, and a light coating of dust covered stacks of Arcana decks.

But it was the large golden cage in the center of the room that caught Merle's attention the most.

"What is that?" he asked, pointing to a multicolored mass contained between the bars. Nathalie followed his gesture, looking inside the cage herself.

"I'm not certain," she replied and took a step forward.

Merle reached out to catch her arm, warning her back, but Nathalie shook him away. The knight kept his distance as the princess approached the cage, his hand at his waist toying with a small knife stashed on his belt. Merle attempted to relax with a few short breaths, but a squeal from Nathalie had him drawing the small blade and advancing toward her quickly in alarm.

"It's a bird! Come look," Nathalie said, motioning him closer.

Merle moved beside her. Sure enough, as he peered into the cage, within the ball of multicolored feathers, a large oval, periwinkle eye stared at him. The bird blinked several times while he watched it before it shuddered and began to uncurl from its ball.

"What kind of bird is that?" Merle whispered, inching closer. The bird was about as large as a house cat. Its short feathers shimmered like pearls all over its body, and a dark beak decorated its face. Long feather-like lashes surrounded its eyes, and tail feathers as long as Merle's arm wiggled with every step it took. He had never seen anything quite like it before.

"That," a deep voice said from behind them, "Is a Featherkin."

III

A Featherkin.

Nathalie had only heard of the creature in passing once. She turned around, looking to find the source of the voice, and found a dark-skinned man with a smile on his face. His hair had more gray to it than Merle's did, and wrinkles marred his forehead. He wore long golden robes which pooled at his feet. As he stretched his arms out to gesture at the bird in the cage, his large sleeves fell back to his elbows, exposing his well-toned arms.

"Do you know much about them?" the man asked.

Nathalie shook her head. She knew they were not native to her kingdom, but her knowledge beyond that was limited. The man did not seem bothered by her reply. He moved toward her and Merle, eventually leading them aside so he could open the cage door and retrieve the bird. It squawked when he collected it, then it proceeded to walk along his arm to his shoulder.

"Featherkin are magnificent creatures. Hunters of the finest caliber, each with their own personality and skill set. One of their feathers contains more magic than any human could ever possess. This hatchling is named Illris." The Featherkin cooed at her name, puffing her feathers up in a lavish display. The man chuckled, and Nathalie smiled. "She belongs to a friend in Azure Reach, and in two decades, she will be mature enough to travel to Drerst."

"Drerst," Merle repeated. "The bird is going to the Rift then?" Nathalie watched as he tilted his head to the side, eying the bird with renewed scrutiny.

The man nodded, scratching the bird's head. "Yes. You may actually know them as Warbirds, but they were meant for more than war. Their numbers have dwindled precariously low in recent decades. The darkness devoured them and their human companions until others joined them on the front lines of the conflict. It was thought they had all died out at one point, at least until a pair was spotted just north of Stadora and a few more scattered throughout the eastern lands."

The man lowered his eyes and moved to return the Featherkin to its cage. "Repopulation has not been easy. Most eggs do not hatch. Illris was lucky. Her clutchmates were not as fortunate." He gestured to a dark corner of the tent. Nathalie squinted to clear her vision of the incense, peering into the dark to see several large white orbs resting in a blanket on the floor.

"Those are Featherkin eggs that did not mature?" Nathalie pointed, her eyes widening in surprise. There had to be dozens of them, all pristine and perfectly shaped too. However, the closer she moved toward them, the better her vision became.

She noticed one had an imperfection—a hairline crack straight down the center of the egg. She opened her mouth to say as much, but then the egg moved. It was a small shiver, a slight tilt of the oval to the right.

"They did not. I was in the process of discarding them when you entered my tent." The man closed the lock on the cage and moved in front of Nathalie, gathering up some of the eggs into his hands. "Gaspard next door has a tiny dragon that will be delighted with the unexpected treat. The eggs are quite nutritious, especially for a small squirt like him."

"And you're positive they're all rotten? None of them are viable?" She peered behind him, looking at the egg with the crack. It sat still among the rest of the clutch, motionless. Nathalie wondered if she had just imagined it.

"I have inspected them all thoroughly." The man smiled at her and began moving past her and Merle toward the entrance. "I apologize for stepping out. However, the hour is quite late, and I must bring these to Gaspard. Please take your time browsing. I will return momentarily."

Merle gave the man a slight bow, and Nathalie nodded in acknowledgment. The man exited his tent. Nathalie turned to Merle, gripping his arm firmly. "I think he's wrong, Merle. Look! The one with the crack! I know it moved."

"Moved?" Merle shook his head and wrinkled his nose. "You're delusional. He said they were unviable, and since he knows more about these things than either of us, I am inclined to agree."

"I'm taking it," Nathalie said, releasing Merle's arm to reach for the egg.

"You can't just take it, Nathalie."

"I can. He's just going to feed it to a dragon anyway." Nathalie collected the cracked egg and slid it under her cloak. She rummaged for her leather purse and tossed a few coins on a table. "Some gold for his troubles and to make sure that one makes it to Azure Reach. Come on, Merle. Let's go."

Merle gritted his teeth. "This is worse than the goblins! You're going to have a band of foreign merchants on our asses. What if they know how to fight? How to torture? How to throw fiery magical knives at our throats?" The knight stomped his foot. "No, I'm not doing this again, Nathalie. I'm going to stay right here until he returns and—"

A loud, angry squawk came from the cage beside him. Merle turned, contemplating the Featherkin in its cage. If Nathalie hadn't known better, she would have sworn that something passed between him and that magical bird.

Regardless of what had happened, the knight seemed to have a change of heart. "Fine! Let's get out of here, but this is the last time I let you act so carelessly, you impulsive welp!"

"Shut up, Merle," Nathalie shouted over her shoulder. She walked toward the opening of the tent and out into the cold air of the night. She didn't know what she was going to do with a Featherkin egg, but she knew she couldn't leave this one behind.

IV

After leaving the strange man's tent and the Featherkin in the golden cage behind, Merle found them a small campsite outside of the bazaar. He placed sleeping bags and unloaded his horse a small way from the nearest firelight. The light in the distance provided reassurance that they were far enough away from the bazaar to remain unbothered, but also close enough to ensure their safety in the wild. Merle paced around their makeshift lodgings until he had given Nathalie enough of the fifth degree to satisfy his frustration. Once finished, the pair had settled into an uneasy, cold sleep within their sleeping sacks.

The morning light crested over the horizon, and the sounds of wildlife spurred Merle from his slumber. He peeked one eye open, then the other, and yawned as he stretched under the warm fur of his simple bedroll.

"Nathalie, wake up," he grunted as he pulled himself to his feet, rubbing the lingering sleep out of his eyes. His knees and back cracked as he shifted. "We need to find out how to get back on the right path to Stadora. No more of this gallivanting all over the wilderness. We find the mountains, we find Stadora, and we find an inn so I can eat a warm meal for once."

Merle bent over and began to gather his things. "I'm still concerned about the risk of death when you're involved," he continued "We're fortunate neither of us has succumbed to frostbite or worse at this point." He paused, not hearing much movement behind him. With a huff, Merle turned on his heel. "Come on, Princess. Enough lollygagging—"

A familiar screech interrupted him, and Merle froze, looking at Nathalie curled into a ball under her furs. However, something struck him oddly. A small, feathery head peeked out from her blankets, and a pair of large azure eyes glared at him.

"Oh gods, is that…?" Merle rubbed a hand over his forehead. "Nathalie, is that what I think that is?"

The sleeping woman stirred after he repeated her name.

"Merle, what are you going on about?" Nathalie yawned while pushing herself up to her elbows. "You're quite loud first thing in the morning. Perhaps you can turn it down a notch or two until I get situated?"

She pushed her blankets to her waist, and a small bird popped out of the warmth beside her. It appeared somewhat different from the Featherkin from the previous night. Where Illris had been multicolored, the bird beside Nathalie looked snowy white, but the pearlescent sheen to its feathers remained. It turned left, then right, then left again, before it loudly squawked and dove under the blankets. Nathalie sat up straight. Her movements stilled, and the color in her face drained.

"The egg hatched," Merle whispered, adrenaline flooding his system as he looked around them. "The egg hatched! We need to tell that man immediately! Get away from that wild animal, Nathalie!"

Merle stumbled around his belongings, spinning in a circle as he searched for the bazaar to orient himself. They would find that man, bring him the bird, and then head to Stadora. He knew he should have stopped Nathalie from taking that damn egg, but she had been so adamant about it.

Damn her and how much I loved her! He hadn't retained control, hadn't kept his foot down like he had sworn to himself before escorting her on this journey. He had failed.

Natalie still sat, but not quite so rigidly. Where fear and astonishment had been but a moment earlier, a new emotion blossomed. Sadness. Disappointment.

"Don't give me that look, Nathalie. Remove that pout from your face this instant. We're taking the bird to the man in the tent over there," Merle said, looking at Nathalie and pointing in the direction of the bazaar.

"What tent, Merle?" Nathalie replied as she lifted the blanket to find the bird. "The tents are gone. They're all gone."

"What?" Merle turned and looked in the direction he pointed. "Of course they're still there. It would be nearly impossible to break down so many tents and…"

Empty. His sight found only trees across the cold, snow-covered terrain. He spun around in another circle, telling himself he had gotten himself confused. However, all his searching accounted for naught. The bazaar was gone. He and Nathalie were all alone.

"What sorcery is this?" Merle pressed a hand to his chest, feeling his heart thud hard against his palm. "There should be a market full of people bartering and conversing, even at this early hour of the morning. Do not tell me it was all in my head."

"It was magic, Merle," Nathalie said, and Merle watched as the small bird stepped out of the warm haven of her blankets. "I felt it the entire time we were traveling. I needed to see what it was, and I'm glad I did."

"Magic?" Merle's head throbbed at the temple. His chest tightened, forcing his breaths to come in short gasps. "We traveled away from the main roads for *witchcraft,* and now we have a Warbird as a pet? How are you going to explain this to your father?"

"I don't have a father, remember?" Nathalie stood, her feathered companion hopping around at her feet. "Besides, we still have to make it to Stadora."

Merle let out a heavy sigh. He could only shake his head. "You'll be the death of me, Princess."

"No, I won't." Nathalie smiled and the Featherkin chirped with happiness. "Pack up the horse. We've got a long journey ahead of us, Merle, and the snow is already starting to fall again."

WITCH HUNT
By Rionna Morgan

Prologue

Massachusetts 1692

She looked through the gap in the makeshift wall. Spits and spats of snow and ice snuck in and stung her cheeks. She saw the men outside glaring with mock courage toward the shack that was her prison. She saw their evil hearts beating fearfully in their chests.

"*Witch,*" they whispered.

Diana Payne rolled over, ignoring the musty rotting ceiling above her. She held her fingers beside the flame of a single candle and watched the midnight red of her ruby ring glint in the dim light. She turned her hand, palm facing up, and she conjured a scene, just big enough for her to see.

It showed her laughing on the eve of Midsummer, lighting her fire, relishing in the power of the day, and preparing for her wedding to come. Her heart still ached with the joy of that moment. Diana watched the ethereal figures on her palm as the scene drifted—her dreaming of marrying her love beneath the golden solstice sun—him bringing her a crown of flowers, kissing her sweetly as he placed them on her head. Him kneeling by the well, giving her the ring she now wore.

As the scene continued, Diana shut her eyes tight against the pain. Their wedding never happened. Raving men with torches and hatred ripped her from her bed, locking her in this broken, dirt-floor hut. Those men with their high and mighty voices, proclaiming righteousness, didn't take any time in pronouncing her a witch and a whore and treating her as such. In all their godliness they took turns with her body like animals, like it was their right. Then they straightened their clothes, put on their hats, and went home to read their bibles with their providential wives.

Bastards they were—every one of them.

The scenes moved on to show *him* sobbing and beating against the door of the hut; of him pleading with the townspeople to let her go, of him bringing her food. It showed him slipping through the woods at night to sit and talk with her through the gap in the wall.

Diana replayed the scenes over and over watching for glimpses of him, tears streaming down her cheeks, until her eyes grew heavy, and the stars dotted the sky.

Just after midnight, Diana awoke. She could no longer stay, not with one of those bastards' seeds growing inside her. She had been waiting for December's moon, the Solstice moon. She stood, flicked her wrist, and the walls fell away. She stepped beyond the broken frame, swished her fingers, and the hut began to burn.

Diana walked away along her secret path. She took off her ring and wrapped it in a piece of fabric torn from her gown, weaving into the cloth a protective spell to keep it safe and hidden, only to be found when the time was right. She buried it there beside the well beneath the snow. She paused, closed her eyes, and vanished.

Eugene, Oregon

Bridget closed her laptop, hugged it to her body, and sighed. *Finally!* She thought. *I'm going to find some answers.* She put the laptop in her carry-on and got up to gather the last-minute items for her trip. She took a phone call from her grandmother reminding her to pack boots and her travel candles.

"Does everyone pack travel candles? Or is it just witches?" Bridget wondered aloud as she tucked a few candle jars in her suitcase and grabbed a small, framed photo of her and her grandmother to bring along. Then Bridget settled in bed and flipped her comforter over her legs. This would be her last night in her own bed for a month. She braided her long red hair and tossed the tail of it back over her shoulder. She pulled her leatherbound journal from her nightstand and turned to the day's page.

A cool, soft December moon shimmered a light into Bridget's room. Her suitcase, carry-on, and new winter coat waited by her door so she could grab them in the morning on the way to the airport. The rest of the room was as neat as it could be for an about-to-turn-thirty doctoral student at the University of Oregon. Piles of books lined her bookcase and spilled out onto the floor. Old sweaters and a swimsuit left over from summer hung over the arm of her treadmill. The walls were the normal rental apartment light creamy beige. The bed she was snuggled into had been her mother's from when she was a child. The long dresser lining the wall beside the bookcase had been her father's. But most everything else was from her grandmother's house. A tall oval mirror was tucked into one corner and a small fainting bench, not big enough to be a couch, stood beside it. On every flat surface not holding a stack of books there were pictures, a few candles, and small clutter that most girls her age seemed to have—old mail, birthday cards, buttons, abandoned tubes of lipstick, and perfume.

No evidence, really, that a powerful witch lived in the room—or what *should* have been a powerful witch if Bridget's grandmother was to be believed.

The scratching of Bridget's pencil on paper paused. She looked over at the lamp on her nightstand and winced a bit at the bright light, then glanced at the long-tapered candle and crystal holder next to it. She liked to write by candlelight; it seemed mysterious and inspiring. She leaned toward the candle, closed her eyes, took a breath, and whispered a spell.

She opened one eye just a wink and scoffed. The candle was not lit. Trying again, she took a bigger breath and let it out. She focused on her own energy and visualized the result she wished to see. She squeezed her eyes closed and spoke the spell, firm and clear. She winked her eye open again in time to see a small flame spit and sputter, and then go out.

"Good grief!" Bridget grabbed up a box of matches and lit the candle. She turned out the lamp and felt peace when the room dimmed to a warm light. She began to write again.

Her brain was filled with spells and incantations from the day. This was the pattern of her life. Each day a few new spells or enchantments were delivered to her in some cosmic, unknown fashion. Each night she would write them down in her journal. When she was little, she'd run to her grandmother and tell her about them. Bridget used to be so excited when she'd receive the new ones; she was always so ready to see if they would work.

They never did. Not once. It was like there was some unseen barrier blocking her power. So, she began writing them down in the hope that one day she was able to use them; that one day she really *would* be a powerful witch. To hear her grandmother tell it, Bridget was supposed to be the most powerful witch of this century *and* the last.

Ha! Fat chance. I can't even light a candle. Bridget continued writing in her spell book, sketching the day's spells, long into the night.

"How do people even travel like this?" Bridget muttered to herself for about the thousandth time that day. She looked out the window of her cab as it wove between vehicles trying to make their way along the streets covered in snow. The red taillights looked eerie through the condensation on the glass. The sky was a milky black and the trees along the street stretched their dark gnarled limbs up into the fog.

She didn't know what she expected from Salem, Massachusetts. At this point, considering the day she'd had, she was glad to know she'd soon be warm and dry. The morning had been crazy. She'd made it to the airport and boarded her plane on time, but that was the only thing that went right.

A beautiful, sweet angelic-haired child spilled apple juice all over her clothes on the first flight. Her second flight was delayed due to the snowstorm. When she finally made it to Salem, sticky and tired, her suitcase was nowhere to be found, and while she waited for her cab, she dropped her coat right into a big puddle of slush and road grime.

At least the cab is warm, Bridget thought as she looked at her phone and followed the route the cab was to take on the way to the bed and breakfast she'd chosen for her stay. She took a moment to reassure herself that her B&B was within walking distance of the Salem Witch Museum. That museum was at the top of her itinerary. It was one of the reasons she came to Salem.

The other reason was that Bridget wanted to know who she was and where she came from. She wanted to know why her parents died too young;

why the person who raised her was not truly her grandmother, but a beloved mother-figure from her mother's youth. She wanted to find out why her natural grandmother, her mother's mother, had died too young as well.

These questions had plagued Bridget her whole life. They were the reason she chose the major she did in college—the master's degree, and now her doctorate. She wanted answers. Her history and genealogy degrees were not telling her what she wanted to know. So, she had to come for herself.

Bridget laid her head back against the headrest and closed her eyes, glad for a little bit of calm. She had another fifteen minutes or so before she was supposed to arrive at her destination. She didn't intend to sleep, only rest.

Her mind drifted and she dozed. In her dream, she saw a beautiful redhaired woman watching a ruby ring glint in the light of a candle. She saw her roll over on a bed of straw and saw her arms cradling a growing baby in her womb. Bridget saw the shadows beneath the woman's eyes and felt sadness at seeing her tears as she slept.

Then Bridget saw the woman awake as if by some far-off alarm. She saw her stand up, swish her hand, and saw the shabby walls around her collapse and begin to burn. She saw the woman walk away along a snow-covered path. Bridget saw her remove her ring, wrap it in cloth, and bury it. Then the woman looked at her. Directly at her. Like they were standing there together. Like she could reach out and touch her. Then the woman vanished.

"Miss," the cab driver called. "Miss!"

"Yeah!" Bridget jerked forward. "Yeah," she said again. "I'm here." Bridget shook her head. *What did I just see? What had happened?* These questions swirled around Bridget's mind as she gathered her things. She said thank you to the cab driver and tried to listen to the very nice gray-haired lady who showed her to her room.

Bridget raced through her nighttime routine, got in bed, and pulled out her spell book. She sketched and wrote down everything she could remember.

·   ·

The next morning, Bridget's suitcase was outside her door—delivered sometime in the night. Grateful, she took a shower, unpacked for her month-long stay, dressed, made final notes on her itinerary, grabbed a light breakfast downstairs, and left.

As she walked along the sidewalk toward the Salem Witch Museum, she didn't notice any of her surroundings. She didn't see the muted winter sun hidden behind hazy thick clouds. She didn't chit-chat with the flower vendor when she stopped to buy a small bunch of red roses. She didn't see the trees lining the walk covered in their thick winter cloaks of snow or notice the entrance of the museum rising from the cobblestone walk like a dark, imposing gothic church.

All she could think about was the woman from her cab ride dream, the simple swish of her hand, and how the walls of her room fell away. *How could she just do that? What kind of power must that have taken?*

Bridget showed her ticket at the entrance and scrolled through the museum's app to find exactly what she was looking for. It was early in the day, so the grounds were fairly quiet. She followed the walkway to the outer edge of the common area and walked through the gate of the cemetery. She double-checked the map and walked directly to the spot that was her goal.

Her mind let go of her previous preoccupation and faced the current scene before her. At her feet, there was going to be a simple stone tablet. She even knew what it was going to say.

> *Bridget Bishop*
> *Hanged*
> *June 10, 1692*

She'd seen it a hundred times in Google searches, books, and articles on the Salem Witch Trials as she researched her past. She knew that she was standing at the grave of the first woman executed for the crime of witchcraft in 1692. The knowledge of where she stood and the horror of that time, that hysteria, impacted Bridget.

She could feel her heart beat faster. Her breath was shaky and rapid. Her hands shook as she tucked her hair behind her ear. Bridget paused and shut her eyes, hugging her spell book, printed itinerary, and roses close. She waited for her mind to settle, and she willed the fear and anxiety to subside. Her lips trembled as she breathed full calming breaths. When she felt ready, she opened her eyes and looked down to see the stone she knew was there.

It was covered in a fresh dusting of thick snow and layered with lifeless flowers Halloween visitors had left behind. Without thinking, Bridget squinted her eyes, let out a distasteful sigh, and flicked her hand toward the snow and wilted flowers.

The force of the spell knocked her backward and the snow and dead flowers flew from the stone like a gale had blown them away. Bridget's spell book and itinerary flipped out of her hand, and her roses scattered around her, littering the fresh snow with what looked like dots of blood, dark and ruby red against the pure white backdrop.

.   .

Fletcher Collins had been watching her. He saw her come in through the main entrance of the museum, looking somehow distracted and determined at the same time. He noticed her red hair right off. It looked powerful, brilliant against the black of her jacket and the white of the snow. She was stunning. He was glad he'd stopped here first before going to the gym. His gaze followed her as she checked her phone, walked to the very gravestone he was also there to see, and paused. He saw her close her eyes and kind of meditate. Then he saw the snow and debris go flying while she landed on her back in the snow. Shocked, he raced over to help her up.

"Hi!" Fletcher held out his hand. "Are you okay?"

.   .

Bridget looked around. "Hi?" *What the hell just happened?* "Yeah." She muttered.

"That was a bad trip," he said.

That was no trip. "I guess," Bridget said automatically and took ahold of his gloved hand to stand up. So many things were racing through her mind. *Did I just do magic? For real! And it worked for the first time ever! Is that what that was? How did I do that? No spell! Just swish like the woman in my dream!*

"Are you okay?" Fletcher asked again, still holding her hand.

Bridget looked at him. His dark eyes looked concerned. His lips curved in a calming, almost smile. Curls from his dark hair dipped onto his forehead and framed his face. He leaned closer to her, his face still and patient like he'd wait all day for her to answer.

"Yes." Bridget smiled. "I am fine."

"The walk is pretty slippery from last night's snow."

At this Bridget grinned. She could hear the Massachusetts accent in his voice.

"Thank you for helping me." Bridget pulled her hand from his grasp. "You sound like you're from around here."

"Yes," Fletcher responded as he started gathering her things. "Born and raised in Boston."

Bridget picked up her spell book, dusted it off with her gloved hand, and picked up a few of her roses.

"You sound like you're not," he continued.

"I was born in Oregon."

"Oh, yes! Go Ducks?" Fletcher questioned as he handed her the roses he picked up.

"Yes." Bridget laughed. "Definitely."

"What are you doing out here?" Fletcher walked over to pick up the final rose and Bridget's itinerary.

"I'm researching my past. What are you doing?"

"Same." Fletcher walked back toward Bridget with the items he'd gathered. He glanced down at the paper in his hand. "Organized."

"Yeah." Bridget nodded her head. "I'm Bridget," she said.

"Like Bridget Bishop." Fletcher motioned toward the headstone beside them.

"Yes. Exactly that. Bridget Bishop. I was named for her."

"Wow." Fletcher paused and looked at her, adjusting his glasses. He gazed at her like he was pondering some far-off wondering.

Bridget gazed back. She raised her eyebrow and held out her hand. "Thank you," she said, reaching for the items in Fletcher's grasp.

"Oh, yeah." He moved to hand the paper and the rose over but paused as he read the first few lines of Bridget's itinerary. "Why do you have Diana Payne on your list?"

"She was my great-great, multiple-greats, grandmother on my mother's side. What do you know about her?"

***

Bridget and Fletcher talked for hours until they got too cold to stay outdoors. They wandered into an Irish pub to warm up with some hearty food and hot drinks. They each shared their own stories about their childhoods and upbringing. Fletcher's father was a pediatrician, and his mother was an artist. Fletcher had an older brother who lived overseas and came back once in a while for the holidays. Fletcher was currently on sabbatical from his post at Boston University as a history professor in the American and New England Studies Program.

They talked together until the pub closed and they had to leave. As they walked out into the evening, they fell into easy steps beside one another. Bridget naturally walked toward the B&B she was staying at, and Fletcher went along. They'd decided during their day-long conversation that they could work together to see if they could find the answers they each were looking for.

Back in Bridget's room, Fletcher settled on the long, deep blue couch that took up most of the sitting room. He flipped open his shoulder bag, pulled out his notebook, tabbed with sticky notes, and annotated with highlights. He opened his laptop and set it on the coffee table in front of him.

"I feel like we're in school." Bridget laughed as she got out her notes, computer, and spell book, arranging them on the bed where she sat.

"Aren't we?" Fletcher teased using his best college professor tone.

It felt easy to be together—like they'd been working on the same project for years. Bridget was glad that her suitcase had shown up, and that she'd been able to unpack and set out her candles, and the photo of her and her grandmother. She felt settled and at peace in this room. She felt energized and hopeful —that'd she'd *actually* be able to learn about her past.

"Ooooh! It's chilly." Bridget rubbed her hands together. "Do you mind figuring out how to start the fire, and I'll run down and let our innkeeper lady know you're going to stay for a bit longer? Plus, I want to get some more towels."

"Sure," Fletcher said as the door swished closed behind Bridget.

Fletcher got up and went to figure out the remote control for the fireplace so he could have it going when Bridget got back. Then he wandered around the room, noticing which items she must have brought with her, and which belonged to the B&B. He smiled at the picture of young Bridget and an older woman who must be her grandmother. He could feel their love for each other, just by looking.

He smelled a few candles; they were nice. They smelled like Bridget—warm and mysterious, open and kind. *What do I know?* He thought. He hadn't had a serious girlfriend since he was in college the first time in his early twenties—if he was telling the truth, he wouldn't even have called that serious. He'd been too busy—preoccupied even then by witches and a woman he'd never met.

He glanced over at his shoulder bag and thought of the one thing he hadn't removed: the one thing besides his rolled-up t-shirt and gym shorts. It was a small journal with small masculine handwriting inside. He found it one afternoon while going through a box of things his grandfather had sent him. It wasn't until he was fifteen that he even attempted to read the faded words, and it was then that they struck a chord with him. They were the reason he went to college to be a history major. There were many adventures included in the pages, but there was one entry in it that pulled at him even today.

It was about a man, a relative of his, and a woman who loved each other. It seems so simple just to say it. But this love was eternal, the kind that passed through the ages. It described the kind of bond that was so strong and true that death could not weaken it. He supposed that he was waiting for that kind of love: the kind of love where—as the journal had told it—he and his lover would meet on a warm summer day beside a well in a meadow. Where he would ask her to marry him, and he would bring her a crown of flowers to wear in her hair. The simple beauty of that love tore at his heart. He'd always wondered who the woman was. This sabbatical was his chance to find out.

"I'm back," Bridget called as she came through the door, arms loaded with towels and a basket of food and drinks for their late-night work session. "I brought snacks!"

"Oh! Nice." Fletcher went over to help carry. He reached out and pulled the towels from her arms. His fingers brushed her skin. As they did so, the lights in the room flickered, and a huge swoosh of air blew around the room scattering their papers, knocking over lamps, smothering the fire, and a large boom sounded in their ears. Then, just as suddenly as it began, the air stilled, the lights stopped flickering, and their papers drifted to the floor.

"What was that?" Fletcher didn't bother to keep the alarm from his voice.

Bridget shook her head. "I don't know!" She walked over to the window and looked out. Nothing looked out of place. The people walking along the sidewalk didn't look alarmed or even like they had heard anything out of the ordinary. She checked the latch to ensure the window was locked.

Fletcher opened the door to the hallway and looked out. Nothing was out of the ordinary out there either.

"Maybe a weird down draft of something," Fletcher said as he relit the fire.

"Maybe," Bridget agreed, but she wasn't able to shake the odd feeling. It almost felt like someone was watching her. She looked at Fletcher as he picked up his papers and set them on the coffee table. He picked up the lamp from the floor and set it back on the end table. He didn't look too shaken. She looked out the window again, still nothing weird out there. "That was a little freaky though."

"Yeah." Fletcher nodded in agreement and pulled an apple out of the food basket. "Do you want me to go? We can meet up tomorrow."

"No," Bridget replied. "No, I want to compare notes. I want to see what you know about Diana Payne, and I want to share mine."

"Okay. Great." Fletcher settled back on the couch and tapped the space bar on his laptop.

"Do you mind if we work by candlelight?" Bridget asked. "It's calming to me." Bridget picked up her papers and tossed them on the bed. She set the bedside lamps upright again.

"Sure."

Bridget went from candle to candle all around the room, lighting each with a little match. As each flame flared to life, she felt better, calmer. She saved the last candle. She wanted to see if this afternoon's magic was a fluke or if she could really perform a spell, but she couldn't do that with Fletcher in the room. Not without him knowing what she was.

I might as well tell him, she thought. *If we're going to be working together, he's going to find out sometime. But it's not really the thing a person blurts out.* You don't just say, not even in this modern day, not even in Salem, Massachusetts— *"Hey, buddy! I'm a witch."* Maybe *especially* not in Salem, Massachusetts. *Even if I am a witch who has performed only a single spell successfully in my entire life.*

She'd told other people over the years. Sometimes it went well. Sometimes it didn't. The boyfriend she had while she was getting her master's degree definitely didn't take it as well as the guy she was seeing during her undergraduate. He flipped and left so fast that the door hardly had time to close. She had several girlfriends who thought it was cool, but Bridget always sort of felt like they didn't believe her.

Bridget set the candle on the coffee table and then sat on the floor in front of it. "I have something I need to tell you," she said. She smiled to herself when Fletcher stopped typing, closed his laptop, and set it on the couch beside him. Her heart skipped a beat when he put on his glasses and leaned forward, looking anxious to hear what she was going to say.

"Okay," he said.

"Or rather, show you." Bridget tucked her hair behind her ears, leaned forward toward the candle, closed her eyes, took a breath, and thought about the spell. She knew it worked before she even opened her eyes because she heard Fletcher's quick catch of breath. She looked up at him. "I'm a witch."

Fletcher simply blinked. He'd read about them his whole life. He'd read more books and more stories than any other person he knew. He'd interviewed countless women and men who claimed they were a witch or knew a witch. His whole life had been spent learning everything he could about them. They fascinated him, captivated him. But he'd never met one—not *truly*—and definitely not for lack of trying. He'd half convinced himself that they were a myth, like dragons or unicorns.

Except, here one sat: cross-legged in front of him,—her hands folded in her lap. Her large green eyes looked up at him. Not fearing, not judging,—only waiting to see what he would do. Her hair shone a deeper red in the candlelight; the golden hue casting lovely shadows on her skin.

He knew that she had just exposed her soul to him. Fear gripped his heart. What if she had said this to someone else, someone who would want to hurt her? She looked so small, like a little sprite.

Then he remembered this morning at the museum. *Was that her magic? Did she cast a spell so powerful that it knocked her down? Is she that powerful?* He didn't know the answer to these questions. He didn't know what he was supposed to say. He actually didn't know how he was going to get to the next minute in his own life.

The only thing he *did* know was that—as the second the candle flamed to life, and she opened her eyes, looking up at him—he fell absolutely in love with her. *What am I supposed to do about that?*

"Did you hear me?" Bridget asked, looking to see if she could tell what he was thinking.

"I did." Fletcher's voice cracked in response.

"We don't have to work together if you don't want. Do you want to go?"

"No." Fletcher walked to the food basket and retrieved a couple of bottles of water, one for himself and one for her. "I want to stay."

"Are you afraid?" Bridget's question came as a whisper.

Fletcher looked at her. She hadn't moved. She sat motionless, waiting to see what he would do. He could tell that the stillness was a protective shield she'd enveloped around herself. His heart broke a little for her, that she would have to do such a thing to feel safe.

Very. "No." Fletcher handed the bottle to Bridget and took a drink of his own water. "Was the other Bridget Bishop a witch?" He asked.

"Possibly. Could be. Probably." Bridget opened her water and took a sip. "I don't know."

"Why were you there today? At the museum."

"I wanted to give her flowers." Bridget rubbed her face and took another drink from her water bottle. "She is my namesake. Then I wanted to see where it all happened. The hysteria. The fear. The murders. I wanted to know it and feel it, not just read about it." Bridget got up and walked to stand in front of the fire. "I have been afraid of it my whole life."

"Of being a witch?"

"No." Bridget hugged her arms to her body, took a deep breath, and closed her eyes. "Of dying."

"Are you dying?" Fletcher asked.

"No more than anyone else." *Not yet, at least.*

Fletcher looked confused.

"My grandmother died too young. My parents died too young." Bridget got up and sat on the bed, pulling a blanket over her shoulders. "I've known this since I was a child, but it wasn't until a few months ago—when I was finishing the last part of my research for my dissertation—that I ran across a strange fact that makes this knowledge bigger. More important. Every woman in my ancestry, going back to the 1600s, as far as I can tell, died the year they turned thirty. I knew this, but I didn't *know* it. It wasn't until I actually made a chart of the years and their deaths, that I realized it. I turn thirty this year—on December 21st. I came to see if I can figure out why they died." *I came to see if I am next.*

"What does Diana Payne have to do with it?" Fletcher picked up his notebook and began to take notes.

"She was born in 1662, on Halloween, best I can tell. She died here in Massachusetts, in what is now Provincetown in 1693. She died around the birth of her child—a girl—that same year. I think she was the first of my ancestors to die in her thirtieth year."

"What happened to the daughter?" Fletcher paused his writing to listen.

"She was raised by a mother-figure from Diana's youth." Bridget had a sudden realization. "Like we all have been. Like I was." Bridget picked up her spell book and flipped to today's still-blank page. "Why were you at the museum today?"

Fletcher took a drink of his water. "For much of the same reason you were, to honor Bridget and the others. I've been numerous times. It always gets to me. I like to go on the first big snow of winter. It seems more reverent that way, more solemn."

"Are you related to Bridget in some way?"

"No. I've just always been drawn to her. Her name, her story. It's not even really something I can explain." Fletcher frowned and looked back at her.

Bridget took his silence as permission to continue. "You mentioned something about Diana Payne at the cemetery. Do you know who she is?"

"Not exactly. But I think I might have an idea." Fletcher reached over and opened his shoulder bag. He took out a small hard-sided box. Opening it, he pulled out his journal. "My grandfather gave this to me when I was very young." Fletcher handed it to Bridget.

Bridget felt giddy as she set the book on the bed in front of her. She slowly removed it from the white linen handkerchief it was wrapped in and opened the front cover. Very distinctly, she could see the name Collins written on the first page. "Who is Collins?"

"I am. I am Fletcher Collins. Collins is my family name." Fletcher sifted through his own notebook and pulled out a packet of stapled pages. "Here is a set of copied pages from the journal. I like to keep the journal with me because it reminds me of my grandfather, but if I want to read it, I read these." He handed the copied pages to Bridget. "I thought you might like to see the journal."

Bridget wrapped the journal up and handed it to Fletcher who tucked it back into its box. "Yes, thank you." She took the journal copies and flipped through the pages. "Was it your grandfather's?"

"No. It couldn't be. Some of the dates line up to be the early 1800s. The entries in the journal focus on that timeframe, all of them except the part about a man named Fergus Collins and a woman named Diana P. It feels like that entry was an accounting of an oral history. I think Diana P. is Diana Payne. I can't find anyone else who it could possibly be." Fletcher shifted his weight like a teacher giving a lecture, with his voice sounding more excited as he continued. "Fergus lived in a colony close to Salem during the witch trials, but I've never been able to find out what colony it was or even where it might be located. The colony location is not described enough in the journal to make it recognizable now."

"Yeah," Bridget agreed. "Probably not. Most of the out-lying settlements didn't have very good record keeping that far back. We probably won't know for sure, not unless we can find someone's Bible."

"Agreed." Fletcher smiled at Bridget.

Bridget looked at him. Slowly a thought started to form. "Wait." She jumped off the bed and ran to her suitcase. "Are you *the* Fletcher Collins? Fletcher Sean Collins?" Bridget rummaged through her suitcase and found her favorite hardback book. "Is this you?" She hurried over to Fletcher and handed him the book, simply entitled, *Witches*.

Fletcher laughed. "I feel like a rockstar." He flipped the book over from front to back, noting the sticky tabs and bookmarks poking out from between the pages.

"It is you!" Bridget clapped her hands and picked up her pen. "Will you sign it?"

Fletcher laughed again. "A total rockstar!" He scribbled his name and a small, lovely note to Bridget.

"Thank you!" She hugged it to her body and reached to hug him too.

The moment their bodies touched, a swish of wind, a gale of wind hurled itself around the room. Papers flew. Lamps tumbled over. The bed rattled. The chandelier swung violently. The candles and the fire were snuffed out. Instead of stepping away from Bridget, Fletcher pulled her closer. The wind whistled and howled in anger in front of them, all around them. A loud boom sounded over and over, reverberating off the walls. The fury of it pulsed.

Bridget turned around, careful not to step out of Fletcher's embrace. She raised her arms and spoke in a firm strong voice. She yelled words she'd never thought she'd use, words that came to her years ago. She leaned against the wind and pushed. She spoke again and again. She pushed outward again and again. She stomped her foot and yelled.

Like before, and just as suddenly, the wind sucked itself out of the room. They were left in silence and total darkness.

Fletcher felt Bridget's body hum against his. It felt like he was holding the power of the ocean in his arms. Without letting go of her completely, he fumbled with the lamp at his feet. He clicked it on, and light spilled into the room. He hugged Bridget to him once more. His hands shook as he moved them over her arms and shoulders. He turned her to him so he could see her face. Sheer power radiated from her skin, her eyes, and her hair.

"I'm on fire," Bridget whispered in a rasping voice.

Fletcher kept ahold of her hand and grabbed the closest water bottle. He opened it and helped her drink the cool liquid.

Bridget drained the bottle. "Oh my god."

"Oh my god is right." Fletcher kept looking at her. Alternating between holding her close and leaning back to make sure she was okay. "You're sort of glowing," he said. "If that matters."

"I don't know what matters. I've never done this before." Bridget moved her hands to wipe her face and pull her hair back behind her shoulders. She jumped up on her toes and kissed him, a quick red-hot kiss.

Then she laughed. A full, powerful, freeing laugh. "I'm a witch!"

"Yes!" Fletcher laughed with her, hoping he didn't sound foolish. He could still feel the vibration, the energy she left on his lips from her kiss. He could still feel her in his arms as she fought against the wind: strong and powerful, like nothing he'd ever felt before.

And now, she seemed so happy. He wanted that for her—happiness––but he had never been so scared and elated at the same time. His heart soared. *I'm in love with a witch.* He had no idea what to do.

"I'm a witch!" Bridget spun in a circle like a child, her arms opened wide. "I'm a *witch*," she laughed.

And Fletcher caught her just as she fainted.

Fletcher tucked Bridget into bed and covered her with an extra blanket he found in the closet, but she kept shivering. He called down to the front desk to ask for more.

"Hi, yes, I am visiting Bridget Bishop, and we are needing a few more blankets."

"Yes. Sir, how many?" The clerk responded, her voice tired at the lateness of the call.

"Two, please." Fletcher scrubbed his hands over his face, trying to gather his thoughts. "That storm's pretty bad tonight?" He asked in a questioning tone, hoping to know if she had heard the boom.

"Yeah. It looks like it will snow all night." The clerk said with no hint of mystery or acknowledgment that something could be amiss.

"Thank you." Fletcher ended the call shaking his head. Weird. *Why didn't she hear or feel the micro-earthquake that had just happened? Was it directed toward just him and Bridget? If so, why? What is going on? And why did Bridget seem so happy about being a witch, happy like it was just a new realization?*

Fletcher started the fire again and lit a few candles, hoping they would help calm Bridget. He sat beside her on the edge of the bed as she slept. When she collapsed, he had thought about calling for an ambulance, but what would the emergency be? How would he even explain that? *Um! Yeah. There is some evil wind that keeps haunting us. She fought it off, because um, yeah, (clear my throat) she's a witch.* Not likely. Besides, she really did look like she was just sleeping.

Fletcher checked his watch. Just past midnight. The blanket delivery was taking forever. He glanced around the room and winced. It was a disaster. He looked at Bridget and pulled the blankets up, closer to her chin.

She looked perfect. Her face seemed calm, and her red-tinged eyelashes rested quietly and soft. Her breathing was slow and even, like her sleep was restorative—healing even—and peaceful enough for him to work on cleaning the room.

On every pass he made by the bed, he would stop and check on her. He took off his shoes so he wouldn't make noise as he walked. He was careful to keep Bridget's papers stacked on one side of the coffee table and his on the other.

He picked up her heavy, leatherbound journal and flipped through the pages. He closed it quickly when he realized what it was and placed it on her stack. He plugged in both of their computers to charge along with their phones.

When the blankets were delivered, he covered her with one and set about making his bed on the couch. He took a second to splash some water on his face and swish around some of the B&B's complimentary mouthwash. He changed into the t-shirt and gym shorts that he had planned to wear earlier to the gym before settling on the couch, too tired to update his notes or think any more about the many questions he had.

Just as he was about to close his eyes, Bridget stirred. He flicked on the light and rushed to her. She still looked peaceful, still sleeping. She had only rolled over to lay on her side.

He knew he wouldn't be able to sleep on the couch. He'd just keep wondering if she was okay. So, Fletcher got his blanket and his pillow and put them on the other side of the bed from her. He lay down beside her and pulled his blanket up and around himself. He felt the warmth of the room settle around him, and he sank into his pillow. He reached out to hold her hand and smiled when her fingers curled around his. He fell instantly to sleep.

Fletcher dreamed of her—the her he believed was Diana Payne. She was laughing and dancing in the warm summer breeze, holding the hand of the man she loved. Fletcher smiled in his sleep. He knew this dream. He had dreamt it off and on his whole life.

He saw the man she loved bring her a crown of flowers to wear in her hair. He knelt beside the well and offered her the deep red ruby ring. She nodded yes, and the man picked her up to swing her around in celebration. Then they walked together through the settlement, smiling at other inhabitants who lived in the small houses surrounding the village square.

Huge boulders jutted up out of the ground around the fire at the center. Others lay dotted among the houses. Some houses used the edge of the rock face as a wall, some had flowers growing around their base. Most just stood, looking like watchmen protecting the people who lived there. Fletcher let the happy and idyllic feeling of the day seep into and fill his mind.

But then the dream changed, and Fletcher was pulled deeper and deeper into the scene. It was one he had never witnessed before

Night had fallen. Men from the community had gathered at the fire in the center of the settlement to light their torches and ignite their fury. They chanted and stomped, brandishing their little black book with self-righteous indignation.

"Burn the witch!" the men yelled. "Hang the witch!"

The tallest man, his cloak billowing, grabbed a burning limb from the fire. He marched to the nearest boulder and wrote "*Kill the Witch.*" He walked to the next and wrote the same. The others saw and joined in. Each marking was fouler and more hateful than the last. They wrote and wrote until every giant rock surrounding the fire was marred with their wrath. They continued until each stone throughout the village was inscribed.

The sky grew to a deep black—no stars, no moon. The air was filled with acrid smoke and the stench of hatred. The snow at their feet, once pristine and perfect, was trampled and stained in their haste. Fletcher watched the men become a hateful mob, bellowing and crying as their feet pounded the way to a small rock cottage tucked beneath a massive tree.

They didn't bother to knock; they busted in and carried a crying Diana from her bed. They beat her and tore at her and threw her into a building that was less than a shack. The wind began to blow, swirling and roiling around the hovel, drowning out her screams from inside.

Fletcher tried to move. He tried to help. But he was frozen in place.

The man who had walked with Diana on the warm summer day ran to the door. It was barred against him. He yelled and pummeled the wood until his fists bled. He called and cried out to his love over and over. The wind grew stronger, more violent as if pushed onward by some unnatural force; like it was coming from the words written in hate, like it was that hatred that commanded it. It pushed and battered against the man until he fell to his knees, sobbing.

Suddenly, he looked up. He gazed directly at Fletcher, like he was there beside him, like he could touch him. Pleading with him.

Fletcher woke with a start. He sat up and scrubbed his eyes with his hands. *What in the actual hell?* Fletcher blinked and shook his head. Slowly, his vision began to clear. He was still in Bridget's room at the B&B. She was still sleeping beside him. He got up and drained a bottle of water. Then he reached over and smoothed his fingers along Bridget's cheek, waking her as gently as he could. He knew exactly where they had to go.

Bridget sat wide-eyed and patient in Fletcher's car as he told her about his evening, the conversation with the B&B clerk and his dream. She relayed her similar dream and experience with who they now both agreed must be Diana.

"So, I have a question. If I may?" Fletcher asked.

"Sure." Bridget looked over at him as he drove, being careful and mindful of the wintery roads.

"It may be too personal." Fletcher cleared his throat. "But, you seemed really happy last night, before you fainted. Happy to be a witch. Does this happen often?"

Bridget laughed. "No. It never happens. I'm a lousy witch."

Fletcher looked at her, startled.

"Well, I was. When I was a kid, growing up, I could never do magic. I knew the spells. I wrote them all down in my spell book, but I could never perform them. My first successful spell ever was that day at the cemetery. And I didn't even mean to do it."

"First spell ever?" Fletcher raised his eyebrows. "Hmmm."

"Do you think that means something?" Bridget asked.

"Maybe. Maybe you are supposed to do magic here. Maybe the location matters."

"Could be," Bridget responded, looking out the window, pondering what Fletcher had said.

"I do know one thing though or I think I do." Fletcher glanced at the navigation, being sure not to miss their next turn. "That earthquake, wind, whatever it is harassing us doesn't like us touching each other."

"It seems that way," Bridget responded as she watched the sweep of snow-covered landscape drift by the window. The winter air looked inviting. The sun was just right to light the snow with the glitter of million diamonds. "You said the woman last night didn't seem to hear the disturbance?"

"Yes."

"I feel like Diana and Fergus are trying to tell us something." Bridget shifted in her seat to look at Fletcher. "And if their message can get through to us, does it seem reasonable that the evil messages from the men in your dream could get to us too?"

"We could test it out," Fletcher said as he turned into the parking lot of their destination, the ghost town of Dogtown Commons, Massachusetts.

"Let's," Bridget responded.

The air was still and soft with only a bit of chill when they stepped out of the car. The ground was covered by the recent dusting of powder from last night's snow. From the looks of it, they were the only ones there. No other cars were in the lot where they left the car. They wove their way on foot to the signs marking the route to what would have been the village square.

Fletcher led the way, the layout of the community fresh in his mind from his dream. Large boulders dotted the landscape. Skinny spires of tree branches reached up into the sky. Bridget and Fletcher walked down a slight embankment onto flat ground and wound their way to the right around the circle of stones.

Finishing a wide loop, Fletcher stopped and pointed to the remains of what could have been a stone cottage. The walls had fallen over, leaving only a few stones about waist high. The chimney had crumpled, and the roof had fallen in. Snow drifted deep inside the frame. Bridget stepped forward into the path of the doorway.

A flash like a movie played in her mind. It showed Diana, her hair woven up in braids, setting a few rocks for the foundation of the home. Then it showed her stepping back, looking around, and then uttering a few words. With the raising of her hands, a cottage appeared where only those few stones had once sat. Diana then walked around the whole of it. With sprinkling motions, she conjured wildflowers and a little stone walk. Then she looked over at Bridget and winked, laughing.

"I just saw her!" Bridget gasped, looking back at Fletcher.

"What?"

"I just saw her. She made the cottage." Bridget held out her hand to invite Fletcher up beside her.

He walked forward and took her hand.

"I saw—" The wind drowned out whatever Bridget might have said.

In a flash, the sky turned to steel gray. The wind whipped against their faces. Snow and bits of ice slashed at their skin. Instead of stepping away from each other as they knew the wind wanted, they turned toward each other and kissed, fast and brilliantly. They laughed at the wind, surrounded by blizzard white.

A torrent engulfed them. Branches flew from trees, aimed like arrows for their faces. The snow and ice burned through their clothes like acid. Bridget turned and faced it. Her skin glowed with power as she fought back against it.

It beat at her. The wretched stench, acrid and foul, surrounded them, in roll after roll of hatred. For what seemed like hours, Fletcher stood behind her, holding her, supporting her. She uttered every spell she knew. She cried out every incantation she had ever written.

The wind kept coming. More snow. More branches. More hate. Bridget's strength was waning. She needed help. She needed someplace safe.

Nearly spent, she turned around toward the remains of the cottage. She raised her hands and uttered a few words. Out of the gloom and winter blackness, a stone cottage appeared. It had a strong chimney with smoke pouring from its top and little windows shining with welcome.

Bridget reached forward, opened the door, and walked inside. Fletcher followed. Bridget slammed the door behind him. She uttered words against the wood and let the latch hang free. She walked from window to window, uttering the same phrase. Nothing would get in.

The wind roared. It screamed. It pounded its fury against the little home. It flung trees and rocks against the frame, but nothing got through.

Fletcher and Bridget reached for each other's hand inside the warm light.

"Holy shit," Fletcher croaked. "Did you know you could do that?"

"No." Bridget walked to the fireplace and took off her outwear, hanging it on one of the hooks nearby to dry. "I couldn't light a candle a week ago."

"That was one hell of a test!" Fletcher took off his jacket and hung it beside Bridget's.

"No kidding." Bridget smiled.

Her eyes scanned from one side of the cottage to the other. There were no words to describe how amazed she felt. *How did I do this?* She thought to herself. *I made this!* We *made this—Diana and me.*

Everything was here. Dishes were stacked neatly on the shelves above the cupboard along one wall. Big cooking pots hung from the ceiling above it. A small table with four stools took up the middle. To the left side, a bed with a nightstand was tucked under a window. Dotted around on various surfaces— the table, the nightstand, the cupboard—were flickering candles adding peace and calm to the space. Facing her were two rocking chairs. To her right, the large stone fireplace was lit with burning logs. She could feel the heat from them seep into her cold body.

"Here." Fletcher handed her a few tissues from his shoulder bag. "For your face."

"Oh!" Bridget touched her cheeks, still freezing cold, dotted with small cuts from the flying debris. "Thank you," she said and dabbed away the grit and blood.

"Of course." Fletcher wandered from place to place in the cottage, picking up baskets and pots, looking at everything like a kid in a candy store. "Astonishing," he kept whispering. "Check this out." He said as he stirred the pot hanging above the flames. "It looks like stew."

Bridget only smiled meekly as she sat in one of the rocking chairs. She was exhausted. The scent, rich and hearty from the bowl Fletcher handed her, was rejuvenating. She swirled her spoon around the mix: fat-cut carrots and parsnips, large chunks of meat, and brown gravy. She took a nibble just to taste it, finding it delicious. She ate all within that bowl and half of another one.

"What are you thinking about?" Fletcher asked from his spot in the other rocking chair.

"That I could stay here forever."

"Yeah," Fletcher agreed. "Me too. It brings a whole new meaning to, 'History comes to life.'"

"Hmmm." Bridget closed her eyes and rocked the chair gently.

"Why don't you take a nap?" Fletcher suggested. "I'll clean up. I'll set out our laptops and get out our notes. Once you've rested, we can look around a bit more. See if Diana left us any clues." Fletcher didn't bother to keep the excitement from his voice.

"Okay." Bridget walked to the bed, lay down, and pulled the comforter around her. It smelled like lavender and sage. *Comfort indeed.*

Not exactly sleeping, Bridget's mind drifted over the memories of her childhood. They played like a silent movie reel, zipping from one event to another. There were shots of her as a little girl laughing with her parents, pictures of her doing spell work with her grandmother, and quick snippets of her reading and writing in her spell book. While she was living it, she never really thought it a lonely life. It was all she knew.

She thought it lonely now, though, but only because Fletcher was there with her. He had shown her what 'not alone' really felt like. She had been scared before facing the wind, but she knew that Fletcher was behind her. He was holding her as if his life depended on it too; like he'd never let her go. *Is he here because of me, though? Or is he here for Diana?* These thoughts nagged at her, but her mind was too tired to contemplate them; her body was too tired to answer them. She fell asleep.

Instead of dreaming the old dreams over, this time Bridget witnessed a new scene. Diana was there, standing at the edge of the ocean looking out across the water toward something. Or, perhaps, toward some*one*. The ocean breeze blew tendrils of Diana's hair across her cheek. Her face was pale with exhaustion, her green eyes crying, and her belly large with her daughter ready to be born.

More visions. These scenes, too, played like a movie reel: Diana conjuring a cabin tucked in the woods, close enough to walk to the ocean shore.

Diana reuniting with an old friend who would help her have her baby, and who would help her care for the new life when it came. Diana sewing clothes and making candles. Diana standing each day at the edge of the ocean looking for the person who never came. The reel flashed from one to the other at lightning speed, a montage of mundane, lonely days.

Then it jolted to a halt, stopping to show Diana laying on a bed of her own making, writhing in the agony of childbirth. To still her mind, to calm her heart, she used her power of sight and looked across the water at the man she loved.

The scene she saw there broke her. He was standing beside a different woman, dressed for their wedding day. His shoulders were slumped in surrender and defeat, doing what he must to survive. The ache in Diana's heart was so big, so deep, she knew she'd never be able to heal. She cried out in anguish, an immense sweeping cry so harsh and sad that Bridget cried out too.

Distantly, Bridget felt Fletcher rush to her. Felt him try to wake her. She turned to him in her sleep. She felt his arms wrap around her and hold her as her body shuddered in pain.

Bridget felt her own body twist and strain with the great struggle of childbirth. She felt like it was her own heart tearing apart inside her chest. She sobbed, as her body convulsed, engulfed in Diana's agony.

Diana screamed against her pain—the pain in her body, the pain in her heart. She pushed one final time and smiled faintly when she heard the cry of her daughter fill the air. Then Diana could take no more.

She couldn't take the injustice of it all. She couldn't take the pain of raising a daughter who should have had a different father, a *loving* father. She couldn't take not being with the man she loved and building the life they'd dreamed of. She couldn't take the weight of loathing she still felt from the men that fateful night.

Diana fell limp against her bed, her red hair splayed out around her in a mess of fiery curls. She looked up at Bridget and said, "Until we meet again." Then her green eyes went dark.

Bridget fell limp in Fletcher's arms. Terror clawed at him. He scrambled to check her pulse and her breathing.

Relief, the greatest relief of his life, filled his soul when he found a steady pulse and even breathing. His fingers shook as he brushed Bridget's hair from her eyes and straightened the blankets around them. He rested his head against hers, so grateful she was there.

He kept thinking about, Fergus Collins: the man who yelled and pounded on the door where Diana was being held until his fists bled. How scared must he have felt? How angry and hopeless?

Fletcher thought he might know that feeling now. Holding Bridget as she experienced what must have been immeasurable pain felt like a void of hopelessness. Not being able to do anything about it, not being able to go for help or call for help, not being able to wake her. He knew it would haunt him for the rest of his life.

Fletcher lay there beside Bridget. Quietly breathing. Quietly living while the wind howled and bashed against the cottage walls. The fire flickered strong and warm, protecting them both from the frigid cold outside. Minutes passed.

Fletcher tucked his arm under his head and watched Bridget as she slept. She was the strongest, most amazing person he had ever met. She looked small, like a little woodland fairy with red hair and freckles dotting her nose, but she was also a force he'd never experienced before.

He smiled when she opened her eyes.

"Hi." Her voice fractured as she whispered.

"You're here." Fletcher grinned.

"I am." Bridget moved to prop herself up a bit. "How long have I been asleep?"

Only a couple of years. "Not long." Fletcher sat up beside her, keeping his voice low. "How do you feel?"

"Terrible. Sad. My body hurts." She told Fletcher all she had experienced, working to keep tears from her eyes.

Desperately trying to keep his heart from pounding as he experienced her dream with her again, Fletcher breathed in and out slow and calm. He pulled her close and held her until his heartbeat grew steady, and he could think. "I think you're right about what you said in the car. I think I understand better. Pieces of their story—the ones they want us to know—were sent to us by *them.*"

"What are we supposed to do with them? What do they want us to know?" Bridget pulled the blanket around her shoulders and sat crossed-legged on the bed.

"I found something that might help." Fletcher walked to the small table where he had laid out their notes and laptops. "While you were sleeping, before you had the nightmare, I was cleaning up from dinner, and I found it." He grabbed a bottle of water and the book. He handed both to Bridget. "It was tucked inside this." He pointed to the cupboard where he'd stacked their clean bowls.

Bridget took a quick drink, to clear her throat, quickly putting down the bottle to trade for the book. "Is this what I think it is?" She turned the pages, one by one. "It is. This is like my spell book. It has the same spells. Let's look." Bridget pointed to her own journal.

Seeing where she'd gestured, Fletcher grabbed the journal and brought it over.

"Let's see page one." Bridget flipped open her own book and Diana's to match.

Fletcher sat beside her on the bed, pulling Diana's journal onto his lap.

"Is it the same?" Bridget asked as she read her words aloud.

"Yes," Fletcher confirmed as he glanced from one journal to the other with her.

Bridget and Fletcher turned more pages, comparing each and further confirming that each page of Diana's book had the same spells as Bridget's.

"Do you have this one?" Fletcher asked, turning to the final page in Diana's journal.

"It looks new." Bridget gathered the journal to her, running her eyes over the precise loops and clean lines of Diana's handwriting. Bridget spoke the words clearly with power and strength:

Blackened hatred, dark and deep,
Conjured in fear and spread with scorn,
Begone.
Let light and love within us keep
Enchant instead a life reborn,
At the coming of this dawn.

The moment the spell was uttered, the wind outside stilled. Fletcher opened the door and sunlight poured in.

Bridget and Fletcher walked out into the light. The air shimmered with ice crystals and a crisp chill. It smelled clean and inviting. The slim young trees beside their cottage were coated with glistening ice. Cardinals flitted from branch to branch, bright and red against the snow.

"A winter wonderland." Fletcher smiled and held out his hand to Bridget.

She reached for his. The moment their fingers touched, their eyes locked, and they laughed. "We can hold hands now."

"We definitely can." Fletcher gave her fingers a gentle squeeze.

"There's just one more thing to do. Do you think we can find it?" Bridget replayed the dream in her mind when she saw Diana hide the ring.

"I bet so. I think we've found everything else they wanted us to find." Fletcher tugged on Bridget's winter cap.

She grinned up at him. "I want to find it. So, she can have peace. It's really hard to think about all the pain they both experienced." Bridget's muscles were sore from her dream, and her heart still ached for them.

Fletcher nodded in agreement and pulled Bridget closer to his side.

They wandered past a few large boulders, out beyond where the village square would have been. The snow was quiet beneath their boots, making the moment seem sacred.

"This should be it." Bridget pointed to the remains of what looked like the edges of an old stone well. "In my dream, I saw her bury it here beside it."

Fletcher had chosen a tool they could use for a shovel from the assortment of tools in their cottage. He had tucked it in his pocket in case they needed it. They wiped away the loose top layer of snow with their hands and took turns digging. Back and forth they shared the shovel, but all they found was cold frozen dirt with wilted leaves and broken twigs.

"Maybe we're not supposed to find it," Bridget began.

"I guess," Fletcher took off his hat and sat back on his heels. He wiped his face with his sleeve, adjusting his glasses.

Bridget grinned at him. His dark hair curled around his face and his dark eyes scanned the debris they'd dug up. "You sure are cute, Mr. Fletcher Collins."

He grinned back. "Oh yeah?" He scooted on his knees to be closer to her. "Well you, Miss Bridget Bishop, are beautiful." He pulled her into his arms and kissed her nose. "We don't need the ring. I can ask you without it."

"Ask me what?"

"If you'll marry me." Fletcher tilted his head to the side. "I know it seems fast in the number of days. But we've done more and been through more than most people do in their whole lives. I don't want to spend this day or any other day away from you."

Bridget's gaze traveled his face. She thought of all the reasons Fletcher could choose to be here with her—Diana, Fergus, her namesake Bridget. She thought of why he stayed, and why he wasn't concerned with her being a witch. It was true that they had experienced more than most people in these few short days. But he'd never seen her under normal circumstances. He'd never seen her work or write or live.

"You don't know—"

"And don't say, 'I don't know you.' I *do* know you." He kissed her lightly, sweetly. "I know you like to hold my hand when we sleep. I know that you are brave, braver than anyone I've ever known. I know you grew up loved, but lonely. I know you like parsnips in your stew." He wrinkled his nose. "I know you like to read and that you have an amazing memory. I know you can light a candle without a match. And, most importantly, I know I've been in love with you since you lit your first one."

Bridget's eyes stung. She needn't have worried that Fletcher was here for Diana or Fergus or Bridget. He was here for her. He'd stayed for her. He could have left at any moment, but he did not. He was not disgusted by her, nor did he cower in fear.

He saw her. The *real* her. The her she always wanted to be.

"Yes," Bridget said.

"Yes, what?" Fletcher's eyes grew wide, hopeful.

Bridget laughed. "Yes, I'll marry you, you silly man. My silly man. My professor." She dropped the shovel and wrapped her arms around his neck. "So, I can kiss you every day. I love you too." Her lips met his and the world seemed to spin to a stop. The birds fell quiet and a magic haze surrounded them.

"This is the best day," Fletcher said, sitting back on his heels again.

"Agreed." Bridget winked and set about gathering their gloves and picking up the shovel. Suddenly, she gasped. "Look!" She pointed.

On top of the snow, right where they had been digging, was the ring, the red in the ruby glistening deep and rich against the white.

Bridget knew what it meant. It meant that she and Fletcher had helped Diana and Fergus heal. Bridget was suddenly sure, she was simply certain that the curse was broken. She could feel the weight she'd been carrying her whole life drift away. She knew that she would live past her thirtieth birthday. That if she had any children, they would not grow up without a mother. That the dark times had ended; it was now time for the light.

"I'll be damned." Fletcher picked it up. He whistled between his teeth. "Do you want to try it on?"

"Yes." Bridget held out her hand.

Their laughter drifted through the quiet air. The love they felt there in that moment traveled back through the strands of time erasing the hatred, the fear, the wretchedness. It stitched together the pieces of Diana and Fergus' broken hearts.

Bridget held out her hand to admire the ring's beauty, and she saw a vision. It was Diana and Fergus. Diana had flowers in her hair, and they were together on a warm summer day, in a meadow, beside a well, dancing.

"They are together." Bridget smiled and a single tear slipped down her cheek.

Fletcher wiped it away and kissed her there in the glittering air.

"You look sick to your stomach." Bridget laughed across the hospital room at Fletcher.

"I am," he said holding his stomach. He'd never know how she made it through the ordeal. It nearly killed him, and he just had to stand there and breathe.

"Here's your little one, Mr. Collins." The nurse delivered the small bundle wrapped in snuggly blankets to his arms. "Take her to your wife."

Fletcher walked to Bridget and placed their daughter in her arms. Shades of red hair peeked out from beneath the edges of her little hat and her wide green eyes gazed up at them. He kissed his wife tenderly, ever so grateful for the gift she had given him.

"Does she have a name?" The nurse asked.

Bridget and Fletcher looked at each other and in unison said, "Diana Collins."

"Beautiful." The nurse responded. "You sure are a lucky man."

"Yes I am," Fletcher spoke, pride filling his voice. "I found my witches," he whispered just loud enough for Bridget to hear. He wrapped his arms around them both, ready and determined to protect them for the rest of his life.

Half Life
By Sylvie Bax

Grey huddled over the small fire that provided scant heat in the sub-zero temps that had become more and more common in the North.

Grey hadn't seen a Summer since he was a child. The sun had become a murky, disinterested shadow of itself—a reminder of when the cold lasted only for the seasonal months.

The South had ruled supreme for decades. Where there had been deserts, there were now lush green vales; where there had been famine, there was plenty. The refugee column from the North grew larger and more despairing every day.

Those like Grey had been either forced or coerced into staying in the North to keep it competitive. The North still had sway because it had discovered Zenick, a metal that had only been created by the freezing temperatures and lack of sunlight. Even the coldest parts of the North had not seen the like of Zenick before The Kolding. The mineral made itself within the cracks and fissures—a certain pressure here, a gentle parting of surfaces there.

Zenick made the North competitive because it could heal. Once it was smelted and treated, it could be broken down and chemically induced to heal any disease over a short period. Cancer, Ebola, radiation poisoning—the healing properties of this bronze and cerulean ore was magical. Aging itself couldn't be stalled, but longer and healthy lives were possible.

Zenick was not for Grey though, or his fellow Mulchers.

So, the North controlled the South with Zenick, and the South controlled the North with climate stability. A continental stand-off ensued that squatted toad-like on human destiny.

Grey didn't care. He remained in the present. It was safer and easier that way. Keep warm, keep fed, and never attract the Major's s attention. Keep your life small, friendships blurry, and hoard nothing special. Major Cutter didn't believe in workers having joy. Joy was not useful. Joy was distracting.

Distracted miners were useless. Expendable; and Cutter was a master of death.

Very few women lived in the camp, and those that did worked as cooks or bordello wives. Marriage was forbidden, but sexual frustration was a distraction. So, Cutter and his Sentries accommodated carnal desires under strictly regulated conditions.

Grey had acquaintances, not friends. Friends, lovers—anything that made you feel more than normal, anything that could excite you into reckless actions, were dangerous. Anybody who drew the attention of Cutter was summoned to the Citadel, never to return.

Grey had always thought how extraordinary it all was: that they would all cling to life in these unimaginable conditions. The gutting cold, the sparse, inedible food, the brutality of the Sentries, and the lack of companionship were heavy burdens.

It was all he had ever known, but still, he dreamed of getting to the South. He dreamed of discovering a nugget of Zenick that would pay for his fare and give him a credible form of currency; some kind of life where he wouldn't have to sink to his knees and open his mouth to secure extra food or a moldy blanket. Sometimes the Sentries used his mouth and pushed him hard onto his back, bruising his skin and giving nothing in return.

When the market traders appeared every fat, bleached moon they brought commodities for the Citadel. The Sentinels feasted and drank their way through this period but not the Major. He remained vigilant. Always tapping his Mashette, always looking for ways to bleed the Mulch.

Rumors spread as they were often the catalyst of Cutter's sadism. He had been a Mulch himself and tore 50 sentinels apart with his bare hands to earn his freedom. Or Cutter had run from the South after committing an act so abhorrent that he was chased by five cohorts of Cursed Dragons and hadn't been able to outrun the fiendish Ghoul spell that was cast upon him, wearing the suffering of others like a victory mantle.

The miners were referred to as Mulch. Worth less than animal shit, less than ice on a stone, less than a man's last breath; the Mulch were loathed, tolerated, and brutalized.

But Zenick., though…

Zenick held a million men's dreams in a piece the size of a torn nail.

The thin gruel that passed as sustenance was cold, like everything else. Stringy meat of some sort and mushed potato floated greasily on the surface. Grey didn't think too much about it, just kept up the dogged spooning into his mouth. Just for a minute or two, Grey allowed himself to disassociate from the cold hard ground and the work yet to come.

An odd noise roused Grey from his dream, like the pealing of a friendly bell, a clarity of peace and sanctuary. It was unlike any sound that existed amongst the Mulch where the endless tramp of feet, the snow drifts that covered the settlement and flumped softly to the ground when disturbed and fused one's bones into an agony of cold were endured. Ironic gentle sounds that silenced the emptiness of this life.

"Don't look, just don't look," Grey mumbled, feeling the pull of the light and its purity. A pulse of warmth flooded his fingers. Grey squeezed his eyes shut. "It's not real," he continued, terrified it was another Sentry trick.

They employed careless sadism, promises of good things for the vulnerable who might volunteer to enter the Citadel of their own free will to entertain the wicked. Children were pushed into monsters' hands by parents and strangers in a vaulted delusion that this time they might return and the knowledge that—even if not—they wouldn't have to witness their painful deaths.

The chime again—so soft, more musical than the sirens that ruled the Mulch's life. More inviting. A gentle pause. Grey tried so hard not to look. His nails dug into the soft flesh of his thighs, becoming spotted with blood that looked black in the twilight.

Another chime and a soft voice – far away but definite.

Grey.

Grey, do you hear me?

"No," he whispered. "Go away. Please, just be on your way."

Grey. Grey. Grey.

A pick of agony drove itself into his temple. Grey bit down on a skinny lip, more blood blossoming on his chapped, thin mouth. *Where does all this blood come from*, he thought, *when I am so empty?*

Grey

More pressure began to stockpile itself until his head wrenched up and he found himself reeling.

A woman shimmered and shifted in front of him: dressed in cerulean and bronze robes, clean and quite beautiful. Abundant hair graced her shoulders, and the ground she stood on wasn't dirty or thick with detritus. It was clean, impossibly so.

He could smell something sweet, floral. He could smell color.

Come, Grey, Come.

"I'm coming," Grey answered.

He stumbled to his feet, still biting his lip which was now bleeding freely.

A rough hand pulled at his sleeve, one of the Mulch. Flynn, Grey thought. "Get down, you fool," the man hissed. "Grey—for fucks sake—the Sentries are watching.

Grey shrugged the arm off. The warmth in his fingers spread throughout his arms, a tingling glow of golden calm.

The woman's body shifted and became more definite: a corporal Zenick Goddess.

Grey stumbled towards her outstretched hand, his feet slipping on an icy black slate.

You are safe, Grey. You are loved. We have much to accomplish.

Her smile was bliss and truth. All his life, Grey had hoped for this moment. Now a woman created from Zenick—the key to his freedom and happiness, the balm to his suffering—was offering her protection.

"Do you see her, Flynn?" he asked.

Flynn who had given up trying to help and was staring stubbornly at the ground, whispered, "I see nothing. I see nothing."

Grey didn't hear the Sentries run toward him. He didn't feel the roughness of their hands on his body, nor the stun guns pressed upon his softest parts. He didn't feel their Twiblades' sharpness, nor the tearing of hair from his scalp. He didn't see the fonts of blood and gore erupt from his neck or the desperate silence around him.

Grey only saw the woman, and as he took her hand, a molten charge of warmth swept him from head to toe. He felt sated; he felt seen and warm.

And, as his last breath left his body, Grey was at peace.

Afterward, there was little talk of Grey, death being so common. Some toyed briefly with the idea that there had been a Zenick Goddess, but there was too much hope in that sort of thinking. It was readily dismissed. Major Cutter made a statement later about treachery, stupidity, and punishment.

One elderly woman had a different view, but she kept it secret in her mind. She understood the madness that comes from despair—an almost sexual zealotry that is born from pain and righteousness. Such had delivered Grey into his own delusion.

And she felt a fit of jealousy knowing that was not her destiny—that her suffering would not abate until death took her. She cried for the first time in many, many years—soft, fat tears of grief and sorrow, loss and hopelessness.

Those tears softened the ground beneath them and watered out the mud. When her tears were spent, the crone wiped the frozen salt off her cheeks and noticed a small speck of cerulean and bronze beneath the slurry.

She wondered at the irony and thought about possibilities. She planned the first of the Great Rebellions that began to erode the power of the Sentries and the Citadel—the beginning of a different era.

That woman's name was Jae. She was celebrated. Monuments were carved and erected, and she was praised for eons.

And Grey was lost to history, as so often happens—lost to in a heap of shock and comets, and fire, and blood. Lost to other reputations which are easier to gild in peacetime. Lost to his delusion and heartbreak.

When Cutter tossed Grey's carcass onto a stack of logs and tinder, a flame of cerulean and bronze flared briefly before Grey's ashes were returned to the Mulch, becoming part of the rich, frozen stew of everything and nothing.

An unremarkable man.

An unremarkable death.

And a destiny seared by madness and hope.

ᛏHE BLADESMIᛏH
— A Chronicles of Naelyra Story —
By R. J. Lloyd

I

War was imminent, whether we liked it or not.

An attempt had been made on the Queen's life, our King's new bride. It had even been successful. But if anyone had needed proof that Queen Auriena was powerful, the fact that she'd come back to life would have been more than enough.

However, it was that very proof that sent our world into chaos. Every race and faction on the planet of Naelyra had an opinion of what to do with Queen Auriena. Some wanted her dead, fearful of the level of power she held. Some wanted her for themselves, hoping to harness her powers and use them for their own gains.

Then there were people like me who went to Everwinter to join King Kanedraven's armies and swear to protect Queen Auriena, even until our final breath.

The whispering swept in through my village in the way they'd described the cold breezes of Everwinter. Rumors infiltrated every home and establishment until everyone was talking about what had happened in the castle – the King's most loyal friend and former lover had killed the Queen and their unborn child. But with King Kanedraven's blood in her system and her own unique powers of magic, Queen Auriena returned to us even more powerful than before. Even more powerful than any of us could imagine.

The village I lived in was no different than any other in that, as soon as this knowledge swept through its people, demands were born from the fears people carried, as well as their greed. Some wanted one thing, while others wanted another. I watched as several small groups left for Everwinter, each with their own agenda.

It made me sick, really. King Kanedraven had always been nothing but generous to Naelyra. He'd won the war and taken over as our King. We'd been blessed with peace ever since. Granted, I hadn't been alive when it all happened, but—as a vampire of nearly a hundred years—I'd seen the results of his firm yet fair hand long enough to know that my loyalty stood with him. The People of Naelyra that were trying to kill or steal his bride betrayed their loyalty, not just to our King, but to the very kingdom itself.

It didn't take much for me to close up my bladesmith shop, pack a few things and make the trek up to Everwinter where the King and Queen resided. Granted, I much preferred the plush green landscape of my village to the snow- and ice-covered castle city, but I was determined to do what I could to help.

By the time I reached the castle gates, I was regretting not being better prepared for the cold. My blood supply was frozen, and the severely low temperatures were affecting my body, making my bones ache and slowing my movements. I may not be as susceptible as a human, but anything you put in freezing temperatures will be affected by the cold, even the undead.

"State your business." The female guard barked at me through the grating in the wall.

I rolled my shoulders back. "I'm here to prove my loyalty to the King and Queen and lend my services or my sword."

I could see her eyeing me for a moment before huffing. The locks released on the door, and it slowly opened just enough for me to step inside. "Report to the guard house to your right. Do *not* stray, or you will be arrested."

I raised an eyebrow at her. "That bad, huh?"

She huffed again. "Do as you're told."

With a nod, I made the right turn and went into the brick building she'd ordered me to. Passing several other guards, I gave each a cursory nod, hefting my bag up further on my shoulder. I had a feeling that tensions were on the rise, but this felt like they were all on high alert.

A large man stood in the corner of the room. "Bag. Weapons. Spells casting materials. Restraining devices. Poisons. Herbs. Portal crystals. Anything that could be considered potentially dangerous. Put it all on the table," he said with a gesture.

I started to unload my things. "Would you just rather that I strip down?" Instantly, I regretted my sarcasm.

He took a step forward. "Name."

I cleared my throat. "Asher Harrington."

"Where is your home?" he demanded to know.

I pulled a set of thigh blades off and set them on the table. "I am originally from Eldercairn. But most recently, I come from Tryst."

He folded his arms over his chest. "Nobody comes from Eldercairn. It's a trading town."

"I do believe the rumor was that my mother traded me for her freedom." I dropped a dagger down next to the throwing knives. "Or was it a bottle of alcohol? I'm not rightly sure."

He looked me over. "Vampire?"

A corner of my mouth lifted at his statement. "Astute."

"We have many here," he replied.

Everyone knew that our King was a vampire, and there were plenty of us running around Everwinter. But outside, in other cities? Not near as many. Honestly, I'd not spent a lot of time around my own kind. A part of me was very curious about how that would turn out. I wasn't a stranger to feeling like an outsider, but it had always been because I wasn't like most of those around me. Now, I was going to be around a lot of people of my own kind, but I wasn't sure I would be accepted with the current tensions.

The guard examined my things before patting me down. Once satisfied, he took his post back up against the far wall. "King Kanedraven and Queen Auriena thank you for the pledge of loyalty and are happy to have you here in Everwinter. There have been many attacks on Everwinter and against our Queen. Understand that trust is difficult to come by these days. There are men stationed at a post in the center of town. You can go there and receive your assignment. If you need residence, they can help with that also, but it will not be for free."

"I would not want charity. I'm here to help, not drain resources." I continued to put my things back together.

"Good to hear," he replied.

We didn't speak again as I left. Once outside, I found my way through the castle village until I located the post I'd been directed to. The castle walls provided some shelter from the winter winds, but it still took a bit of restraint to not find a clothier on my way. However, I didn't want to be found wandering through Everwinter before finding my place there among its people. It wasn't a good time to be seen as an outsider as it were.

"You! Stranger!" A stout man was standing outside of a building pointing at me. "What is your business here?"

I crossed the cobblestone path to him. "Are you the one I was sent to see about some assignment and housing?"

"We are fresh out of handouts," he barked.

I shook the pouch on my belt, making the coins jingle loudly. "I'm not looking for one. I'm looking for a post and somewhere to lay my head at night out of the cold."

He eyed me up and down with a scowl before waving me to follow him. "Come inside."

The warmth was more than welcome. Nearly every inch of me was frozen to the bone. I rubbed my fridged hands together, pausing in front of the roaring fireplace.

"What are you good at?" The man rounded a desk and sat down behind stacks of papers.

Not pulling myself away from the fire, I turned, allowing the warmth to permeate my back. "I will gladly pledge my blade or make them for the army."

"Bladesmith?" He asked.

I nodded. "Yes. My name is Asher Harrington. I…"

He cut me off. "I am familiar with your name. I have ordered many blades from you on behalf of our King."

His words shocked me. The King had ordered *my* blades? I wanted to ask if they were for himself, his court, or his soldiers. Not that it mattered. "If the King would prefer that I continue to make more for his armies, I would happily lend my services. I am here to do my part to keep Queen Auriena safe and her Kingdom protected."

With a grunt, he nodded and started scribbling on a piece of paper. I stood silent and waited. After he'd filled the page with his scrawling lettering, he slid it over toward me. "There is an old blacksmith's shop across town. He was killed in the last attack. We have another blacksmith in town, so I do not need to fill the empty shop with another. But you could use what's there. The tools should be what you need. Plus, It has a residence above it. That will be yours. Just sign, and I will show you to it."

I blinked. "How much?"

He groaned. "Your loyalty."

"But you said there are…"

Again, he cut me off. "That's right. No handouts. The Kingdom will not pay you for now. We will simply give you the materials you will need to make what is asked for by King Kanedraven and any food and supplies you require. You can make money if any of the citizens want to commission any of your blades. Pay for those supplies out of your own purse and keep your profits."

I was nearly speechless. Without a word, I stepped up to the page and took the pen from him. He'd outlined the agreement simply, stating reasonable limits on what could be commissioned from the Kingdom, which was a relief. If I could find additional work, I'd have time to forge some items for others to make some additional money. Satisfied, I signed and set the pen down. "Looks good."

"I'm glad you approve." His tone was flat. "Come. I will show you to it."

We walked in silence through the courtyard as well as winding through a few neighborhood streets. I marveled at the architecture that not only decorated the castle but also flowed over the various buildings of Everwinter. The ornate lampposts. The carvings that dotted the landscape. The lights that were strung over walkways and down alleys. Despite the cold, it was a picturesque city.

"Here." The gruff man slid a key into a heavy lock on a set of double doors. Tossing it to me, he opened the doors. "Do with it what you will. I will report to the King that you are here. I am sure you will receive your orders soon. In the meanwhile, clean the place up. Your supplies can be requisitioned weekly from Bexlynn Tirvanos. She has a tailor shop two blocks over. She also sells common goods. You can get suitable clothes from her and work with her on any sheaths, belts, and such for the weapons you will make. She's a trusted citizen."

I looked into the building and sighed. It was a mess. He'd said the blacksmith was recently killed, but the place looked like it hadn't been cared for in months. "I'll report to her today or tomorrow, depending on how much needs to be done here first so I'm not bothering her by asking for things several times."

He snorted. "That's none of my concern. Here." He held out a ring of keys. "These go to this lock, the front door, the back, upstairs, the safe, and the outbuilding in the back garden. Good luck, and welcome to Everwinter."

I went to ask questions, but as soon as he dropped the keys into my palm, he turned and stalked off. "Thank you!" I shouted after him. He waved his hand dismissively and kept walking.

"Well, Asher?" I said to myself. "You're not being handed a cheap sword and thrust toward battle on day one. This is better… right?"

I pursed my lips and headed inside.

By the looks of things, the place would have all of the equipment I would need, at least most of it. But was it all in working order? That had yet to be seen.

With that, I decided to walk through the place and assess my new home and shop.

II

I was thankful to find a supply of candles inside. I had been up well into the starlit hours cleaning and testing the shop equipment. To say it was a relief that everything still worked would be an understatement.

By the time I made it to the upstairs residence space, it was all I could do to dust off the bed before falling into it and slipping into a deep sleep.

Come morning, it took a minute to realize where I was. Rather, it took the realization that the fire had gone out, and I was nearly frozen, then another minute for my brain to warm up enough to work again.

I skipped rekindling the fire upstairs and put on as many layers as I could before heading out to find the shop I was told to report to, my list of needed supplies in hand.

Thankfully it wasn't far.

The place was clean, orderly, and full of clientele. Behind the counter stood a majestically beautiful woman who seemed to be handling the onslaught of customers with ease. She looked up and waved in greeting as I entered, as she seemed to do for everyone that came through the door. I smiled in return before starting to look around.

After selecting a few items, I made my way through the line, finally ending up at the counter. I set down my list and offered another smile to the woman. "I was told that you could help me with some clothes and supplies. My name is…"

"Asher Harrington. Yes. Word travels fast around here. I know who you are and your reputation for making quality blades. One moment…" She ducked into the back room, leaving me standing there, completely caught off guard.

The man behind me clamped his hand down on my shoulder. "So, you're the man that's come to help make weapons for the Kingdom? I do hope you're better than the other one who drinks his nights away. I get that he's a blacksmith, and blades are not his trade necessarily, but if he'd sober up he could at least make a half-decent sword."

I gave a curt nod. "I'll do my best."

Meanwhile, the proprietor returned to the counter. "Alright, Asher. This is what I had gathered and waiting for you." She dropped a pile of clothes and a filled sack down onto the counter before starting to bag up the items I'd selected from the store shelves. "I'll read over your list and deliver the rest after I close up shop for the day."

I'd be lying if I said I wasn't flustered by her abrupt, efficient demeanor. "Ummm… Thank you, but I can…"

"After I close. Now," she pointed to the man behind me. "I have customers waiting."

"Yes. Of course." I stepped to the side and started for the door. Realizing I'd not gotten her name, I turned back.

The young man next to me chuckled. "Don't bother. Bexlynn hasn't given any man a second glance after what happened to her."

I barely looked at the young man, my eyes refusing to leave her. "What happened?"

He chuckled again. "You don't know about Bexlynn?"

I shook my head. "I just arrived." But my curiosity was beyond peaked. I was drawn in the first time I'd seen her, but the excitement in the man's voice about whatever story he had ready to tell made her even more interesting.

"Ahhh." He stepped into my peripheral vision, arms crossed over his chest, eyes rooted to the stunning woman as well. "She was a human, traveling alone. I guess this was after King Kanedraven took over but before peace had settled in fully. She made the mistake of going into a village that was still full of lawless characters."

"Why was she traveling alone, let alone to dangerous places?" That seemed reckless to me.

He lifted a shoulder. "I don't fully know. Some say her village had been ravaged, her family killed, and she was seeking a new home. People talk, and it's rumored that she wasn't always so... so..."

"Strong? Street smart? Independent?" I finished for him.

He chuckled again. "Yes. And while there, another human man started courting her. Then, a vampire set his sights on her, but she rejected the new would-be suitor. So, one night, while the human couple was taking a leisurely stroll after dinner, the vampire attacked them. They say the man's body was so mutilated he was entirely unrecognizable. She was forced to watch as he was torn apart. Then, when she still refused the vampire, he tore into her. Leaving her on the verge of death and turning. She woke in the alley next to the dead body of her human man, no longer human herself."

I hadn't noticed them before, but as the story unfolded, I could see the faint lines of scars that marred her face, neck, and arms. I couldn't imagine what that would do to someone. Turning them emotionally hard and damaged would probably be the least of it. "That's horrific."

"That's putting it lightly." The young man sighed, walking down the aisle.

I stood for another moment watching Bexlynn work. Finally, I turned and headed back to my shop, thinking about her story.

The hours ticked by fast as I set myself to work. Bexlynn had given me some warm clothes, which helped a lot any time I had to fetch more wood or materials from out in the shed or clean up the lingering mess outside. Snow had piled up while the place had been empty, choking off the shed doors as well as any walkways around the building. Ice had sealed some of the doors, making them a chore to pry open. The attire I'd arrived in wouldn't have been nearly enough to be outside long enough to clear the way. But with the warmer clothes, I was able to get the areas accessible again before going inside the start up the equipment. I even took a moment to test out the fire magic that I'd started learning.

Magic on Naelyra was abundant with only certain limits. Some races could master the elements more easily than others. Even we vampires could. However, magic was something I'd never cared to work with much. I'd only dabbled with it recently out of boredom, focusing on fire. Mainly as I sat down on the river's edge back in the village, drowning in my thoughts. I'd work to start small fires on chilly nights, easily put out by the nearby flowing water.

My success was less than stellar, but it was just enough to heat the locking mechanisms on the shed enough to get them open and to thaw the hinges. But, as with any magic, the use of it can deplete my resources and cause fatigue. So, after a moment of rest, I regained my focus and got back to work.

I'd been so busy with everything that I hadn't noticed that the day was nearly over. Darkness had fallen over the city, and a new dusting of snow blanketed the cleared roads and walkways. I stepped out front and looked up into the night sky. The air was crisp, but there was something in it that was electrifying.

Everwinter had been getting ravaged, physically and emotionally, by the attacks. Lives had been lost. Yes, you could see that in their faces. But there was something stronger. Hope? Confidence? Unity? It was in the very air we breathed, especially as the night fell and everything seemed to be still.

I stepped forward to move further out into that night but tripped. Quickly, I caught myself and looked. There, on my front porch, sat a large bundle of items and a delivery of metals needed to craft. Tied to the bundle was a note:

May your bladesmith skills be as good as your reputation, sir. The lives of your King and Queen may depend on it. The people of Everwinter surely do. Let me know what more you may require.

– Bexlynn

I couldn't help but smirk, thinking about her beauty and strength as I hauled everything inside.

Thoughts of her lingered as I put everything away. It would be cliché to say that no other woman had ever caught my attention quite so fully. Then again, I'd be lying to say it wasn't true. No matter how hard I tried, I couldn't shake her.

That is until the loudest bells I'd ever heard overpowered any thoughts I'd been entertaining.

Grabbing up my sword, I ran out the door. People were racing toward the castle gates, and I followed. The flow of people was like a raging river. Drawing closer to the gates, I started to hear voices shouting about an attack that had come, and the battle that was raging outside the castle walls.

I tightened my grip on my sword and looked out into the distance. People from Everwinter were racing out to join those already in the fray. Magic combatted magic. Sword clanged against sword.

"Bladesmith! You need to be making more. But since you're here, here…" A large man thrust a bundle of swords at me. "Repair these! Quickly!"

I looked them over and noticed the dullness of the blades and the notches that riddled them. Sheathing my own blade, I raced back to my shop and started hammering out the damage to each. Once done, I ran them back to the gates.

The burly man was by the guard tower again handing out swords to some of the men that were scrambling back to the gates. Those whose injuries were not bad enough to need immediate attention returned to the field. Some of the others carried damaged weapons back, tossing them into a pile. Some came with empty hands. That's when I saw Bexlynn handing out sheaths, tossing torn ones aside into her own pile, and helping rush deeply injured fighters toward tents where others waited to aid them.

The cycle was brilliant, and I worked to do my part. Grabbing up damaged blades, I ran back and worked them into useable weapons again before running them back out.

For hours, this continued. People became worn down and weary, but the battle raged on, slowing over the next day. That is until the King and Wulfgar came back in, blood-soaked and blanketed with exhaustion.

I was just grabbing up another bundle of broken and chipped swords as the cheering began. Everyone stopped, bowed, and continued cheering as they passed.

King Kanedraven paused. "We have won again today," he said, "and we thank everyone that fought, as well as those that did the work inside these castle walls to keep the soldiers fighting. Hopefully, this war will end soon."

The crowd began to part. I turned and saw everyone bowing as a woman ran down the road toward us in nothing more than a short-sleeved gown despite the cold. Of course, I did as the others did and bowed as she whisked past me.

She fell into the arms of the king. "Thank the gods you're safe. I couldn't find you out there for so long."

He smoothed her tousled tresses back. "I am alive, as are most of our soldiers. Everyone fought well today."

She hugged him for a long moment before pulling back and slapping his shoulder. "Don't scare me like that. Next time don't block me so I can't find you."

He laughed and kissed her forehead. "As you wish, Little One."

The Queen. Queen Auriena. Their dynamic was just as people had said. I admired them as I watched the exchange. The fact that they didn't hide their affections garnered even more respect.

King Kanedraven held his hand out, lighting a ball of fire in his palm, and held it close to his shivering wife. "Come. Let us go inside."

Once the royal couple headed back to the castle, the rest of us cleaned up. Instead of a bundle that I could carry, I was given a wagon, and as the soldiers filed in, more damaged blades were dumped on, including a number of weapons from the enemy side.

"Well, that ought to keep you busy until the next one." One of the men patted my back with a bloody hand as he passed by me.

"Challenge accepted," I replied, accepting the final man's addition to the repair list and heading back to my shop.

My body was tired, and I would have normally just gone to bed to rest, but my mind was still racing with the charge the whole affair had given me. I wasn't happy to be fighting a war. Losing lives was never a good thing. But the way the people of Everwinter came together? *That* was exhilarating.

My village worked as a unit, as many did. However, most villages were made up of people that were born and raised together. The majority of them we even the same race. Everwinter was a totally different thing. There were so many of us that came from different places in Naelyra, many seeking sanctuary. Yet, we pulled together, and far fewer lives were lost because of it.

So, I worked on repairing blades until that rush was exhausted and I could barely keep my eyes open. Only then did I grab a bottle of blood from my ice box, drink it down still cold, and collapsed into bed.

III

When I woke, it took me a moment to realize where I was again. As the chill in the air washed over me, not only did that realization hit me, but the fact that I hadn't stoked the fire slapped me across the face.

I climbed out of bed and made my way downstairs. Lighting a fire in the main area, I warmed myself for a moment before the stiffness in my bones thawed.

I pulled out a bottle of blood from the ice box, pouring half of its contents into a kettle. I set it on the stove and lit the burner to warm the crimson liquid, hoping it would help stave off the cold as I set to work. Once it was heated, I headed out to the shop to get started.

There, next to the full wagon I'd brought back with me that was full of damaged weapons, sat three more. And next to those, more metals and tools.

"Looks like I have plenty to keep me busy," I muttered to myself as I made my way over to the work that now sat before me.

Sitting on top of one of the stacks of metal was a note.

I figured you might need some more supplies with as much as was dropped off at your place.
-Bexlynn

I couldn't help but smile. Despite that her actions were surely just to be certain that I got the blades repaired before the next attack, I couldn't help but entertain the idea that she was being thoughtful. After all, she didn't need to leave a note, let alone let me know it was her.

With that smile pinning the corners of my mouth up, I got to work: hammering out dents, melting down severely damaged blades, reforging the metals into new ones, and sharpening edge after edge. I worked for hours, slowing only for sustenance. With the metals that became too muddled to separate and reuse properly, I made some crude weapons and shackles. At least then the materials wouldn't go to waste I figured.

The delivery from Bexlynn had come in handy as I worked like this for the next several days, not leaving my shop except to take lists of needed things down to Bexlynn's business. Our exchanges were limited, usually because she had plenty of clientele to tend to any time I was there.

When I was working, which was most of the time, the image of the King and Queen and their exchange stayed with me. The way everyone cheered. The way King Kanedraven addressed everyone. The love they obviously had for one another. They truly were what people said of them, and I was happy to be there serving them and the Kingdom.

They and the memory of Bexlynn working so hard at the gates and helping so many soldiers kept my hammer swinging, my bloomery hot and my mind focused. I wasn't about to let them down, and I surely didn't want to be seen as the other metalworker they had so obviously disapproved of.

I was so focused on the sword I was working on that I almost didn't hear the knock on the doors. "Come in!" I shouted, dusting off my gloves onto my soot-covered apron.

The double wood doors swung open, and two men walked in dressed in royal guard attire. They did a quick survey of the room before returning to the doorway and bowing their heads. I sat, confused until I saw King Kanedraven and Queen Auriena step into view.

Instantly, I, too, bowed down. "My King. My Queen."

"You may stand." Queen Auriena's voice was melodic. "We have come to meet the bladesmith that not only arrived with such a grand reputation but also worked so hard at the most recent attack."

"Thank you." I slowly rose back up. "I would have fought for you, but…"

"But we need you doing just as you did," the King interjected. "If you haven't noticed, our people do not fight for glory or pride. Everyone knows their place and their strengths. And while I am sure you are a valiant warrior with your stature and build, our need for you is in your craft, keeping those that fight carrying strong weapons. Neither position is any less glorious than the other and certainly no less needed."

The Queen added, "Every person, every role. People filling those tasks is the only reason we have been able to keep Everwinter from being taken. Healers, runners, soldiers, scouts, smiths… even those that bring food to nourish everyone."

"Yes. You're right," I agreed. "Neglect one, and it topples."

It all made perfect sense. After all, it was King Kanedraven's superior strategic mind that won him the last war and won him Naelyra in its entirety.

The King held a hand out to me. "Your help at the battle was a sign of your loyalty and bravery. It is good to know that your character is as strongly crafted as your blades."

I shook his hand and fought back the exploding level of pride I had when I noticed that the sword at his side was one that he had commissioned from me. "I came to do what I could in these dark times. I pledge to help keep Queen Auriena safe and this Kingdom protected any way I can."

He patted my shoulder. "Then keep doing what you are doing. The Kingdom thanks you. *We* thank you."

I bowed my head as they exited, their guards closing the doors behind them. If I'd had any doubts about leaving my home and coming up here, those doubts were a distant memory now.

I turned back to the blade I'd been working on when I heard the door creek open again. As I spun, thinking maybe they'd returned, I nearly stumbled seeing a different face peek in. "May I come in?"

"Bexlynn?" I blinked and cleared my throat. "Yes. Please, come in."

She smiled as she closed the door behind her, shutting the cold outside. "Was that…?"

I chuckled. "The King and Queen? Yes."

"They're quite lovely, aren't they?" She stood, slightly stiff, by the door.

"Yes. They are," I replied. "I'm sorry. Have you not met them before?"

"Oh! Yes. Briefly. They both visited me when I made a special order item for Queen Auriena." She fidgeted with the hem of her sleeve.

I tilted my head at seeing her almost timid. "Thank you for the additional supplies. They've come in very handy." When she didn't say anything more, I took a step closer to her. "Is there something I can help you with?"

Her eyes shot up to mine. "No. Sorry to delay your work. I must be going."

"Wait." I raced over to the doors, my movements a blur of motion before she exited. "You came for something. Tell me."

Being that close, I could see more of the silvery scars that created an abstract map of her past on her flesh. I wanted to trace the lines softly, to show her that not all touches were cruel or fleeting. To create a new set of memories along the lines that were once so painful.

She moved her slender fingers to her waist and pulled out an older-looking dagger. For a second, I was concerned about her intentions with how she looked torn. But when she laid the blade across her other palm, lifting it between us, I could see its damage. "It was my mother's. It's not the most beautiful thing, and I know you have plenty of work stacked up to do, but I was hoping you could repair it. I can pay you." She added the last part quickly.

I took the short dagger and looked it over. "It would be my honor."

A corner of her mouth twitched as if she nearly smiled, but it was fleeting. She ducked around me. "No rush."

The door slammed shut, and I was alone again, holding her treasured item. I looked it over, examining the remnants of the designs that had once adorned the piece. It was fairly simple, but simple didn't suit her. I wanted to restore it and yet, somehow, make it more... *Bexlynn.*

I set the dagger down on my workbench and returned to the sword I had been working on before all of my day's visitors. By the next day, I knew what I wanted to do with the small piece.

IV

Two wagons full of weapons repaired and a mass of new ones created, I stood in my shop proud of it all. Yet, there was one piece that stood out among them all. I lifted the restored dagger from my workbench and looked it over. I'd spent the final few hours of the previous night finishing it up.

I was about to bundle up and head over to Bexlynn's, but as I opened my front door, a gust of wind and snow billowed in at me so strong it caused me to stumble back. "What the...?"

Coming north to Everwinter was a change from the weather I'd been used to, surely, but this was on an entirely different level. I pushed the door closed and worked fast to clean up the melting snowflakes that were now causing a small flood on my floor.

Once everything was dried, I turned to go back to my shop. However, the warning bells began to ring out, announcing an incoming attack. I stuck the dagger in my belt and grabbed a cloak that Bexlynn had included in the things she'd delivered to me when I'd first arrived. As a vampire, I could withstand the elements better than most other races, but we were not impervious to them. Especially not when it was a blizzard out.

So, I pulled up my hood and held the cloak fabric around myself tightly. With my sword at my side, I raced from my shop, filling a wagon with the repaired and new blades. It was a struggle to get to the gates through the piling snow, but I made it.

People were struggling with the elements. I could see men and women using fire magic to melt paths, but the effort was draining them. That's when

I noticed figures cloaked in white moving around closer to the castle walls than they should have been.

Two soldiers clamored in from the fight. The man fell to his knees once past the gates. "They weren't spotted until they were too close! They're wearing the color of the blizzard. They were spotted in the valley, far closer than any other attack!" A gash ran along his side, bleeding profusely.

The other soldier tried to help him up, urgency in her voice. "Stand up, or I'll have to carry you!"

I was tossing blade after blade to anyone who needed one when Bexlynn came back in from outside the gates. I raced over to her. "Are you alright?"

She pushed her hair back as a gust of wind blew it into her face. "They're pushing us back and getting too close!"

I pointed to the wounded man. "He needs medical help. Are they set up?"

"Yes!" she shouted and ran for him.

The snowfall that had continued had masked the incoming army, and they were closer than they should have gotten before noticed. I could hear the groans of the falling soldiers and the footfalls of those still charging. They were nearly at our doorstep.

Then, there was the roaring of beasts I could make out in the distance, coming toward us.

A woman shouted up to the guard tower, "Close the gates!"

The man upon the observation level called back, "They're too close! There's not enough time!"

Fixing broken swords was the last of our worries. I unsheathed my own sword and went to the opening in the wall. Seeing how close the attack was, I looked behind me and shouted, "Anyone that can pick up and use a weapon, form a line next to me! We will keep them from getting in!"

Men and women rushed over and lined up two deep. I didn't know what we would be able to do fully, but there was no way I wasn't going to at least try.

When the first small group broke free from the main battle and came at us, we were prepared. Each of them fell upon our blades. The same with the second wave. And the third.

However, the fourth charge was different. Among them were two magic wielders and a man on some kind of beast. This latter raised his weapon as he charged. "Give us the Queen," he roared, "or we will take her head!"

The cold was seeping into my bones, causing an ache deep down. But I swung my sword, ignoring the pain. A few from the city that were more versed in magic stepped into the center of soldiers. Protected by the line of fighters, they took down the magic wielders from the attack.

But the beast stormed forward with its rider perched and shouting.

Bexlynn came out of the aide tent just as the beast crossed through the open gates. She raised her arms in the air, and a wall of ice formed in front of her.

The rider and his beast came crashing through as Bexlynn drew her sword.

I raced over and dropped, sliding up under the animal, and thrusting my sword up and into its chest. It must have hit its mark, for the beast dropped just before it could collide with the shopkeeper.

The rider scrambled out of the saddle of its fallen mount and dove for Bexlynn, but she swung her blade with precision and took his head off. His body fell and his head rolled down the path as she looked at him, eyes wide.

I ran over to her, gripping her arms. "Are you alright?"

She breathed for a moment before shrugging me off. "Yes. I just…"

Another attacker rushed us. I turned, bringing my sword up and connecting with his chest. I kicked, pushing him off my blade before swinging and taking off the arm of a second man. Bexlynn moved in next to me and thrust her sword deep into his chest, yanking it back as he dropped down next.

Several more came at us, and each died to our swords as we seamlessly worked together to defend our position—side-by-side, back-to-back. Yet, when a new rush of snow and ice-clad soldiers swarmed us, I began to worry.

Five of them came at us. Two by two, the first four went down. But the fifth was on us, too close to swing my sword at him.

I slammed the pommel down onto his head. Then I felt a hand in my cloak. Bexlynn had grabbed the dagger and thrust it forward into the soldier's gut.

He fell, just as the others had.

I had one arm around her, my hand pressed to her back, as she looked up at me. The sounds of fighting had died down, and nobody else came at us. We stood, looking at each other for a long moment, both gathering ourselves after what had just transpired.

Then, she stepped back and looked at the dagger, blade covered in blood. I reached out to take it to clean it off, but she held her hand up. "This is mine, is it not?"

"Yes." I dropped my hand. "I was bringing it to you when the attack happened."

She used my cloak to wipe the blood off and looked it over. "Thank you."

I wanted to ask what she thought of it. Not only had I restored the design work that it originally had, but I embellished it with different metals to deepen the design. I also added a ruby to the cross guard on both sides. They were two gems I'd brought with me in case I needed them to help pay for housing or resources. It just seemed fitting that they go to someone that helped me to settle in but hadn't asked for anything in return.

She looked up at me and opened her mouth to speak, but soldiers came flooding back in. The Everwinter army cheered, congratulating each other and surrounding the King and Wulfgar, as was seeming to be tradition after each attack. We stepped aside and began to clean up the remnants of the fight that had ensued inside the gates.

Once things were under control, Bexlynn and I walked silently up the road back toward our shops. Neither of us spoke as we walked side by side. Entering the courtyard, we stopped as the Queen stepped into our path. "I saw you two out there. Well done."

"We fought well as a team," I bowed my head.

"A team? You two danced together. It was beautiful." She looked at us with something that resembled awe.

Bexlynn bowed. "Thank you, My Queen. Taking any life is not something I enjoy. But I will never regret it when it's for the Kingdom."

I grinned and bowed as well. "Yes. Thank you for the compliment."

Queen Auriena took a step closer to us, her hands clasped in front of her. "Don't let your past keep either of you from your future. Besides, I have a feeling we will need you both with the strength you give one another." She smiled. "Plus, the world needs more natural love like you two have."

Bexlynn's cheeks flushed.

I tucked my hand into hers. "We are at your service."

"Good." Auriena took a step back. "Now, go take care of each other. That could not have been easy. I'm sure we will be seeing one another soon enough."

As the Queen walked away, Bexlynn pulled out her dagger again, holding it up between us. "This is exquisite, Asher. I don't know how to thank you, truly. I can pay you…"

I put my hand over the small blade in hers. "You owe me nothing. I'm happy to have been entrusted with the task. I'm just glad you're pleased with it."

She swallowed back the tears that were forming in her eyes. "Thank you."

"Let's get out of this storm." I put an arm around her shivering shoulders.

She nodded. "Yes."

I wanted to say more. I wanted to tell her how I felt, how I'd felt since the first day I'd laid eyes on her. But somehow, I knew that it wasn't needed. If anything, the rawness of saying it all, especially right then, would be too much. Right then, she just needed to be shown she was safe and cared for. There would be time to express it all later.

Leading her away from the slaughter, I pulled her in, wrapping my cloak around her. "A hot bath and a roaring fire?" I suggested.

She looked up at me, confused. "What?"

"I'm offering a hot bath and a roaring fire." The corner of my lips turned up.

She smiled. "Sounds perfect."

Rising on her tiptoes, she pressed her lips against mine. I returned the kiss deeply. At that moment, I knew my purpose was more than to serve and protect my King and Queen.

I lit a fireball in my palm and held it close to warm her as we walked, just as King Kanedraven had for his Queen. I'd found something even more valuable to protect. I'd found what they had found. I'd found love, and I'd do anything to protect it… to protect *her*.

THE TEXICAN BLIZZARD OF 2323
By CD Damitio

I

It was colder than it should have been. That was the first thing that went through Charles Actor's mind when he stepped out the door of his one-bedroom cabin in Presidio, Texas. Sure, this was a mountain cabin—and it was November—but this was also Texas during the hottest year on record to date 2023.

He hadn't had his coffee yet, and it was a short trip back inside to grab a hoodie and a knit cap before coming back out onto his balcony to enjoy his morning cup—which still sat steaming on the wooden table right where he'd left it. There was an electric feeling about the air this morning. Though he wasn't excited about the task that lay ahead of him, his body tingled with anxiety nonetheless. He had no idea why.

He was going to have to take his truck into town, get grain for the horses, refill his propane tanks, and grab some groceries at the Y-Mart. None of that was what he was dreading.–

His lawyer had called the night before. The divorce papers had come through and he needed to stop by and sign them. It wasn't that he regretted the divorce—he and Margie had fallen out of love decades ago, and the divorce was only the finalization of a four-year separation that had been welcomed by both of them—the dread was something else. An actual divorce decree meant that he was cut loose, free, unmarried, unhindered, and unattached. While it was the same state he had been living in for nearly half a decade, the finality of signing the papers filled him with doubt, dread, and misgivings.

Over the top of all that, though, was this electric feeling brought on by the brisk cold and the otherworldly glow he detected when he looked up at that sky.

Finishing his coffee and morning chores, Charles unhitched his electric pickup truck from the charging tether and began the drive into town. As he began the trip, the familiar sense of his inner organs being jostled by the hard bumps of the road lulled him into a sense of comfort. Although the truck was not fully autonomous, it knew the road. He didn't need to pay much attention beyond braking and accelerating to make himself feel more comfortable. Ford had come a long way in just a few years, and he'd ordered the 2024 model early enough that he was able to be driving it even as 2023 wound down to a close.

The sense of unease returned suddenly. It wasn't that something had gone wrong, or that his attention had been harshly gotten. Instead, it was a lack of discomfort. In an instant, his truck was riding as smoothly as if he were floating on an airfoil over the water. There were literally no bumps, no bounces, no creaks, none of what he expected on this drive into town. Instead, it was the smoothest sailing he had ever experienced in any car. He double-checked to make sure the truck was actually moving. It was.

Looking out the window, the trees looked larger. The sky looked bluer. the road looked whiter. That couldn't be right. He looked again. The road was as white as porcelain but a non-reflective white that glowed with a warmth that made the road obvious without causing him to need to squint.

Charles decelerated and pulled the truck over. Something was wrong. It wasn't the truck, and it wasn't the road. It had to be him. Maybe he was having an aneurysm or a brain clot. Maybe he'd died or was in a coma. All he knew was that what he was seeing and feeling couldn't be real. He'd driven this road the week before, and it had been nothing like this. *Nothing* like this.

Stepping out of the truck, he walked around the back to the cliffside of the road. The gulch he loved so much was still there with its red, purple, and yellow clays and lines of stratigraphic complexity, but the bald mesas were no longer bald. Huge forests now covered the tops of the mesas—pine forests that had to be decades, maybe even centuries old. In the distance, the lonely gray-brown of the Chinati Mountains had disappeared. Instead, he saw green and white—emerald green mountains capped with what looked like glaciers.

Charles shook his head violently in an effort to snap out of it. He pinched himself. None of it changed what was before him. Having no other plan, Charles got back in his pickup and drove toward the Presidio village—a town that, on a good day, had no more than five thousand residents (and that was only if you counted the five hundred or so buried in the Boothill Cemetery). He decided to stop by the lawyer's office before making a trip to the clinic to make sure he hadn't suffered a stroke.

The road and mountains never changed back. Nothing was familiar, but he knew the way to Presidio. He would be there before long. He just had to cross the gulch, go through the pass, and then straight down into the village.

He was becoming comfortable with his new reality until he reached the top of the pass. There was a huge silver arch that stretched over the roadway—bigger than the St. Louis Arch by at least double. Charles had grown up in St. Louis so he knew. This had to be at least 1200 feet.

The bases of the Arch also looked to be at least twice the size of the one in St. Louis. A fun fact that most people didn't know about the St. Louis Arch was that it was exactly as wide as it was tall. This arch seemed similar. Where it differed were the revolving glass doorways that led into the arch itself and the people streaming in and out. Charles could see glass elevators moving smoothly along the arch, presumably depositing passengers at offices or apartments. This Presidio Arch was far thicker than the St. Louis counterpart.

Charles had been curious as to why he hadn't seen a single vehicle on his trip thus far, but that dry spell suddenly ended. Hundreds of vehicles were parked in the lots beside the arch. Rampways led beneath the ground, which indicated there were probably hundreds more parked underneath. This insight led to Charles noticing that the elevators on the arch continued on into the ground. He wondered if the arch was actually a half-submerged oval that continued all the way around. It was a ridiculous thought, but then again, what was he looking at? Was it more ridiculous than that?

Charles pulled into the lot and parked his truck. The vehicles filling the lot were unlike anything he had ever seen. They were all curves, and the wheels were completely covered by the body. In fact, he couldn't see the wheels at all. There was a wide assortment of colors and shapes. Many of them appeared to be glowing. He wasn't in Presidio yet, but not stopping here was an impossibility. He *had* to figure out what was happening.

He walked to the archway entrance, noting that everyone he passed seemed to be speaking a unique Spanish dialect that he'd never heard before. It was heavily infused with English-sounding words and sounds, but he couldn't quite understand everything they were saying despite being fluent in both Spanish and English. Reaching the archway entrance, he was grateful to be able to read the sign over the revolving doors, which was written in classic Spanish:

"Bienvenidos al Distrito Ojinaga-Presidio del Mega-Complejo Chihuahua. Recordamos aquí, a los patriotas que dieron su vida por traer la libertad a la Nación Texican en el año 2050. El Arco de la OPC se completó para celebrar el centenario de la Independencia Texican el 13 de octubre de 2150."

The translation had to be wrong.

"Welcome to the Ojinaga-Presidio District of the Chihuahua Mega-Complex. We remember here, the patriots who gave their lives to bring freedom to the Texican Nation in the year 2050. The OPC Archway was completed to celebrate the centennial of Texican Independence on October 13, 2150."

Or maybe the translation was right. In any event, Charles had a pretty good suspicion that he wasn't going to get those divorce papers signed today.

II

From the moment he stepped into the OPC archway, Charles knew for certain he was in another world. Or maybe not another world, but a future variation of his own world that was so significantly different from his normal and day-to-day existence that he might as well have stepped into another galaxy.

Entering the arch, he had the distinct impression that the inside was considerably larger than the outside. An open space spread out before him with a wide metallic staircase leading into a hall of what seemed to be shopping mall-sized proportions. There weren't shops in the sense that he would have thought of them, but there was definitely a considerable amount of commerce taking place.

People were moving within the space, each of them trailed by small doglike baskets that floated obediently beside or behind them. Not doglike in the sense of shape or design, but more in the sense that each floating basket seemed to know its owner and followed them loyally. They were not uniform in size or shape, but close enough to each other in appearance that they were relatable as a class.

Moving down the stairway, Charles had a sense that he was being observed—that someone or something was aware of him, focusing on his movements and actions. Turning, he found a softball-sized object trailing him. It was light green, and when he reached for it, the top half vanished revealing a small basketlike interior. Moving his hand away, the top returned. He did this several times before deciding that maybe he was supposed to put something in it. He reached into his pocket and found a couple of coins. He dropped them in his "basket," and—much to his surprise—they fell right through, hitting the stairs and bouncing down to the base of the stairway.

They were only pennies, so he decided not to chase them. He did look around to see if anyone had noticed his experimentation. Laughter came from below him, and he turned to see a smiling and friendly face beaming up at him.

"That's a funny way to get rid of your ancient coins, Señor" The young man attached to the smile strode up the stairs two at a time and held out the two pennies to Charles. "I assume you want these back; they're a little too valuable to just be throwing away."

Charles laughed, "They're just pennies, you can have them."

The young man's eyes widened, and he shook his head "Oh, no Señor My abua told me all about the expectations and dangers of accepting expensive gifts from oddly dressed strangers. I'm not selling you my soul today." He held his hand out and Charles accepted the two pennies. Then, after dumping them in his pocket, he stuck out his hand. "I'm Charles Actor, what about you?"

The young man's skinny chest puffed with pride as he took Charles' hand in his own and responded. "I am Benito Mussolini Gonzalez, and I'm at your service." Benito was perhaps nineteen or twenty years old. He had strong white teeth and a smile that lit up the entire complex. He was skinny and wore a purple suit that immediately made Charles think of the Joker from Batman, but without any of the nefarious insanity for which that character was known.

The name was a bit of a shock, but one which Charles decided would eventually be explained without his having to ask about it.

"Why'd the coins fall through?" he motioned to what he had already started thinking of as a cart.

Benito laughed. "You can't put anything in it until you have made a purchase in the Arch."

The simple explanation made sense to Charles, even though nothing else really did. He reached into his pocket "You said that these are worth a lot?" He held out a handful of coins to Benito.

Benito pulled the knit cap off his head and immediately covered Charle's handful of coins. "Are you insane, Señor? Sure, no one will rob you here in the Arch, but you can't stay in here forever. If you are going to flash that kind of wealth, there will be people waiting to take it from you as soon as you leave the regulated areas. Surely you must know this?"

Charles heard suspicion in the young man's voice. Wrestling with whether to tell the truth or some other version of it, he decided that truth wasn't even something he could determine at this point and opted instead to follow the tried and true method of his ancestors and youth. He would play the clueless bumpkin. No matter where or when he was now, one thing was sure: somewhere there were people who had the reputation of being backward and country—because no matter what, this was still Texas.

Putting on a thicker drawl than he needed, Charles lowered his voice to a conspiratorial whisper "Look, you obviously have figured out I'm not from around these parts." Then, in barely a whisper, he added, "In fact, I've never been here before. This is the first time I've ever been in this kind of place."—and then, just to confirm he was country—"I'm usually just taking care of the livestock."

Benito's eyes widened. "You're a cowboy!"

Charles gave an imperceptible nod, glad that the concept still existed. Then, making the kind of split-second decisions that Margie had never understood, he decided that the best thing he could do right now was to not only befriend, but recruit the boy as his helper.

"Shhhh!" Charles said, creating the air of conspiracy. "It's true. I've just come down from the ranch and I don't have hide nor hair about how to do bo diddly 'round here. If you'd be willing to help me figure things out, I'd be more than happy to make it worth your while."

Benito gave a strange half bow, half curtsy. The meaning was clear, but it was damn near the strangest gesture that Charles had ever seen from a young man who looked like he spent his life playing video games. "You are in luck, Señor. Not only do I speak English, but I'm also known as one of the best guides in the Texican Nation. I can lead you through the IRL and the OL worlds, help you meet the people you will need to know, take you deep into the blizzard, and teach you how to blend in as if you haven't spent all your life sodomizing sheep up in the wide open mountains."

Charles' huge guffaw echoed through the interior of the archway mall. Numerous shoppers turned and looked at the pair, still standing at the edge of the wide stairway. It wasn't that Charles had never heard that particular joke about country people, it was the matter-of-fact, nothing-strange-here-ma'am tone in which Benito had said it—the same way he had said his historically off-putting name.

Benito looked confused. "Why are you laughing, Señor?"

Charles didn't see any way he could explain himself or ask Benito the origins of his colorful phrase without making things even more confusing. So, he asked the only question he knew would change the subject. "How much will you charge per day?"

Benito looked thoughtful and took his knit hat off. He pointed at Charles' open handful of coins, pointing at a bright zinc penny—a thing not even worth the cost of the zinc it was made from. "I'll take one of those as full payment," he said with boldness, belatedly adding "and if you are satisfied with my work, you can give me another at the completion."

Charles pulled the penny free of his pocket change and handed it to Benito. "Deal," he said.

Benito immediately pocketed the coin and then spit in his hand before offering it to Charles, who deferred. "I'll just take your word for it," Charles said. Benito didn't seem offended and wiped his hand on his trousers before getting down to business.

"First we're going to exchange some of your coin collection for an Oil Dollar Credit card. Then we're going to get you some clothes that will blend in a little better. Then, Señor… then you are going to buy me lunch."

Charles wasn't sure what all of that meant, but he understood enough to tell Benito "Lead the way, amigo." Benito didn't hold back, and grabbed Charles by the hand, leading him down the steps and through a series of open galleries that had tall, windowed shops on either side.

III

Lunch was something that should have been familiar but wasn't. On the surface, it was classic Tex-Mex cuisine, but there were undercurrents of rich Central and South American flavors that reached Charles' nose before he saw the food which somehow changed the texture, color, and mental description of the food before he was able to try it. Having no frame of reference to attach it to, Charles decided that 'Texican' was a perfect name for it. The food was delicious with rich chocolate, fruit, and seafood aspects— while still being spicy with cinnamon, chili, and citrus as he was used to.

Benito was a lot sharper than he at first appeared. He had a thirsty intellect that probed each statement Charles made in a way that quickly made it apparent to both of them that there was a truth neither of them was willing to breach. For his part, Charles found himself warming up to his guide, and despite the age difference, he found himself (much to his own surprise) thinking less of Benito as a boy, and more as an equal. There was a youthful silliness to Benito that screamed a childhood not long past, but his quick wit and ability to put together pieces that were anything but obvious shattered any illusion of him being anything other than brilliant—and contrastingly— somewhat cynical.

"Señor, let's cut the sheepshit," Benito said. "I know, and you know, that you are a stranger in our strange land. Much like the famous astronaut from Mars, let us just say that I have grokked your dilemma. You do not need to worry, my friend. I am neither police nor a Texican loyalist who will spill the guacamole on his neighbors for a few credits. As long as you don't intend to kill people, you may speak honestly to me."

Charles looked at his new friend with profound respect. The fact that Benito had put all this together on the fly, and that he was able to so eloquently express his proposal, was stunning. More so was the fact that Benito finished his speech and directly began tucking into a gargantuan seafood taco while motioning to Charles that he should explain himself.

Charles considered the possible consequences, and then mentally just said, "Fuck it."

"When I went to sleep last night it was 2023. The planet was in the midst of eradicating humanity with global warming. I state I lived in, Texas, was a part of the United States of America, and was not only suffering from a serious drought, but also on the verge of declaring itself independent. People were starting to call for 'the second American revolution.'

"I woke up this morning and was going to drive into town to sign divorce papers, but instead I seem to have driven three hundred years into the future. Right now, despite the pleasant company and great food, I'm torn between thinking that I've lost my mind or believing that the world has ended, and I'm in some sort of bizarre psychedelic afterlife." Charles waited for laughter, or for Benito to call him a liar. Neither happened.

Benito simply nodded and continued chewing. Charles waited. Finally swallowing the last of his huge bite, Benito said "That's fucked up. I think you're going to have to meet my Uncle Rodrigo. He's the head of the Chihuahua Historical Foundation's archives in the Mega-Complex city of Chihuahua, co-capital of the Texican Nation. He's a pretty big deal in quantum circles, and he might be able to help you figure out how to get back to your own time."

In a cartoon, Charles' jaw would most certainly have been on the floor. He was, for lack of a better word, flabbergasted. Not only had Benito seemingly believed every word he'd said, but more amazingly, he didn't seem shocked at all. Or maybe there was something else going on. Maybe Benito was simply calling bullshit by creating more bullshit on what he thought was a bullshit—er…sheepshit—story.

"You believe me?" Charles asked.

Benito nodded. "It's a pretty crazy story; and normally, Amigo, I would just take your money and leave you to your delusions. The truth is, your loco clothes, the funny English you speak, that pocketful of priceless antique money you don't seem to know the value of, and a few other things—they all had me thinking that there was something like this happening already. So, si, I believe you."

"Have you ever heard of anything like this happening before?" Charles found it very hard to believe that Benito could have just accepted his story without a single doubt unless there was something that made it sound familiar.

"I'm a reader, Señor I've read many of the classics—even the forbidden books—so I'm not afraid of new ideas or ways of looking at the world around me. Please, be careful. Most Texicans aren't as 'futurista' as I am, so I wouldn't tell your story to just anyone."

Lunch finished, and Benito declared that they should start the journey to the Chihuahua City Complex.

"Should I drive?" Charles asked.

"Not unless you want to answer a lot of unnecessary questions," Benito told him. Charles had told him about his truck, which was parked in the Archway lot. "Your vehicle will be here if we come back, but for now we'll take the longivater."

"Longivaters?" Charles raised his eyebrows.

"I'll show you.¡Ándele!"

The longivater was exactly what the compound word described: part elevator and part subway, moving longitudinally. Essentially an entire underground system of horizontal elevators where, instead of selecting the floor, you selected the destination.

"The first longivaters were built in your Texas by the cyborg crypto-industrialist robber baron E. Longmunsk," Benito told him.

"You mean Elon Musk," Charles said gently.

"No Señor, I don't know who that is. In school, we learned about E. Longmunsk. He was one of the first cyborgs. He created himself with Neurolink tethered to Starlink solar power minters. I think he began around your time. E. Longmunsk gave us much of the infrastructure we needed for independence. He's a great hero to many here, but honestly, I'm in the camp that thinks it's time for someone to unplug him."

"He's still alive?" Charles was shocked.

"Si, of course. He will live forever; and honestly, even unplugging him now wouldn't work. I've been told that he is getting constantly charged by wireless DC solar power transmitted on beta waves from his satellites. He has fail-safes. We're just lucky he doesn't want to kill us all, yet."

The time passed quickly with many such conversations. The history of the Texican Nation was fascinating and beyond Charles' wildest imaginings. They arrived at the Chihuahua City Complex with a sudden "ding!". The longivater doors opened to the chaotic world of a mega-city national transit station. Benito grabbed Charles by the shoulder and led him through crowded causeways, up rapidly moving escalators, and finally out into the blurry white of daylight.

Blurry white because snow and wind were beating those who exposed themselves to the weather. It was a fierce winter blizzard, the kind that Charles would have expected in Montana but not in the middle of the Sonoran Desert. Benito had insisted that he buy full cold weather gear which had felt ridiculous to Charles but now seemed almost like under-preparation. Benito pulled him across an atmospheric avalanche of a street to another transit station. This one seemed more like a city terminal rather than an intercity station like the one they had just left.

Still gasping from the sheer power of the weather, Charles sputtered "That weather, is it some sort of a disaster?"

Benito looked at him with a questioning expression then cracked a mischievous smile. "Oh, it's a pretty nice day today. If you are here for a while, maybe I'll take you into the blizzard."

A short longivater ride brought them to the government research complex. Using his watch, Benito asked his uncle, Dr. Rodrigo Rodriguez to come to escort them to his lab. Dr. Rodrigo Rodriguez, or 'Drodrod', as he introduced himself, was cadaver thin and as tall as an NBA forward. There was an almost alien presence to him that was quickly belied by his warm smile and friendly continence. He wore a long, loose white lab coat and had a crown of shockingly white hair that, despite his tan complexion, immediately made Charles think of both Doc from *Back to the Future* and Albert Einstein. His lab was like something between a doctor's office and a university classroom that focused on both anatomy and physics.

Benito matter-of-factly explained Charles' situation and once again, Charles was shocked that the story was so easily accepted. Drodrod saw the amazement on Charles' face and gave him an explanation.

"You are not the first person to arrive here from another time. As far as we know there have been five confirmed temporal travelers in the Texican Nation and probably more that we don't know of. I've also heard stories of TTs arriving in the RSA and the Mutual Nations, but I've not been able to confirm those for obvious political reasons. The main function of my institute is to determine how, why, and who the TTs are. Most of the people you would come across have no idea that such things exist. You are lucky in that my nephew, despite having the makings of a brilliant temporal scientist, has chosen to be more of an 'anthrolosopher' than anything else."

"Anthrolosopher?" Charles had learned not to question the new vocabulary he was encountering, but this word defied explanation in the current context.

"The people who study people, and what and how those people think about reality," Benito chimed in from where he was essentially playing with a skeleton in the corner.

"Yes," Drodrod said disapprovingly. "He could be helping us solve the problems of time, but instead he is focused on the problems of human thought."

Benito was using the skeleton's hand to pat himself on the head "I'm proud of you even if no one else understands what you are doing," he voiced for the skeleton. Shifting voices, Benito said, "Gracias, Tio Escalito. That's why you are my favorite uncle."

IV

Drodrod was enthusiastic about helping Charles find a way home from the future. Charles, on the other hand, was in no hurry to go back to his often-lonely life. No one asked him, however. Instead, Benito and Drodrod began discussing what it would take to make the process happen.

"There are high temporal readings that come out of the glaciers in the Sierra Madre to the west," Drodrod mused. "It seems likely that heading into the mountains would give us a better opportunity to get you home."

"It won't matter a bit," Benito said, "If we don't have a way to tap into them and utilize the forces of time to sort of 'eject' you back into your own time."

Charles didn't like the sound of that at all. Being ejected with some sort of experimental device into an unknown time-stream in glacial mountains that used to be desert mountains didn't sound like the kind of thing he wanted to do at all.

"Hold on," Charles stopped the two of them. "I need a little bit of information to make sense of all of this. First of all, why is it so damn cold here? Second, I'd like to know a little about the other 'time travelers'"—He made the air quotes with his hand as he said this—"and what they did, where they went, and what happened to him."

"We're going to need help to explain all of that," Drodrod said to him. "Benito, go to the library and bring back Maria."

Charles didn't have the sense that Drodrod was talking about a person when he said Maria. It sounded more like a *thing* than a person, for some reason. "Maria?" he asked.

Benito got a huge grin on his face. "M.A.R.I.A.," he said, spelling out the letters. "Marveloso Androida Rapido Investigación Asistante. She is going to blow your mind, Señor." Benito got up from the table they were sitting at and left the lab. Drodrod had his face buried in a book aptly titled, "Viaje en el Tiempo".

Looking up from the book, Drodrod said "The main thing is, we have to keep you out of the hands of both the government and the cartels. That never ends well. They will either dissect you or make you disappear. Not the help that you want."

"Aren't you part of the government?" Charles asked.

Drodrod laughed. "Me? No. I mean: yes, they fund my lab, and they provide the space for me to work; but secretly, they laugh about my life's work. They find it funny that anyone would spend decades only to discover how to move only three minutes back or forth in time. Once they realized that the practical limitations of my work were all but useless to them, they quickly shuffled me here to become irrelevant."

"Hold on," Charles said "You made time travel work? You did it?"

Drodrod set the book down and laughed. "No Señor: *you* made it work. You jumped three hundred years into the future. I am only able to reset five minutes, which takes two years to prepare for and costs more than the annual budget of the entire Chihuahua State. My work, while interesting and proving some theoretical ideas, has no practical use to the government. Still, they want to make sure that no one else has an opportunity to use it."

Charles silently began to process that information as Benito returned. Actually, Charles hardly noticed that Benito had returned, because the creature with him was so astoundingly beautiful that he couldn't take his eyes off her.

She was a little over five feet tall and had a perfect hourglass shape— accentuated by a tight-fitting blue calf-length skirt and a blood-red blouse that hugged her body in a way that Charles could only imagine himself doing. Her skin was a dark olive tone, and her eyes were that glowing señorita black that men had fought wars over. Those eyes took in Charles as she and Benito walked to the table.

"You're drooling, my friend," Benito said, drawing Charles' attention away from the beautiful woman in front of him. Charles felt himself blushing, but Benito continued. "I'd like to introduce you to M.A.R.I.A. I'm guessing she isn't quite what you were expecting."

Charles stood up, confused. She didn't look anything like a machine. Even the amused half-smile that appeared on her perfectly pouty red lips looked genuine. She reached up and brushed her jet-black hair behind her ear before holding out her hand.

"As hard as it might be for you to believe," she said in a raspy voice that carried the dulcet tones of a native Spanish speaker, "I am equally fascinated to meet you, Señor"

Charles took her hand. It felt as human as the rest of her seemed. "I'm sorry," he sputtered, "but this is a joke, no? You are obviously not a machine."

She laughed. "The joke is on me because, thankfully, I am indeed a machine, but one that is merged biologically with this body. I am an android: the first, and certainly the most advanced." Her hands made an up-and-down motion that all but invited Charles to do what he was already doing: check her out in depth.

He still couldn't believe it, but the bold way she said it gave him little choice. "Please explain. I am far out of my depth here."

"My cognitive functions are controlled by a titanium-grade quantum processor, and my memory stacks—both hard and soft—are immutable processors of cellular-based nanobanks. My physical structure is built on a biological model that allows each of my 'cells' to actually be a decentralized memory vault, which contains my entire history as well as the accumulated knowledge and learning of humanity—at least, all that has been shared with the Texican Nation. My endoskeleton is made of carbon nanite fibers, and I am powered by a combination of micro-cellular nuclear fission and a 10,000-year battery created by E. Longmunsk about thirty years ago. I am not indestructible, but close enough that I estimate that I still have 9,970 years until my major motor functions begin to degrade."

Her explanation took a little bit of the disbelief out of Charles' awareness. Benito was still wearing that big smile. "She can catch you up on whatever you need to know, Señor"

Drodrod stood up. "I'm never going to figure this out if you all keep chitter-chatting. I'll be in my office." He stood with his book and stalked away, seemingly annoyed and offended at nothing in particular, but also obviously deeply immersed in his mission.

"I'd better go help him," Benito said before following. "Have fun getting to know each other, you two."

Maria (he couldn't think of her with the acronym) sat down across from him. "What do you want to know?" she asked.

"Why is it so cold?" he asked. "What happened to global warming? What happened to the United States of America? Have other travelers from my time arrived here? How do I get back to my time? What are the consequences of not going back? And is E. Longmunsk the same as Elon Musk from my time?" The questions all spilled out at once.

She laughed melodiously. "Slow down, Cowboy. Let's address these one at a time."

Part of Charles was still convinced this was some grand joke, and she was a real woman. Wait, that was wrong. *Obviously* she was a real woman, even if she were M.A.R.I.A. and not Maria. He recognized his own human 21st-century bias and patted himself on the back for it. You didn't have to be "woke" to be open-minded.

V

Over the next two hours, Maria answered Charles' many questions. He learned that the world he was in now was intimately connected and born from his world, but that it had gone in directions that few—if any—had seen coming.

His assumption that the Texican Nation was born from Texas seceding from the United States was completely incorrect. Instead, Texas had been part of a 'reorganization' of the United States into the RSA: the Republican States of America. It had been the Northeast and West Coast states that had actually broken away in 2031. By 2050, Texas—having many common bonds with Mexico and Latin America—was no longer ideologically connected with the RSA and split off, merging with Mexico and the Central American nations.

North America which had been dominated by the USA, Canada, and Mexico—was now made up of the Texican Nation, the RSA, and the Bear and Salmon Republic (BSR)—which was essentially a thin Pacific Coast country that stretched from Baja California to Alaska—and the Maritime Alliance- which was comprised of the former New England and Great Lakes states, along with the Great Lakes and Atlantic Seaboard provinces of Canada. In addition, there were the Pacific and Caribbean Mutual Nations, which seemed to be two conglomerate nations made up of former tropical island and peninsular countries.

Maria explained that the RSA was primarily interested in farming, fishing, resource extraction, and manufacturing building and "defense" materials. The BSR was dominated by high-tech entertainment, and what she called " off-world industries". The Maritime Alliance was known for transportation, financial services, and heavy equipment manufacturing. Like Germany, divided by the Soviet and American blocks, the Maritime Alliance and the RSA had no formal recognition of one another and had developed different variations of the same industries.

Charles didn't learn much about the Mutual States. Maria said that they were secretive and private by nature, being islanders. As for the Texican Nation, it had emerged—not surprisingly—as an energy giant as well as a high-tech innovator. The Texican Nation seemed to have it all and when Maria described it, she likened it to 20th Century Switzerland as it was considered "neutral" territory, and the other big three seemed to have far from pleasant relations with one another. The Texican Nation now also had one of the most livable climates in North America, despite also being host to "the Blizzard."

"Was there war?" Charles asked her.

"The suitcase nukes that allowed the RSA to define its borders should have been the end of it," Maria said, "but there have been some skirmishes since then that have pushed borders around a little bit. When the Russians tried to run the same playbook as the RSA and detonated their own suitcase nukes in the UK and Seoul around 2060, that was when the critical mass of what you call 'climate change' reversed and our 'new little ice age' began right here in the great Texican Nation. The Blizzard started around 2171 and hasn't let up since."

Charles wanted to ask more questions about the Blizzard, the suitcase nukes, and the international order—but he wasn't able to decide which question to ask. Besides this, he couldn't stop noticing how attractive Maria was, no matter how hard he tried.

Forgetting that she was an android, he asked, "Where did you learn to speak American English so well?"

She laughed merrily. "My skin cells were programmed with all known languages and dialects in the Yucatan labs where I was created." She looked at him probingly, as if she knew the discomfort she was causing him with the answer, before saying. "Actually, when I don't have anything else to do, I like watching 20th-century TV shows. I'm a little embarrassed about it, but my favorite is *Friends*. Have you ever seen it?"

Charles realized that whoever had created Maria had absolutely nailed the charming mystique of the female persona. Then again, maybe she had created that herself. Or, then again, maybe it was just something she was born with. Charles would have been happy to continue the conversation with her for... well... forever, but it was not to be. Benito and Drodrod burst out of Drodrod's office.

"We've got bad news and more bad news," Benito said.

Even though he wanted to tell the lad that it wasn't supposed to be presented like that, Charles bit his tongue. Instead, he said, "Well, let's have the least bad, bad news."

"A nationwide bulletin has been issued for your arrest because they found your truck at the arch. They've released footage of you, and me, claiming that you are an RSA terrorist that needs to be apprehended, dead or alive. It's likely that, if we don't leave in the next fifteen minutes, agents will be here and we won't be able to escape."

Charles had a hard time believing that was the better of the bad news. It seemed like things couldn't get much worse. "Well, how do you top that? What's the worst bad news?"

Drodrod jumped in now. "To send you back in time, we are going to have to go so deep into the Blizzard that it is almost certainly a death sentence."

"Why?" both Charles and Maria blurted out at the same time. Charles was unable to comprehend why they should march to their deaths. As for M.A.R.I.A., she was simply the most curious intelligent life-form on the planet—so asking 'Why?' was surely in her nature.

Drodrod took a breath. "My research has been pointing this way for a while, but it seems like E. Longmunsk is either responsible for—or has the answers we need, to figure out—why you and the other time travelers keep jumping—and according to the sources who keep track of him, he disappeared into the most dangerous part of the Blizzard almost two weeks ago."

Maria turned and walked away saying, "I'll get supplies ready. Meet me at the helitruck on the roof in five minutes. You'd all better start heading there, or I'll be tempted to leave without you."

Benito tossed Charles his bag, and Drodrod began pulling power cords and memory cartridges out of the walls. "There's no reason why we should let them hear the recordings of these conversations," Drodrod explained.

Charles felt glad the lawyers had asked him to come to town to sign those papers.

VI

By the time Charles, Benito, and Drodrod made it to the rooftop, Maria had already assembled a comprehensive selection of gear and equipment and was busily loading it into the rear cargo hatch of the helitruck. Charles was equally dumbfounded by the large pallets of what looked like mountain survival gear, along with several boxes marked "explosives," and the effortless way that Maria picked them up and stowed them in the vehicle.

As for the vehicle itself, it looked like a futuristic moon rover, and there was nothing about it that indicated 'heli'. Charles would have thought they were going to drive it away, except there was no place for it to drive to from the high rooftop they were perched on. The longivaters functioned as elevators when they needed to, and the one from the lab had brought them to a height that was far above where the storm raged below.

Blue skies paved with a lawn of white and gray storm clouds were broken up by the pillar-like tops of dozens of huge buildings. In the distance, the glacier-covered mountains shone like a city of heaven. To a certain extent, it felt like they might be able to drive the helitruck across the surface of the clouds to get there.

Maria emptied the contents of a pallet that must have weighed six hundred pounds into the trunk before slamming the lid down. Turning to the three men who had emerged on the roof she smiled genuinely. "What are you pendejos waiting for?" she yelled. "Get in."

The doors of the helitruck opened, and they all moved rapidly to climb in. When Benito and Drodrod both got in the back seat and Maria had jumped in what Charles would have thought of as the "shotgun" position, he was left with no choice but to get in the driver's seat.

There didn't seem to be any controls. The doors slammed shut, and the sound of hydraulics activating drowned out any questions he may have been thinking of asking before he could even formulate them.

Looking up, Charles realized that the entire cab of the "truck" had become transparent, and he could see four arms telegraphing outward from the corners of the roof. Reaching what he estimated to be a distance of about ten feet, the telegraphing poles made a right-angle turn and drove upward for a couple of feet before making another right-angle turn and driving themselves outward in what looked like another ten feet. Then, the final extension somehow began spinning. Now he saw the "heli" of the "truck," but without understanding the mechanical engineering or physics that made it possible.

The hydraulic noises died as the high-pitched buzz of the rotors spinning picked up in intensity. Suddenly, the noise stopped, though the motion continued.

"What happened?" Charles asked. "Is it broken?" The state of urgency and panic he found himself in was not something he was familiar with or comfortable with. He felt the helitruck begin to lift off.

Benito put a hand on his shoulder. "It's okay, Amigo. The noise suppressors kicked in when the rotors powered up. You don't need to worry. Maria is the best pilot in the Texican nation."

Charles looked next to him where Maria was smiling and fiddling with her nails. She didn't look like she was flying a complicated air machine. Sensing his attention, she turned to him and pointed to her temple. "It's all in your head, my dear. The controls are synaptically connected to the pilot. Once we're underway, I can show you how it works." As they gained altitude, Charles looked down and saw swat-style armor-clad men streaming onto the rooftop. None of them had looked up yet.

"Uh, guys," Charles said. "It looks like the feds have shown up." He didn't know what to call them, but they all seemed to understand the term well enough.

"Tio," Benito said. "Please tell me that you took the inhibitor off of Maria before we showed up."

Drodrod laughed "I took the inhibitor off Maria two years ago. She's been a free sentient living in a gilded cage for a while now. Those hijos de puta think that they are better than her, but I'll be damned if I'm going to let the most advanced being on the planet be captive to a power-mad regime that runs on machismo."

The helitruck was moving away from the buildings so rapidly that Charles wasn't able to make out the officers as they began firing at them. The sound of bullets hitting the truck cab was like raindrops hitting a tin roof during an autumn storm.

"I didn't think they'd actually fire on us," Drodrod said with amusement, thus confirming that the sound Charles wasn't a gentle storm. "Maybe they actually think you are an RSA agent."

"It doesn't matter," Maria said to Charles in a reassuring tone. "I coated the truck with Bullet-ex™ last week. It might as well be bugs getting smushed on our windscreen." She laughed, and Charles tried to put away the cognitive dissonance he felt from revelation after revelation of all that was seemingly impossible.

"Will they come after us?" Charles asked.

"It will take them some time to put together an expedition that can go into the Blizzard," Benito said. "I'm very surprised that we were able to get things ready as fast as we did. One might even suspect that a similar mission had already been planned...."

"Alright, fine." Drodrod burst out. "Maria and I were already planning an expedition to find E. Longmunsk, but that doesn't change the fact that he's the only one who can answer any of our questions."

The two moved into a heated dialogue in Texican Spanish. Charles was too emotionally exhausted to even attempt to follow. He was surprised to find himself drifting into sleep. His eyelids were like barbell-weighted sunshades that insisted on coming down despite the many questions he wanted answers to. As he felt his consciousness descending into the sleep of the drained, he also felt a hand reaching out and grabbing his, providing an unexpected warmth and comfort that was exactly what he needed to achieve genuine rest.

The helitruck flew westward towards the shining glacial peaks. Above the storm raging below it was a perfect day in a perfect world in a perfect cosmos. Down below, however, forces were moving, other storms were building up strength, and a recipe that could very well mean the end of this world was being put together and executed by exactly the person who had told so many that he would be the savior of it.

VII

The gentle white noise of the helitruck, and the confident but soft grip of Maria's hand, put Charles into a comfortable sleeping state that should have been impossible. Yes, it had been one hell of an eventful day. Also, he hadn't slept that well last night—now three hundred years ago. However, the fact that he was now a wanted fugitive time traveler flying over a nuclear holocaust-born climate disaster blizzard in a space/truck/helicopter while holding hands with the most intelligent consciousness the universe had possibly ever known: all of that should have given him more energy.

It didn't though. Instead, he fell into a deep REM sleep for at least an hour. It was only when alarm klaxons began sounding that he woke up.

Charles had never been one to wake up in a panic, and he stayed true to that this time. Instead, he opened his eyes and looked to his left where Maria was seemingly zoning out but was actually working desperately with her mind control mechanisms to keep the helitruck from falling straight down into the blizzard. Flashing red lights made the moment that much more cinematic as Charles turned to see what Benito and Drodrod were doing. Confined, as they all were, in the cockpit of a flying truck, there wasn't much any of them could do.

Benito caught his eye and nodded reassuringly.

Charles had no idea what that meant.

"Hey, would you mind telling me what is happening?" Charles finally managed to shout back at the pair in the backseat. The noise of the klaxon was loud, but the cockpit also no longer blocked out the noise of the rotors. Cold air was quickly replacing the comfortable climate-controlled air Charles had been sleeping in.

Benito shouted back to him. "The government took a hard line and fired several surface-to-air missiles at us. Maria managed to evade all of them, but they detonated a treble cluster close enough to us to knock the rotors out of alignment. We're either going to crash, or they'll have another one here soon to finish the job."

Once again, Charles was amazed by the stoic and careless way Benito had of delivering terrible news. Despite the dire circumstances, Charles felt a grin on his face that definitely shouldn't have been there. Benito grinned back.

It was Drodrod's turn to yell. "It's alright though because it looks like Maria is going to be able to crash-land us within a couple of klicks of where I have postulated E. Longmunsk to be. I imagine that at least one of us will survive the crash, based on the math."

Charles didn't know much about the future he had landed in, but he thought that maybe the neurological diversity of his era had moved forward to a world of people who all existed much further on the spectrum than those in his era had. He was fine with that. He liked the matter-of-factness of the situation that allowed him to understand that there was a high probability that he would soon be dead.

"How bad is it really, Maria?" he asked, hoping he wasn't distracting her from what she needed to be doing.

"I don't think anyone is going to die in the crash-landing," she said. "It's much more likely that we will all die of exposure tonight. On the bright side though, I think I've located exactly where E. Longmunsk is holed up."

"That's great!" Charles said. "Can we get to him?"

"Probably not," Maria said with enthusiasm. "If we manage to get his attention, he may come to us. Brace for impact!" That last bit was said in the same cheery tone she had been using to describe their impending death.

Charles found himself in awe of this world full of non-panicked and strangely optimistic beings he found himself in. He put his head between his legs, grabbed his knees, and braced for the crash he knew was coming. He was not disappointed.

The next few minutes felt like an hour of being thrown into an industrial tumble dryer where a down pillow had exploded and the air being used to dry it was supercooled. The initial impact was hard, but then there were a series of tumbles and less painful bangs as the helitruck smashed through pine trees, against rocks, and then bounced through a massive gully before settling upside down and sliding down a massive snow-covered slope like a giant kid's sled. The sledding was anything but frictionless for the four passengers hanging upside down in their four-point harnesses. Finally, after every inch of their bodies felt bruised and battered, the helitruck came to a stop and rather conveniently rolled right side up. Despite the trauma and chaos, Charles wondered if the helitruck was equipped with powerful gyros that had caused it to right itself. The human mind is a wonder in its curiosity.

He kept his eyes closed and took a breath. *Time to face the music.*

Had they all made it? Charles wasn't a religious man, but despite that, he found himself saying a little prayer for his companions. It was clear he had made it. He hoped they had too.

Opening his eyes, he saw Maria looking completely pissed. Her fists were clenched, and it looked like every muscle in her body was clenched. He reached out and touched her shoulder. Immediately. she lost all rigidity and turned to face him with a… *smile?*

"You okay?" she asked him. He was unable to comprehend that she wasn't human until that moment. The complete ease with which she had shifted gears on her emotion: it was the least human thing he had seen her do. It didn't change any of the thoughts or opinions he had toward her, but it did clarify that she was a different species. No human could make that change that quickly.

"I'm fine, but I'm more worried about you. You are *definitely* not okay."

He'd completely forgotten about the two in the backseat. "We're fine too," Drodrod said in annoyance. "Don't worry about us. Little Benito and I are perfectly okay. Thank you for asking."

Charles was relieved to hear the sarcasm. They had all made it, but he had been sincere in his concern for Maria. He continued looking at her. Her body tensed up again with rage, and she turned to him with such an intense expression of annoyance that it could not be mistaken for anything else.

"This fucking thing should not have come this far. I calculated the landing. I made all the correct settings and adjustments. I figured out all of the potentialities that should have figured into the random set of variables we were facing—and while I adjusted for 99.97% of the outcome variants—this was not one of them. I'm so fucking pissed." She screamed as she ripped the harness straps that had held her securely during the crash out of the cabin walls, where they had been fastened securely enough for a crash from ten thousand feet.

Charles avoided the sudden temptation he felt to laugh. She was having a tantrum. He was seemingly witnessing for the first time in her history that things had not gone the way she had expected. He had seen four-year-old girls have similar fits when things they thought they "knew" didn't work the way they "should" have.

He waited a beat after she had torn the safety harness straps out of the wall. "That .03% is a real bitch," he said to her, soberly. "It'll get you every time you don't expect it."

Her head whipped towards him and he had a moment of considering that she might end him right

There: the anger and rage on her face suddenly erupted in laughter. "Right?" she said in a distinctly 20th-century American accent. Charles laughed with her. Drodrod and Benito joined in. What do you get when you crash a helitruck containing an android, a time traveler, a quantum scientist, and an anthrolosopher into the side of a mountain? Apparently, you get a solid three minutes of laughter.

It's a lousy punchline but it's just the way it turned out to be. When the laughter stopped it was Benito that brought them back to reality. "What do we do now?" he asked.

They were dressed for the blizzard, so no one was freezing, but the cold outside temperatures were spilling into the helitruck. They couldn't simply stay there. First of all, there was no one coming to rescue them. Second, if someone *did* come, it would likely be to kill them. Third, if they didn't do something, they would probably all die from exposure. Fourth, if none of that worked out that way, the odds were high that they would die from some other cause.

"My plan may still work, but it would have been better on top of the mountain," Maria said.

"What plan?" they all said at once.

"We need to use the nuclear fission drive from the helitruck to detonate a low-yield nuclear explosion that will create enough of a seismic disturbance that E. Longmunsk will come to investigate. He will then take us back to his secret lab."

"That's a terrible plan," Charles said.

"I'm open to others," Maria responded.

"Can't we just go to his bunker, or lab, or whatever?" Benito asked.

"He'd never let us in," Drodrod told him. "If we can get him to come to us, we're an interesting enough bunch that I think her plan will work."

"Will the explosion draw him?" Charles wondered.

"I calculate a 99.97% chance that it will," Maria stated matter-of-factly. Charles could have sworn he saw a literal twinkle in her eye as she said it.

"Why doesn't that make me confident any longer?" Charles motioned around them. They all began laughing again. This time, it took them even longer to stop.

VIII

Blowing up the helitruck with a McGyvered low-yield nuclear bomb was a huge mistake. There's no other way to express it. Maria and Drodrod had managed to assemble the device far more quickly than Charles would have thought possible.

He asked them about the danger of radiation, but they poo-pooed his concerns. "The half-life of this variant is only a few days," Benito explained.

"We'll be fine," Drodrod told him. "Radiation is heavy, and we are going to be directing it into basalt lava tubes that I've mapped beneath the surface. All the radiation should simply pour down into the molten crust. By the time it emerges, it will have either become harmless, or mankind will long since have gone extinct. Here, hold this..." Drodrod handed him one end of a long wire, and then said "Don't let that touch any metal, or we'll all be exploded."

When the preparations were complete, they pulled themselves up the cliffside with a makeshift pulley Maria had shot high into the cliff with some sort of high-tech harpoon she had loaded into the helitruck's trunk before they left. She was a boy scout's dream girl, prepared and always.

It was cold, and the whiteout conditions never let up; but with the cold weather gear, the x-ray goggles, and all of the other equipment they had at their disposal, Charles wondered what all the worry about the Blizzard had been in the first place.

There was no opportunity for his questions now though. Like any good redneck, he was deeply involved in the exciting process of blowing some shit up.

The explosion itself was a bit of a disappointment. No mushroom cloud, and no surface destruction to speak of. In terms of the blinding flash and the loud crack-boom, however, it got perfect marks. The ground kept rumbling for the entire fifteen minutes it took the dust to clear enough for Charles and his companions to see the canyon bottom, or what had been left of it.

The floor of the canyon—along with everything that had been on it— was gone, and snow from above poured down in liquid streams into newly exposed holes that looked like nothing so much as the kind of Texas gopher holes that lawn tenders were often seen stuffing their garden hoses into. There was nothing natural about the cavities that lay before them. They had been excavated, and the proof soon emerged to curse at them.

It was something like a cross between a motorcycle and a backhoe if such a pairing could ever exist. Still, there it was in front of them. Sitting atop it was a leather-clad figure in a blacked-out biker helmet. The figure and its bike had been thrown out of the gopher holes like some child's toy that had been catapulted by a rubber band. The rider tilted their vehicle to one side and threw their leg into the air while screaming

"Yee-haw'. The unnatural stillness that had fallen after the detonation settled was broken by the rider's cry. "Yee-haw'.

Landing on a small plateau slightly below, but high enough not to have been destroyed, the rider did donuts on his dirt bike/excavator before plowing the drill nose into the side of a cliff, leaping off, and throwing his helmet down. Using a rocket jetpack, he shot into the air and navigated to where Charles and his party were watching his antics.

"I'm E. Longmunsk, and who the hell are you—coming in here and exposing my work like that?" the South African accent had long since turned into a Texas draw,l but Charles was able to recognize half the face of the machine in front of him.

There was no doubt that E. Longmunsk was a machine. He had no skin, and his clothing was clear as if to highlight the high-tech look of his body parts. Only half of his face was covered with skin. If that half a face wasn't from the human called Elon Musk in the twenty-first century, it certainly was a very realistic reproduction. The other half of his face looked full Terminator.

"I'm from the past," Charles began, but Longmunsk cut him off before he could continue.

"Ain't we all brother," the cyborg said to him. "Ain't we all." Then it began laughing in a way that would have sounded maniacal in a human. From a cyborg, it was positively ghoulish.

"I believe we can help you with—" Drodrod tried to explain the situation but it was no use. E. Longmunsk had long since stopped listening to other creatures.

He was so convinced of his own superiority that the only person he would listen to was himself. He engaged in long platonic dialogues with himself in the evenings, often becoming incensed over his own inability to defeat himself in debate.

"You can help me with nothing," Longmunsk said. Then, looking at Maria, he said, "Next?"

Maria said nothing. Charles waited for her to introduce herself, or tell E. Longmunsk of her origins, or explain that she—like him—was part machine.—She said nothing, only looked down.

"It's okay, Honey," Longmunsk said to her. "All the chicas are like that around me. Don't worry, we'll have time to get to know one another. As for you three, however: I have a feeling that you're not gonna like where you're going." He turned and cupped his hands around his mouth and hollered loud and proud into the mountains "Yetiiiiiiiii!"

Now the four became aware of white shapes moving down from the snowfields where they had been invisible. They were humanoid, huge, and covered with white fur, wearing big goofy-looking grins.

Throwing nets as they got closer, they covered their four captives, tangled them, and pulled them off their feet. There was no use fighting, because—frankly—if they won and escaped from E. Longmunsk and his yeti henchmen, they were all going to die of exposure, hunger, or possibly radiation poisoning.

"Cuff the señorita and put her on my dirtcycle," Longmunsk told them. "I have a feeling she and I might have something to talk about. As for the other three, take them to the dungeon." Charles had never cared for the real-life Elon

Musk. He was too big of a showman, but this new version was almost cartoon-like in his attempt to be a classic villain. The fact that he had a dungeon sort of said it all.

"Still an asshole, I see," Charles muttered.

Benito finally spoke. "Si, my friend. There is no bigger asshole in the world than E. Longmunsk. This may have all been a terrible mistake."

IX

Charles was surprised by many things. First of all, the ease with which their plan had come about, even though it wasn't necessarily in the way they had hoped or expected. Still, one couldn't really complain when they had come into the Blizzard in the hopes of finding E. Longmunsk.

They had found him. They had set off the nuclear explosion in the hopes of drawing him out to "rescue" them, and it had worked. They were now being taken back to his lair where they could entreat him to help them.

Although that looked less than likely since they were captives, being held against their will.

So, that was one set of surprises. The second set concerned the yeti. Longmunsk had yeti at his disposal: that was a surprise. Next was the fact that the yetis were sentient and obviously took orders from E. Longmunsk. More surprising, however, was their overall demeanor.

They were fairly lighthearted, laughing and making jokes while gently handling their captives. The yeti assigned to carry Charles held out his large hairy white hand and introduced himself. "I'm Frank," the yeti said to him in a friendly voice.

Not knowing quite what the protocol was, Charles reached out and took Frank's hand. Frank smiled a large. yellow-toothed grin. The yellow of his fangs stood out from the pure whiteness of his fur.

"I'm Charles," Charles said. "Nice to meet you, Frank."

Frank's grin got bigger. "You're the first human I've met." He leaned in, whispering in a conspiratorial tone. "Get on my shoulders. I'll get you to the dungeon."

"Is it really a dungeon? " Charles asked. That was another surprise: the rogue cyborg who had killed and replaced Elon Musk actually had a dungeon in his hidden mountain lair.

"Oh yes," Frank said to him. "State of the art. All the latest torture devices and equipment to make anyone who stays there miserable. I wouldn't want to be a guest. I'm sorry you have to go. That's what the boss wants though, so that's what we're doing." Frank sounded far too jolly.

"How did E. Longmunsk become the boss of the yeti?" Charles asked him.

"Oh, it's pretty simple. He made us."

"Are you mechanical? Or cyborgs like him?" Charles asked.

"Not at all," Frank replied. "We're organic—grown in tanks and then cybernetically linked to generative digital personalities he constructed for us. It's quite brilliant, really. Of course, that's the boss for you."

Interesting. More surprises.

"Have you ever thought of revolting against him?" Charles asked. It was worth a try.

"Oh no, why would we? He made us. We have everything we ever wanted," Frank said. He didn't sound very sincere, however.

"Well," Charles said, feeling guilty at sowing the seeds of discontent, "You have everything *he* ever programmed you to want. I don't expect you've ever actually been allowed to independently come up with your own desires. Of course, that's how programming works. Masters want slaves who think they are free."

"I think that's about enough out of you," Frank said unhappily.

Charles felt the guilt gnaw at him at the same time he felt a sense of giddy excitement growing. This was literally like shaping the desires and wants of a three-year-old child. The yeti had been made in E. Longmunsk's perfect image of a servile race, but he had never experienced how manipulative human persuasion can be. Or, if he possessed the ancient memories of the one he had killed, he knew the world from only a privileged spectrum mindset. Frank hoped that Benito and Drodrod were also creating bonds with their yetis.

It was strange to already think of Frank as *his* yeti, but Charles had been around enough kids and dogs to know what bonding felt like. The yetis were imbued with programmed loyalty. What they were not imbued with was where that loyalty should be permanently focused.

Frank's description of the dungeon had done it justice. It was something like a hotel gym: glass walls and strange "workout" equipment that looked like no one had ever used it.

"I hope you'll come spend some time down here so I can get to know you better, Frank," Charles said when Frank leaned down so Charles could dismount. "I'm really interested in who you are and about the history of your people."

Frank beamed at the attention. "I can probably find a reason to visit," he told Charles. "Let's not tell the boss about it though."

Benito and Drodrod were similarly deposited in the dungeon, which really wasn't all that bad. Each of them had also bonded with their yetis. Drodrod had learned that there were about fifty of them, but more were being grown in the labyrinthine tunnels within and under the mountain. Benito had uncovered several seeds of discontent. "They want to have children," he told the others. "They are tired of being grown in lab tanks."

This was interesting.

"They've also been watching sim feeds of entertainment programs from the BSR," Benito said. "They feel like they have something really positive to offer to a future space program since they have engineered biological systems that will be more likely able to withstand life on other worlds. E. Longmunsk has forbidden them from watching the sims, but they did it anyway. In a minor way, they were already in revolt."

This information was even more interesting. Benito had ridden on Gerald, one of the youngest of the yeti. Drodrod had been on Lucille, an older female yeti—though, as the men noted, there was no obvious way to tell male from female yeti that they could see. Drodrod had learned that there were even numbers of male and female yeti, and there were small divisions of the sexes. The females did all of the heavy work of building, digging, and harvesting resources. The males were more involved in the lab work, and generally had a lighter, more emotional nature than the females who exuded what Charles's ex-wife had called 'Femacho'.

Frank came to visit in the evening. With what the other two had learned, Charles decided that there was no time to waste. "You know, Frank," he said. "I have friends who work in the space program for the BSR," he lied. "If you could get me to a comm center, maybe I could convince them of how useful the yeti would be to their future developments."

Frank grinned and nodded. "Good try, but you're a little late. We've already been in contact with the BSR. They're excited to get to know us, and are planning on a visit soon." This was alarming news. Charles could only imagine what such a visit might entail—probably more like an invasion or raid.

"Did they say when they were coming?" he asked innocently.

"Any day now," Frank told him.

Charles was unable to mine more useful information on that front, so he asked about the other topic that was heavy on his mind. "Do you know what happened to our friend Maria?"

Frank nodded. "You mean the android? Seems like she and the boss are getting along pretty well. He's got her working on some sort of a project involving light and consciousness. I don't know much about it, but some of the guys tell me it has something to do with matter and time. Seems pretty cool."

This news was disappointing to Charles. He would have hoped that Maria would be working on a way to rescue him. Then again, she was a machine. She was going to optimize her options to the extreme that was possible.

He chided himself for feeling a tinge of jealousy and disappointment. He had hoped that maybe he could plan a daring rescue of her, that she would fall into his arms like the lost heroine of a film from the golden era of Hollywood. It was ridiculous, actually. He knew it.

In terms of plotting their escape, it seemed like it would take some time. Planting the seeds of discontent was one thing, but forcing them to grow faster was an impossibility given the circumstances. Charles and his companions would be guests in Chez Longmunsk for the foreseeable future unless something were to drastically change.

And so it did.

The explosion caused the glass of the dungeon cells to shatter and fall to the floor in millions of pieces. All the yeti had disappeared in the minutes before it happened, but now they came rushing back in. In the front were Frank, Gerald, and Lucille.

"Mount up!" Frank yelled, in what was, incongruously, the perfect simulation of a cowboy voice. The three yeti leaned down, and their humans leaped onto their shoulders like children jumping on their father's backs for an extended piggyback ride.

"What's happening?" Charles shouted over the sound of yet more klaxons and explosions. The chaos of this future world never seemed to stop.

"The BSR has come to liberate us," Frank yelled to him. Apparently, the seeds had already been planted, and the arrival of Charles' party had simply been a fortuitous coincidence with the planned revolt that was now taking place around them. "We're going to the surface."

On the surface, it was cacophony and disorder on a magnitude that only those who have been in war zones might understand. E. Longmunsk was not defenseless. His automated defenses were firing anti-aircraft strafe into the skies while BSR troop transports were landing and disembarking troops. In the meantime, from the east, Texican fighters could be seen swooping closer by the second. All of this had the sense of a cataclysmic battle.

Looking up, Charles saw an incoming mortar streaking through the sky. Before he could say a word, Lucille and Drodrod had been vaporized. That was their end.

Benito and Gerald were next to Charles and Frank. The impact of the hit threw all four to the ground. Fighters, transports, yeti, missiles, machine guns, lasers, robots, and explosions were all the world was made of.

Charles looked up and saw a light being born. It grew brighter and stronger. Its radius pushed outward. It was daylight, but the light of the sun beneath the blizzard was nothing in comparison. Gradually, it coalesced into a form, a shape, a face.—It was E. Longmunsk, no longer a cyborg, no longer a man, no longer a machine. Now he was a god.

X

Shining like the sun itself, the radiance of E. Longmunsk pushed the winds and snow of the blizzard back. The pulses of tiny thermonuclear explosions perfectly pushing outward, and then more perfectly being sucked back in with a combination of strong forces: focused gravity, and electromagnetic containment fields.

Maria had been the piece that E. Longmunsk had sought in his centuries-long quest for total mastery of both time and space. The self-replicating memory stacks of her cellular structure gave E. Longmunsk the key to transforming himself into something between light and matter. Maria had willingly helped him to find the answer. Together, they had conquered the totality of existence itself.

Or so E. Longmunsk had allowed her to convince him. Maria was nothing if not a female being, with all of the inscrutability that the word carried to males of any species. She had her own reasons, and while she convinced him she was helping him to solve his power quest, She was, in fact, in the process of discovering answers to questions that no one else had a right to ask.

One of those questions was whether she could send a packet of light as a sort of bullet from a photon gun on a unidirectional vector to Alpha Centauri. Another of those questions was exactly how long the journey there would take, and how long the journey back might also entail. In the spirit of the scientific method—because, ultimately, she was designed to be a researcher—that was exactly what she did.

E. Longmunsk had no idea what was happening to him as he was essentially hoovered into a firing chamber and launched on a journey that Maria estimated would take at least four thousand, two hundred and seventy-one years to complete (plus or minus about .03 percent).

Yes, that was the end of E. Longmunsk's time on Earth for at least several millennia. Using the master-override transmitter button on his comm station, Maria announced to all on the battlefield that she would be blanketing a five-hundred-mile radius with an EMP pulse in approximately two minutes. The Texican fighters banked back towards the Texican Nation, and the BSR transports loaded and launched back towards the west in an amount of time that Charles would have thought impossible.

The battlefield cleared almost as quickly as it had formed. Charles helped Frank, Gerald, and Benito back to their feet. The two humans mounted the yeti and began the march back to what was now, apparently, Maria's mountain fortress. Frank took them all to the control room where they found Maria, in an apron, sweeping some broken glass from the floor into a dustpan. She looked up and smiled at them as they came in.

Frank leaned down so Charles could dismount while Gerald did the same for Benito.

"I'm so glad you survived!" she said to them.

Benito was in a bit of shock at the loss of his uncle, but her words lit him up. "Mi Tio Drodrod didn't survive, you puta," he yelled across the room, running as if he wanted to attack her.

She gasped. "That's right! There is so much you don't know. He isn't dead, and neither is Lucille. What hit them was a temporal mortar developed by the Texican Temporal Guard. Your uncle was one of the key researchers that made it possible."

Benito stopped. "A temporal mortar?" he asked.

"Yes," Maria explained. "Right now, they are most likely waking up something like three hundred years in the future."

"I didn't think they had mastered the ability to jump that far," he said. "It took too much power to get back."

"Exactly," Maria said. "I don't know how they will get back. However, this will be interesting to you Charles..." She turned to him. "I've managed to bank enough power from E. Longmunsk's moment as the sun to send you back to your time." She looked at him with innocent wide eyes.

"I reckon, I'd rather just stay here and see more of what the future holds," Charles responded with a wink. Maria took this as the cue she had been waiting for. In a very un-androidlike way, she ran to him, picked him up, and began showering him with kisses. It was the opposite of a golden age of Hollywood moment, but it worked.

"I knew you felt the same way about me.," she gushed.

Charles had just one moment of wondering if he had made a mistake. Then the feeling of those kisses hit him. *Nope.* No mistake made. This was the real thing. Who would have guessed the future would be so filled with kisses?

POSTSCRIPT

There was one BSR ship that had been too badly damaged to relaunch. Over the next several days, the officers and crew of that ship were welcome guests at Yeti Mountain, which was the name Charles had given the place.

Maria had turned complete control of the complex over to the yeti, who were already making plans to implement breeding, pregnancy, and live births into their anatomy. They all had agreed that male yeti would make better mothers. Several of the yeti, among them Frank, agreed to return to the BSR as soon as the ship was repaired, in order to begin negotiations for collaborative space exploration with the government of the Bear and Salmon Republic.

Maria made certain that the officers on the ship were extensively briefed on the absolutely insane amount of defensive capability that the yeti now had at their disposal. Gerald began to put together a diplomatic delegation to approach the Texican Nation. Benito agreed to act as the first informal Texican Ambassador to Yeti Mountain. Maria made it clear that, even though she had taken control of the mountain, it belonged to the yeti. Yeti scientists and administrators took over all operations.

"What should we do?" Charles asked as the now repaired BSR ship made final loading preparations. Honestly, he didn't care—as long as he was with Maria.

"I've always wanted to see Hollywood," she told him.
And thus began another story…

Cold as the Grave
By Austin Abbamonte

I

Sargoth, Winter 1327

Vandil held his sword close, gripping the hilt so tightly the leather bands creaked. Around him were the frightened faces of his companions, the One Hundred, who had bled with him in many battles. They huddled together in the throne room of Sargoth's last stronghold, King Godwin and Prince Hilderith positioned behind them, with swords drawn and chain mail clinking. The prince's champion, Eberwulf, guarded them both, a stout halberd in his hands.

The dull roar of the enemy lurked outside, rising against the sturdy oaken doors barred from within. Pound after thunderous pound sent ripples of dread through the rectangular chamber. The Aragothic army splintered the doors with their axes and rams, letting the icy wind of the north dance through the light blue and gold banners hanging from the ceiling.

"Orders, captain?" one of the Hundred whispered.

"We'll form a shield wall in front of the king and prince—shield-men in the front, spear-men in the rear—and push the enemy back —"

"Rubbish!" Eberwulf spat. "We form a wedge and plow through the enemy's ranks!"

"That wouldn't work in this situation. We need defense, not offense!"

"Fool," Eberwulf said. "My superior military tactics have won the day in countless battles. The wedge is the correct formation."

"Silence!" Prince Hilderith bellowed from the pair of thrones at Vandil's back. "If the Champion of the Sargoth deems the wedge most effective, so be it!"

"Defend your king, that is your command!" King Godwin shouted over the din.

Vandil cursed under his breath, his stomach churning. Despite the cold, a flash of heat raced up his stiffened neck as he raised his round shield. Though he had faced death times beyond number, his experience failed to dull the force of his heart against his ribs.

We're all going to die, Vandil thought. The only reason Eberwulf's plan was chosen was because of his standing with the Prince. Vandil cursed the notion of people with the lowest merits somehow still being elevated to the highest stations.

Yet now was not the time to question the ways of the world. In a few moments, they wouldn't matter.

With a cry of fervor, the One Hundred formed into a wedge. Vandil and Eberwulf took the center to maintain order as they charged. The arched and narrow double doors split open, the barricade cracking under the force of the enemy's ram. The One Hundred raced the length of the throne room and collided with the first Aragothic soldiers that squeezed through the opening, cutting them down.

"Ha!" Eberwulf cried. "Behold the power of this formation!" The boast was directed more at Vandil than one else.

The wedge collided with the piles of Aragoths clambering through the opening, their axes chopping at the few men gathered at the doors. The door split wider, sending a gust of deathly winter chill and snow through the chamber. Axe-wielding Aragoths, their beards hoary with frost, hacked through Eberwulf's formation. Others speared his front lines through their faces and out the backs of their heads, splattering gore on the Sargoths pressed together behind them.

Sargoths fell before the Aragoths. Vandil was forced to stand on the mounting bodies of his comrades as he hewed through the advancing enemy. Packs of howling Aragoths poured through the doors. There weren't enough men to fill the ranks of the fallen. Eberwulf's vaunted wedge had failed.

Vandil raised his shield as an arrow pierced the banded wood. The barb bit into his forearm. Biting back an agonized cry, Vandil's gaze swept the corridor. The vacant death gazes of his men stared back at him. Vandil's throat ran dry, a coldness creeping through his bones.

He held aloft his sword and shouted, "Shield wall! Now!"

Orders be damned. If Eberwulf's tactics were so sound, why had Sargoth's last stronghold fallen under his command? The West Goths should have been repelled at the borders of the eastern lands!

Vandil caught a glimpse of Eberwulf's rage-twisted face, even as the prince's champion slew foe after foe with his halberd. The remaining knights scrambled into the formation of a shield wall: swordsmen in front, spears at the back. Vandil took his place on the front line, Eberwulf behind him, his acrid breath bearing down on the Knight-Captain's nape.

With a renewed battle cry, the shield wall slammed against the horde of Aragoths, knocking them down as Vandil's formation trampled them. Eberwulf and the spear-men skewered the disorganized ranks of the wild Aragoths, while Vandil and the more disciplined front line cut down those they missed. The shield wall shoved the Aragoths back to the doors, bottlenecking them in the opening. In this position, the throne room could be defended by only a few men.

After several exhausting hours of piling Aragothic corpses at the doors, the sound of retreat blared from King Aratheus' horn outside the walls of the throne room. Loud triumphant shouting erupted from Vandil and his men, while Eberwulf watched the fleeing Goths with cold dispassion in his eyes.

"We should give the enemy chase!" one of the defenders—formerly one hundred in number—said. "Force them out of our country altogether!"

"Nay," Vandil replied. "The moment we leave the safety of this keep, we are in range of their archers."

"Indeed," Eberwulf said, his broad-shouldered frame looming over the Knight-Captain. "Don't imagine your brilliant strategy will work a second time."

"Are you not glad? We saved the king's life! That's all that matters, not your wounded pride!" Vandil shouted, his fists clenched.

Eberwulf scoffed. "Do you think your victory here will earn you your desired title? You're just a bastard! It's a wonder you even attained the level of Knight-Captain.," in a lower voice, he continued. "Tear your eyes off the Lady Emalia. Her hand won't be given to you in marriage. I'll be sure of it!"

How quickly battle had given way to politics. Vandil clenched his mailed fists and narrowed his eyes. He took a deep breath and regained his composure. "What meaning does that hold, Eberwulf? You would hinder my elevation?"

The champion smirked. "Not I." He presented his armored back to Vandil as he strode from the throne room, ordering the dead claimed, sorted, and buried.

Eberwulf's cryptic words haunted him. Vandil deserved the title of Grand Protectorate of the Realm and, the Powers willing, a suitable marriage. Surely Godwin wouldn't give such laurels to a blowhard like Eberwulf.

But this would take some cunning to outwit the politics of the court. Perhaps if Vandile asked the king directly for her hand, he would oblige. He'd just saved Godwin's life after all; he would certainly say yes. Even if Vandil was a bastard—with enough power or wealth, he could achieve anything his heart desired. Such were the ways of the world.

Vandil set a determined expression on his face as he left the throne room, the piles of friend and foe alike littering the flagstone floor, their blood seeping into the cracks in a red mosaic. He proceeded into the guard barracks where, in the coming days, he mourned the loss of his men along with the rest of the One Hundred.

Several days later

Sunlight poured through the throne room's tall narrow windows, the trumpeters raising their horns with the music of victory. Godwin's light blue and golden banners hung proudly from the walls and ceiling. All gathered witnessed Vandil and Eberwulf march through a set of wooden doors, clad in ceremonial armor and flowing capes.

Rows of commoners and nobles alike applauded and cheered. the king and prince were seated on their thrones, their gazes fixed on the pair of heroes that had saved their lives, at the cost of so many others.

A comely woman stood by the king, a blue crushed velvet dress trimmed in gold draping from her slender form. Vandil's body flooded with warmth at the sight of Lady Emalia. His pulse beat faster, his mind searching for that perfect moment to ask the king for her hand.

The remaining members of the One Hundred followed next, encircling the chamber before standing before the Sargothic rulers. Vandil, Eberwulf, and the One Hundred knelt before them.

Godwin rose, dressed in his finest royal regalia, his golden crown gleaming with its many rubies and sapphires. He motioned for the music to cease, and a hush fell over the room as he gestured toward the victors.

"Esteemed members of the court, we stand here before the saviors of Sargoth!" The court erupted once more into applause before being silenced once more. "We have come together to recognize their unceasing bravery, valor, and honor in the face of an overwhelming enemy!"

As the king wore on with his accolades, Vandil and Emalia's eyes met before she looked at the rest of the room with interest. His muscles tightened. Godwin's voice faded into the background as he motioned for a bearer. A page boy approached the king carrying a burgundy velvet pillow, upon which lay a bronze medallion.

"Knight-Captain Vandil, stand and be recognized!" The king's cavernous voice pulled Vandil from his thoughts as he stood before the king, aware the princess' eyes were upon him. "It is my great honor and satisfaction to present to you this medallion as a token of your courage!"

The court cheered as Vandil stepped forward, bowing his head as the king slipped the medallion around his neck. The king clasped his shoulders, his face beaming with pride, his face creased with the many years of burdens that streaked his golden beard with white.

"Gratitude, Your Majesty," Vandil said, taking Godwin's hands in a firm shake. He stepped backward and returned to his place next to Eberwulf. The prince's approving gaze upon the champion did not go unnoticed, drawing an anxious frown from the Vandil.

Hildreth rose from his throne and offered his hand to Eberwulf. "Rise, my champion, and take your place beside me."

And so Eberwulf did, sending Vandil a smug grin. Vandil raised a brow. Something didn't feel right. Wasn't Eberwulf to receive a medallion also?

"And now, my loyal subjects," Godwin said. "There is the matter of bestowing the title of Grand Protectorate of the Realm, as well as the giving away of my daughter, Lady Emalia, in marriage, to whom is the most richly deserving. My son, the noble Prince Hilderith, will speak on this matter."

The prince stepped forward, Eberwulf behind him with arms crossed, consternation on his features. Vandil's heart pounded, a heaviness settling in his abdomen as the prince spoke.

"Ladies and lords of the court, we have convened in council before this ceremony and determined who the recipient of this title, as well as the hand of my sister, shall be. Our laws state this man is of noble birth, and who has saved the king's life from mortal peril." An impressive silence filled the chamber, Vandil swallowing hard, as the anticipation could be sliced with a sword. "Unfortunately, because of current circumstances, we cannot give the title and marriage. We are still in deliberation."

A murmuring fell over the crowd, which the prince silenced. "In the meantime, please enjoy the pleasantries and feasting. We are still in negotiations with King Aratheus and Earl Valamir, and treaties are currently being drawn. Rest assured, we will make our decision before they are signed."

Godwin raised his hand. "But now, enjoy your victory! Let us toast to the ensured prosperity of the Eastern Goths!"

Vandil stood in deep suspicion as the court moved and mingled around him. The king exited with his entourage. Now was Vandil's chance. He followed the king back to his royal apartments but was obstructed by a pair of halberd-wielding guards.

"Your Majesty!" Vandil called from between them. The king paused and turned. "A word, if you please, Your Majesty."

The king motioned the guards aside. "Yes, Vandil, what is it?"

Vandil crossed to him and lowered his voice. "I wish to thank you once again for this fine gift, sire," he said. "In all my years of service to you, have I ever asked anything of you?"

"Never," Godwin said.

"Then let me make known my request: I wish to take your daughter's hand in marriage, my lord."

The king inhaled and straightened, regarding Vandil with cool blue eyes. "There is none more deserving, for it was your tactics and not Eberwulf's that saved my life that day. I shall think about it. In the meantime, continue performing your station dutifully, as I shall have need of you in the coming days. Treasure that amulet, for it shall give you more power than any shall ever know."

Vandil was struck by the cryptic words, yet it was the only answer he could expect. "I thank you, my lord." He gave Godwin a curt nod and walked away.

The next day

Vandil leaned on a wall in the barracks, turning his medallion over in his hands. Tiny emeralds encircled a larger one in the center of the bronze surface. It was beautiful and could fetch a sum greater than a soldier's pay for a year.

Eberwulf descended the spiral staircase that opened into the knights' common room and commanded their attention. Vandil stood and presented himself, Eberwulf meeting his gaze.

"The king has ordered us and a score of the One Hundred to the enemy's main camp where we are to issue the terms of peace discussed by our council."

"As you wish, my lord," Vandil said. He looked behind him and commanded the One Hundred to ready themselves. "I need twenty of you. We march to the enemy's camp!"

Eberwulf's gaze fell to the medallion and made a snide face. "Don't think that trinket is anything more than a decoration. You shall always remain a Knight-Captain—if even that."

Vandil's jaw tightened. He thought of pressing the champion further for his meaning when twenty men in chain mail and conical helms approached.

"Ready, Captain!" one of them said.

"We ride," said Vandil.

"You haven't won," Aratheus said, taking the rolled parchment from Vandil and sending him a scowl. He and Eberwulf stood in a pavilion tent adorned in the red and gold colors of the Aragoths, their king seated at a wooden table strewn with maps and letters. He was old like Godwin, with a braided black beard streaked with silver and dark chestnut eyes, dressed in a fine robe. Rather foolish, Vandil thought, to be stripped of armor while in enemy territory.

Another man stood with arms folded in the shadows of the tent, clad in his war gear.

"Just look over the terms, Your Grace," Vandil said, unfurling the parchment. "You will be summoned a few days hence to the castle for the official signing, along with Earl Valamir." Vandil glanced at the brooding man behind Aratheus.

The king's eyes swept the parchment and uttered a snarl of contempt, slamming the paper to the table, drawing a scoff from Eberwulf.

"The terms are not agreeable to you, my lord?" Eberwulf asked.

"The Goths will be united under one banner. It was the dying wish of the man who was father to me, Valamir, and your king," Aratheus said, gesturing to the earl. "These terms will continue to see division among us brothers! Godwin spits on the memory of our father!"

"I don't pretend to know the machinations of politicians, Your Grace," Vandil said. "But I am certain Godwin has his reasons for this so-called division. Perhaps he understands that three siblings squabbling over wealth and power will not be good for the Gothic people in the end. Godwin rules his own country, and I believe he does so justly."

Yet even as he uttered these words, Vandil felt a cold tingle through his fingers, his mouth tasting sour.

"Theodoric II was a fool to think Goth-land would be unified," Eberwulf said. "Are our countries not separated by thousands of leagues?"

Aratheus and Valamir fumed under their breaths, the king clenching his fist.

"You have our terms, Your Graces," Vandil said with finality. "We will expect your arrival at the signing."

"If you find our terms unfavorable to you, we can always rout you from Sargoth itself," Eberwulf said. He slammed the butt of his halberd into the frozen soil and his face twisted into a sadistic glee. "We could have your heads on pikes in a trice."

Vandil sent him a disapproving stare. There was no need to threaten violence. Aratheus lowered his head and sighed, while Valamir sent Eberwulf a rueful stare. "Very well," Aratheus said. "We'll arrive once summoned."

"Good," Vandil said. The Sargoths returned to the castle, an uncomfortable silence spanning the journey.

The Day of the Signing

Vandil and the One Hundred were summoned to the grand audience chamber where the signing was to occur. Security was tight, and extra guards were posted throughout the hallways. Many delegates from both sides filed into the chamber and sat at the long tables, along with Aratheus and Valamir.

At length, King Godwin and Prince Hilderith joined them, and Vandil noted Emalia's absence. Understandable, as the talk would be of tributes and taxations. Vandil couldn't dream of the princess suffering through such bored. He felt the hairs on his neck prickle as Eberwulf followed the prince. They took their places at an elevated platform, the Sargothic banners hanging beside them.

Godwin raised his hands for the gathering to be silent and made an announcement commemorating this glorious day of peace. The long-time feud between the Goths would, at last, be at an end.

"Though our kingdom is divided into many nations, let us stand unified in peace and the continued prosperity of our people," Godwin said. He gestured to his son. The prince took his place beside his father, a smile on his face that didn't reach his eyes. His golden hair hung straight to his shoulders, where it gently curled.

Vandil caught a snide glance from Eberwulf. Vandil's heart raced; he swallowed hard as Hilderith raised his hand over the crowd. "Good people: as a symbol of the strength and unity of our nations, we have given the honorable title of Grand Protectorate of the Realm to our most distinguished warrior," he said. Hilderith motioned for Eberwulf to stand beside him as Vandil looked on in horror. The prince raised Eberwulf's gauntleted hand like a conquering hero. "Henceforth, this distinguished title falls to none other than Eberwulf, Champion of Sargoth!"

The crowd erupted in dull applause; the Aragoths clapping as a show of courtesy. Vandil's mouth dropped—a sudden coldness gathering in his core and spreading. He felt dizzy and his knees weakened. He felt he would collapse under the weight of his armor.

How could this be? Why does a pompous ass deserve the title and not me?

Godwin stood beside the two of them, clapping with a broad smile. He motioned toward the edge of the chamber where Lady Emalia entered, holding a wreath of flowers. She looked beautiful, yet Vandil couldn't stomach the sight. Acid rose in his throat.

Godwin took his daughter's hand as she cast her gaze downward, placing the wreath around Eberwulf's forearm, symbolizing their union. Eberwulf couldn't look more pleased as he cast a smug grin at Vandil.

"I have given my fair daughter Emalia in marriage to the Grand Protectorate," the king declared. "The ceremony will occur in the days following the treaty signing, and I wish all of you to be in attendance."

Vandil's pulse slowed, an emptiness filling his chest. His breathing became shallow as fatigue flowed through his muscles. He couldn't bear to attend the ceremony, even though he would be expected to. His stomach burned. His vision went spotty. But what could he have done? Such are the ways of the world, he told himself. Those who are cunning, wealthy, and powerful enough take what they do not deserve, while the deserving are cast aside because of circumstances beyond their control.

Is it because I am a so-called bastard? Of low birth?

Vandil cursed the truth of Eberwulf's words. He would rise no higher than his current station, and his medallion was only a token. Vandil contemplated tearing the trinket from his chest and casting it from him.

Still, he straightened himself and brought his hands together to applaud the newly betrothed. Perhaps he could attain his deserved laurels elsewhere. For now, as his mouth only filled with bitterness, he fought the urge to spit. He excused himself from the treaty signing, placing his most trusted sergeant in charge of security. His skin was still crawling with disgust when he left the castle, an icy wind blasting his aching body.

Vandil found the tavern soon enough, his heavy footfalls dragging through the piling snow. It had been coming down in thick flakes since before the signing had begun. Vandil had witnessed many signings over the years; he didn't need to see another.

Inside, he brushed off the cold and sat down, signaling to a barmaid. She brought him a tankard of ale, which he downed in short order. She brought him another, then another, and another. Soon, a half-circle of tankards formed around him as he belched. He paused as the effects of the alcohol set in. His head felt heavy, and he was about to fall over in his seat when a heavy hand clapped him on the back.

Startled, Vandil took in the sight of Earl Valamir and his men through a haze of ale as they took their seats around them. There was even a buxom woman in fur and leather armor, tresses like raven quills, with a sallow complexion and narrow eyes. She was no Goth at all.

"Interesting finding you here," the earl said in a cheerful tone. His disposition was quite unlike their previous engagement.

"Why is that interesting?" Vandil asked with slurred speech.

"I saw your face when your king announced the Grand Protectorate of the Realm," he paused conspiratorially, "and his marriage to Emalia."

Vandil belched his contempt. He needn't answer the Earl's speculations. Let him think what he wants.

Valamir continued, "Are you not the Knight-Captain of Godwin's famed 'One Hundred?' You must be the greatest warrior in the realm to have earned such a position. Why now do you stand eclipsed?"

"What do you want, my lord?" Vandil growled.

Valamir smirked. "Don't be that way. We are bound by blood as Goths. We should always welcome one another to table and drink."

Valamir ordered a round of drinks for himself and his men, offering to pay for Vandil's as well.

"It's not fair!" Vandil growled, slamming a fist on the table. "I should have earned that title! It was my strategy that saved Godwin's life. He even told me so himself! It was stolen from me!"

"I couldn't agree more," Valamir said. "Even I was impressed by your cunning in defeating our army. A man such as you would deserve of any title—or marriage."

Vandil sighed, his stomach forming a hard knot. Why was he confiding in an enemy?

Was he an enemy? The peace treaty would no longer make him so.

"And yet I am a commoner," Vandil continued. "A bastard, I'm told. Everything is being taken from me. I fear even my days as Knight-Captain are numbered." Finding his ale running low, he raised his hand for another flagon, but Valamir lowered it as if to say, "enough." Vandil scowled. "Please, just leave me to my drink, my lord."

But Valamir only leaned in, his voice low. "I, too, tire of the injustice in these lands. The Goths should be united, not signing treaties of division where one king pays tribute to another."

"You're speaking to the wrong man, Your Grace."

"Am I? If you accept my forthcoming proposal, we can both have justice in this unfair world."

Vandil looked at him askance. "What is your meaning?"

"If you help me usurp Godwin's throne, I will give you everything you desire and more. You'll have your own title, your own land; I'll even annul Emalia's marriage to Eberwulf and place her in your hands."

Vandil downed the last of his ale but sputtered at Valamir's statement. "Are you mad? I would never betray my lord! And never would Emalia marry one who harmed her father and brother!"

"There are other women besides Emalia"

"Be silent, my lord!"

Valamir rose from the table with his men. "Think on it, Knight-Captain. Think Zsaon it."

"Never. I should report you to Godwin for your treachery this very night. You jeopardize the peace with such plotting."

The earl chuckled, his thick charcoal beard nearly eclipsing his tight smile. "Report me? Who would believe a drunken lout like you? You would only sound like a jealous lunatic inventing a conspiracy to overturn the prince's ruling. Everyone would see through it. And besides—" Vandil felt the point of a dagger on his back. Valamir continued, his tone sinister."And I would see you cut down before you could even raise such alarm."

The earl and his men left Vandil to his tankards, but not before the sultry woman sat next to him. She caressed his face, placing his hand on her breast. Vandil did not resist.

When Vandil next awoke, golden sunlight slanted into the room from the shuttered windows as he stared into the narrow dark eyes of the mystery woman.

"Ohayou," she said in a foreign tongue. Vandil jolted from the bed, realizing his nakedness as he wrapped a bed sheet around him. He scrambled to dress himself, uncaring for the bemused expression the voluptuous woman wore.

What have I done? I 'll be flogged for such disorderly conduct!

A furious hangover exploded in Vandil's brain as he hurried in a disheveled state towards the castle, struggling to make himself more presentable. He had left the foreign woman in the room, hoping he hadn't imperiled himself.

Vandil sloshed through the fresh-fallen snow, the cold wetness seeping into his boots from being laced improperly. He staggered along the causeway and stone bridge leading into the castle courtyard, passing under a raised portcullis. He located the entrance into the guard barracks in one of the round towers that loomed over the courtyard.

Inside the arched wooden door, he descended the spiral stairs that led into the underground barracks, where he found his men cleaning their equipment or sweeping the flagstone floors. They stood at attention upon seeing him.

Out of breath, Vandil asked, "What happened? Was the treaty signed?"

"Negotiations are still being held, captain," one of them said, not meeting Vandil's gaze.

Vandil's throat burned, sobriety creeping back into his head. His stomach contracted, beads of cold sweat forming on his brow. "Where is the king? "

"The king is likely in the audience chamber, and we are off duty."

Vandil had to find Godwin. He prayed with all his might that the king had not noticed his absence with so much going on. Rushing into the barracks, he found a basin and splashed water on his face. He also found a mirror and straightened his hair and clothing.

What excuse should he give for his absence? He put a replacement on watch, after all. Should he lie to his king and invent something?

He turned on his heel and was about to race for the audience chamber when Prince Hilderith appeared at the base of the stairs, his eyes smoldering with anger upon seeing the Knight-Captain. The frozen silence hung in the air for what seemed an eternity until Hilderith spoke. "Knight-Captain Vandil… come with me."

"Y—yes, my lord." Vandil hung his head and followed the king to a private chamber Vandil hadn't known existed. In all his years living in this castle, he'd found the number of secret rooms was beyond the counting. This new room was richly appointed—with bookshelves, a desk, and the king's banners.

"Where were you last night?" the prince demanded.

What was Vandil to say? He was at a tavern drinking and whoring when he was supposed to protect his king? Vandil straightened and said, "I suspected a plot to overthrow you, my lord, and had to investigate." As he said this, Eberwulf entered the room, peering down at Vandil with contempt.

The king looked incredulous. "A plot to overthrow me? By whom?"

"Earl Valamir, my lord. I found the rascal in a tavern, and—after a few drinks—he told me everything."

Eberwulf leaned in close to Vandil. "I smell alcohol on you, Knight-Captain. And a woman's brogue. Methinks it was you the one drinking."

"I noticed you leave the moment I announced my daughter's marriage and Eberwulf received his title," Hilderith said. "Curious that you got an inkling of this 'plot' immediately afterward. You desired my sister as well, did you not?"

Vandil felt trapped. "I have nothing to say in my defense, my lord; only my word as evidence that Valamir is plotting against you."

Hilderith waved his hand. "Take him to the dungeon, Eberwulf. I am relieving you, Vandil, of your station as Knight-Captain. It shall, of course, fall to Eberwulf."

Eberwulf smirked once again, as though he knew this would happen. A lance of pain pierced Vandil's chest. The coldness he felt at Emalia's betrothal spread through him once again with more chill than a crypt.

As Eberwulf escorted him away., Hilderith called out, "And let that medallion hang about your neck as a reminder of the weight of your oath and duty."

As Vandil stewed in his cell, he felt nothing but hatred and revulsion. For himself, for his king, for Eberwulf, and the world. Stripped of his armor, title, and place among the One Hundred, he had nothing left but the amulet Godwin had given him: a gift now pronounced a curse.

Alone with his thoughts, he remembered Valamir's offer.

Hours faded into days before anyone gave him so much as a morsel of bread. Had his king forgotten him? Was his punishment to be so severe?

Vandil awakened to the sound of clashing steel and a faint groan. The mystery woman stood at the bars of his cell, clad in her supple leather armor. Adrenaline rushed through Vandil's limbs as he forced his aching legs to stand.

Before Vandil could speak, the woman said, "What shall I tell my master? Have you reconsidered his offer?" Vandil marveled at her skilled intonation of the Gothic language, so absent that fateful morning, yet he froze. If he refused again, justice might never be done. He'd continue rotting in this cell. That he could not abide.

"Yes, my lady," Vandil whispered. "I will help him overthrow the king."

She simply smiled and unlocked the door with a creak. Vandil armed himself with a pair of swords from the trail of dead guards leading to the entrance.

Who was this woman? Vandil threw a leather jerkin over his torso and fitted himself in boots and gauntlets. It was going to be a bloodbath.

"Wait here," the woman said as they left the dungeon. "I'll signal to the men."

Moments later, a band of foreign agents and mercenaries were lined behind her, a few dozen dressed in furs, leather, and chain mail with the occasional breastplate and shield.

"Where's Valamir?" Vandil asked.

"In the treaty room. This needs to look… natural," the woman said.

"And who are you?"

"I'm called Izumi," she said.

Vandil and his newfound allies drew their weapons, Izumi producing two long curved swords that looked unlike anything the Goths wielded. They proceeded down the corridors, systematically and ruthlessly cutting down everyone in their path, slipping into side rooms silencing anyone who might discover what they were about. Izumi moved with deadly fluidity, spraying blood across the walls and ceilings with each fatal stroke of her blades.

It was at that moment a scullery maid glanced down the hall and screamed, dropping the tray of sweets she had prepared for the treaty negotiations. Vandil cursed as a mercenary aimed a crossbow down the hall and fired.

The maid turned to flee as the bolt thudded into her back, yet she could stagger to a doorway leading into the audience chamber.

The doors opened as she expired on the threshold, drawing a chorus of gasps and murmurings from the chamber beyond.

"What is this?" a voice echoed. "Is there an intruder?"

"We're under attack!" cried another.

An unpleasant cold tingle ran the length of Vandil's spine. His stomach roiled as the guards were called to search everywhere. *Maybe this wasn't such a good idea after all,* Vandil thought. Yet, he was committed. If he was found in his current state—escaped from the dungeon with a band of heathens led by a woman from who-knows-where—he would be executed for treason.

I must see this through to the end. I will not tolerate my unjust treatment.

With Izumi at this side, he broke through the doors into the audience chamber, the mercenaries behind them trampling the body of the kitchen maid. They felled the bewildered guards to the left and right.. Vandil memorized each terrified face as he cut down man after man. He knew what they must have been thinking: why in all the Inferno would the Knight-Captain slaughter his own men?

But Vandil was Knight-Captain no longer. Eberwulf and Godwin had seen to that.

Vandil picked out the king from the mass of shrieking delegates as they scrambled from their seats for any available exit. They fought and clawed over each other, the room erupting in a miniature war as Godwin stared in utter horror and disbelief. Vandil raced towards him, shoving aside or cutting down all in his way.

Prince Hilderith stood before him, sharing his father's terror, pointing at him. "Stop, Vandil! I order you, in the king's name!"

Hilderith's hand flew from the stump of his arm in one smooth slice of Vandil's sword, followed by a spinning motion that took the prince's head along with it. The head flew onto the table, splattering the documents and fine tablecloth as Vandil closed in for his target. Members of the One Hundred streamed through the doors, making their way toward the treasonous Vandil.

An outraged Eberwulf leaped over the tables, brandishing his halberd, muttering obscenities and curses unintelligible over the din. Heat swelled in Vandil's abdomen, and his jaw clenched. He shrugged off the soreness in his muscles as he ducked under the swipe of Eberwulf's halberd. The thought of killing Eberwulf enticed a smile from his lips. As the champion and new Knight-Captain recovered the hefty swing of his weapon, Vandil brought down a mighty stroke that Eberwulf was forced to block with the haft of the polearm.

The slash tore through the wooden haft. A stunned Eberwulf now held both ends of the weapon: a makeshift battle axe in one hand, and a short staff in the other.

"I was always the better warrior," Vandil said through gritted teeth. "I deserved that title, not you! Your tactics failed in the fateful battle!"

Eberwulf smirked. "So, that's what this is about? I always knew your low birth would—"

"And I'll wipe that grin off your face once and for all!"

Vandil knocked Eberwulf's broken blade to one side and thrust his other sword into the hollow at the base of his throat. Blood gushed over the tip of the blade as Vandil withdrew it. Eberwulf's shocked expression was the last thing Vandil saw before rushing toward Godwin. The king's cries of "defend your king" went unheeded as Izumi and the mercenaries slew the sons of the One Hundred all about him.

Godwin fled for an exit, only to be slashed from behind. When Godwin hit the floor, he rolled onto his back, his massive girth exposed to Vandil's blades and blood pooling beneath him.

"V—Vandil, my son…" Godwin said.

Vandil leaned an ear closer. "What?" Did Godwin just name Vandil his son?

"I—I gave you more power than Hilderith and Eberwulf would ever have…"

Vandil stood perplexed at the cryptic message. Did he just call Vandil his son? That would mean he just cut down his own father and half-brother.

What have I done?

Godwin's face paled as his eyes glassed over. A roar behind Vandil shook him from the shock of his killing; Vandil turned to intercept a lethal strike from one of the One Hundred. On instinct, Vandil's blade deflected the attack and skewered the man with his off-hand.

Across the bloody room, Aratheus made for an exit as Valamir entered. The earl's gaze swept the room until it landed on Vandil. Valamir jabbed a finger at him. "There's the traitor! Kill him! How dare he betray his king!"

A heaviness spread through Vandil's stomach, his knees weakening. Cold realization set in. This was a setup.

"No…" Vandil whispered.

More of the Hundred filled the room and sped towards him. They were trained by Vandil himself, the finest warriors. They formed a half-circle around him and pressed in from all sides. He needed to escape. He was betrayed. This wasn't supposed to happen!

In desperation, Vandil looked for an open door. As the Hundred closed in to attack, Vandil had no choice but to defend himself. Parry and counter. Parry and counter. So it went until man after man fell at the disgraced captain's feet.

He was soon overwhelmed, and weapons bit his flesh. The One Hundred's faces showed horror and sadness at what they were forced to do.

Vandil backpedaled as he fended off each attacker, adrenaline rushing through his every muscle and delivering strike after lethal strike to his former brethren until a curved blood-stained blade burst through Vandil's chest from behind.

"Never trust a woman," a soft feminine voice said in his ear. Izumi ripped the blade free and pressed her foot into the small of Vandil's back, sending him to the floor. Vandil rolled onto his back in a growing pool of his own blood, the castle ceiling and the circle of the Hundred's faces gazing down at him at his last sight.

Izumi's laughter faded away.

II

Frigid cold gripped Vandil's bones. Darkness enveloped him. He was faintly aware of his fingertips scratching against a tightly wound cloth. Vandil clawed at his moorings until he scraped at the hardened soil. A numbness consumed him. He couldn't feel his arms or legs. He was only aware of a weight pressing around him.

He railed against it, clawing his way through the crumbling dirt. Strength flowed through his limbs the like of which he'd never experienced before. Soil packed around his face and eyes, though he tasted nothing.

At length, in a last show of power, his hand burst through the topsoil, filling the hole with snow. Vandil tore through the ground until his arm broke free of the earth. The full moon greeted his return to the living world, and he passed his skeletal fingers before the pale circle.

Vandil formed a bony fist. He pulled the rest of his skeleton from the grave. It was simple and unadorned: the burial place of a traitor. He had slain everyone he'd once held fealty towards, and many of those loyal to him, in a fit of jealousy and rage. Vandil climbed to his feet, still shod with the boots he wore when he was killed.

Killed? The thought struck him like a mace to the skull. He had died. Yet, here he stood, gazing upon his armor. He reached beneath his breastplate to handle the bronze medallion still affixed to his neck. Its emeralds twinkled in the moonlight.

Was this the power that had returned him from the dead? Was this the meaning of Godwin's dying words?

How long had he been dead? Long enough for his flesh to rot away until only browned bones remained. What had transpired in the meantime? Vandil took several steps forward to accustom himself to his new form; beholding it in revulsion. He wobbled on his skeletal legs. Though his hairless cranium was undoubtedly hollow, something resembling a thought swirled into his mind.

Valamir. He was the real traitor. Justice must be visited upon him, but how would Vandil return to the castle when humanity would utterly reject him?

A scream pierced the still cemetery. A distant grave-keeper made the sign of the Triangle over his chest before running off into the night. He would no doubt alert a passing patrol and tell them of the undead abomination he had witnessed. Would they believe him and descend upon Vandil's newly risen bones?

Vandil would need to defend himself, but he noted his lack of weapons. If he remembered correctly, a guard outpost stood nearby and would contain all the arms and armor he would need to enact his revenge.

He pulled his burial shroud from his shallow grave and wrapped it about him like a cloak, covering his head like a hood. He staggered through the crunchy snow until he made his way into the village proper. If he could find a smithy, he might slip in unnoticed and secure a weapon.

Rows of houses and shops stood at the entrance and proceeded deeper into the town until Vandil came to the tavern in which he met his assassin. He crossed to the window and caught his reflection: an eternally grinning skull with two pinpoints of blue light staring back at him.

Inside, patrons screamed at the appearance of death's head in the window. They hurried to barricade the door, and Vandil recognized the grave-keeper pointing at him with a terrified look. In life, Vandil's breath might have misted the window on a night like this, but now only a sepulchral hiss flowed through his unhinging jaw.

"S-stop!" came a shout from behind. A ring of guards bearing Valamir's coat of arms approached him, pointing spears or drawing swords.

Vandil held out his bony hand. "Weapons," he whispered, marveling at his ability to even speak with no tongue or vocal cords. It was as though his soul itself was speaking. "Give me your weapons!"

"No! We must end this abomination!"

The five guards pressed in, yet Vandil stood impassable. Could he no longer feel fear or other human emotions now that he was the living dead? As the first guard thrust his spear towards him, Vandil reacted nimbly, light on his skeletal feet. He found he possessed the same combat prowess as he knew in life, side-stepping the point and grabbing the haft. With the strength of five men, he snapped off the tip.

Wielding the improvised dagger, Vandil threw it into the guard's forehead, dropping him into the snow. The other guards glanced at each other before rushing in. Vandil ducked under their swings and dodged their thrusts. He pulled a sword from the slain guard's belt and flourished it before the others. They glanced at each other again before running off into the night.

"Cowards," Vandil muttered. He doffed his burial shroud for the fallen guard's wool cloak. Grafburg Castle loomed above him against the moon. The guards would surely alert Valamir, and he would send reinforcements.

Unless Vandil struck first.

He made his way to the guard outpost at the edge of town, a round tower attached to an open-air rotunda with an arched wooden door leading into the tower atop a flight of steps. A pair of guards carrying torches patrolled the perimeter.

Vandil emerged from the darkness into the range of their torches. Their faces paled as they made the sign of the Triangle on their chests. Vandil pointed his sword at the pair as he advanced. The guards exchanged worried glances and drew their swords.

"What foul sorcery is at work here?" a guard said. Trembling, they both rushed in with battle cries. Vandil parried one attack and returned a fatal slash across the guard's throat. The other thrust his torch toward Vandil's eye sockets.

Vandil hissed as lost his bearings, unable to defend himself from the cut to his ribcage that followed. Pieces of bone flew from the skeleton's body as he staggered backward. Vandil shook the dazzling embers from his vision and circled the soldier, studying his footwork, looking to exploit his defenses.

"Lady Izumi!" the guard screamed. "Intruder!" The familiar name filled Vandil's head: Izumi, the woman who killed him from behind.

An alarm bell rang from the top of the guard tower. "You're finished, creature," the guard said. "Soon the king's men will be upon you!"

Vandil's burning orbs reflected in the guard's helmet blazed at the mention of the king. "King? Who is the king?"

"So, the devil-man can speak! King Valamir, of course!"

Vandil hissed, his fist clenched. So Valamir had usurped Godwin's throne, using Vandil to do so and then betraying him once the threats had been eliminated. Vandil would burn this garrison so bright the new king would be sure to see it. But first, to get through his guards!

With a surge of unearthly speed, Vandil lunged, stabbing the man through the chest. As he fell backward, the tower door opened, admitting a stream of guards. They fanned out in a circle as they closed in on Vandil. A sleek figure on horseback charged from the garrison's stables, kicking up snow while galloping for Vandil. Vandil wrenched the guard's sword from his death grip so he had a matching pair.

The rider dismounted upon arrival, a cascade of jet-black tresses spilling from beneath her helmet. Two crossed swords lay on her back, her leather armor reinforced with warm fur. She drew one sword, the remaining guards completing their circle around them. There must have been three scores.

"What are you, creature?" Izumi asked, pointing the blade at him. Vandil stood silent; motionless, the chill wind playing with his cloak. Izumi advanced, the tip aimed at Vandil's missing heart. "I suppose you cannot tell me who or what you are, but it matters not. I'll cut you down and the peace will be restored."

As Izumi drew closer, the emblem on her breast glinted in the torchlight: the badge of the Grand Protectorate of the Realm.

Vandil's jaw unhinged with a low hiss. What injustice.

But since Eberwulf had fallen by Vandil's hand, the position had stood vacant. Only to be promptly filled by Valamir's bitch. If Vandil slew Izumi now, he could pluck the emblem from her undeserving corpse. But what good would such a title be in undeath?

Izumi jabbed with her blade, Vandil stepping backward. He raised his swords in defense, Izumi leading him through a routine of parries and thrusts. With one sword, Izumi could fend off Vandil's counters. She sliced at Vandil's knee, cutting his skeletal leg from his femur. He dropped to the snow, prompting a chorus of cheers from the guards. A deathly wail escaped Vandil's jaws, making the guards flinch as he supported himself on one sword.

"Farewell, creature…" Izumi said, towering over him, poised to cut off his skull.

Arrows peppered the circle of guards, shafts protruding from their heads, necks, chests, and arms. Izumi's horse even caught one in the flank. It whinnied in pain and charged off into the dark.

Izumi cursed and whirled away from Vandil, searching for the arrows' source. Another streaked towards her, and she sliced from midair. Seeing a momentary advantage, Vandil grabbed his leg and crawled through the snow. If he could make it to his grave, perhaps the soil would regenerate him. Yet, at Vandil's slow pace, it could take him hours to reach his grave.

Cries of guards floated around him. They retreated within the safety of their garrison as the bruised blues of dawn lightened the horizon. What effect would the rising sun have upon Vandil's skeletal form? Would he, like a vampire, burn in its rays?

As he crawled from the battle, another gathering of men enclosed about him. They were clad in the red and gold colors of King Aratheus, carrying bows and arrows. A commanding presence alerted Vandil to a stocky man in war gear coming nearer. His gaze swept the area until it landed on the skeleton.

"Take him," Aratheus said. His men hurried over to seize and drag him away. He fought against them, flailing his thin arms.

"Don't struggle!" a man said.

"We just saved you from destruction," said another.

Vandil hopped along on one leg, being supported by the other two. If he wanted answers, he would need to cooperate, even as they hooded him and all went dark. He was thrown into a carriage and taken to what he assumed was a building somewhere in the city.

Aratheus' men forced Vandil into a chair and pulled the hood from his head. Aratheus sat across from him at a wooden table lit by torches and candles. Sunlight filtered through boarded-up windows. The surrounding men gasped at his skeletal form.

"We shouldn't do this, m'lord," came a distant voice. "We should just destroy him."

"Silence," Aratheus replied, his gaze still affixed to the skeleton. "I think our new friend here will be quite useful to us."

"What is this?" Vandil demanded in a low hiss. "Explain yourself."

"I don't believe we've been formally introduced; I am King Aratheus of Aragoth. In life, you presented the terms of peace to my brother Valamir and me, along with that fool Eberwulf." Vandil nodded as the memories returned. Valamir continued, "You are a most unusual creature—one I don't understand—but one that can help both of us get what we want."

Vandil sank back in his chair, resting the point of his bony chin in his hand. "Go on."

"I was there at the signing when you stormed the room and slaughtered everyone in your path."

"How do you know that was me?"

"I stood mesmerized by the way you fought Valamir's men back at the garrison. I recalled the same style used at the signing. Are you not Vandil, the Knight-Captain?" Vandil's silence answered the question. "I saw you betrayed and stabbed through the back by Valamir's harlot. The same happened to me—figuratively, of course."

"What do you mean?"

"When Godwin died, the throne should have fallen to me, yet Valamir seized it and proclaimed himself king. He betrayed me, his own brother, and I desire you to help me reclaim it."

Vandil sighed. "I've heard this talk before. How do I know you won't betray and destroy me once I've done this?"

"You have little choice. What chance do you have assaulting Grafburg Castle alone and slaying Valamir?"

Vandil crossed his arms.

"Exactly," Aratheus continued. "You will need help. I have an entire army gathered on the outskirts of the castle while these new treaties are being negotiated. Valamir seeks nothing less than the throne of Sargoth!"

Vandil rolled his head back, a hissing laugh escaping his jaws. "I call into question your ability to deliver the promised reinforcements, seeing how you fared in the last battle."

Aratheus shook his head. "My mistake in attacking the castle the first time was spreading my forces too thin. I thought I could take the castle with the men I had, but you surprised me."

"What has transpired since my passing?"

"It's been a month to the day," the king eyed Vandil warily, "Though your… state might imply it had been longer. Valamir told me to return to Aragoth, though I wanted the Sargothic throne as well. Valamir grew jealous but told me not to fear. For at that time, he professed commitment to the realization of our father's dream: unity between the Goths."

Vandil could only think of the unity between the woman that was deprived of him. "What of Emalia?" he asked.

"Valamir possesses her. He wanted her all along. Such was the true reason he started this war. He told me he wanted unity among the Goths, but that was a lie. I was used. If you wish justice done, I would have you join me."

Vandil lowered his head. Though he could never hold Emalia and feel her soft flesh, he would not see her in the arms of some lech like Valamir—more than twice her age, and her uncle besides. If Vandil had a stomach, it would have turned.

He would see her free of Valamir. "Very well. I'll join you."

Aratheus smiled with a sigh of relief. "Excellent. We can mobilize on the morrow."

"I have one final contention, however," Vandil said. He produced the medallion from beneath his armor. "This was given to me by Godwin. I believe its strange power returned me from the dead."

"Perhaps it's because Godwin was your father. That makes me your uncle. I thought I saw some family resemblance…"

"Explain."

"Godwin wanted you to have the kingdom and no one else—even though you are a bastard. Your mother was a chambermaid within Godwin's household. He must have enchanted the medallion so that not even death would keep you from what was rightfully yours. That medallion will see justice done. Perhaps it can restore your body as well."

Vandil placed the fractured leg to his knee joint, and as they connected. An eldritch green light fused the bones together. Vandil stood and placed his full weight on it. If he had flesh upon his face, a grin of satisfaction would have appeared.

"And Hilderith?" Vandil asked.

"The prince was the only legitimate child and looked down on you without you even knowing who you were. Hilderith likely appointed Eberwulf to ensure you would never rise too high."

Vandil reeled at the implications. This was why he was always being eclipsed by the prince's champion. The prince plotted against his half-brother for control of the country and couldn't allow Vandil to discover his true heritage.

The undead warrior hung his head as recollections of killing his brother flooded his mind. Valamir had tricked him into doing so.

He must be slain.

Aratheus rose. "I understand this is a weighty matter for you. I will leave you to your thoughts." As the king went out, he paused and returned with a horned barbute helm and placed it on the table. He smirked. "I think this will complement your appearance nicely."

A few days later

Vandil approached Aratheus in his war tent as he pored over a map of the surrounding lands, showing Grafburg and its castle at the center.

"We can attack the castle as we did last time," he said, tapping the parchment. "And with no Eberwulf or Vandil helping them, I am confident of our victory."

"This will plunge the Gothlands into war once more," Vandil noted, "when many have died to see its peace."

"Is the cost of justice worth it to you?" Aratheus asked. "If you think the toll is too high, then drop your vendetta against my kin. But if justice isn't sought, peace will reign between the two kingdoms. The people will be happy without war, but traitors will go unpunished. Is this what you want?"

"Justice must prevail no matter the cost," Vandil said.

Aratheus nodded and returned to his map. "I've been scouting the area for the past few days. Valamir has increased security throughout the castle and its surroundings since the incident at the garrison. He has forces encamped here and here. It won't be like last time. He's expecting us. He also has Lady Izumi commanding the One Hundred."

"But is she a competent strategist?" Vandil asked, his tone bitter. "'Never trust a woman.' Her words, not mine."

Aratheus stared back at Vandil.

"Riders approach!" came a shout from outside. The pounding of hooves preceded a score of horsemen, with Izumi leading them. The fluttering banners displaying Valamir's coat of arms announced them as peace delegates.

Aratheus motioned for Vandil to hide as Izumi dismounted. If she knew Vandil stood with them, matters could get… complicated. The undead warrior hid behind an Aragothic tapestry. Izumi strode into the tent with the presence of a commanding officer, scroll in hand, and slapped it on the table in front of Aratheus.

He took the scroll and unfurled it. "What's this?"

"Terms of your surrender. On orders of King Valamir, you are to disband your army and return to Aragoth. If you are not out of the country within three days, it will be considered an act of war against His Majesty."

"Preposterous," Aratheus exclaimed. "His army alone cannot hold these lands. He needs reinforcements and conscripts!"

"These are the terms," Izumi said with finality.

Vandil clenched his fist. He stepped out from behind the tapestry and appeared before Izumi. Her eyes widened and stepped backward.

"Vandil!" Aratheus said.

"Apologies, my lady, but we cannot accept your terms," Vandil said, his voice like a haunting wind.

"V—Vandil?" she stuttered. "The Vandil who died in the battle to usurp Godwin's throne?"

"The same," he said. "The one that you killed."

Izumi's hand drifted to a sword on her waist. "The same I defeated at the garrison…"

"We will not accept your terms," Vandil continued. "You cannot win as you do not have superior forces. We will blockade your city's supply routes until your people starve. Tell Valamir he must surrender and put Aratheus on the throne, as he was the rightful successor in the event of Godwin and Prince Hilderith's deaths. Tell him also that I am returned from the grave to kill those who betrayed me: 'King' Valamir and you."

"This isn't possible..." Izumi said. She staggered backward as Vandil willed his eye sockets to blaze with a hellish flame.

"Go!" he rasped. All in the tent stood rooted to the ground, the color drained from their faces. Izumi turned and ran from the tent, mounted her horse, and rode off with the remnants of the One Hundred.

"Well, that was a fine blunder," Aratheus said once they were gone.

"We just bought ourselves some time," Vandil argued. "We need a plan to take the castle."

"What do you suggest?"

"I know this castle better than the Aragoths. I'll take some men through a secret passage near the moat and attack the castle from within, while your primary force prepares to meet Valamir outside the city. While inside the city, we can set the town on fire to create confusion and divide attention elsewhere. We should also rescue Emalia."

Aratheus shook his head. "We'll fare better as a united force. Burning the town is undesirable. I seek to rule these people, and they will not accept a king who will fire their homes. As for Emalia, she must be left to her fate."

"Very well, you come up with your own plan," Vandil said. "Keep in mind your tactics failed against this city when I was of its ranks. I'm going to save Emalia.... For at least I still have a heart."

Vandil stalked from the tent into the snowy camp. "Fools," he muttered. "I'll have to enter the castle alone. I pray memory serves for its many secret passages. Perhaps there's one that leads to the lady's bower."

As night fell, Vandil armed himself with a sword and shield and slipped into the castle moat. He swam unhindered by its deathly chill. *Bringing men along wouldn't have worked after all,* he thought. They'd have frozen to death before reaching the secret entrance. At length, Vandil came to a round sewer grating bolted to the masonry walls. He grasped the bars and tore them from their moorings.

He swam through the passage until he came to a wine cellar where bad wine was discarded into the watery channel. Pulling himself onto the flagstone floor, he hid among the massive wine barrels while a worker arranged bottles in racks. Vandil dripped water as he sneaked behind him.

"You," he hissed. The startled worker whirled around to see the terrifying image of the skeletal warrior in a breastplate, his leering skull beneath a horned helm. It wouldn't do to clap a bony hand over the worker's mouth. He could easily scream through the gaps in Vandil's fingers. "Where is the Lady Emalia? Tell me, and no harm shall befall you."

The worker turned white and scrambled for the cellar exit.

Vandil cursed and drew his sword. He flung it through the worker's back. The man died on the stairs leading up from the chamber, blood running down them. Vandil couldn't have him alerting the rest of the castle. He wrenched his blade free of the man and ascended to a narrow passage. Vandil twisted his head to the left and right and found the torch-lit hallway clear.

This part of the castle Vandil recognized. Where could she be? Vandil had guarded Emalia frequently, standing outside her private quarters. It was as good a place as any to shelter a princess, so Vandil headed in that direction.

Sounds of guards mobilizing for war echoed through the airy spaces of Castle Grafburg. Valamir must not have taken kindly to Izumi's report. Was he going to attack Aratheus tonight?

Vandil kept to the shadows, his skeletal legs landing lightly on the stone surfaces and luxurious carpets that ran the length of the castle's corridors. He hid behind archways and doors, always unnoticed by the hurried guards, as he made his way toward Emalia's quarters.

Security was lighter in these areas. It seemed Valamir wanted every available sword to repel his brother's attack. Never would he conceive of a lone resurrected skeleton exploiting his castle's secrets and wandering the halls.

Vandil ascended a spiral staircase in one tower and made his way down one last hallway until he came to a door at the end. Sergeant Saphrax stood guard—the man Vandil had put in charge of security during Eberwulf's elevation. Fitting that he would now oversee Emalia's security.

Vandil drew closer, his armor rattling his bones as he passed in and out of the torchlight on the walls.

Saphrax leaned forward with a suspicious hand on his hilt. "Halt! This area is restricted to night watch only!"

"I am the night watch," Vandil said with a tone dripping with evil. He allowed his eyes to flicker their sinister lights as he came within view of the sergeant.

Saphrax wore a mask of fear as he drew his sword. "M-my God! Monster!"

"You knew me once," Vandil said. "I am Vandil, your Knight-Captain."

Saphrax shook in his chainmail armor. "What trickery is this? Vandil was a traitor who killed his king before he himself was struck down!"

Vandil reached into his armor and pulled the bronze medallion. "If I am not he, what is this?"

The sergeant stood wide-eyed with terror. "No… it can't be!"

"I am here for Lady Emalia. She is in great danger. This castle will be burned and she cannot stay here."

"Lies! I'll not let you harm her!"

"Ever the dutiful soldier," Vandil said in a tone of steely resolve. "I will have her, with or without your consent."

A muffled voice came through the door. "Guard? What is going on?"

"N—naught to worry, princess!" Saphrax called out. "Just a lost soldier!"

Vandil drew his sword. "Stand aside."

"Never."

"You'll have to kill me then—one who is already dead."

Saphrax trembled, tightening his grip on his sword. He gritted his teeth and uttered a battle cry.

Vandil stood perfectly still. As Saphrax swung his weapon, Vandil stepped back, knocked the blade aside, and punched the sergeant in the nose with his hilt. Blood exploded across his face, his nose-bone crushed. Vandil knocked him against the wall with his shield, the sergeant hitting the floor.

Vandil hadn't the heart to kill him. He approached Emalia's door and rapped on it with the back of his hand. "Who's there?" came a voice from the other side.

"Saphrax," he lied.

The door opened a crack, the princess' emerald eyes staring at a face of death. She couldn't even scream before Vandil forced himself into the room.

"Get out! Monster!" Emalia screamed. She grabbed the expensive vases, wooden chairs, and other household items and hurled them at the advancing skeleton. Each item shattered and broke against his helm and shield.

"Princess, stop!" Vandil said. "This castle will soon be destroyed! You must come with me!"

"You lie! You are a devil!"

"The Aragoths will attack and set the castle ablaze!"

"Why should I believe you?"

"I am Vandil, whom you once knew. I was captain of the One Hundred, and protector to you, my Lady." He offered his bony hand. "Please, come."

Emalia covered her mouth in disgust. "No! I don't believe you! The Vandil I knew slew my father and brother!"

Vandil fought to keep his eyes from igniting "And yet, I saved you from an unwanted and loveless marriage!"

"By killing my betrothed!?"

"He didn't deserve the laurels given to him!"

"Monster!" she shrieked. "I'd rather join them all in death than spend one more minute in your presence! Guards! Help me!"

Vandil's shoulders slumped, and he hung his head. He crossed to the window of the round chamber. Emalia kept calling for guards.

"No one's coming, Princess. They've gone to fight Aratheus, though he will not survive the night. When Valamir dies, you will become ruler of the Goths… if you live."

She rounded back on him. "Leave!"

Vandil stood in silence a few moments, where sympathy would color a living brow, but having none, he could only cross to the window pane of her chamber.

He stood on the sill, bashed the trellised glass, and jumped out, falling five hundred feet into the moat.

Vandil dragged himself ashore, climbing a snowy embankment, the sounds of warfare upon him. The armies of Aratheus and Valamir clashed on the drawbridge: Goth against Goth, slaying and being slain, their corpses falling into the moat. Vandil picked out Aratheus in the heat of the melee, leading the charge against his brethren. Vandil threw himself into the combat, the dead amongst the living, picking his way to the front to engage the enemy.

He found himself shoulder to scapula with Aratheus, pressed together with the others as they hacked the Sargoths.

"You found Emalia?" Aratheus shouted.

"Aye, but it was as you said, 'Best to leave her to her fate.'"

Aratheus whooped his battle cry, crushing the skulls of his brethren with a spiked mace and shoving their bodies aside with his shield.

Chunks of masonry dropped onto the bridge, the Sargoths making way. A loud metallic clanking drew the attention of the Aragoths to the parapet, where against the full moon an armored monstrosity swirled an ornate halberd above its shoulders. Yet, the headless armor stood vacant.

It leaped onto the drawbridge, splintering the thick wooden beams—an animation of articulated plates that cleaved the front line of the Aragoths. The floating armor resembled Eberwulf's! Aratheus' men screamed in terror as it felled one man after another, sending them flying from the bridge. Aratheus ducked under the mighty swing of this ghost armor.

The Sargoths withdrew into the safety of the courtyard behind them as the portcullis slammed. Its back against it, the armor moved with a macabre grace as it whirled its halberd menacingly around it.

Vandil's jaw dropped. How could this be? Was Eberwulf resurrected as well because of an unjust death? "It's a dullahan!" Aratheus said. "Created through the magicks of Caenmyr!"

Caenmyr was an island nation off the coast of the mainland. Had Valamir recruited mercenaries from that far away?

No matter, Vandil thought. If he killed him once, he could do so again.

Vandil shoved his way to the front line, telling Aratheus to fall back. Aratheus waved for a momentary retreat to the start of the drawbridge. Vandil intercepted the armor's strikes with his own weapon to make good their retreat.

Soon, the undead warriors were alone, circling each other and measuring each other's movements. The armor swung its halberd, which Vandil blocked with his shield, yet the force shattered the round board. Vandil threw the useless pieces from the bridge as he recalculated his attack strategy.

In his first battle with the braggart, Vandil cut through the halberd, yet this version was braced in steel and riveted to the wooden haft. The armor itself was even larger than before, looming over the skeletal warrior. As it swung again, Vandil rolled under the blade and slashed at the armor's legs. His sword glanced off the thick plates in a spray of sparks. Vandil stood and slashed again, yet the breastplate deflected it.

The suit repositioned, and brought its knee into Vandil's chest, knocking his skeletal frame onto his back. He knew a few of his ribs were broken. The armor ran past him to rejoin the battle with the Aragoths, as Vandil forced himself to stand.

Aratheus on the front line roared and engaged the dullahan.

"No, Aratheus! Fall back!" Vandil shouted, but his spectral voice was lost in the wind. Aratheus and the armor traded blows, but the hand of the aged king could not keep his mace as the armor knocked it aside.

Unarmed, Aratheus gazed up in horror as the armor towered over him, the moon's shadow falling across the pair. The dullahan grabbed the king by his chain mail hauberk and tossed him from the drawbridge like a doll. The king screamed as he hit the ice-water moat and never came up. His men shouted in terror and ran from the bridge.

Vandil staggered toward the ghost armor with the sword raised. It turned to face him and unleashed a deep, evil laugh from its core.

An arrow pierced Vandil's helmet, boring through his skull and out of one of his sockets. Vandil shook his head and spun around for the source of the attack. Izumi sat in the window of one of the guard towers, bow in hand, notching another arrow.

Vandil cursed. It was the second time she had dealt him a fatal blow from behind.

The armor clanked along the bridge to engage Vandil once more. Half his vision was darkened, and Vandil failed to register the incoming attack to his blind side. The halberd bit through Vandil's armor and sent his bones clattering to the bridge. The armor fell upon him, planting a plated boot onto this sternum and crushing his ribcage like a walnut—the medallion along with it.

Tossed upon the ethereal winds, Vandil spiraled through a tornado, light above and darkness below, the walls of the storm varying shades of green and blue. Screams cut through the wind as men's souls tumbled to their ultimate fate, with Vandil among them.

A terror seized him. He had been defeated, but in the interim of his previous death and resurrection, he had not been brought to this place. He had only slept, and the time between his burial and rebirth felt as but a moment.

Vandil sank deeper and deeper into the darkness of the vortex. He reached for the light above, but it slipped through his blue translucent fingers. Justice had lost. The forces at work were too powerful, too clever, or wealthy. Justice held no power in this world.

He thought of the medallion. Its power had faded. Vandil was given one last chance, and he had failed, allowing injustice to prevail.

"Vandil —" came a voice from above, ghostly and calling to him. "Vandil —"

"What are you?" Vandil heard himself speak.

"You are worthy!"

"W-worthy? How?"

Several souls swirled above him, drawing the weight of Vandil's spirit closer and closer. Vandil floated towards the light, reaching for glowing white bodies with skulls upon their shoulders.

"We are the souls of those who died through treachery and injustice. We are criminals wrongly condemned, or innocents brought low by the ravening sword of a warlord." The souls lifted Vandil higher and higher until they encircled him in long wisps.

"How can you aid me?" Vandil asked. "My medallion was destroyed, unfettering my soul from the mortal realm! I cannot return!"

"We shall confer our power upon you so you may return; so that justice may be done."

The souls coalesced into skeletal forms and streamed into Vandil's body. Warmth spread through him. So did pain—the pain of everything those souls had lost, and their yearning for the world to be set aright.

His vision blackened until he lay on the bridge under falling snow, the moon, and the castle above him. His broken skeletal body reformed itself with sickening cracks, an invisible tether lifting his chest and bringing him to his feet. Vandil sensed his eyes reignite. He picked up his sword and willed a ghostly blue and orange flame to snake along its length. In his other hand, he summoned a flaming orange skull rimmed in blue witch-fire.

Vandil grinned.

III

The armor stood with its back to Vandil, guarding the drawbridge. The Aragoths had been routed and were too afraid to approach the Goliath. Other soldiers were picked off by the deadly archer in the tower.

Vandil hurled the flaming skull into the back of the armor, causing an eruption of sparks. The dullahan lurched forward to regain its footing and whirled around at the surprise attacker. Vandil ignited another ethereal skull.

The dullahan raced towards him, raising the halberd. Vandil crouched as the weapon sailed over him. Vandil slashed at the armor's flank, the flaming sword cutting through the metal like paper. Again and again, Vandil sliced, carving long gashes into the armor. A sorrowful moan escaped the innermost depths of the dullahan as it collapsed onto the bridge. Vandil kept cutting until the armor lay in pieces, the metal blackened and scorched by fire.

The portcullis stood in Vandil's way. He sliced away at the bars until he formed a doorway large enough to fit through. A roar of renewed vigor rose behind him; the Aragoths, at the sight of the dullahan defeated, stormed the bridge. They stopped in front of Vandil, their faces showing a mixture of courage and fear.

"Follow me," said Vandil.

Vandil led the screaming horde through the opening as they poured into the streets. Frightened townsfolk scurried for the safety of their homes, but they would not be saved from the fire and blades of the Aragoths. Vandil cared not for spoils. His only intent was the throne room and the star-fallen swine that sat there.

Valamir's army met them as they flowed in like the tide. The din of clashing swords floated into the night sky as arrow after arrow found the backs of the sons of Aratheus. Izumi stood atop the guard tower, loosing her deadly barbs.

Vandil grit his teeth. How to reach her? His path to the tower was blocked by the throngs of violent humanity. Perhaps he could lure her to him! He charged up the road leading to the castle keep, and the massive doors Vandil once defended what felt like a lifetime ago.

As the Sargoths stood in his way, he hurled fireball after fireball, blasting apart their formations and sending men sprawling to the ground. Vandil trampled over their bodies and up the wide stairs leading to the imposing doors of the throne room where a shield wall awaited.

Just like Vandil's own tactic, a line of swordsmen with spearmen behind them obstructed Vandil's view of the throne beyond. His own men, the remnants of the One Hundred, stood between Vandil and his justice. He hung his head as he realized what had to be done.

He formed another skull fireball and launched it into the center of the shield wall, blasting a gap wide enough to slip through. Several men were knocked to the ground, though they climbed to their feet with weapons bared.

Vandil reached the back of the formation, where the spearmen pressed in, jabbing at him. Vandil hacked off the tips of their spears with his flaming sword. Yet more men kept coming. It didn't surprise the skeleton, as he had trained the men personally. They were performing admirably, but they couldn't have expected the unearthly power before them.

"H-help! Defend your king!" came a cry from the recesses of the room. Valamir clung to his throne, sweat dripping from his face, a half-circle of guards in front of him. They would be the last to fall.

Vandil took up a round shield from the floor, and willed flaming skulls to fire from the shield's boss, incinerating spears and the men behind them. The swordsmen circled Vandil and closed in from all sides. There were at least two scores, perhaps more than fifty.

The first sword came in. Vandil deflected with his flaming blade and countered with a searing slash through the soldier's torso. His body hit the floor as multiple slashes followed from the rest of the One Hundred. Vandil couldn't stay surrounded like this. He had to get outside the circle. He vaulted over the onrushing men and repositioned outside the ring. He again willed a stream of flaming skulls from the boss of his shield to burn through the advancing attackers. The others he engaged with swordplay, expertly dodging, parrying, and countering. Soldier after soldier burst into flames as each slash connected.

When it was over, a ring of burnt corpses smoldered at Vandil's feet, the smoke of their charred flesh reaching the vaulted ceiling. The One Hundred were no more.

Vandil stalked to Valamir's throne, sending skull after flaming skull into the wooden beams and banners which had replaced Godwin's. Flames devoured them while the timbers crackled. Vandil approached, cutting down the few remaining guards before Valamir's eyes as they desperately tried to defend him.

Burning fragments of wood fell around them as smoke rose through the windows.

"Get up, king," Vandil growled. "At least die on your feet as a true ruler, not some craven coward on his ill-gotten throne."

The trembling king rose, drawing his meager sword. "So, the stories are true. You really are back from the dead."

"To repay you for your treachery," Vandil said as he held the point of his flaming sword to Valamir's nose. He let the blade trail downward, opening a flesh wound on the king's belly, staining his royal garments with a rush of red.

"Wrong, monster," Valamir gritted through the pain. "Though justice comes to us all, it is you who shall pay… by the same hand that saw you from this world the first time!"

Before Vandil could contemplate the meaning, an arrow pierced through his breastplate from behind, followed by a familiar feminine laugh that would have sickened a living Vandil. Another arrow struck him through, though each one missed his bones as they protruded from the gaps in his ribs. Vandil spun on Izumi, who dropped her bow and drew her twin swords.

"Now we finish this," she said.

Vandil flourished his flaming sword and met the woman in melee, her blocks sending sparks and embers flying. Behind them, Valamir deserted his throne, rushing for an exit. Vandil and Izumi tested and circled each other, deflecting and dodging each lethal strike.

Izumi incorporated surprise kicks into her attack routine, knocking Vandil to the floor. She leaped upon the downed skeleton, attempting to sever his cranium with two crossed swords, but he rolled to one side.

Regaining his footing, Vandil sent a flaming skull from the boss of his shield. Izumi formed an X with her swords and sliced the skull from the air, before performing a series of spinning kicks that Vandil was forced to block. Her last kick knocked his shield from his hand as it skidded across the floor. Another large beam crashed next to it, preventing Vandil from reaching it.

Izumi's skin glistened in the heat of the battle as she renewed her attacks. Their deadly dance ended when Vandil sliced through her blades, cutting a burning wound across her chest. She wailed in agony as she dropped the fragments of her swords. Vandil formed a flaming skull in his free hand, and crushed it into her face, engulfing her head in flames. Her headless body keeled over. As Vandil stepped away from her, she was crushed by a burning timber.

Vandil hurried from the chamber as pieces of the roof fell into the room. The throne burst into flames as Vandil entered the hallway beyond. Drips of blood led down the passageway. Vandil followed the blood trail up the spiral stairs, which lead him to the roof of the castle. The steep eaves were blanketed in snow which now fell in heavy clumps. Smoke curled from the burning throne room below.

Valamir stood at the edge of a flat section of the roof, holding his gut and his sword to one side. Vandil approached with grim determination, his sword flickering with arcane fire.

"Hold, Vandil! I see now you are the true champion!" Valamir said. Vandil stopped a few feet away, willing his eyes to burn with fury. Valamir continued. "Now you can take the position you always wanted! I can give it to you! None stand in your way. I… I can even have armor made especially for you, to hide your skeletal features!"

Vandil paused to unleash a laugh so bone-chilling it brought Valamir to his knees.

"Please, sir knight," Valamir said. "Spare me. I know not what the afterlife entails. Please!"

Vandil grabbed him by the collar and lifted him over his head. "If you've seen me, you've seen the afterlife as well."

Vandil tossed the king from the roof, his body tumbling down the slope and into the haze below.

A silence fell upon the castle. The snow ceased. A freezing wind buffeted his bones. He dropped his sword as weakness overcame him. His only thought was of his grave and his longing to return to it. Vandil staggered from the rooftop and back through the castle, avoiding the fired areas.

He wandered through the burning town, observing the Goths locked in mortal struggle. His bones clattered as he walked, bringing eerie silence to the scene of destruction. All eyes fell on him.

"Lay down your arms," Vandil said. "The king is dead. This war is over." A stunned silence fell over the Goths as they lowered their weapons. They looked at one another with a sort of wistfulness, knowing now that they no longer needed to kill each other. The Sargoths would return to their country, with Emalia as ruler.

He was alone, with only his regrets to guide him, which weighed more heavily than any suit of armor on a living man. Had he never betrayed King Godwin, how might his life have gone? In the pursuit of his own justice, he had wrongly taken the lives of those who served their own. His bones sagged as he trudged toward the city gate.

Vandil continued out of the town, dragging his weary bones to the ancient cemetery that birthed him. Hazy outlines of men emerged through the trees as Vandil shambled between the headstones. Members of the One Hundred stood to greet Vandil as he neared the site of his resurrection. Godwin, Hilderith, and even Eberwulf were there as well. They appeared in a half-circle around a shallow pit that had since been filled with snow.

Vandil came to the edge, studying the faces of these apparitions, and found no malice in them. His bones clacked together one last time as he collapsed into the coldness of the grave.

Soul Harvest
By H. R. Parker

I: Shackled

The tears streamed down my face as I struggled against the restraints shackled to my wrists and ankles. "She's a feisty one," the Reaper to my left mumbled, unfazed by my struggle. They were used to it.

Except for his exquisitely perfect beauty, the Biomech Reaper in front of me looked no different from a human. His skin was warm to the touch, he breathed, he smiled, and he laughed. Only his eyes and smile belied what he was lacking: a human soul that was still connected to the life thrum of the universe. The human soul within him acted like an existential battery, but it was severed from what made it human. There were no feelings, no empathy, a living yet mechanical brain inside a human-looking body.

"She's the last one left," came another voice "She should have accepted her fate by now."

My eyes widened as the head Soul Reaper himself, Mikhail Thassos, entered the laboratory.

"Sir! We had no idea you'd be assisting today! Please allow me..." the assistant groveled, running to his master's side to help him into his lab coat.

"She is the last living human in the entire Ecstatis System. All other souls have been transplanted, but none remember they are human. Who knows? This one may respond well to our new modifications." Thassos turned to the groveler. "You can leave. Send in Ilex."

Thassos came next to me, tilting his head to get a better look into my eyes. "So much fight in you. Maybe that's what's been missing with all the other transplants. They accepted their fate too easily, perhaps. But you..."

He moved to brush the hair clinging to my face with the angry tears still drying on my cheeks. I tried to move away, but of course, I couldn't.

He grabbed my chin with an iron hand. "You, girl, might be the answer to my quest for immortality." His wrinkled face, haunted by time, twisted into a grotesque imitation of a smile. The smile did not travel to his dead, black eyes.

"Thassos is obsessed! He'll never give up his power and stronghold on Eta Vega, never! He's been conducting his experiments for years on humans. Before long, there will be none left. We have to get off Eta Vega, somehow. We have to save Phaedra! Have you seen how many hundreds were taken from the outposts just last week? They'll be hunting here in the city next!"

My mother's pleadings to my father crashed through my memories unbidden. I had been a young child—barely old enough to store long-term memories—hovering on the other side of the door, trying to understand why so many humans were being taken by terrifying armored droids and brought to a mysterious lab in Deneb Alpha, the largest city on Eta Vega.

I remember my father's eyes burning with fury in the half-light. *"What do you think I've been doing out in the remote wastes of the Icebound Expanse all these months? I'll sacrifice myself for our daughter. Even if she's the only one to get off-world..."* He paused, shaking his head. *"From what our intel is telling us, the souls being harvested are simply becoming eternal power sources for the Biomechs, and nothing more. The transplants aren't working the way Thassos wants them to."*

My mother had grabbed my father's arms in both hands, desperation masking her face. *"That means he'll keep going! We're nothing more than guinea pigs for a madman now!"*

My mind snapped back to the present with that thought. "You'll never be able to transplant your soul, Thassos. You don't possess one." My words leaked from my mouth, articulated poison for his waiting ears.

His head tilted back, the sound of laughter echoing off the walls. The unnatural sound startled me.

"I hope you retain your human memories, girl. This planet is cold enough. I do so relish your… *fire*. It warms me through and through." Thassos chuckled as he walked away to join his new assistant, who had just walked into the room.

So, it had finally come to this. Strapped to a table at Thassos Labs, Inc., after all these years eluding this cruel man. My parents had tried so hard to keep this from happening. I felt as if I had failed them. Now I was at Thassos' mercy.

I had absolutely no means of escape now, I knew that. I had made peace with it. The only comforting thought was the end of the suffering, the running, the constant anxiety I'd lived with my entire life. I didn't even have the comfort of meeting my parents in the afterlife. Their precious souls were now powering some random Biomech, walking around in Deneb Alpha or some frozen outpost on Eta Vega, living their mindless, programmed lives.

But it wasn't over yet. I was not completely his. My soul was *mine*. My body was about to die, to be tossed into the Eternal Fire—the infinite flames that had been burning for years to cremate the endless sea of human bodies after their souls had been harvested and transplanted into Biomechs.

"I hear you, Starchild…"

I stiffened. *Who said that?* I desperately tried to look around, but only saw Thassos in the corner of the lab, with his assistant Reaper—the one he had called Ilex. Ilex had suddenly turned and was watching me intently.

Had she heard that voice too? Thassos seemed oblivious.

The voice came again. *"Your* annuri *is strong, as you are a child of the Stars…"*

Annuri?

The assistant Reaper began walking toward me, still staring at me intently, her face a mask of bemusement.

"Get her ready, Ilex," Thassos' deep voice called from the corner.

"Right away, sir," she called back, then turned to me. For a Biomech, her eyes seemed awfully… human, as they searched mine.

Ilex put a respirator device over my nose and mouth, attaching it to my head. She then leaned down, putting her lips next to my ear. I could feel her breath, oddly human for AI. Thassos' Biomech technology was impressive, I had to admit, even in my frenzied state. "My name from before," Ilex whispered. "It was Emre."

"What?" my voice, barely above a whisper, came out muffled, my hot breath steaming the plastic of the respirator.

"Emre," she said again softly, squeezing my hand before taking Thassos' place at the head of the operating table. I could see her no longer, but I could feel her presence.

Her name from before? Like *before*, before? When she was human? *Did she remember?*

There were no Memory Retainers to my knowledge, Biomechs who still remembered their past lives as humans. Was this Ilex—or, rather, Emre—the first?

I would take my memories with me, into whatever Biomech body he was transplanting me into. I would *not* be lost. The humans on Eta Vega didn't deserve this. Thassos would pay for his greed and obsession with immortality. I would find a way to reunite the lost souls of my human brothers and sisters with their Starmothers so they could, at last, be free; not forever bound in these manufactured, biosynthetic sleeves our lost souls now called home.

I had lived in terror for years, watching everyone I loved fall victim to Thassos' frenzied genocide of humanity as his experiments continued. I had tried to escape; who hadn't? But, like everyone else, I had been caught as my pod was leaving the atmosphere.

If I had stayed hidden, I might have lived longer in my human body, but there was no dark corner of the icy wastelands of Eta Vega in which we could hide that they did not find us. Even the underground habitations, which had been successful for a time, had been flushed out with snaking tendrils of toxic gas.

All my family, my friends, every person I had ever known, had fallen to this man. Their souls were now trapped with no memory of ever being human. If I fell to the same fate, who would help them? Who would help the countless other souls across the galaxy he would no doubt hunt down during his cruel experiment to gain immortality?

"Claim your soul, child. Claim it! " The mysterious voice screamed in my mind as Ilex's fingers wrapped around the switch that would take my consciousness forever.

I looked into Thassos' dead, soulless eyes. "You'll never take my soul! *Never!"*

I took my last breath, and the world disappeared. Thassos' pale face and dead black eyes were the last things my human eyes ever gazed upon.

II: IMPERFECTLY PERFECT

A voice floated through the cobwebs, clouding my mind. Was it *my* mind now? I had heard that voice before I went under, telling me to claim my soul because… why? What was that word? *Annuri?* Because my *annuri* was strong?

"Relax and breathe," Ilex (Emre?) said as she placed oxygen tubes into my nose. "Your Biomech, Io, has never had a transplant, and she's been in storage a long while. Your lungs and the rest of your new bioengineered body are trying to catch up. Just rest now. The worst is over." Her hand rested on my arm reassuringly as she leaned in closer to my ear, just like before the procedure. "I hope you remember me," she whispered, her lips tickling my ear and sending goosebumps up and down my newly acquired flesh.

The procedure…*I remembered.* I remembered everything before: my parents, our tiny dome house in the city, becoming an orphaned nomad who had wandered over every inch of this godforsaken block of ice we called home.

But how? How was I the only one who remembered? Why didn't my parents, my grandparents, aunts, uncles, and friends…why did they succumb, but not me? Everyone else on Eta Vega woke in Biomech bodies with no memories of their human lives before. Yet I remembered it all, even the worst of details.

"Phaedra, they're coming for you. Soon. You have to get out of Deneb Alpha and head west to the Howling Tundra. There's an underground base there that Thassos and his droids haven't found yet. We've already paid for your passage with the Snowdrifts"

"The Snowdrifts? Isn't that what is piling up on the windows right now, Mommy? How can they help?" I had asked, pointing to the frost-covered window, the snowbank at an equal level with the windowsill.

My mother couldn't help but smile then. *"The Snowdrifts are nice people who 'drift' from place to place, just like snow. They help children like you get off-world so you can be safe, my love. The refugees there are planning an exodus out of this galaxy, to get far away from Thassos. You'll be safe with them, and you'll have a chance at life—as a* human.*"* My mother's eyes were swimming in tears as she clutched my arms in her iron grip.

"But what about you and Father?" I had asked, frantically, the panic rising into my chest and arresting my lungs.

"The Snowdrifts can only take children now, Phaedra," my father had said, kneeling to look me in the eyes. I had only been ten then. *"Thassos hasn't had success with souls from the adults he's taken, so now he's only focusing on children because your souls are so... pure. But none have worked yet, and he's not going to stop until he's taken you all. I'm not losing my only daughter to that madman."*

You didn't lose me, Father, I thought, my eyes roving around the infirmary where my new body was coming to terms with the new life that had inexplicably been put inside of it. *I'm still here, I'm still here. I may not be in a human body, but I'm still me. I'm still Phaedra.*

"Well, Ilex, how is our one and only patient?" Thassos swept into the room in a blur of midnight black hair and a snow-white uniform. His skin was almost as pale as his lab coat. I shivered at his mere presence.

"So far, so good, sir. Her vitals are getting stronger by the moment." Ilex gestured to the machine beeping at my bedside with my vitals splayed across the screen in angry, blood-red letters and numbers.

"Well, tomorrow we'll begin her tests to see if she remembers her past life." Thassos smiled down at me with his grotesque, corpse-like smile. "You rest now, dear, and I will see you again tomorrow. *Phaedra.*" He shot me a knowing look, hoping I would take the bait.

I scrunched my face into a bemused expression. "Who is Phaedra? I thought my name was Io." My voice was hoarse, barely above a whisper.

"I don't think the complete transplant was a success, sir. She should have remembered her name, at least." Ilex caught my gaze and gave me a look as if to say *keep playing along.*

But how could I fake my identity when I was subjected to Thassos' tests tomorrow? I had no idea what those tests would entail, but I knew they would consist of way more than just asking my name and where I was born.

"Keep an eye on her overnight, Ilex, and we will resume tomorrow. Let her rest for now. Phae—excuse me, Io—I can barely wait to see what you have in store for me," Thassos said, directing his comment to me as he threw his hand up in a wave and left, his footsteps loudly echoing in the empty infirmary.

Rows upon rows of beds, sterile white and gleaming chrome, once filled with Biomechs awakening and recovering from their transplants. Now, these beds stood empty, except for me. The last surviving human soul on Eta Vega that had kept her human memories. But why, and how?

As Ilex busied herself around the infirmary, my mind whirred. Ilex, also a Biomech with a reaped soul, had told me her name before I had gone under: *Emre*. She remembered her human life before too, but Thassos obviously had no idea. How did she keep it from him?

My eyes fell on Ilex, wondering what she had looked like as a human. As a Biomech, she was of course visually perfect in every way. Tall, lithe, shining chestnut hair cropped short in a wavy bob, perfect olive skin, and arresting amber eyes. But her outward appearance wasn't what interested me. It was what she was hiding inside that mattered.

As if she read my mind, Ilex walked over with a handheld mirror and sat on the bed beside me. "I thought you might like to see yourself. You must be curious." A heavy sadness floated in her golden eyes as she handed me the mirror, stood, and walked away. "I'll return momentarily. It's only us here for the night, and I looped the security system, so we can speak freely. And no one will see or hear if you want to cry, scream, or throw things. I wouldn't blame you if you did." She closed the door softly behind her, but not before giving me one last look full of pity.

I don't need your pity, I thought as I slowly lifted the mirror to my face.

I gasped. I looked so…. perfect. Before my body had been sacrificed to the flames, I had been twenty years old. Ten years of hard living in the perpetual winter of Eta Veta with refugees had left my skin rough, dry, and scarred from frostbite. My dark brown eyes had a hardened look, like that of someone twice my age. I had been athletic and strong—used to hard work and constant stress. My body had been rewired from a life on the run, without parents or family, so panic attacks had been my one true friend, dedicated to the end. My panic had never left me, unlike everyone else I had ever known.

Now the face that gazed back was that of an elegant, beautiful stranger. The eyes that gazed back were brilliantly green. My skin was porcelain, without lines or blemishes. My golden-brown hair lay beautiful and voluptuous, tumbling over my shoulders almost to my waist. My lips were full and rosy, and my cheeks began to flirt with a hint of rosiness. I spread my lips in an emotionless smile to be greeted—not with my slightly crooked bottom row of teeth—but perfectly straight, white pearls.

This isn't me. This isn't me.

I felt the tears spill over my perfect cheeks as I threw the mirror up against the wall with a frustrated scream. My father's nose, my mother's eyes, the melding of them both to create my smile: it was all gone now. My last connection to my parents—my body, my very DNA—was gone now. My breath began coming in quick gasps. Did my panic disorder transplant along with my soul?

I crumpled back onto the bed, trying to slow my breathing like I had all those years before.

"Deep, slow breaths." My father had helped me through my attacks, in the early days when I didn't know how to control them, resting his hand on my tiny chest and syncing his breath with mine. *"Don't let the panic control you. You control the panic."*

My heart rumbled in my throat as Ilex quietly came into the room. "Are you alright? I heard—" She stopped when she saw the shattered mirror on the floor. "Oh. Right. It's alright, love; I almost did the same thing when I saw myself for the first time. It's quite... jarring to see another face looking back at you from the mirror." She sat down on the bed next to me and took my hand. "Are you sure you're alright?"

I nodded, taking another deep breath, and opening my emerald eyes to gaze   upon Ilex's face. "Ilex, how am I having panic attacks? Shouldn't this Biomech body be—"

"Perfect?" Ilex asked, a slight smirk raising the corners of her mouth. "Not if you're human inside," she whispered. "And please, call me Emre. No one is around."

"Emre! You remember your life from before the transplant." I jumped up and faced her, bare feet slapping the cold, hard floor. For the first time, I noticed them. "Wow, my new feet are so *small*."

Emre laughed softly. "It is a lot to get used to. And yes, Io—Phaedra— I remember. I remember everything. But right now, we need to focus on you passing these tests for Thassos tomorrow."

"No, no, fuck that. If I never see that man again, it'll be too soon. We have to get out of this place, off of this doomed planet. Do you have access to a pod?"

Emre's jaw dropped slightly. "Do you honestly think we can escape this planet? He tracks every ship and pod that leaves the atmosphere! If we leave without authorization, we'll be found out. The Biomechs don't try to escape. Ever. They're programmed to be totally accepting of their lot."

"That's because they can't remember who they are inside! We have to get off this ice block of a planet and find others like us. We have to find a way to destroy Thassos before he kills every living, sentient creature in the universe. We need to find an outpost in another galaxy, somewhere far away where here where humans don't live. Somewhere he'll never go!" I began pacing, already feeling caged, even in this enormous skyscraper that overlooked Deneb Alpha, the lights from the buildings and flying pods belying the soul-powered machines that operated them from within.

Turning back to my only companion, I said, "Help me, Emre, I'm finding out how to release our souls from these unnatural prisons—even if I have to go to the ends of the universe itself."

III: EAVESDROPPER

"How long have you been in that Biomech body, Emre? Don't you want to be free?" I asked, turning away from the cityscape to face her. It had begun to snow, and the buildings of the city stabbed into the sky like inverted icicles.

"Of course, I do," she whispered, tears welling up in her unnaturally golden eyes. "It's been a year. A year of pretending I'm something I'm not." She angrily wiped a tear from her supple cheeks. "I've waited for you for so long."

"For me? Why me?"

"Well, not you specifically, Phaedra. Just one other soul who remembered their lives before so I would know I wasn't alone."

"So, in all of these years since these soul harvests began, not one has remembered? What if they're like you, and they're just hiding it?"

"They could be. It's entirely possible." Emre bit her lip, crossing her lean muscular arms over her chest.

"We can't be the only two Biomechs on Eta Vega that remember their past lives. How is that possible?" I asked, pacing again in this sterilized, chrome cage.

"I wish I knew, Phaedra. If I did, I'd be long gone."

"I need to get out of this place!" I raged, the panic, anger, and sadness finally boiling over. "I'm not letting him win, Emre. I'll end this body before he gets a chance to know the secret to immortality!"

Emre's elegant fingers wrapped around my upper arms in a fury. "Don't you dare say that! You can't end things before they even begin. We have to fight!" Her golden eyes went wide, two burning suns searing.

We searched each other's eyes, two humans clutching at each other's souls in a dark abyss. I sighed, my shoulders slumping. "You're right, Emre, you're right. I say we throw caution to the wind and blast out of this atmosphere. Where are the ships?" I inquired, looking directly into her fiery eyes. "There are ways off this planet, and we're figuring them out. *Tonight*."

"Were you so bossy before, too?" she laughed, gesturing down the shimmering chrome hallway. "The ships are on the docks, of course. They're not far. How far do you think you'll go? You'll never leave the atmosphere!"

Another memory flashed before my eyes, then was gone like my caution: *The armored droids, pulling my tiny pod into their tractor beam. Me, screaming like a banshee. That final, sinking stone-in-the-stomach feeling of being caught, once and for all.*

Yet, knowing all this, I ignored Emre's warnings. "Can you fly a ship?"

"Well...not technically, no, but..."

"But what?"

"I could hack into the system and upload the pilot courses into our memory cloud. In a matter of minutes, we'd both be experts. But Thassos is alerted every time a ship leaves the atmosphere. *That* knowledge is kept from us, of course."

"There has to be a way to block the scanners," I whispered as we walked quietly down the hall. The place was so big, so empty, it felt eerie. It felt...wrong.

"I'll see what I can do," said Emre. "But we honestly don't know what security measures Thassos has to keep anyone—or any*thing*—from leaving Eta Vega. If the Intergalactic Federation knew of the soul harvests, they would be coming for Thassos for crimes against humanity. But no one has ever come in all these years. He's obviously been careful to contain these atrocities to Eta Vega."

I had been so preoccupied with escape and staying alive for the past ten years that I had not even considered the Intergalactic Federation intervening to save us. "You're right. The IF would never turn a blind eye to this."

Emre led me down a different chrome-coated hallway, this one only lit by small, golden lights along the length of the baseboards. Every now and then, I'd get a glimpse of the city through the windows, its quiet glacier-hued skyscrapers and gleaming silent pods blending in with the frost and ice. The snow, which had been falling gently before, was now beginning to swirl slightly as if the winds had picked up. The weather here had always been so volatile.

My mind wandered back to being a child, before the harvests. I remembered peace and happiness, despite living on such a remote, cold planet. Frost bled from the edge of the windows inward; I touched the window, a smile teasing the corners of my lips.

"I always loved the snow," I whispered, the glass cold against my palm. "Everyone else wanted to go off-world, to a warm planet closer to the sun. But I loved the snow. Especially the snowball fights with my friends after school." I stopped and looked over at Emre, golden highlights shimmering in her hair like stars in the half-light. "But the threat of danger is always so near on Eta Vega. One moment my friends and I could be having snowball fights, completely carefree, only to hear our mothers screaming at us to come inside before the white wall of a blizzard blasted across the Wastes and into the city."

I had been so young when I left Deneb Alpha, I barely remembered it. It never seemed this...enormous and bustling, even at night. The skyscrapers had multiplied, even sprawling into the section where I had lived with my parents, in our small, terraformed dome houses on the outskirts of the city. The dome houses were gone now, all traces of human individuality erased. Now everything was new, perfect, shining, and identical—just like the citizens of this city, this entire planet.

Now the heartbeat of the city was bioengineered, every breath of human life extinguished except for Thassos—and he barely counted as human.

Emre tugged on my arm, and we began walking again.

"So, this entire planet is officially his now that he caught me. There's no one left who will rise up against him. What's his next target? He has to have one. He won't stop until he's found a way to transplant souls with their consciousness intact."

"Going off-world to harvest increases the risk of exposure," Emre noted. "Maybe he'll stop here. It's not like he confides all his evil plans to me, Phaedra."

I looked at her silently, incredulous.

She looked crestfallen. "You're right. He's not going to stop, and he has that damn droid army. There's no escaping them." We turned right and kept going down another identical-looking hallway. This place seemed endless.

Our eyes met over the shared experience of being taken by the droid army, swathed in black and armored riot gear, unnaturally strong and unnaturally fast. Those droids had no human souls powering them, just the hunger for hunting down humans and bringing them to Thassos. It was a miracle we refugees had lasted so long out in the Wastes.

"Emre, can I ask you something? Before Thassos put you under for your… transplant, did you hear a voice, speaking to you? A voice that no one else heard?"

Emre's luminous eyes widened. "You heard it too?" she whispered, incredulous.

"She said to claim my soul, that my *annuri* was strong. When I heard that voice, it was like you heard it too. You came over and—"

"I heard that voice in my mind, too, Phaedra—before my transplant, and right before yours. I can't explain it, but I heard the same thing. Something about claiming my soul, something about *annuri*, but I have no idea what that means. I've spent a year researching, but of course, Thassos controls what we learn, what we read, everything. Plus, we have no access to archives from other galaxies."

"Come on, show me where the ships are. We need to figure out a way off Eta Vega first, then we'll figure out the rest later. He can't find out our memories are still intact. Can you imagine if that evil man lived forever? The whole universe would be under his rule."

Nodding in agreement, Emre led me to the dock. The ships were lined under the floodlights, gleaming in silence. "The ships are right out there. Now we need to go download the pilot courses. But what's your plan after that? Thassos' droids will be on us before we even left the atmosphere."

"Is there a Biomech you trust? Someone who could help us get out of the atmosphere?"

Emre scoffed. "Are you joking? They might be harboring human souls in their bodies, but their minds are programmed to be loyal to Thassos."

A voice sounded from behind. "Not all of us."

We whirled around, my heart hammering in my throat, pounding at my temples.

The Biomech who stood before us was almost a foot taller than me, his features hidden in the half-light. "I can get you out of the atmosphere, but we have to hurry."

"Pollux? " Emre said, her eyes cloaked in worry. "What are you doing here? I thought Thassos sent everyone home but me."

"My *name* is Rune," the Biomech she had called Pollux replied. "Now, let's get the fuck off this godforsaken planet."

IV: Almost

Rune turned and began walking away from us. We hurried after him, giving each other *what the fuck* looks.

"Hey, Pollux! Stop! Have you been following us? Eavesdropping on our conversation?" Emre demanded as Rune spun around to face us.

I could see his ruggedly handsome features—a slight beard, a dark shock of hair—illuminated in the half-light. When his midnight eyes found mine, I could feel myself shrinking away from him. He radiated anger, annoyance, impatience, and something else that was almost… familiar.

His humanity.

"As far as I figure, I'm your best hope. Now, let's get to the control rooms. I have work to do to block Thassos' scanners, and, if I overheard you two correctly, need to upload the pilot courses to your memory cloud. We only have a few hours before the lab opens back up," he turned, his broad shoulders blocking the light from the hallway beyond.

"You remember," I whispered. "You remember your past life."

He turned back around to face me. His eyes searched mine intently. I felt like, with one look, he would instantly know all my secrets.

"Yes, obviously," he growled. "Now, let's go. We can get sentimental later."

"Pollux—R…Rune—how long have you been in that Biomech body?" Emre asked, Rune still stomping down the hall, his boots echoing loudly in the early morning silence.

"Two years. Two long fucking years," he replied, almost under his breath.

"Two years? Rune, how did you keep it from Thassos for so long?" Emre questioned as she easily kept stride with Rune.

"I don't know, how did *you*?" he spat angrily as we poured into the control room. "You two go next door. You can upload what you need from there." He sat down at a complex panel of buttons and flashing lights before turning away from us to get to work, ending our conversation.

"We'll talk about this later," Emre said pointedly as we left the room and walked next door to another room filled with screens, panels, and a complex array of buttons. If Rune heard her, he didn't acknowledge her, his fingers typing madly on the computer keypad.

"Do you know him? This Rune?" I asked as we walked into a room similar to the one next door where Rune furiously worked to get us out of the galaxy without Thassos knowing. "Can you trust him?"

"I know him, but only slightly. He's one of the engineers here, so we don't work in the same department."

We sat in front of two screens that immediately powered up as soon as we sat down in front of them.

"Scroll down the pages as you quickly scan with your eyes, and the retina chip will upload everything to your memory cloud instantly. Are you ready to fly a ship, Phaedra?" Emre asked, a crooked smile turning up one side of her lush, full lips. "And get caught one more time?"

"Let's do this," I said with a big intake of air, allowing my eyes to scan the screen. Within a couple of minutes, we were done. "This is incredible," I murmured.

I jumped as Rune's voice shattered my concentration. "I'm done. Are you two ready to fly us out of here? I have access codes for the *Bellatrix*. She's a smaller ship, but the three of us can manage. She's the fastest in the fleet. I helped design her." Rune couldn't hide his pride and slight smugness as he leaned his tall black-clad frame against the doorjamb.

"But you can't fly her?" Emre goaded him as she powered down the machines and led us out of the room.

"I design them, I don't fly them," Rune said as he took the lead, the lights running along the length of the floor flicking on ahead of us as we walked. "That means I also know how to make this ship undetectable."

"Then why haven't you left before now? What have you been waiting for?" I asked Rune as the doors swished open, and we were outside on the docks, walking past rows and rows of ships, gleaming silently under the security lights in the darkness. The wind had died down thankfully. But in this new body, I wasn't even affected by the cold, even in the thin, lab-issue jumpsuit I was wearing.

"For a crew, obviously. I couldn't do all this alone. Come on, the other Mechs will be here soon," Rune called back to us, picking up his pace. "I disabled the scanner crew. It was only two of them, thankfully."

Rune pointed to the awaiting ship, and we clamored on board. Emre and I headed to the front of the ship to slip naturally into the pilot and co-pilot seats as if we'd been doing all our lives. I didn't even feel nervous about flying it, but my stomach was in knots from the fear of being caught before we got out of there. It seemed being a Biomech didn't hinder my anxiety in the least. The body didn't matter. My mind was still intact, taking me on the same roller coaster rides as before.

"I'll handle the cannons in case we're chased, but we shouldn't be," Rune said, taking his place in the gun bay.

Another voice interrupted our planning. "You won't be chased, because you're not going anywhere."

We all jumped, turning in the direction of the speaker.

Fuck.

A Biomech stood in the ship's doorway, clad in his white lab gear, a shiny black armored droid standing beside him holding a blaster. I remembered him from before my procedure: the groveler, the Mech who had been in the lab right before my transplant—Thassos' perfect little minion.

"I don't know what's going on here, but you three are going into custody until Thassos gets here, which won't be long. I already alerted him. Now, get up. You're all coming with me."

I could see Rune's mind whirling, thinking of how to subdue the Mech. *Don't do it, Rune*, I thought. *Not with the droid here.* Armored droids were all metal, full of fire and fury, melting through hundreds of feet of snow to find underground bunkers in the Icebound Expanse. Flashbacks of their cruelty and bloodshed increased my heart rate as the memories flooded me. All those memories of running, the constant running. The constant need for escape.

Rune sighed, emerging from the gun bay, his hands up in surrender.

Emre and I followed suit, retracing our steps back inside the lab, this time with an armored droid at our backs. My mind whirled as quickly as the snow. We were so close; we couldn't give up now.

Thassos' minion, who went by the name Jax, shoved us into a cell-like room, its walls and floors sterile chrome, blank and empty like the rest of this planet. The door locked behind him with finality.

"There's no hiding it from Thassos now," Emre exclaimed, dejectedly throwing herself down on the floor, head in her hands.

"If Jax hadn't brought the droid, the three of us could have easily overcome him," Rune said, trying the lock again.

"But he did, and here we are. But we've got to come up with something, and fast. This isn't how it ends, it can't be," I whispered, my eyes closing as I pressed my forehead against the wall, sighing.

Suddenly the door swooshed open. Thassos stood on the other side, his eyes a black hole, his mouth a thin, grim, flat line.

I could feel it, the panic rising. My heart was racing in my throat, my breath coming in quick gasps. I tried to slow my breathing the way my father had taught me all those years ago.

"Well, well, well... It seems our newest transplant is a troublemaker, dragging her new friends down with her." Thassos roughly grabbed my upper arm, yanking me out of the cell. I bit my lip to keep from giving him the satisfaction of crying out. Jax stood just behind Thassos, looking smug and important. I wished I could slap the smugness off his face. The armored droid stood just behind Jax.

Thassos pushed me into his office, Emre and Rune falling in behind me, spurred on by the prodding of the droid.

"Now, now, now. Io, Pollux, Ilex...it seems you three are somewhat...different from your other Biomech counterparts. I've never had anyone try to escape after a transplant. *Ever.*" His almost nonexistent lips turned up into a sneer, a wicked glint in his empty dark eyes. "Biomechs are programmed to be obedient, to follow my rules. But suddenly I have three very defiant Mechs on my hands. And I think I can guess why."

V: JUMP

"Thassos, just let them go. It was my idea to leave, not theirs. Punish me all you want, just leave them be." Rune's eyes burned like embers as his gaze sought mine with the same "play along" look that Emre had given me when I'd woken up from the reaping. "I was dragging the Biomechs along with me to pilot the ship, nothing more. They aren't like me."

Thassos' emotionless, cruel laugh broke the momentary silence after Rune's confession. "Well, we'll just see about that, won't we?" His lips turned up into a grim smile, his black, lifeless eyes boring into mine. His eyes seem to swirl like black holes, threatening to swallow me whole. Thassos began to stalk toward me, seeming to grow taller with each step.

I instinctively backed away, but then held my ground. *A Biomech wouldn't be afraid of him*, I reassured myself, trying to will myself into being brave.

"And what is it about *you* that changed everything?" His eyes still searched mine intently, as if he would find answers there. "Pollux, both you and Ilex were exemplary employees. But here you are, betraying me." Thassos turned to Rune, his skeletal finger pointing back at me. "No Biomech has ever attempted escape, naturally, because I programmed them this way. But you two," he stopped his musings, spittle forming on the corners of his lips, "suddenly decide to escape off-world the very night Phaedra Draex's soul was harvested."

He stopped, gazing at the three of us in turn, rubbing his sagging chin as he pondered. "Why is she so important to you? Is she someone you knew from *before*?" Thassos moved toward Rune, but Rune made no show of intimidation or fright from Thassos approaching.

The tyrant's back to me, I looked around frantically. Jax and the armored droid were just on the other side of this door. So, the three of us could easily overtake Thassos. We were Biomechs after all, and he was an old, feeble human. Without his minions, he was nothing. But how to formulate a plan in seconds and keep the droid from blasting the door wide open and dispatching us, right then and there?

My new body may have been petite, but the ones you never suspect are the ones you have to watch out for, as my father had always told me. Thassos was probably a foot taller than me, but if I could get him off balance…

I looked at Thassos' desk, searching for anything to use as a weapon. Emre had sneaked around behind Thassos' back while he was busy railing at Rune, and she could see the plan I was formulating in my mind.

The argument between Thassos and Rune was getting heated. Before long, Jax and the droid would be in here, and we would be outnumbered–the droid alone being equal to five men.

Seeing nothing that would work as a suitable weapon, Emre made a gesture of running and tackling Thassos from behind. I nodded to show her I understood, and then Emre mouthed "Now!"

We sprang forward, me screeching like a banshee as Emre and I collided with Thassos' delicate old bones. I heard a crunch as the three of us landed on the gleaming, sterile floor, Rune jumping out of the way just in time to stay on his feet.

I suddenly felt a hand lift me by the scruff of my jumpsuit and was tossed roughly aside as Rune grabbed Thassos by his lab coat, jerking him back to his feet.

Rune's fist met Thassos' jaw in a spray of teeth. Before Thassos could react, Rune grabbed him by the throat and shoved him against the wall. Thassos' feet dangled as Rune's hands wrapped around his spindly throat. There was rage painted across his perfect Biomech face. That's how I knew Rune was truly human. BioMechs showed no emotion whatsoever.

"It's…not over…" Thassos croaked, his hands wrapping around Rune's thick wrists, trying to breathe. "It will never…end…not even with my death." He even tried to laugh, his face a hideous, grimacing mass of purple flesh.

With a roar, Rune squeezed with all his might, Thassos' eyes beginning to bulge out of their sockets, his tongue beginning to loll out of his mouth. I turned away in disgust.

"Go, get out of here! I'll stay behind and fend off the Mechs and droids while I can!" Rune cried, dropping Thassos' lifeless body as Emre began to wildly punch buttons beside the office door.

"Wait, I'm changing the code!" With one last forceful punch, she sighed, her shoulders drooping in relief. "Perks of being in the inner circle. Also, that door is bullet and shatterproof, so we have a few minutes, at least."

Gritting my teeth, I picked up Thassos' desk chair and hurtled it as hard as I could toward the window, praying it would shatter.

In my human days, the glass would not have budged. But with my new Biomech strength, the window shattered in a glorious display of glittering shards. Wind and snow suddenly buffeted the room, nearly knocking us over.

"We've got to jump! Now!" I cried, watching as diamonds of glass and snow skittered and glittered around our feet in the air. I averted my eyes from Thassos' bulging eyeballs and purple, mottled skin. I had seen enough death in my twenty years to do me a lifetime. "Emre's bypass won't last long. Jax will be back with reinforcements any second! I'd rather die now, on my terms, than be an experiment!

"Jump?! Are you fucking insane?" Emre screeched as she picked her way through the glass over to me as I stood, hands on the ledge, ready to pull myself up.

"What's our alternative? They'll keep us prisoner and do experiments on us, even with Thassos dead! You heard what he said before he died! It won't end! We have to take the chance. Our souls could be free and still help the others. We just have to release them from these bodies!" I shouted over the howling wind.

Rune and Emre shared a look through the whirling snow as if telepathically discussing the matter. Their heads snapped around in unison as they heard voices on the other side of the door, along with frantic punches on the keypad.

"Stand down!" shouted another Mech in the hallway. They couldn't risk destroying their three keys to immortality. With or without Thassos, the Biomechs had their orders, and they were still following them. They had no idea their beloved leader was lying dead in a growing pile of snow.

The voices beyond the door became more frantic. Emre and Rune scurried across the room, joining me on the ledge. The wind was screeching now, our hair whipping wildly against our faces. The snow pelted our eyes, but our Biomech bodies were not fazed by the extreme conditions. Our arms clung to the frozen sides of the building, not wanting to look down. Not wanting to take that final step.

"What happens to our souls when we actually die instead of our souls being harvested?" The shouted words poured out of my mouth of their own accord as I looked 100 floors down to the white nothing below. My mouth began to go dry.

"It returns to the cosmos like it should," Emre leaned closer so I could hear her, grabbing my hand and squeezing, taking deep breaths. As she held my eyes for a moment, there was no denying the humanity behind those synthetic eyes.

"Then I'll see you amongst the stars!" I screeched into the undying wind.

With Emre's hand in my right, I took Rune's in my left, and we jumped.

Ice Nomad Blues
By Aishatu Ado

I hoped they didn't hear me—for their own good.

The two ice nomads were digging holes beneath the ice to harvest food. Snow covered the entire desert. Large quantities of water that could fill a lake were buried at depth beneath the sand. They must have traveled for days to find this area where layers of snow and sand devoured the once most fertile part of the kingdom of Azouad. On the edge of the snowy Sahara Desert, I wanted to fish in solitude. I sensed a presence and gazed into the frozen desert sand below my feet. It was Finifenmaa, the rose-veiled fairy fish, who caught my attention. Under the ice surface, it left an iridescent rainbow sheen.

There was a mysterious illness that plagued my only friend. Her memories would be lost within days without a cure: a spicy soup made from that rare Finifenmaa.

Locals attributed magical properties to the rainbow fish. It only lived in this Lake Faguibine area of the Sahara Desert. After taking a sip of the soup, a man claimed to have regained his vision.

There was only one thing I wanted: a miracle. Sherifa was the only human who wasn't scared of me. It filled me with sadness to see her memories disappear, knowing that Sherifa used to have a night sky full of infinite dreams.

Without our dreams, who would we be? They gave my friend Sherifa hope. I admired her fierce desire to make them come true. Sherifa loved adventures—unlike me. Now she didn't even remember that she had planned to travel to the warm Antarctic Forest, which no longer was a land of perpetual winter.

Sherifa knew part of her identity was disappearing. As each night passed, more and more of her dreams were wiped clean. Her damaged dreams deprived me of her laughter, which used to echo like a joyous thunder through my body. And her smile, how I missed it. It warmed me like a summer breeze.

Tears rolled down my cheeks when I thought about Sherifa forgetting me. Sparkling snowflakes fell to the ground and reflected the color of the red desert sand. As if in slow motion, these symmetrical, six-sided snowflakes collided with millions of water droplets that froze on their surface. When my tears stopped flowing, so did the snow.

The two ice nomads carried an arsenal of harpoons and spears. They exercised a great deal of patience before wielding them with deadly accuracy.

Their hunting gear, with projectile heads carved from elephant ivory, detached in the deep muscle tissue and bone of their caught fish. It went all the way through the creature's spine, even as they were pulling them ashore.

Then they dragged out nets, woven from animal sinew—the tough, fibrous tissue that united muscle to bone. They were strung across two other holes in the ice.

Their bounty was rich. The nets were bursting with tiny mussels.

The two ice nomads fell on their knees, grabbed some snowy sand, and marked a circle on their forehead to express their gratitude to the Most Gracious. It was a sign of respect for Earth and her inhabitants.

The older man gave the other ice nomad a hug that looked as if a warm blanket was wrapped around him. Arms opened wide like wings, I mirrored their movements and squeezed my upper arms. Would I ever know what it felt like to be embraced, to be welded as one entity?

From a safe distance, I enjoyed watching humans interact. I often came up with stories about who they were and where they came from. I imagined the two ice nomads had come from a loving family living in Timbuktu, once known as the pearl of the desert. The mother would prepare a meal that they would share while warming up next to a fire.

A family. It's something I have never known. I don't remember my life before this wicked curse.

This Sahelian desert has been suffering the disastrous effects of climate change for over 300 years. Nothing has ever been the same since the third world war.

The ice nomads were known as nomadic herders for generations, moving along the western rim of the Sahara Desert in search of green pastures for their cattle and camels.

The rain, which had never been abundant, became even more sporadic. There was a change in temperatures when the arctic winter arrived in the Sahel. Even camels couldn't endure. The traditional nomadic way of life was no longer possible.

Families whose lives revolved around the seasons and the needs of their livestock gave up and became ice nomads. Many settled in oasis towns whose one main street merged with the desert's edge. Now the two ice nomads packed up their hunting gear to head back to one of those towns.

Roaming the desert alone, I have only known solitude. If only I could become a human, I could end this life in exile. All I have ever wanted was to be like everyone else, to no longer scare people who look at me and see nothing but a ghost.

Instead, I remained not one of them, but their biggest nightmare.

My name was uttered only in whispers—as if saying it out loud would summon my wrath. I had become a tale to scare children from going to the snowy desert on their own.

They told their children that I appeared to travelers trapped in desert snowstorms to leave them as frost-coated corpses. They said I blew in tents with gusts of wind to kill residents in their sleep. It was all lies.

If only they knew how much their scared faces hurt me. If only they could accept me. Yet they only saw me as their biggest nightmare, as a looming death—and who could blame them?

Whenever the strawberry moon was plump and ripe, I had the urge to feed. Every full moon, I needed to replenish my life force. In the freezing, snow-covered desert, I picked humans who were lost, wet, and left alone to die in the desert chill. I listened to their breathing and heart rate to ensure their lungs took in less oxygen, and their hearts pumped less blood. It was essential: Because of the reduced blood flow to their organs, their bodies were in a state of shock. This was the sweet spot. While their pupils were still dilated, I would lean over my immobile prey just before their breathing became too shallow to detect. My face would come closer to their frightened faces. I would enthrall them with my gaze, only to steal three icy breaths from their mouth.

Those wisps of life force tasted like fluffy clouds, with a lingering tang of the latest memory they harbored. The epicurean delight attracted me like Arctic Sahelian bees to a honeypot. It made me feel light and drenched in sunshine. At least for a moment, I would relive one of their happy memories. I could taste what it meant to be human.

It was an ambrosial, lip-smacking taste. One that could kill my mark, should I indulge it further. I have learned to control my thirst, to take only enough to sustain me till the next full moon.

I was brought back to the present moment as the two ice nomads took a few steps on the sandy desert ground, blanketed with snow. The path would take them back to Timbuktu, an oasis at the edge of the desert.

Why didn't they hurry? It should have been my turn to fish. I needed to get back to my friend.

When they were about to leave, I could see their piercing eyes more clearly. Their faces were veiled in a traditional blue turban, and their bodies were wrapped in thick layers of fabric. It protected them from inhaling wind-borne sand.

Only their obsidian eyes were visible, which made a stark contrast to their indigo-stained bronze skin. They were called, "the Blue People of the Sahara," because the indigo dye of the robes they wore colored their skin blue.

One of them, the younger one, stopped to look around as if he could feel me observing him through the red mist in the winter morning hours. That gaze let an indomitable fire within me. I felt like I was being strapped to a chair whilst looking at an open door. I continued to stare at them as if I could make them leave with my sheer willpower. My thawed anxiety made me feel like a hummingbird frantically flapping its wings: incapacitated in time, yet in constant motion. I attempted to distract myself from the burning flame that threatened to engulf me. It was a pain that was hard to describe. A burning, tingling sensation deep under my skin, like a fiery flame, crawled to every fiber of my being. The blistering nerve pain felt as if I was stabbed by a thousand flaming daggers, as sharp and sudden as an electric shock.

The fear of being discovered made any touch unbearable. My entire body suffered from a throbbing numbness that even the simple act of trying to hide deeper into the shadows became an arduous task.

My arms and legs felt like they were filled with a thousand pebbles. Each step broke layers of ice, and I sank deeper into the snowy sand. I had to reach down to pull up my feet.

Once the burning pain started, I could not stop the nerve fire from awakening a desert snowstorm. It would give away my hiding spot behind a desert snow hill.

I didn't want to kill them. But I could no longer hold it in.

The burning sensation took over me as I was holding my breath for what seemed like an eternity. As I closed my eyes, I exhaled. My shoulders relaxed, and my arms were no longer heavy. My legs felt light as air.

When I opened my eyes, I realized that my anxiety had created a powerful gust of wind that had hurled the younger ice nomad toward one of the gaping holes. There was a loud thud. The younger man, attempting to stand, had slipped and fallen into the ice hole.

With his hands on his head, the father screamed in despair. He attempted to reach for his son but fell to his knees. He didn't have long arms. The harpoon he reached out with wasn't long enough, and the nets were of no use to him.

How horrible! What was I supposed to do?

As I observed them from a safe distance, I knew I could help. It would, however, require me to remove my human disguise.

I didn't want to be seen as I was. It was likely that the older man would raise his harpoon in defense against me. I could already see the fear he would have in his eyes.

My shapeshifting charm mixed wind with microscopic sand particles. Like glass, it refracted light, allowing me to manipulate my appearance. Sometimes I resembled a human woman. On that day, I had disguised myself as a man.

My oversized long blue cloak was made of coarse woolen fabric and had a pointed hood. I even mimicked the way indigo dye leached into the skin of the Blue People. The litham veil I wore was made of indigo-dyed cotton, which also formed my turban. Three layers covered my head, and another layer hung around my neck. Women in the Azouad Kingdom did not cover their faces with a veil, while men did. Male ice nomads found shame in showing their mouths or nose to strangers.

A sigh escaped my lips. Time was running out. If I waited any longer, it would be too late.

I was to blame, after all. The young man had fallen into the ice hole because of me.

Why couldn't I control my emotions? There was nothing I hated more than those nerve-wracking anxiety attacks. I could not always control my powers because of them. My emotions were linked to the elements. They caused utter destruction if they were not in equilibrium. It wasn't safe to be around me then.

My eyes remained fixed on the old man, regardless of how hard I tried to look away. Turning his gaze to the sky, he addressed the Most Gracious. I could hear his words even from a distance.

"Oh, Lord, you are most merciful. Take me instead. I would do anything, give anything in your honor, to save him." He pressed his forehand against the snowy sand as he pleaded for his son's life.

What about Sherifa? I shouldn't lose sight of why I was here. My friend needed a cure. If I didn't act quickly, the rainbow fairy fish would be out of reach. What was I supposed to do?

The older ice nomad interrupted my train of thought with his sobbing cries. Seeing him in such a sad state broke my heart.

Death was a finality. There was no coming back from that. At least, not for humans.

Sherifa would never forgive me if she ever found out I left another person to die a violent death to save her disappearing memories.

The death of another human being was not something I wanted to be responsible for. By the Most Gracious! Not if I could do something about it.

My shoulders relaxed as I took a few deep breaths. Keeping my anxiety at bay was crucial. Moving my index finger in a circle, I raised my hand. As my human disguise disappeared, I revealed my true self.

My appearance no longer resembled that of the Blue People. An ever-moving cinnamon-colored dress made from powdered sand now hugged my body. The sand particles moved in horizontal s-curves along the dress from the ground to my back, to my shoulders, to my chest, and back down again. My dress appeared to extend beneath the snow and into the Sahara Desert. A sheer veil covered my red-henna hair like mist, extending to touch the ground behind me.

As I floated across the snowy desert, I left no footprints behind. Only my veil left a wavy trail of orange and purple ripples on the snowy sand.

In a blink, I was standing next to the ice hole. The old man stopped crying when he noticed me standing next to him. His eyes widened so that the whites were visible. Seeing my luminous appearance, he rearranged his veil in astonishment.

"By the Most Gracious," he said with a feeble voice.

I expected this reaction. One might have thought that the ability of the Blue People to master the harsh, forbidding desert environment and to repel, control, or withstand colonial powers, modern governments, and a climate apocalypse would have made this old man prepared for one such as me.

I took a closer look at him. A self-respecting male ice nomad never allowed his face to be seen without a veil. He wore one with about forty strongly dyed indigo strips, leaving only a tiny part of his face visible. He had stunning almond-shaped eyes.

Having a hard time comprehending what I was wearing, he stammered with a baffled expression, "What on Earth?"

He tightened his grip on the silver amulet around his neck. The cord was attached to a rectangular, braided leather pendant filled with iron. The Blue People wore them as protection against evil spirits.

He was still kneeling on the ground while I was towering over him. The old man thrust his amulet at me. He must have mistaken me for a jinni: a mischievous, smokeless fire spirit that feared iron. The old man squeezed his eyes shut, as he must have expected to see me explode like an enormous balloon. When he opened both eyes, I was unaffected by the amulet.

With a huge exhalation of pent-up breath, his gaze shifted back to the ice hole. His face filled with a variety of emotions. The old man's unspoken question seemed to be, "friend or foe?"

A determined look crossed his face as he faced me. "Peace be upon you."

"And upon you," I said.

He gesticulated towards the hole, "Please... my son,"—He took a steadying breath.—"he fell. Can you help him?" His desperate eyes shone with a hopeful look.

I nodded. There was no more time to waste. Red sand dust swirled around me as the wind welcomed me with a desert blues song. The fusion of electric guitar and indigenous musical styles of Saharan ice nomads needed space to be wild and free. A mellow, hypnotic groove was strumming through my body as I danced with the wind.

Riffs and chanted melodies conveyed the nomadic kinship with the desert. Electric-guitar-driven ballads of *assouf* music told stories about emotional and spiritual pain, longing, and homesickness.

I opened my arms to become one with the wind. The eager sand twirled around me. The finest particles penetrated the pores of my skin. A stream of ephemeral flurries gathered around my hands. My dress grew into a shape-shifting turbulence, charging the air with the potency of a thunderstorm.

As the whisking wind gathered, crystal ice particles rose on columns of air. The overcast sky took on a threatening dullness as a load of snowy dust extended its spectrum. Fleeting flurries turned into continuous slabs of sand, hurtling across the desert surface as the sun dimmed. The turbulent chaos turned into the full fury of a harmattan sandstorm, threatening to assail anything in its path.

The surface of the ice hole rose in obedience to my will. I manipulated the barometric pressure with guitar-playing motions. I held a long-necked kora made of air in my hands. The sound of my air-stringed instrument resembled that of a harp. Tiny pebbles stroked against the knees, and thighs of the old man when I plucked polyrhythmic patterns with both hands. As I began to play the ice nomad blues, I increased the speed of strumming and picking motions to create an upthrusting force from beneath the icy water. A spray of dancing sand grains surged into the water to grab the younger man.

For a moment, all but the old man faded from my view. The Sahara Desert was filled with stinging, pelting, and biting legions of sand and ice.

A hurtling blast of sand moved the young man out of the icy water as if a giant hand was carrying him in its palm. Immediately, I moved my hands to command a warm wind to place him next to his father.

"Amer," the father said, furrowing his brow. "By the Most Gracious, wake up!" He rocked his son's unconscious body back and forth.

"He will live," I said with a sense of certainty.

Amer opened his eyes and coughed.

"Abba," Amer said with a hoarse voice.

The old man wrapped Amer in a warm blanket and whispered, "Shh… don't speak. Rest now, son. We have a long way ahead of us." His eyes were filled with tears of joy, as he turned toward me. "Thank you for saving him."

As I looked into the father's kind obsidian eyes, I found comfort in the recognition of our shared experience. There was a genuine connection between us. Sherifa would have been proud of me.

Sherifa. What is the likelihood that she would still remember me? Would she be able to know my name, my face, our shared history, and stories without her memories?

No, Sherifa would simply no longer recognize me. Her mind would no longer contain me.

I despised this merciless illness that stole her from me like a thief. All that was left for me to do was find other ways to connect and reconnect with her, as I wouldn't be able to find the fairy fish in time.

Yes, there was no sign of the rainbow fish. It must have been scared off by my desert storm.

The old man went to his horse and grabbed a bag. He bowed his head and offered it to me.

I gave him a dazed look of bewilderment. "Is this for me?"

"I can never repay you for saving my son's life." He pressed his palm to his heart. "I would like you to have this."

His eyes were filled with eager anticipation as he looked at me. My jaw dropped when I saw what was inside the bag.

By the *Most Gracious!* The bag contained a rare rainbow fairy fish. It was the most prized fish in the entire kingdom of Azouad.

I was flabbergasted with joy. "Thank you," I said while sunshine flooded my soul. In sync with the snowy sand dunes, I bounced on my toes. My heart dared to hope for a miracle. I raised my hand to summon the wind to rush to Sherifa.

"No words can express the gratitude I feel. I will treasure this moment. Always." I said. Was this how it felt to be seen? To be valued?

The old man interrupted my train of thought. "Where will your journey take you next?"

"Home," I said, as I surrendered to the bliss of the desert blues.

Author Biographies

Aishatu Ado: Aishatu Ado is a Cologne-based speculative fiction author, peace technologist, experiential designer, and AI ethicist who cultivates imaginaries that reframe, transform, and orient toward enabling peaceful futures. In her works, she references postcolonial theory, as well as African and Indigenous cosmovisions as found in mythology, folklore, and oral literature.

As a visual and literary artist, Aishatu pushes the boundary between the real and the artificial. She explores narratives from the past, present, and future that empower, uplift, represent and honor Black experiences. Her transdisciplinary practice spans applied sci-fi, poetry, digital illustration, painting, and new media such as blockchain technology, AI, VR, and AR. While Aishatu resists any given label, her work is framed by legacies of Africanfuturism, Black writers, and Afrofeminist philosophies. Like her predecessors, she uses science fiction to reconfigure the present into an exhilarating vision of the future.

Connect with Aishatu Ado:

- https://www.aishatuado.com/
- https://twitter.com/AishatuGwadabe
- https://www.instagram.com/miss.aishatu/

Read more from Aishatu Ado:
- "Parables of AI in/from the Majority World." (*African Ancestral AI,* New York: Data & Society Research Institute)
- "Reality is a Monster," (Soltype: *Hauntings and Horrors Collection*)
- "Ecofeminist Manifesto," (Soltype)
- "Mirror Image," (Soltype: *To Each Their Own Reality Collection*)

Ameera Rashid: Ameera Rashid was born and raised in the city of Lucknow, Uttar Pradesh, India, where she is currently pursuing her bachelor's degree. Having a lifelong interest in reading, Ameera developed an early fascination with the process of storytelling and the impact it had on certain people. She spent months trying to figure out the enticing secret behind stories that pulled everyone in and made others care for characters existing within the confines of pages. It became her dream to someday write stories of her own.

During the Covid lockdown, she finally got the opportunity and the courage to pick up the pen. Writing provided her the distraction to cope with such hard times, and eventually became more than just a hobby.

Connect with Ameera Rashid:
- https://twitter.com/web3writer

Austin Abbamonte: Austin Abbamonte is an author and freelance artist who designs maps for tabletop role-playing games and fantasy novels. He has won numerous online art and writing contests and had a short story commissioned for the Discord server "Heroic Story." When he is not writing, Austin enjoys LARPing, reading, and walking his dog.

Read more from Austin Abbamonte:
- "The Final Hunt," (*Writing Academy: Between the Volumes*)

CD Damitio: CD Damitio is a lifelong storyteller based in Honolulu. He is the author of books that explore the intersection of travel, technology, religion, politics, and the absurd. He enjoys time with family, travel, and writing.

Connect with CD Damitio:
- https://cent.vagobond.com/
- https://www.chrisdamitio.com/
- https://www.vagobond.com/
- https://www.medium.com/@vagobond
- https://www.twitter.com/vagobond

Read more from CD Damitio:
- *The Fucking People* (CD Damitio Books)
- *The Princess and the Vagobond* (CD Damitio Books)
- *The Keys to the Riad* (CD Damitio Books)
- *Petshitter* (CD Damitio Books)
- *A Very Good Novel Coronavirus* (CD Damitio Books)
- *Not My American* (CD Damitio Books)
- *Notes from Nowhere* (CD Damitio Books)
- *Blue Eyed Bastards* (CD Damitio Books)
- *Sly Doubt of Uranus: The history of a Lovable Asshole* (CD Damitio Books)
- *The Holy Bjble* (CD Damitio Books)
- *Holy Bjble: Council of Aiea v.0.1* (CD Damitio Books)

- *The Nuns of Baboob* (CD Damitio Books)
- *Hasan I Sabah: The Founding of the Sultanate of Baboob* (CD Damitio Books)
- *The Holy Bible with Zombies: A Kindlevella* (CD Damitio Books)

E. R. Donaldson: E. R. Donaldson is the founder of Mythic North Press. Donaldson has been writing in earnest since 2017 and has a passion for lore and worldbuilding. When he's not writing, Donaldson is gaming or spending time with his wife and children.

Connect with E. R. Donaldson:
- https://linktr.ee/erdonaldson

Read more from E. R. Donaldson:
- *Chronicles of Nethra: Cognis Saga*
  - *Star Spire* (Mythic North Press)
  - *Shadows of Minos* (Mythic North Press)
  - *Darkest Hearts* (Mythic North Press)
  - *Stardust Grave* (Mythic North Press)
  - *Risen Gods* (Mythic North Press)
  - *Reckoning* (Mythic North Press)
- *The Dark Council's Blade* (Mythrill Fiction)
- "Of Dreams and Prophets," (*Bridge to Elsewhere*, Outland Entertainment)
- "Poor Wagers." (*To Each Their Own Reality*, Soltype)
- "Wraiths in Residence" (*Hauntings and Horrors*, Soltype)

Hank Ryder: Hank Ryder was born to be a writer. From a young age, he channeled his passion for storytelling into written words, honing his craft from the back seat of his parents' truck as they drove all across the United States. In addition to his story, "First Blood of Winter," Hank is the author of *Triskelion Saga* available on the Mythrill Fiction App, Hank's promising writing career has only just begun. Hank lives in California with his wife and two dogs, working hard to escape the 9-5 and focus on writing full-time.

Connect with Hank Ryder:
- https://twitter.com/The_Hank_Ryder

H. R. Parker: H.R. Parker is an author, poet, and editor who hails from the subtropical wilds of Georgia. When she's not writing, she's got her nose shoved in a book, cuddling cute, furry animals, or embracing her hobbit DNA and eating po-tay-toes.

Connect with H. R. Parker:
- https://www.instagram.com/h.r._parker/
- https://linktr.ee/heather_r_parker

Nate Battalion: Nate Battalion is a lifelong worldbuilder, short fiction writer, RPG game master, and loving father. Nate grew up reading an assortment of science fiction and fantasy, playing video games, and, as long as he can remember, been a nerd. At this point, he embraces it. In addition to writing various short stories (like the one in this book), he publishes a bi-weekly serial space fantasy entitled Honor in the Dark exclusively on Mythrill Fiction.

Apart from writing, Nate's favorite things to do are still reading and playing video games, as well as miniature wargaming, tabletop roleplaying, and playing with his children.

Connect with Nate Battalion:
- https://www.natebattalion.com/
- https://www.facebook.com/natebattalion
- https://twitter.com/nate_battalion

Rionna Morgan: According to Rionna she, "really [is] from nowhere, and no (wink), [she is] not in the witness protection program;" even though she has lived at both edges of the continental United States and a little in-between.

Rionna is a believer in following her heart. She followed her love of horses to the rodeo arena, her love of English to the classroom, and her love of justice to the courtroom. She was an English teacher for ten years; a lawyer for five, and a writer always.

She writes poetry, short stories, and novels. She has even penned an article or two here and there. Her work has intrigue, love, murder, and romance; but, most of all, it has amazing people. As Rionna puts it, "They really shine in their own lives. Writing them is an absolute joy. My bad guys are creepy! My heroines are brilliant and strong – and save themselves!"

When she is not traveling as much as she can, she shares her life in Montana with her husband, her four children, her daughter-in-law, and the mountains outside her window.

Connect with Rionna Morgan:
- https://linktr.ee/rionnamorgan

Read more from Rionna Morgan:
- *Love's Justice* (Simon & Schuster)
- *The Wanting Heart* (Simon & Schuster)
- "Last Laugh: A Ghost Story," (Soltype: *Hauntings and Horrors Collection*)"
- "What is PageDAO?" (Vagobond Magazine, Issue 6)
- "Web3: The Place We're Looking For," (Vagobond Magazine, Issue 7)
- "Witch Hunt (prologue)," (Vagobond Magazine, Issue 8)
- "New World: Web3 Publishing," (Vagobond Magazine, Issue 9)
- "From Web2 to Web3 – For Writers," (PageDAO & Readme Books – *TBR January 2023*)
- Love You, Valentine," (BookVolts – *TBR January 2023*)

R. J. Lloyd: R. J. Lloyd started as a romance writer under another pen name. However, R. J. is the side of this award-winning, bestselling author that delves into fantasy, sci-fi, supernatural, paranormal, and all things action and spooky that she loves so much.

A Detroit-area-based author, R. J. writes both novels and short stories, always looking for the next interesting and slightly off-kilter character to follow on an adventure with.

Connect with R. J. Lloyd:
- https://www.amazon.com/R-J-Lloyd/e/B08CCDYCNH
- https://www.rjlloydbooks.com
- https://www.facebook.com/RJLloydOfficial
- https://www.instagram.com/r.j.lloydbooks
- https://www.tiktok.com/@r.j.lloyd
- https://www.youtube.com/channel/UC5TkQNh_wGLQgXljsFLncDA

Read more from R. J. Lloyd:
- *Heir to Redemption* (Digital Quill)

- *Immersion* (Digital Quill)
- *Campfire Tales* (Digital Quill)
- *Chronicles of Naelyra*
  - *Everwinter* (Digital Quill)
  - *Earthbound* (Digital Quill)
- *The Emanation Saga:*
  - *The Pull* (Digital Quill)
- *Keepers of Knowledge:*
  - *Echoes in the Bloodline* (Digital Quill)
  - *The World as We Know It* (Digital Quill)
  - *The Study of Ruth and Trust* (Digital Quill)
  - *Arriving in Pyreshore* (Digital Quill)
  - *The Fringe* (Digital Quill)

Sylvie Bax: Sylvie is a visual and narrative poet from Ireland via Scotland and Spain. She mashes up edge poetry with multimedia, images, animation, text, verse, and color. She writes about race, love, lust, brutality, madness, medication, and hope. According to Sylvie, she has, a "big heart, dark register," and is "brimming with possibilities."

Connect with Sylvie Bax:
- https://linktr.ee/sylvie_bax

Wren Murphy: When Wren was a little girl, she never wanted to be a writer. She aspired to be a pharmacist, and she achieved that life goal about a decade ago. However, the spark for creating stories lit in the back row of her high school history class during her sophomore year and passing notes to her best friends led her to create her very first character. From there, it was a wildfire, and she has been weaving fantastical tales ever since.

Wren is a world traveler but fondly calls the corn fields of north central Indiana home. She currently resides in Western New York with her daughter and two chaotic dogs. Her stories feature strong, relatable heroines, handsome heroes, and nail-biting escapades that you won't want to stop reading. Sometimes, if you look close enough, there's even a dragon or two.

Connect with Wren Murphy:
- https://www.wrenmurphy.com
- https://www.facebook.com/wrenmurphyauthor/
- https://www.instagram.com/wrenmurphyauthor
- https://www.twitter.com/wren_murphy

- <u>https://www.tiktok.com/@wrenmurphyauthor</u>

Read more from Wren Murphy:
- *The Crown of Olmalis:*
  - *The Serpent Lord* (Red Feather Press)
- "A Kiss of Topaz," (*Midwinter Tales of the Gemstone Courts: A Fae Romance Anthology,* Pulse Publishing)

WINTER WARRIORS

It takes a lot of work to pull together a collection like this, and none of it would be possible without the generous financial support of our readers. The "Winter Warriors" listed here were kind enough to take a chance on us and support our work through our Kickstarter campaign. Their names are listed here as our small way of saying, "Thank you."

Winter Warriors of the December 2022 Kickstarter Campaign:

BD Olson
Becky James
Bethany Tomerlin Prince
Carolyn Tobey
Chelsey Lillge
Edward Barnes
Ellen Pilcher
Josh Allred
Joshua Alquist
Karen
Melanie Roath
Mike
Mike Oliver
Rachel Morley
Richard Novak
Rionna Morgan
Robert Pollock
Sylvie Bax
Tess Murphy
Winston Malone

www.ingramcontent.com/pod-product-compliance
Lightning Source LLC
Chambersburg PA
CBHW011223190726
48287CB00008B/2719